OF POWER & DARKNESS

FORSAKEN BY THE GODS
BOOK 3

T. B. WIESE

OTHER BOOKS IN THIS WORLD

- Of Spirit & Hope
- Of Blood & Secrets
- Of Power and Darkness

To everyone who reads this series ...
If you have not yet had THE moment, I hope you do. That
moment when you know deep in your soul that you are enough
- just as you are.

AUTHOR'S NOTE

**Please take care of yourself and your mental health

Of Power & Darkness is an ADULT fantasy that contains elements such as: abuse, anxiety, loss of a loved one, explosions, blood, torture, death, infanticide, emotional abuse, gore, violence, profanity, PTSD, light religion, and sexually explicit scenes.

PRONUNCIATION GUIDE

Hello wonderful reader,

First off, I want to preface this with - if you find it easier or more natural to pronounce these names another way, go for it! This is your story now. Have fun.

But, if you're curious how I pronounced these names, here you go...

characters
    THAEIA: They-ah
    NOR: rhymes with four
    VALSAN: Val-san
    KEIR: rhymes with fear
    NEZERA: Nez-er-ah

places
    SODOLES : So-dough-leys
    KAPROS: Ka-prose
    ALOPSON: Al-op-son
    DRAKAM: Drah-kum
    KA CRUMMENS: Kah Crew-mens

AKARETH: Ah-car-eth
OXTARA: Ox-tar-a

creatures
PRAZAR: Pray-zar
HAGRAVEN: Hag-ra-ven
BASILISHOUND: Bas-ill-ish-ound

AKARETH DESERT
COLISEUM
ALOPSON
FOX OF THE NORTH
CAPITAL
KA CRUMMENS
CAPITAL
DRAKAM
DRAGON OF THE
CENTRAL TERRITORY
KAPROS
BOAR OF THE SOUTH
OXTARA
CAPITAL
COUNTRY OF
SODOLES

WHAT CAME BEFORE

HERE'S A REMINDER OF WHERE WE ENDED IN BOOK TWO ... THE FINAL CHAPTER

THAEIA

My hands tighten even more on the bars, and my head shakes slowly. No. That can't be true. I'm not ... he's not ...

"Ah, I see you really didn't know. Interesting." He waves his hand again with a dismissive gesture and I focus on his tattoo. ROMMAR. Channel. Four stars climb his light brown skin. He sees the direction of my gaze and smirks. "Ah, yes." Running a finger down his arm, he traces his tattoos. "My gift allows me to take on the power of anyone near me. That range has grown over the years, granting me access to so many different kinds of magic." His self-satisfied tone grates on my nerves. "But not only can I use their magic, I can amplify it, making it more, making it mine."

Keeping his head tilted down, he aims his look at me,

eyes staring at me from under his lashes. "You are my antithesis." He drops his gaze again and resumes slowly pacing the edge of the line. "All the females of my line have your ... affliction. They have for generations. Every filthy female born of my seed, my father's seed, his father's seed, has possessed"—his narrowed eyes find me again, shimmering with hate—"the Void."

I release the bars, relaxing my hands at my sides, my left hand hovering over my thigh sheath. "You're lying. Why—"

"Generations ago, your kind were used to moderate, to constrain, to *punish*. And they were quite effective. Until you women got it in your head you were more powerful than the rest of us. It is a little-known fact"—he chuckles to himself, and my fingers graze one of my blades—"well, I guess it's not known anymore. Long ago, three sisters with the power of the Void staged a coup, taking Drakam from its previous ruler. So I guess I should be thankful for your wretched curse." He chuckles again and it sounds manic, the sharp tone echoing off the low ceiling. "It was a bloody affair, and all but one sister died. She held her position by swearing to leash her Void."

My body tenses at that. Leash the Void? How?

"She contained that disgusting nothingness within her, but when her youngest son came for her seat of power, she abandoned her vow ... but it was too late. Her son killed her and began what our family refers to as 'the cleansing.'"

Vomit burns in my throat, and I gulp it down, my eyes burning as my mind guesses where this story is going.

The toe of his boot taps the line as he smiles at me. "He saw the danger of your kind. And while he couldn't prevent his seed from creating female babies, he *could* control whether those babes lived or died."

My hand falls from the hilt of my knife. I stand in stunned silence. Every female baby born to the Drakam line ...? For generations? Sweat breaks out on my forehead, and for a moment I'm dizzy. But I clear my throat before asking, "How have you kept this secret?"

He chuckles, turning to walk the line back the other way. "History is written by the victor. It took time to erase the records of your kind, and even longer for the memory of you to fade." He waves his hand yet again. "And it became well known that the Drakam line could not produce female children."

I think through what little knowledge I have of the Houses, specifically Drakam. All sons. No daughters. I shake my head. "All the bonded. *Your* bonded. She can't have agreed to this. Someone would have come forward. Someone would have stopped this" He's lying. He has to be lying. This can't ...

He throws back his head, barking a laugh. "They don't know. My bonded is beautiful, and too sweet for this world, but she's not the brightest. Stillborn. Every bonded knows that if the Drakam seed takes and produces a female, that child will be stillborn. They are warned, and to spare them the trauma of going through such an ordeal, they are drugged heavily for each birth. So you see, *daughter*, the lie is intact and easily upheld."

How many of my sisters has this monster killed? The image of Fara on her knees flashes through my mind. She must have gotten me out, gotten me to Saph. But why did she come back here? Why put herself back in the path of such danger? Why not hide with Saph? My hand shifts to hover over my blades again. "Why are you telling me all this?"

A sudden calmness falls over his face as he stops his slow progression along the line. "Because you should understand what is at stake for me, and what I'm capable of. I'm telling you so you are grateful for the opportunity I'm about to offer you."

I sneer. "Grateful?"

The door clicks behind Severn, and the same son from before comes in. My heart drops into my stomach with a thud. Halee lays in his arms, her hair swinging over his arm, her body limp. Severn sees the look on my face, and grins, waving that godsdamned hand again. "Don't worry. She's alive. We just couldn't have her furry little friends interfering."

My arms begin to shake from the rage that burns through me. Halee is alive because she's useful to Severn in some way.

"Let her go. She's not part of this, whatever *this* is. You have me. Let her go."

He tsks, taking a step back from the line. His son sets Halee down at Severn's feet, shooting me a look filled with loathing before leaving the room again. Severn moves to stand behind Halee. "When I saw you at the Games, I was sure you had come to kill me. To kill my sons."

"You blew up the Coliseum."

"I had to protect what is mine. But then I realized ... I might have been squandering something great. My ancestors were afraid of your kind, but with the right ... *management*." He actually licks his lips. Gross. "Can you control it?"

I force my gaze up from Halee to blink at him. Control what?

He waves his hand at me, and I swear I'm going to cut it off. "Your power. Can you control it?" Should I lie and say yes? I didn't even know it was controllable. He hums at my silence. "Let's test it."

My eyes drop to Halee. *No.*

A single thread of his shirt unravels and drops to the floor. It snakes over the stone, then lifts into the air, stiffening. When the light of a torch hits it just right, it gleams with lethal sharpness. The point moves towards Halee.

My arm is a blur as I grab one of my knives and throw it at Severn's head. It hits an invisible barrier, clattering to the floor loudly. I stop myself from throwing another. I only have so many blades on me ... six more to be exact.

"Tell me what you want. Just let her go."

"That is up to you." He waves his hand, and I'm clutching another blade before I can think about it. I keep myself from throwing it, but it's a hard-won battle as he says, "Stop me, and she lives. She gets to go home."

Panic steals my breath. How? I search for some flaw in the barrier he has constructed between us, but I can't even tell where it begins or ends. I don't know what magic is available to him right now. How? Think.

He takes one step forward so his boot lands next to Halee's head, and the needle-sharp thread hovers over her neck. "Use your power to stop me. Take my magic, Thaeia."

That's the first time he's used my name, and it sounds dirty. I've never hated my name so much. In quick succession, I whip three blades at him ... face, chest, gut. Two hit his barrier and fall, the third stops mid-air right in front of his stomach. The knife turns slowly to face me, then flies forward. As soon as it hits my Void, it loses the momentum of the magic propelling it and clatters to the floor.

Severn growls. "Go on!" He cackles madly. "Stop me!"

The thread-turned-blade presses to Halee's skin, and a bead of blood wells up. She stirs, moaning, moving her head, causing the thread to go deeper.

Shit! I look around frantically, another knife in my hand. I grip it so tight, the leather hilt creaks. My other hand comes to the bars, squeezing one tightly as I press my body against the cold iron. "Please."

He just raises a brow at me. I hold my breath and bear down, willing my Void to expand. Just a few inches. That's all I need. I plead with the gods, desperate. *Please, if anyone is listening, please.* I imagine pushing my Void outward. My lungs burn as I beg my Void to save Halee.

Opening my eyes, my breath wooshes out. Nothing. The thread still presses to Halee's throat, and now her eyes are open. Her confused gaze falls on me, and her voice cracks. "Thaeia?"

Severn drops his voice in warning. "Last chance."

Absolute terror and rage sharpen my vision onto my father. "I will kill you." Keeping my eyes on him, I shout, "Halee, use your magic, NOW!"

Severn sighs. "So disappointing."

Halee's eyes go wide, and her body arches as the thread slices deep.

"NO!" My blade falls from my hand, but I don't hear it hit the floor. Halee's blood pools around her, soaking into her dark curls. Her body jerks, her hands weakly reaching for her neck. Slowly, like the sun setting, her body goes still, her arms falling to her sides, her gaze emptying.

Severn tsks. "This is your fault, Thaeia. You could have sav—"

A force explodes out of me, and Severn takes several steps back, eyes wide with fear for the first time since he entered this room. *Yes. Let me see your terror,* Father. *Tremble before me.* The force pulses out of me again, stronger. My Void spreads like the shockwaves of an explosion. My entire body tingles as hundreds, then thousands of powers snuff out against my Void. The edges of my vision darken, and I grin at Severn who raises his left hand, arm trembling. His lips form my name, but I can't hear it. My gaze drops to the floor, to the bright red blood, to Halee's open, unseeing eyes.

My heart shatters into a million pieces. I'm torn apart. There's a ringing in my ears, and I realize I'm screaming. The next pulse that comes from me is so powerful, the bars shake. I grab them, my screams growing louder. My fingertips are black, like I dipped them in soot. With every pulse, the darkness spreads, crawling up my fingers, over my hands.

I have the vague thought that I should be worried, or panicked, or ... something, but I'm not. I'm just angry. So angry. As the black overtakes my wrists, a word circles my skin, created by the absence of the darkness spreading up my arms. I fully expect to see QUED, the word for Void, but instead I read, KURKODAM. Forsaken.

A laugh bubbles up through my despair. Of course.

Abandon all hope, those who enter my Void, for we are all Forsaken. The darkness creeps up my arms, tendrils curling around my biceps. Severn's eyes go wide, the whites standing out stark against his brown skin and the brown of his irises. He backs away, keeping his eyes on me as he leaves through the door.

I shout after him, my voice so filled with rage it doesn't sound like mine. "I will kill you! Severn Drakam! I WILL kill you!" My hands loosen on the bars, as I continue to yell, "I'll kill you! I'll kill you!"

My knees buckle, and the pulsing power slows then stops. I hit the floor, pain shooting up my legs. I don't care. Halee's lifeless arm is splayed out from her body, as if reaching for me. I need to get to her. I ... She needs me ... My shoulder presses to the bars as I reach through. My blackened fingers stretch, and the iron digs into my chest. My body slides down parallel with the bars, and my cheek presses to the cold floor. My fingers scrape at the stone, reaching for Halee's outstretched hand.

"Come on Halee, wake up." My fist slaps the cold stone floor. "Come on. Come on!" She doesn't move. The blood around her is darker now. My hand falls flat. A sob tears from me. There's a crashing sound from somewhere, but I can't stop staring at Halee's blood, her life force. My body goes numb. I can't breathe. The darkness recedes down my arms, the script around my wrist disappearing. All I see is blood, so much blood—the consequences of the secrets kept from me my entire life.

My broken mind catches on those words, repeating over and over until I'm sure I've gone mad. *Blood and Secrets. Blood and Secrets. Blood and Secrets.*

Now ... on to book three

OF POWER & DARKNESS

CHAPTER 1

THAEIA

"Kɪʟʟ her and get rid of the bodies." The voice of my *father* coming from the dark hall beyond this empty stone room snaps my attention away from the blood slowly cooling on the floor.

I sway slightly as I push myself off my stomach and to my knees. Severn Drakam's revelations still pound against my skull, my brain reluctant to accept the fact that he's my father, and that for generations the males of the Drakam line have been murdering their female babies in secret to prevent the Forsaken magic, my magic, from manifesting ever again.

Godsdamned fucking bastards. All of them.

Four guards file into the room, safely on the other side of the bars splitting this room in half. One raises her left hand, but when her magic fails to respond, she frowns and drops her arm back to her side. A corner of my lips lifts into a smile. *That's right, bitch. You're in my Void.* But my smirk morphs into a scowl as another of the guards locks a bolt into a crossbow, aiming at me. The last two bend down, one wrapping his meaty fingers around Halee's arm.

Before he can move her even an inch, a scream rips out of me. "Don't touch her!" The sound coming from me is unnatural, echoing off the walls and low ceiling. The bars I now have my hands wrapped around actually vibrate, and I notice the strange darkness creeping up my hand, staining my skin black.

Everything seems to slow down as I watch the ink-like shadow bleed up my arm, leaving behind the natural color of my skin to spell out the word KURKODAM—Forsaken. I touch my fingers to the black creeping up my arm, half expecting it to stain my other hand, but no, it's in my skin. It's in me. As I stare at it, I realize it's not actually black. It's a deep sapphire blue, like ... like lightning flashing behind dark clouds reflected in a stormy sea. It's ... violently beautiful.

Movement draws my attention away from the seemingly living mark of my power. The guard with his hand wrapped around Halee's arm is breathing a little faster, his eyes darting to me then to the one holding the crossbow as he grunts, "Hurry up and shoot her. Let's get this over with."

I don't even glance at the crossbow. No. All I see is Halee's skin, stuck to the floor by her dried blood, pulling and tugging as the guard starts to drag her away. He doesn't even bother to pick her up. He. Drags. Her!

No! They can't take her. We won't let them!

I blink, confused. The four guards lay crumpled on the floor. The one that held the crossbow just a second ago—the one closest to me—has blood trickling from his nose from where he landed on his face. He's still breathing, but lying like that, he might end up choking on his blood if he doesn't wake up and move. What the fuck happened?

My eyes drift back to Halee, now flanked by the passed-out bodies of two guards. Her open eyes are dull, and her pretty black curls are soaked in her blood. I know there's pain inside me, sorrow so deep it might fracture the very core of who I am, but it'll be okay. Everything will be okay.

I let my rage block the pain ... for now. I'm so angry. *We're* so angry. At the gods for forsaking us, at how people treated us growing up, at my father, at his sons, at my birth mother for not noticing what was happening or just not caring enough, at Saph for not telling me ... So much fury, and it keeps building inside us. *Yes, let it build, let it break us apart. Let us free!*

Fingers wrap around my forearm, tugging. I don't turn to see who has a hold of me. I don't care. All that matters is the anger, the rage ... My shoulder pulls painfully as I'm yanked again. There's a voice, but I can't make out the words through the pounding in my ears. The cold iron bars dig into my palms. Or maybe it's my body that's cold. When I'm pulled back again, I wrap my entire arm through the bars, hugging them.

"Thaeia, let go. We have to get out of here."

I don't recognize the female voice, but I still don't turn to see who is trying to pull my arm out of my socket. I can't look away from Halee. I manage to yank my shoulder free of their grip, surprised at the strange calmness in my voice as I say, "I can't leave her. I won't. I need to fix this."

There's a moment of silence then a huff behind me,

followed by a shuffling. Footsteps fade, and I sink back to my belly, arm stretched through the bars, fingers scraping against the stone floor. If I could just reach Halee ... I don't know, but I can't leave her like this. Alone. Like she died. Alone and afraid. Because of me.

The darkness staining my hand recedes to just the tips of my fingers as my sorrow begins to push at my anger. It hurts. Too much. The pain of losing Halee threatens to hollow me out until I can't breathe. But I suck in some air, telling myself over and over that it'll be okay. I just have to get out of here with Halee, and ...

In order to function, I need the rage. I force myself to recall Lord Drakam, my *father's* face as he killed her—all to ... what? To force my power to come out? Grabbing hold of the fury that flares up, I use it to fuel my muscles —to move, to act, to get out of here.

There's movement on the other side of the room at the open door leading to the hall where the guards came through, and I push to my feet, blade in hand, ready for whatever comes next. I hope it's Lord Drakam so I can sink my knife into his heart and watch the light leave his eyes. But the shadowy form that moves through the door is too small. *Shame.* Still, I keep the knife in my hand just in case.

A woman strides into the room, and I blink. I know her. The Poison mage from the games. "Vesper?"

She shoots me a quick smile and a shrug. "I wasn't about to drag you by the arm through this massive estate, so ..."

"What? How did you ... What are you doing here?"

"I've been keeping an eye on you, Void." She looks around the room as she crosses to me. Vesper tosses a bundle of fabric through the bars, and I clumsily catch it.

The grey fabric smells musty, and I recognize it—a similar style cloak that I've seen shrouding the faces of my attackers these past weeks. I flick my gaze back to Vesper and she nods at the cloak. "Found a bunch of those here in the estate in a room no one was probably supposed to know about." She sounds pleased with herself, and I almost smile. Almost. She goes on, "I may be jumping to conclusions here, but I think it's safe to say Lord Drakam sent those grey-cloaks after you." She shrugs. "Anyway, put that on. I don't think you're getting out of here without hiding your face."

I don't want to get out of here, at least not until every Drakam is dead by my hand, but I shrug into the cloak as Vesper's gaze flicks over the unconscious bodies of the four guards as if they are mere pieces of furniture. Her fingers scrape through her short, blond hair as she says, "I couldn't find a release mechanism for the bars. And it's not magic, cause, well ..." She waves a hand at me, one brow raising at my left arm which is now only tinted a shadowy black along the tips of my fingers.

I point with the blade in my hand. "There was a stone that depressed when Severn's son stepped on it."

"Is that who that was? Hmm. Shoulda killed him. Oh well, next time." I'm not sure what she's talking about as Vesper crosses to where I pointed, stomping on a few stones before one clicks under her boot. The bars slam into the floor and I sprint the short distance to Halee. Ignoring the deep gash in her throat, I push a few curls off her face. Her features turn blurry, but I swallow my tears, stroking a finger across her cheek—a cheek that was always tinged with a pink blush for one reason or another. She's so pale now, her dark skin devoid of the color, the life, the spark that made Halee, Halee.

But it'll be fine. Everything will be fine. I just have to—

A hand comes to my shoulder, squeezing. "I'm sorry, Thaeia. There will be time to mourn later. We have to go. This entire place is in a panic since all the magic just went pfft." I look up at Vesper, questions spilling through my mind. *All the magic? Everyone in the estate? What am I?* She crouches, shifting Halee's body before taking her over her shoulder. "We need to move while everyone is distracted and before more guards come." She grunts as she adjusts Halee. "And they will come. So let's get a move on."

My gaze snaps to the door. Severn. I need to end this. He's not going to let me go easily, and I won't rest until he's dead. Vesper sees the direction I'm looking and shakes her head. "Later. Revenge later. I'll even help. Now, we retreat to fight another day. You need to sort out your magic."

My magic.

I hold up my left hand, looking at my wrist. Without the inky whatever-it-is covering my skin, the Forsaken mark is invisible.

Vesper snaps her fingers a few times in my face. My gaze flicks to Halee's body lying limp over her shoulder. Vesper is right. There's no time. I need to get Halee out of here ... get her to ... Turning, I curl my fingers into my palms, nails nearly breaking the skin. Running a hand down Halee's back, I fist her shirt, now stiff with drying blood, determination in my voice. "Let's go."

I collect the knives I threw at Severn, sliding them into my thigh sheath with a vow that they will find their new home deep in Lord Drakam's heart. Without another word, Vesper and I stride from the room. As we cross the large space, I just now notice the door that I first came through with Severn's son is standing open. I could have sworn he locked that. They wouldn't just leave me in an unsecured room ...

Vesper digs in a pocket with her free hand, producing a key. She waves it in the air with a smile before sliding it back into her pocket. My brows pinch. "Who are you?"

She chuckles. "Just someone who's really good at getting into places and finding things."

"You said earlier you should have killed Severn's son ..."

She shrugs. "I was trying this new thing where I don't kill everyone who gets in my way. So, no. Drakam's son isn't dead, unfortunately. He *is* temporarily blind and paralyzed."

"You can produce different toxins and can control their levels?"

"Yup. At least I could, until whatever it is you do unleashed on us all."

Flexing my hands, I stalk down the hallway after Vesper. How long ago was it that I followed Severn's son down this corridor? Minutes? Hours? It feels like days.

I stop, grabbing Vesper's arm. "Wait. Fara."

"What? Who or what is a Fara? Seriously, Thaeia, we need to keep moving."

"We need to find Fara. She saved me, as a baby ... I think. Severn is going to kill her, if he hasn't already."

"Look. My arms are full right now. I don't have magic. No one does. People are panicking, and panic easily turns to anger that turns into violence. You get me? We can't go traipsing through this giant estate searching for one woman who may or may not be alive." She shifts Halee again, and I bite my lip, unsure of what to do. Vesper sighs. "But this is your shit show, so ... what do you want to do?"

I say a silent apology to Fara, promising to come back for her as I take Halee's hand. The feel of her lifeless fingers against my palm solidifies my decision. "We're leaving."

The dim light of the room behind us casts my shadow before me like a wraith of death. I grin as another wave of ... something ... bursts from me, lifting my hair from where it hangs down my back. Death indeed. My *father* made a grave mistake in not killing me as soon as he had me alone in that room. He thought to use me, to use my *power* to leash other mages. I trail my left fingers over the wall as we go, and as my anger builds, the smoky darkness climbs my arm, curling all the way up and around my shoulder, settling like the long sleeves I used to cling so desperately to. My nails scrape over the stones.

Vesper winces. "Is there any way to reel that back in?"

Pulling my fingers away from the wall, I wiggle them in front of my face. "Not sure."

"Well, if we run into anyone on the way out, which is likely, my magic would come in handy." I glance at her wrist. VUEDATH. Poison. She shifts Halee's body, nodding at my own wrist. "You think that was always there?"

I turn my arm one way then the other, looking at the scrolling letters of my power. KURKODAM. Forsaken. Like a secret message. Like a sick joke. Shrugging, I press my fingers to the wall again, trailing them along the stones. "Don't know. Don't really care."

"It is interes—"

We round a corner, coming face to face with a wide-eyed man.

Severn's son. He blinks, rubbing at his eyes, and sways slightly as if Vesper's Poison is not yet completely out of his system. Something close to euphoria blooms through my chest. I didn't think I'd have this opportunity so soon. A strange voice in my head giggles, *How wonderful.*

I push the hood of my cloak back, and Vesper scoffs, "Defeats the purpose of the cloak, idiot."

I ignore her as Severn's son's lips pull up in a sneer, his left hand flexing. The muscles of his forearm ripple, drawing my eyes to his tattoo. DORKRAKK. Darkness. Fitting. Asshole.

Vesper steps closer to me, whispering, "Now would be the time to rein it in, Void. I need my magic."

I smile, palming one of my knives, twirling it between my fingers. "If I could ... and that's a big if ... then this fucker would have his magic too." Vesper sighs, shifting as if she's going to put Halee down. I stride forward, a shiver of excitement stealing down my spine at the flash of fear in Severn's son's eyes. "Don't worry, I'm used to having no magic. This won't take long."

The man before me fumbles for the long dagger at his waist, and I laugh. "You should run ... *brother.*"

His scowl deepens, hatred flaring across his face. "You're no sister of mine. My father should have killed you on sight. I'll fix that."

I chuckle again, pointing my knife at his chest. "You can try."

CHAPTER 2

KEIR

I grit my teeth, leaning over the neck of my horse as she gallops into Rokvale. The capital city of Drakam is in a panic, forcing me to slow. My magic went out over half an hour ago. It came back briefly, my hounds whining as they reappeared mid-sprint. But then they'd winked out once again. And my magic hasn't come back since.

Something is horribly wrong.

When I rushed out of my estate after my father told me about his past with the woman who raised Thaeia as well as his theories about Lord Drakam, I was anxious to catch up to Thaeia before she got too far into Drakam territory. I got hung up at the border, the Drakam guards not wanting to let me into their territory. A growl rumbles from my chest as I recall trying to be 'diplomatic' with them. I'm such a fool. I wasted so much time talking.

Finally, the need to get to Thaeia made me act, and I called several Spirits, quickly knocking out all the guards.

Then my magic disappeared, and my nerves shot into full-blown panic. Getting to her became a compulsive need, driving me to go faster, rest less, push harder ... just to find her.

Now, as I'm forced to pick my way through the city, I'm wound so tightly, my back aches. A woman on the side of the street rubs her tattoo as she yells, hysteria in her voice, "What's going on? What happened?"

"It still won't work. My magic. My magic," another woman says as she walks down the middle of the road, her eyes glazed as if she's in shock.

I rein my horse around her and am distracted by soft crying coming from the doorway of a shop to my left. A young boy who can't be any older than fourteen, sits on the stoop, cradling his left arm in his lap, tears falling to his tattoo.

As I turn down the main street, an older man peeks out his window before darting back inside. He slams the window shut and draws a curtain just as a green-clad guard of House Drakam shouts at me.

"You! Turn around. No one's allowed down this way."

I raise a brow, ready to run him over if needed, but a swarm of people rushes him. Over a dozen citizens crowd the guard, everyone shouting at once. He tries to keep an eye on me, but I trot right on by. A woman grabs the guard by his shirt, actually shaking him. "What's going on? What's happened to the magic? It's gone!"

The guard struggles to untangle himself from the press of bodies, holding up his hand. "We are looking into it. You all need to return to your homes."

Shouts drown him out, and I kick my horse into a canter.

House Drakam looms several blocks ahead, the gates closed and guarded. I skirt the estate, sticking to side streets and shadows. I know this city fairly well since I've traveled all over Sodoles with my father and Captain Daria in service to Alopson.

Tracking back a block, the scent of hay and horse manure hits me a few moments before the public stable and carriage house come into view. The sign with its peeling paint swings in the slight breeze, and a horse stomps its hoof from within the small barn. Before my mare even draws to a stop, I swing my leg over her neck and hit the ground. A woman rushes out, and I realize that I left in such a hurry, I don't have any coin on me. I pat my pockets and fish around in the small saddle bag, hoping to find something.

A gasp draws my attention, and I turn to face the wide-eyed woman before me. She has smile lines along the edges of her hazel eyes, and her straw-colored hair is pulled back in a tight tail. She blinks a few times, and I pat my pockets again, irritated at this holdup. "Um. I don't have any—"

"You're Lord Keir Alopson."

Honestly, I'm surprised she recognized me. People usually don't see past the Spirit fire and my hounds. I figured I'd be anonymous without my magic waving like a literal red flag letting everyone know who I am.

The woman clasps her hands, her cheeks turning pink. "I've been to every Games since I was five. The first time I saw you ... gods! And every Games you just got better. More and more stars. But this year. The Games. Your match against that Void woman. The explosions.

Gods! You were right there! I saw you, watchin' the team competition right from the edge of the arena. Such chaos! I've never—"

I hold up a hand to stop her rambling. Yes, I was there, I don't need to relive that, though I know she means no harm. "I'm sorry. I'm in a bit of a rush, but I don't have any money. I, of course, will pay. I just—"

"No! Oh, gods no. Please." She reaches out, taking my mare's reins, and curls the leather around her hand. "This is my place, you see. I'll take great care of her. Don't you worry, Lord Keir. No charge. Wow. Lord Keir at *my* stables. You almost don't seem real. I can't believe you're here! Wait, why are you here? Are you here about this magic blackout? Is it that Void woman? Is she here? People are sure up in arms about it. I thought for sure the horses were going to break out of their stalls when people started screamin' and yelllin' like fools. I figure there's nothin' to be done, so why lose my head over it. The magic'll come back. Or it won't. Though I don't have anythin' impressive" —she waves her left hand, but she's moving too fast for me to read what her magic is, and there are no stars climbing her arm—"so I don't really miss it all that much. But I guess someone like you is feelin' this blackout pretty bad, huh?"

I open my mouth, but her eyes go wide once again, and she waves her hands, the reins flopping. "I'm so sorry. You said you were in a rush, and here I am blabbin' on. You go on now, and don't you worry about your mare here. She's in good hands."

Despite the anxiety clawing at my stomach urging me to move, to find Thaeia, I smile. This woman reminds me of our young stable hand back home, Arabell, if she were fifteen years older. I ask, "What's your name?"

The woman's blush deepens. "Kit."

"I thank you, Kit. Would you happen to have a coat or cloak or something with a hood that I could borrow?"

She licks her lips, a brow raising with a little smile. "I think I can help ya there. Wait right here. I'll be back real quick."

Kit jogs off, my mare trotting happily behind her as if she knows a meal and some rest await her inside the stables. I look up and down the street nervously. The stables are tucked back from the busier parts of the city, and though the sounds of people yelling can still be heard, I'm alone on this little side street.

Kit rushes back out, dark fabric balled in her fist. "Hope this fits. You're a tall fella."

I smile, taking the pullover from her. It's loose at the bottom and swings around my hips as I pull it on. It must hit her calves when she wears it. The material is scratchy with a faded grey and blue pattern running all over it. I slip my arms through the sleeves that only make it halfway down my forearms. But I'm not worried about covering my arms. Reaching back, I pull the wide hood over my head. The fabric is thick and heavy, smelling strongly of horse, which I don't mind, but it's stiflingly hot.

Kit clicks her tongue. "Yeah, a bit small. Sorry, it's all I had. I only wear that in the winter when I'm muckin' stalls."

"It's perfect. Thank you. I'll be sure to bring it back."

"Pfft." She waves her hand, her entire face turning red. "Don't worry about it. Now off with ya. I've kept ya long enough with my blabbing. Good luck with whatever it is you're doin'."

I give her a little smile then jog down the side alley back towards the Drakam estate. As soon as I push out of the shadows, someone runs into me, stumbling, then keeps going without looking up. I trip over a man sitting right in the middle of the street curled into a tight ball, and two people erupt from a doorway to my right, arms wrapped around each other as they tumble out into the road. As soon as they stop rolling, fists start to fly. Gods, these people lose their magic for a few hours and they lose their minds.

I push through the chaos, moving towards the east side of House Drakam. As soon as I'm away from the main thoroughfare of the city, the crowds thin. People here seem to be hiding instead of fighting. Good.

The fingers of my left hand flex and clench over and over with the need to get to Thaeia. Stopping at the edge of where the city ends and the estate grounds begin, I look across the short expanse to the high stone wall of House Drakam. I spot the tall hedge I'm looking for. The way seems clear, so I duck my head and force myself to walk and not run across the empty stretch of grass until I get to the tall line of bushes. Pushing through a narrow section, I'm grateful for the thick pullover as the exposed ends of sheared branches poke at me. This is definitely tighter and less manicured than the last time I used this hidden entrance. Visiting territory leaders and their council use this entrance to avoid the public eye. Well, they used to anyway. This seems like it hasn't been used in months, maybe over a year. I know it's been at least three years since I've been here.

I pause, fishing in my pocket for the key. I didn't bring money, but I brought this—my father's key that opens this hidden gate in the perimeter wall as well as a secret entrance into the estate. Lady Kapros has one too, and she and Lord Drakam have keys to a similar entrance to

House Alopson. There's a third key for House Kapros, though now I'm thinking we should change our lock back home.

It sounds like a bell tolling my arrival when the gate squeaks open, and I grit my teeth as I pull it closed through the tangle of branches and vines. I pause within the shield of the hedge, poking my head out. I don't see anyone, so I shift to work myself free of the stabbing branches, but then I hear running footsteps. I freeze, stepping back to make sure I'm hidden just as five guards run past, weapons drawn. They round a corner, and I wait until I can't hear them before I shove out of the bushes and sprint across the grounds. I slam against the wall, breathing hard. I keep my back pressed to the stone as I reach for the hidden latch that will open the secret door. My finger finds the keyhole, and I slip the key in, turning it slowly, trying to make as little noise as possible.

A hiss of sound accompanies the opening of the door, and musty air huffs in my face as I push into the dark hall. I sputter as a cobweb sticks to my face, and I carefully close the door behind me, slipping the key back into my pocket. Running my hands down the wall as I work my way deeper into House Drakam, dust coats my fingers, confirming this entrance hasn't been used in a long while. I can't help but wonder why, but I'm grateful.

There is light ahead, and I know this hall empties into a receiving room of sorts. Shadows move through the light, and I know I won't be able to hide much longer. But that's okay. I'm inside the estate. Now I just have to find Thaeia.

I blink against the brightness of the room as I step into the chaos. I hug the wall, hood still drawn as staff run in and out of the room with no obvious objective. A woman hides under a table, tears streaking down her face, her round eyes darting back and forth. A guard grabs a man wearing a white apron, shaking him. "Get back to the kitchens." The cook just shakes his head, his mouth open, but no sound comes out. The guard growls, practically dragging the man out of the room through a pair of doors hanging off their hinges.

Pushing into the fray, I aim for the doorway, but a body slams into me, and I hit the wall, my shoulder screaming in protest for a second. I grip the man before he falls to the floor, but he doesn't even look at me. He just shoves out of my arms and runs towards another man who's glowering at him, blood dripping from his lip. The two trade punches, and I move on.

I flex and clench my left hand, willing my magic to come back. Nothing.

I make it out of the room, down a wide hall and into another large room. I have no idea where Thaeia could be, but I know she's here, and I'll search the entire place room by room if I have to. I leap over the back of a sofa, running towards shouting coming from another room. A woman darts in front of me, tripping over the edge of a chair, her skirt tangling around her ankles. I grab her arm, keeping her upright before moving her out of my way.

Several guards back out of a narrow hall on the other side of the room, blocking my way out. One guard falls over a table, the wood clattering to the floor, and she sprawls to her back. More guards retreat into the room, facing away from me as they watch whatever is happening in that hall.

A voice booms out. "No one interferes. She's mine."

Shit.

The guards fan out, creating a semicircle as a broad

back steps out of the hall. Sweat dampens his green tunic, and his muscles flex as he raises his arm, deflecting a blow.

And there she is. Thaeia's messy hair is pulled back, a wildness in her eyes I haven't seen before, and that's saying something. A grey cloak like the ones worn by the attackers at the Coliseum and my estate swirls around her. She rears back, punching out. But it's a feint. One of Severn Drakam's sons, Sidian, shifts to avoid her swing, leaving his right side open. Thaeia swipes, the steel of her knife flashing, coming away dripping red with his blood.

Sidian hisses, holding out a hand. "Sword."

A guard slaps the hilt of their blade into Sidian's waiting palm. The lord swings it twice, then points it at Thaeia. "Time to die."

Thaeia shrugs out of the cloak, the grey fabric billowing to the floor around her feet. Rage ignites through my veins when I see blood on her hand.

No, it's not blood. It looks as if her arm's been inked or like she dunked her hand in black paint. I brace on the balls of my feet, ready to sprint through the wall of guards and stab Sidian in the back, but I'm shocked into stillness as the Poison mage from the Games steps out of the hall into the room. Vesper? I think that's her name. She was on Thaeia's team when the explosions went off. She was down in the arena during all that chaos ... She's from Alopson. But she's here. Why? How? I shake my head, noticing what is definitely blood staining one side of her clothes and the two wicked-looking daggers in her hand. She stands at Thaeia's side, a grin on her face, her blue eyes sparkling. "You'll have to take us both down." Her eyes flit to me, and she jerks her chin. "And him."

How she picked me out of the group so quickly, I don't

know, but my breath leaves me like someone punched me in the gut as Thaeia's eyes snap to mine. There's pure rage in their golden depths. But under that, there's ... pain. Devastating agony. *What has happened?*

I shove my hood back and dip my head at her. "Hey, Fox Slayer. Sorry I'm late."

Her anger bleeds away, and for just a moment, tears pool in her eyes. The look on her face guts me. She didn't think I was coming for her. That thought is both devastating and infuriating. Next chance I get, I'm going to make sure she knows she can count on me, no matter what. She will understand that she's etched herself onto my heart and there's nothing that will keep me from her side.

Sidian looks over his shoulder, his eyes narrowing on me before he barks. "Take him."

"No!" And just like that, the rage is back in Thaeia's eyes. A burst of ... something punctuates Thaeia's scream. My hair flutters, and the darkness that covers her arm spreads across her chest and up her neck. Her beautiful golden eyes turn black, and even as a shiver creeps down my spine, I can't look away. She is stunning, and I know I'd follow her anywhere. Still, this isn't good.

Vesper staggers, clutching her chest with a grunt. "Rein. It. In. Thaeia."

I don't have time to see anymore as five guards rush me. I duck under the swing of a sword, slashing my dagger across their thigh, deep enough to sever muscle. A fist connects with my side, and I grunt as the air is forced from my lungs. I don't feel the pain, though. All I feel is the need to get to my Fox Slayer. I throw my elbow back, and the cartilage of a guard's nose crunches. I'm yanked back, someone fisting my shirt so tight, it nearly chokes me. Bending at the waist, I spin, coming up behind them to bring my arm down, breaking the hold. I have to get to Thaeia. Turning, I raise my dagger and lift my other fist to protect my face, but everyone has stopped. Vesper has a grip on a guard's wrist, keeping his blade from punching into her belly, but they are both looking at Thaeia and Sidian.

My skin turns clammy as dread fills my stomach like thick oil.

Thaeia has her stained left hand wrapped around Sidian's throat. His sword is sunk deep into her side, but it's as if she doesn't notice the blade in her flesh. There's just rage in her eyes. If fire burned black, that would be what's in her gaze. Sidian's eyes bulge from his face, his mouth open, little gasps coming from his lips. My brows furrow. She doesn't have that tight of a hold on him.

Though, the look on her face ... There's something inside me, screaming, *This is wrong. This isn't her. Whatever this is, she's not in control.* Cautiously, I thread my way through the stunned guards. I reach out to Thaeia, but it's like trying to press through Nor's Gravity magic. Before I can reach her, she steps closer to Sidian, his blade sinking deeper, but she doesn't so much as flinch. Her nose nearly brushes his, and when she speaks, the hairs on my arms and the back of my neck stand up.

"How many times did you stand by as your father murdered my sisters?" It's like another voice is layered over hers ... like her Void is manifest and ... speaking through her. Sidian's skin pales as Thaeia asks, "How many?"

His voice cracks on a whisper. "I don't know."

Thaeia's grip is loose around his throat, but her arm shakes as she bares her teeth at him. I take another step towards her and nearly crumble under the pressure of whatever is emanating from her. The sound of feet shuffling tells me the guards are backing away, and several more straight up run from the room, abandoning their lord in order to escape Thaeia's wrath.

And I can't say I blame them. It feels like my bones are being crushed, or sucked dry, or ... it just plain hurts. But I reach for her. She doesn't look at me or the last of the fleeing guards. Thaeia keeps her hard gaze on Sidian as her eerie double voice says, "Well, now it's our turn. We're going to wipe out the males of your line. Your brothers, your father, anyone who knew and did nothing." She runs her finger down Sidian's throat as I struggle to get closer. I expect him to pull his sword from her side and strike her down, and I'm not sure if I can reach her in time with this ... power holding me back.

But then I notice a trail of Thaeia's inky blue-black shadow sticking to Sidian's neck where she trails her touch. His skin seems to ... shrink as Thaeia—or whatever is inside of Thaeia—actually chuckles. "There's something poetic about you dying by our power, don't you think?"

Our power? Oh, gods. I push against the pain, my fingers finally wrapping around her right forearm. My knees buckle, and I hit the floor hard, but I keep my grip on her. I won't let her go. There must be a few guards who've stayed because gasps sound from behind me, and when I look up, Sidian is ... shriveled is the only word that comes to mind. Thaeia taps him with her finger, ignoring my grip on her arm as she says, "Your life is *Forsaken*."

It feels like I'm being scraped out from the inside. It's hard to breathe. My skin itches. A wave of dizziness has me swaying on my knees, and my grip on her loosens. This is wrong. But how do I stop it? How do I stop her?

Sidian topples to the floor with a sickening crack, his sword sliding out of Thaeia's side with a sucking sound that makes me wince. His lifeless eyes stare up at the ceiling. When I look at Thaeia's face, all I see is darkness, rage, sorrow, pain ... I don't see my Fox Slayer at all. Wrapping my other hand around her arm, I tug until she finally turns her gaze down to me. I nearly gasp with despair when there's no recognition of me in her eyes. I can't catch my breath as she cocks her head, looking between my hands on her arm and my face. She's terrifying, like she's trying to decide if I'm friend or foe. But she's glorious. Fiercely beautiful. But not Thaeia. Not my Thaeia. She is lost somewhere in this darkness.

All I can manage is a whisper. "Stop, Thaeia. Please."

For a long moment, she just stares at me, and I feel my death looming. Not like this. Please. If she kills me, she won't come back.

Vesper chokes out a shout. "Thaeia! You're killing him!"

My right hand drifts down to her wrist, and I give her a little squeeze. "Fox Slayer, come back to me."

She blinks down at me, the black bleeding from her eyes, the roiling shadows quickly retreating from her skin until only the tips of her fingers look like they've been dipped in soot. She falls to her knees, and the intense pressure scooping out my insides vanishes like a bubble popping. I pull her to me, wrapping her in my arms, holding her tight. She exhales on a sob, and I hear her heart breaking in the sound.

Her voice cracks. "You came."

I pull her into my lap, wrapping one leg over hers,

holding her tighter. I think I need this as much as she does. Seeing Thaeia like that, taken over by whatever that was … "You are mine, Thaeia. Of course I came. I always will."

There's so much more I want to say, but movement catches my eye. I curl my arms around her, pulling her even closer, ready to defend, but it's just Vesper. My breath hitches as she carries Halee's body out of the hall, skirting the toppled furniture, and gently lays her on the closest sofa.

Oh, gods. My eyes meet Vesper's, and I flick my gaze to Halee then back to her. Vesper shakes her head.

No. Oh, gods, no.

I press my hand to the back of Thaeia's head, holding her to my chest. She mumbles something, but I can't understand her. I try to shush her, stroking her hair, but she pushes against my chest. She stares up at me with … hope.

Fuck.

And then she says the worst thing that could have ever passed her lips. "Bring her back."

Vesper gasps, and I take a slow breath, trying to control the visceral reaction her words cause. When I don't say anything, her tone becomes a little more desperate. "Keir, bring Halee back. Call her Spirit and put her back in her body." I'm shaking my head as tears shimmer in Thaeia's eyes. "Please, Keir. Bring her back. Please. She didn't deserve that. Please. It was my fault. Please. Please. Please." Her fists ball my shirt, each of her pleas hitting with the force of a physical stab, ripping me open.

But she doesn't understand what she's asking of me. My stomach churns and vomit burns my throat. Sweat breaks out across my skin just at the thought of doing what Thaeia is begging me to do. I'd do anything for her ... but not this. Never this. I'm still shaking my head when the inky blackness starts crawling back up her arm, and that double voice screams her desperation and pain at me, "Bring her back!"

CHAPTER 3

NOR

THIS IS BAD. This is very bad.

Luckily, we still had our magic when we got to the Kapros-Drakam border, and Valsan just confused the shit out of all the guards so we were able to gallop right through. But not long after, our magic just ... vanished. For a moment, I thought Thaeia had somehow found us, and I whipped my head around, looking for her. Aimee did the same, but no Thaeia.

We've been riding for hours, days. My ass hurts from so much time in the saddle, and my back aches. We're all exhausted, our nerves stretched thin, but we can't stop. The capital of Drakam is now less than an hour away. Will Thaeia be there? Halee? What happened to cause Thaeia's Void to explode like this? I flex the fingers of my left hand around the reins.

This is bad.

Owen's voice pulls me out of my head. "Do you think she'll be there?"

I don't bother to look at him, because I don't know. But Valsan shocks me as he says, "Yes." I cock my head at him. I'm so tired I nearly sway in the saddle. He slows his horse, and we all do the same, though Miles takes a bit longer to pull his horse from his racing gallop. He hasn't said a word since our magic went out. Aimee twists and turns, cracking her back, and Owen stretches his arms over his head as Valsan continues, "I don't trust Drakam. They've been stirring up trouble since the Games."

Aimee keeps her gaze on the road, asking, "Plan?"

Valsan cracks his neck. "I'll request to speak with Lord Drakam. Captain Silas if that fails. Diplomacy first."

Miles visibly stiffens in his saddle, shaking his head but says nothing. None of us respond. I'm too lost in my spinning thoughts of Thaeia and what the absence of our magic means. *Are Thaeia and Halee even in the capital city or in Drakam at all? How the fuck are we going to find them? Is Thaeia okay?* I roll my left wrist. *No. I don't think she is. Her Void has only expanded in the past when something traumatic happened to her. Does that mean ...*

I want to talk this out with Valsan. Okay, I want him to make this knot in my stomach go away. I want him to tell me everything is going to be okay. But I don't turn to him, because I don't want him to give me platitudes. I don't want him to lie to me because he thinks I need to hear the words.

We all look ahead, down the long, nearly empty road leading to the capital city of Drakam, Rokvale. After a few minutes, Valsan steers his horse close to me. The breeze brings me his leather and wood-smoke scent, like a gift, and I take a slow inhale. Just the sound of his deep voice loosens some of the tension straining my muscles.

"Are you okay?"

Shit. I really need to work on keeping my thoughts from parading across my face. Though, even if I had the best poker face in the country, I think Val would still be able to read me. I shake my head, but keep my thoughts internal.

His arm flashes out, gripping my reins, pulling my horse and his to a stop. Aimee and Owen look over their shoulders at us, but Valsan tilts his head towards where Miles continues on, and they move to follow him. Valsan takes my hand, and I shift to face him. Our horses dance in place, uncomfortable with being pressed against each other, but after a few seconds they settle, and I sigh. Lifting my left hand, I stare at my tattoo and the three stars climbing my arm. "This is bad, Val."

He just nods, his hand warm around mine. I ball my left hand into a fist, then release it, dropping it into my lap. "I keep thinking of worse and worse reasons for this to have happened. I'm spinning. I'm terrified ... for so many reasons. I ..."

His hand leaves mine, but only to cup my face. My facial hair is longer now, almost a full beard. It feels good as he scrapes his fingers through the bristles, gently pulling me to him. "I know. I can't promise we'll fix this, because I don't know what *this* is. But, Nor"—he runs his thumb over my lower lip, and I barely resist the urge to lick him—"I can promise we'll find her. We'll find them both. I'm here. I'm not going anywhere. I'm with you. Okay?"

"But—"

"Nor. I'm with you."

My chest is tight, but not in an uncomfortable way. In a way that tells me I'm loved. And I love him. I nod, and he presses his lips to mine. Reaching up, I place my hand over his where he still cups my face, holding him to me as we kiss. When he pulls away, I tighten my fingers around his, keeping him close.

"Val, you are ..." I take a deep breath, looking into his eyes. "Thank you. Wherever you are, wherever you go, you are my home. You are my heart."

He smiles, pressing another slow kiss to my lips before saying, "And you are mine, Nor."

We shift in our saddles, letting our horses pull apart, then pick up a quick trot to catch up to the others. My mind still swirls with horrific possibilities, but now there's a sliver of peace calming me slightly. That's what Val does for me. He doesn't silence the noise in my head—I don't think anything can do that, but he turns down the volume, allowing me to breathe.

We travel in silence as the press of the jungle that frames the road thins, and houses start to dot the landscape, growing more frequent and getting closer together. The city finally appears on the hazy horizon, and I wipe sweat from my face before pinching my shirt and fanning it away from my sticky skin.

"Why would you think I had anything to do with this?" The shout spills from a house on our right a second before a man stumbles out backwards, tripping down the single step into the yard.

A woman follows him out, rage pulling her lips back as she shoves him again. "You were doing something in that locked room of yours you never let me in! Then the next thing I know, my magic is just gone! Everyone's is gone. How do you explain that, Murphy?"

The man holds up his hands, shaking his head. "I don't know. It wasn't me!"

"Bullshit!"

The woman rears back to shove him again, but he grabs her wrists, tugging her off balance before snarling in her face, "Push me one more time, I dare you."

Fear flashes through her eyes, but then she lands a solid kick to his shin. The man curses, raising a fist, and I flinch. Before I can even think of getting down to stop the fight, Valsan is there. His large hand holds the man's arm, keeping him from connecting with the woman's face. Murphy snarls, yanking back, but can't manage to pull out of Valsan's hold. "Hey. Let me go. Mind your own business."

Valsan steps between the two, but keeps himself angled so he can still see them both. Aimee is now on the ground as well, her arms crossed, but her posture is poised and ready to jump in if needed. Valsan smiles as he moves into the man's space, causing him to involuntarily back up, giving the woman additional space. "Violence is my business." Godsdamn, his voice holds such command, it sends a shiver down my spine all the way to my toes. "Now, I know tensions are high, but we all need to do our best to stay calm and remember, we are not the products of our magic. We are more. We are human. We are Sodolerian."

Murphy and the woman blink at him before they both duck their heads as Valsan continues, "This is scary for everyone, but that just means we must be extra kind to each other. We need to help each other through this, and hopefully our gifts will come back soon. Maybe gather your friends to say a prayer at the chapel?"

The woman's head lifts, and she nods, but she doesn't

do a good job of hiding the small scowl on her face as she glares at Murphy before going back into the house. Murphy shrugs. "Sorry about that."

Valsan leans in. "Don't apologize to me. You threatened her. You are both scared and reacted poorly when you should be supporting each other. Do better." And with that, he turns, striding back to his horse.

Well, fuck me. I love him so much.

I gasp, clutching my chest. Valsan actually stumbles, falling to one knee, and Aimee staggers back catching herself on the side of her horse. My legs scream with pins and needles as I leap from my mount. It's hard to breathe. It feels like I'm being hollowed out. I crouch next to Val, placing a hand on his back. He shakes his head, his face half-hidden by his hair as he tilts it up to look at me as he whispers, "We have to go. We have to find her. She needs us."

I marvel at him through the agony. He's thinking of Thaeia even as he clutches his own chest in pain. Slowly, the waves of sucking pressure pulling at my insides lessen and then fade to nothing. I lift my left arm, clenching my fist, but still nothing. Damn it.

"What the fuck was that? That's the second time that's happened. It feels like someone was ripping out my intestines like scraping seeds out of a pumpkin." I almost laugh at the very accurate description as Owen's horse dances in place, tossing its head.

Valsan gets back to his feet, then we're all mounted back up. "We need to keep going."

We kick our horses into a fast canter, and I will the city to get closer faster. The tension in Miles' back makes it seem like he's ready to snap at any second. He still hasn't said a word.

An agonizingly slow fifteen minutes later, and we pass into Rokvale. The fear and violence we witnessed between Murphy and the woman is amplified tenfold here in the city. People dash across the street, ducking into stores and homes, slamming doors. There are shouts, and people crying. A few wander aimlessly, eyes glassy, fingers of their left hands twitching. This is like something out of a horror novel. The clothing store on our left has no windows. They're not broken or shattered, just gone. A large hole in the street forces us onto the walkway. A section of the roof of a house is missing, and all the fruit on the trees lining the road is withered and rotten.

All the things magic has created, and held together, and repaired ... it's all gone. This never happened with Thaeia's Void before. She has evolved again, and I can't stop the tremor that shivers down my spine. What if ...

I shake my head, not allowing my old fears to take root. I know Thaeia. I trust her.

Carefully, we pick our way through the chaotic streets, and more than once, I hear Owen grumble incoherently under his breath.

"Captain Valsan!" We all turn at the shout to find a green-clad Drakam guard jogging our way from around a corner. We head towards her, stopping right in the center of the road. She glances at all of us before focusing on Valsan. "You shouldn't be here."

Val just raises a brow. "I think you could use the help. What's going on?"

Her left hand flexes as she shakes her head. "Not sure. All the magic just ..." She makes a fist then quickly opens it, spreading her fingers. "Poof."

A scream sounds behind us, and the guard flicks her gaze past Valsan. He jerks his chin. "You have a job to do."

She grinds her teeth as she stands straighter. "And you should go home. If this is going on in Kapros as well, I'm sure you're needed there."

Shit. What if this has happened across the entire country? I glance at Valsan's back. Of course he'd want to be in the capital of Kapros, keeping his people calm and safe until everything returns to normal ... *if* things return to normal. But he's here, for Halee, for Thaeia, for me.

The screaming cuts off, but then several shouts ring out. The guard sighs, pointing her finger at the fighting mass of people. "Hey! Break it up. Go home."

Valsan aims his horse north, towards the Drakam estate, and I realize Miles is already three blocks ahead of us. House Drakam looms, its stone, wood, and metal facade towering into the sky, the closed scrolling iron gates blocking the way. Scores of guards stand at attention on the other side of the thick bars.

How the fuck are we going to get in? And is Halee really in there? Thaeia?

One of the guards closest to the center of the gate calls out, "Stop where you are!" Miles keeps going, and the rest of us kick into a canter to catch up. The guard calls out again, this time raising his hand. "Stop, or we'll shoot."

I follow the line of his hand to the top of the solid stone wall surrounding the estate where several guards lay on their stomachs, crossbows pointed at us.

Valsan shouts, "Miles!"

My eyes go wide. Miles ignores his captain and keeps going, and with seemingly perfect timing, my magic churns to life in my gut. Miles leaps from his horse and throws out his left hand. Large vines explode out of the ground, wrapping around the gates. The metal groans and shifts as the bars are pulled apart. The rest of us surge forward as a crossbow bolt sails towards Miles. Owen throws up a shield of Ice, and the bolt slams into it. A gust of wind hits Miles so hard, he's blown backwards. I send my Gravity magic to cushion his fall, keeping him from slamming into the cobblestones. A flash of Light flares from one of the guards, and we all shield our eyes.

Then it goes eerily quiet. I blink away the dots still dancing in my vision, and when I look around, everyone is just standing around, Confused expressions on their faces. Ah. Valsan, now off his horse as well, steps forward, placing a hand on Miles' shoulder. Miles looks at him, his brows furrowed as Valsan's magic muddles his thoughts, calming him.

The guard who spoke earlier scratches his head, a bit of fear laced in his question. "What's going on?"

Valsan turns to our group. "Come on. Quickly, while I have them."

I'm about to jump from my horse when Thaeia's Void slides around me once again. Shit. A few of the guards shake their heads, casting off the last of Valsan's Confusion magic. Swords lift and point towards us. Crossbows aim down, and tension spikes through the air. Our group skids to a halt, and Valsan raises his hands, palms out. "Look, we just—"

A clang rings out as a large rock slams into the warped and twisted iron bars of the gate. We all swivel to see a large crowd headed down the road towards House Drakam. Their eyes are pinched with anger and fear. A few hold makeshift weapons; kitchen knives, mallets, hammers, shovels ... and some hold actual weapons; swords, daggers, and even crossbows. Another rock sails through the air, slipping between the bars of the gate, and a few guards jump out of the way to avoid being struck.

The guard that spoke to us shouts, "Go home! Everyone turn back and return to your homes."

A man at the front of the advancing crowd yells, "Where's our magic?" The mob surges, their shouts turning into a war cry. The sky fills with thrown rocks. One hits Aimee's horse, and it rears, but she leans into it, keeping her seat. Valsan swings back onto his horse, glaring at the guard. "Let us in. We can help."

The guard shakes his head as a fist-sized rock clangs off the mangled bars right in front of his face. He glances at the gates and the holes in the ground where Miles' vines had punched through, then narrows his eyes at Valsan. "Fuck you."

Valsan wheels his horse around, raising his arm, taking the hit of a thrown stone against his forearm. He drives his left heel into his horse's flank, yanking his reins, barely dodging a crossbow bolt fired from the crowd.

Fuck. Without thinking, I thrust out my left arm, forgetting about the Void. I'm forced to duck to the side, avoiding a few rocks, but one makes contact with my thigh. Thankfully it's small and wasn't thrown with much force.

Once again, Miles has gone off on his own, racing his horse east along the estate wall into another section of the city. Valsan moves to follow, and the rest of us do the same as the Drakam guard shouts, "Warning shots."

The thrum and wack of crossbows being fired sounds behind us, and when I look over my shoulder I see several bolts sticking out of the ground at the feet of the front line of the mob. There's a moment of silence before the people let out a bellow and charge forward with renewed anger. They rush the gates, shaking them. A few slip through the gaps left by Miles' magic, but they are quickly either subdued or cut down. Several try to climb the gates only to be struck by a sword or crossbow bolt. This is horrible. The guards are killing their own people. I watch a man fall from near the top of the gate, an arrow in his chest. The crowd parts, some fanning out along the wall, searching for handholds, and start climbing. More people flood from the city until it looks like ants pressed against the gates and walls, trying to force their way into House Drakam. The rush of bodies is too much for the guards and the damaged gate, and several people make it through, charging down the stone drive towards the front doors of House Drakam.

When I focus forward, I'm met with a rush of even more people running past us heading towards the riot. Their bodies brush against my legs, and my horse throws his head as a few people bounce against him in the crush. If I'm knocked or pulled down, I'll have to move with the mob to keep from being trampled.

But after a few minutes of sheer mayhem, the press of the angry crowd thins, the shouts dimming behind us as we push further into the eastern section of Rokvale. I follow Valsan and the others, breathing a little easier now that we're out of that chaos. I look around at the buildings, wondering where we're going now.

We turn a corner and are met by silence. The street is empty. The sun slants shadows across the road, and a stray piece of paper tumbles across the street on the breeze. Miles pulls to a stop, spinning his horse to face us. We all dismount, securing our mounts to a post around the side of a milliner's shop. The shadows on Miles' face are so dark, his eyes seem hollow. His jaw flexes, and I think he's about to finally say something, but Aimee speaks up first. "We could try to blend in with the mob and get in that way."

Miles nods his agreement with that plan, but then a loud crack booms from the direction of House Drakam, and a plume of dust billows into the air.

Well, that can't be good.

CHAPTER 4

THAEIA

HALEE'S BODY is draped across the sofa behind me. Her absence is like a depthless pit of darkness hollowing me out. But it'll be okay. Everything will be fine now that Keir is here. But why isn't he doing anything?

I search his face, asking, "Keir?"

He won't meet my gaze. Sweat drips down the side of his face as he just shakes his head. Realization hits, and I wobble to my feet. He needs me to get away from him so he can call up his magic. I don't care how far I have to go, for Halee I'll cross the damn sea if that means Keir can bring her back. Pulling away from him I jump to my feet, ignoring the pain in my side. He reaches for me, but I back away, glancing around the room, looking everywhere but that couch. I sprint across the absurdly plush rug.

Gotta get away. Keir needs his magic. It'll be okay. It'll be fine. It'll be okay.

I'm brought to a stop as Vesper jumps in front of me, my chest slamming into hers. *What the ...?* I jerk back, but she grabs my shoulders, shaking me. My palm presses to her chest. "Vesper, let me go. My Void ... I have to ... Keir needs his magic ... Halee ..." A sob catches in my throat, but I manage to swallow it down. *It'll be fine.*

Vesper shakes me again, and when I try to rip out of her hold, a loud slap resounds around the large room. My cheek burns, but I go still as she says, "Thaeia. Stop. Think. Your Void has stretched throughout the city, maybe farther. We need to get out of here. The guards will be back ... with reinforcements. And if Lord Drakam finds us here with *him* ..."

My brows furrow as I follow the angle of her gaze. Vesper still has one hand tight around my shoulder, so my neck pinches slightly as I turn and see ...

"What? Who is that?"

Keir pushes to his feet and approaches me like I'm a rabid animal. *What the fuck?* He holds out a hand as he takes another slow step towards me. "What do you remember?"

My eyes threaten to shift towards Halee, but I resist, keeping my eyes on the shriveled body curled up on the floor. "Lord Drakam." I shake my head, not even close to ready to talk about that. "I ... Vesper came, and ... we were leaving. To find you. I had to find you. For Halee. And then ... then ..."

I pinch my brows, biting my lip. When neither of them says anything, I snap my head around to meet Vesper's gaze before spinning back around to face Keir. It's there in the look on his face—pity and fear. I know the look well. Waving a hand at the body on the floor, I say, "Are you saying *I* did that?"

Keir keeps his arm raised before him, now only two steps away. Vesper shifts her grip from my shoulder and pats my back like I'm a child. "You don't remember?"

I blink at the man on the floor. His skin is too tight, and it looks as if his muscles have been sucked out of his body somehow. His open eyes bug out from his gaunt face, his thin lips cracked. I shake my head as bile burns my stomach. Keir reaches me, tugging me into him, and I let myself fall against his chest as I whisper, "I don't. I ... I really did that? Why? How? Who is he?"

Keir strokes my back, but I feel him shift, and a second later, Vesper is moving across the room. When I start to lift my head to see what she's doing, Keir cups my cheek, turning my gaze to him instead. "That is Lord Drakam's son, Sidian."

I recall when I first arrived, and a flash of Sidian leading me down the dim hall spills through my fractured mind. He didn't say much, leading me to that room where my *father*, where Halee ... That dried-out body on the polished floor looks nothing like the man who led me to my current misery.

Vesper comes to our side, Halee draped over her shoulder. "So, you understand, we need to go. You killed one of Severn Drakam's sons."

Nothing seems to be getting in. The hollowness inside me just consumes everything they're telling me before I can feel any way about it. Keir steps back, deftly taking Halee from Vesper, tenderly cradling her against his chest, though I know it would be easier to carry her like Vesper was, over his shoulder. I should carry her. It was my fault, but the thought of having her dead body pressed against mine ...

The room sways, and I dig my nails into my palms.

When that doesn't work, and darkness begins to creep in, I press my fingers to the wound in my side. I don't remember how I got stabbed, but the pain that lances from my waist, around my back, and up my spine snaps me out of my impending faint.

Keir frowns at me, but when I don't say anything, he takes a step closer as Vesper strides across the room, ducking her head out into a hall, looking one way then the other. "Come on. I have a way out."

Keir nods in her direction, indicating I should precede him. My legs move automatically, and as I cross the room with Keir on my heels, I stare at Sidian. Why can't I remember doing something so ... awful? It looks like it was a painful way to die, but still, I feel nothing. That's probably not good.

Shouting comes from somewhere outside, but it's distant and muffled as Vesper leads us away from the noise. Keir whispers to her, "I had my own way in, but how'd you manage?"

She smiles over her shoulder, turning a corner like she's lived here her whole life. "It was easier than getting into House Alopson, so you can be proud of that, Lord Keir."

He huffs behind me. "We'll come back to that later."

Vesper just winks, taking another corner then starts down a narrow flight of stone steps. They wind around, and I trail my fingers along the wall, noticing the deep blue stain on my fingertips. The air grows warmer when we exit the stairway, and Keir and I follow Vesper into the kitchens. Steam curls from a large pot sitting on the stove. Three loaves of fresh bread sit in a row on a clean marble table running the length of the room. There's only one person here, and when we enter, she freezes with her whisk raised, white foam dripping from the tip. Vesper waves, snatching a cube of seared meat from a sizzling pan which looks like it was recently abandoned over the open flame. She pops the steak into her mouth, blowing on her fingers as she mumbles around the mouthful, "Nothing to see here. We're just on our way out."

The lone cook just stares as we weave through the room. But we all pause, heads whipping around back towards the stairs as a bellow rings down from upstairs.

"Sidian! Noooo!"

I know that voice. Lord Drakam. My *father*.

Wincing, I look down at where Vesper has a death grip on my arm. She shakes her head, and I realize I had turned around, ready to storm back upstairs. Why do I keep blacking out? I look at Halee cradled in Keir's arms and shake my head. I'll deal with my father later. Right now, we need to get out of here so I can figure out how to give Keir's magic back so he can fix what I've broken.

The three of us rush through the kitchen, and Vesper opens a door, the hinges squeaking softly, and we step outside. I blink against the harsh rays of the sun. The air is heavy with humidity, and it smells like rain, though right now, there's not a cloud in the sky.

Silently, we do our best to stick to the shadows of the estate. The crunch of boots on gravel gives us enough warning to duck behind a group of large barrels just as a trio of guards jog past. One says, "They just keep coming from the city. Magic needs to come back soon, or we'll be in real trouble."

Another says, "It did come back for a second there. Maybe it's like trying to come back or something?"

The first guard responds, "Who the fuck knows."

We have to shuffle around the barrels to remain

hidden as they pass. A touch of flesh brushes against my arm, and when I glance over, Halee's shoulder is pressed against mine. The edges of my vision flash with little stars, then start to go dark. I sway, but Vesper wraps her fingers into my hair and tugs, hard, whispering through gritted teeth, "Stay with us."

I nod. Vesper rises to a crouch and jogs across an open space with Keir and me right behind her. Twice more, we have to stop and hide as guards rush around the grounds, a bit of panic on their faces. I don't know what is going on, but it's working as a distraction, so I'm thankful for whatever is causing the chaos on the other side of the estate.

I'm not really paying attention as I blindly follow Vesper. All I can think about is Halee. I haven't looked back once, but I can picture her all the same. Her arms limp and folded against her body, her beautiful curls bouncing over Keir's arm, the drying blood ... so much blood. My chest is too tight. Over and over I see Severn Drakam, my *father*, flick his wrist to send that blade across Halee's throat. Again and again, I see her terror, her pain, her blood. It's on a never-ending loop in my mind, and I fear I've gone mad.

Shadows fall over us, and I blink. We're in an alley in the city. When did we leave the estate grounds? How? Vesper stands in the darkness, arms crossed. I feel Keir behind me, but I don't turn around. I can't.

Vesper says, "We're out, but I doubt we're safe. Either of you have someone or someplace in Drakam we can trust?"

All three of us are silent for a moment when something breaks through the torment of my blood-soaked memories. Blond hair, a bright smile, clear, hazel eyes, and always either a rag or a glass in hand. I nod. "I might know someone."

Keir steps closer, but still, I don't turn as he whispers, "Layla?"

I nod again. Vesper looks to Keir with a question in her eyes, not fully trusting me right now. I don't blame her. I don't trust myself. Whatever Keir does behind me must appease her because she uncrosses her arms. "Lead the way, then."

My lips quirk to one side. "Actually, I'm not sure where to find her. All I know is she lives in Drakam. I don't know if she's even in this city."

Vesper lets out a little chuckle, rolling her eyes. "Then that's not as useful as you seem to think."

Keir shifts. "I know where her tavern is. It is here in Rokvale."

Vesper raises a brow. "That's good. So what's with that look on your face?"

"Well, she's in a busy part of the city, right off the main thoroughfare. You can see the front gates of House Drakam from her front door."

Vesper sighs. "Not ideal."

My fingers curl into my palms. "I'm sure there's a back way in. There's always a back way."

Vesper's smile grows, and she winks. "Indeed." She looks back over my shoulder, speaking to Keir again. "Think you can get us there? Quietly?"

Keir doesn't respond. He strides past me, leaning down to whisper in my ear. "I'm here, Fox Slayer. You're not alone."

I refuse to let my tears fall, though I want nothing more than to collapse into Keir's arms and just cry for days. I'm so tired. So angry. So ... scared. Gritting my teeth,

I finally let my gaze land on Halee. If it wasn't for the blood, I'd think she was just sleeping, or maybe passed out. I keep my eyes on her, silently promising to keep her safe once Keir has brought her back.

Keir sinks further into the shadows as he moves down the alley, and Vesper goes to follow him with a cautious look back at me. I nod, forcing my feet forward. Everything will be fine. We'll find Layla, ask her for help, for a place to hide, and Keir will fix Halee. It'll all be okay. I'll get control of my Void again, and everything will be back to normal. Everything will be fine.

CHAPTER 5

NOR

VALSAN LOOKS BACK, his weight on the balls of his feet. I can tell he wants to go back, to help put a stop to the riot. I place a hand on his shoulder, bringing his attention back to our group as I say, "We can split up. Miles and I can find a way in. You and the others—"

"No." His voice barks with soft command. "We stay together." Taking a deep breath, he rolls his wide shoulders. "We'll use this. We'll keep our distance, skirt the estate, look for an opening."

I cross one arm over my stomach, absently rubbing my elbow just to give my hands something to do to keep from grabbing and kissing him. "Isn't there anyone in the Drakam guard who might just let us in? You're well-known, Val, and well-liked. Isn't there someone ...?"

He scratches his beard, and Miles shifts his weight from foot to foot, obviously anxious to keep moving, to do *something.* I know how he feels. Valsan scrapes his fingers from his jaw back through his hair. "There is a private entrance, but I don't have the key, it's with Lady Kapros. But, maybe ... there might be someone ... but I imagine it's all hands right now to handle the situation with the citizens."

Owen says, "Angry mob."

Valsan sighs, but nods. "For now, let's move, see if we can get in on our own."

Miles turns on his heel, stalking down the alley without a word. We follow, moving parallel to House Drakam, slowing at each intersection to peer down the streets towards the estate wall.

The next cross street is only a few steps away, but Miles jerks to a stop, flattening himself against a wall, pushing into a sliver of shadow. Before I can blink, the others have done the same. I'm a bit slower to react, and Aimee's hand wraps around my forearm, yanking me out of the street and against the wall. I feel my cheeks heating with a blush of embarrassment, but then the loud clomping of footfalls draws my attention to the cross street. A dozen citizens jog by before I lose count. They're running towards the estate in a tight group, but they don't seem angry. They're whispering amongst themselves, and as they move past where we're hiding in the shadows, a trio of men come running from across the intersection. A few at the back of the group slow, then wave their hands. One says, "Come on. We're headed to the main gates. Someone heard that Lord Drakam is coming out to speak."

As the three newcomers join the group, another one says, "There are rumors that that Void woman from the

Games escaped the Akareth desert and slipped through Alopson."

A woman wrings her hands. "You mean she's here?"

"That's the rumor. Maybe Lord Drakam knows."

My body goes rigid, and adrenaline tingles through my blood as someone else asks, "If that Void woman really is here, I'm sure Lord Drakam will get her to give us our magic back. He's powerful enough."

A young man who looks barely out of his teens sneers, "I don't imagine power matters when it comes to that abomination. Though, I'm sure if she's dead our magic will come back just fine."

Damn it. We need to find Thaeia. The crowd has moved on, and I blink at the now-empty street. I can't help but wonder if something like this is happening in Kapros and Alopson as well. Are the three Houses of Sodoles under threat of collapse all because of Thaeia? I clench my fists. Doesn't matter. I have to get to her. I just got her back. I'm not losing her now.

My mind conjures an image of her rolling her eyes at me, and I internally smile, knowing she can take care of herself ... but against an angry mob?

Miles darts forward, shucking his Kapros-guard vest as he strides after the group headed towards the main gates. The black material of his vest lands on the walkway with the boar crest of House Kapros face up. Valsan just stares at it for a second. There's something close to pain in his eyes, and I'm not sure if it's from seeing his House emblem lying in the street, or the fact that Miles so easily discarded it. But he shakes it off and shoves off the wall, scooping up Miles' vest and follows after the angry Plant mage.

Do I follow? When Owen and Aimee stay put, I stick to the shadows with them.

Just as Miles moves to kick into a run, Valsan comes up behind him, grabbing the back of his arm. He holds on to Miles, walking next to him, keeping their pace slow. Valsan leans into Miles, saying something to which Miles just balls his fists. Valsan keeps talking, and I'm waiting for Miles to either shove away from his captain, or nod in agreement ... something. But he does nothing, just grits his teeth. Eventually, Valsan straightens and looks over his shoulder at us. With some silent communication, Owen and Aimee stride down the street, each shedding their vests, turning them inside out before sliding them back on. They stick to the shadows as much as possible, and I can't help but feel out of my depth with this group. With Thaeia and Halee gone, I'm now the only civilian of the bunch. These people have trained together for years. And here I am, stumbling along.

To further prove my thoughts, Aimee's arm snaps out, slamming across my chest to keep me from walking right into a giant hole in the street. Owen steps around it, and Aimee and I go around the other way, pieces of the sidewalk broken and crumbled in the absence of the magic that must have once fixed the damage.

Once around the hole, Owen and Aimee quickly jog to catch up. I stumble into a sprint to keep up, watching as Val turns his vest inside out like the others, hiding the emblem of his House. But will that be enough? He's pretty well-known.

We join Val and Miles, and we all move down the street. As we approach the ever-growing crowd, Val tilts his head at his guards. Aimee and Miles peel away from us, blending into the crush of people. Owen goes in the opposite direction, aiming a smile at someone, picking up a quiet conversation, asking questions.

Valsan hangs back, falling into step with me. His fingers curl through mine, lifting my hand, and without missing a step, presses the back of my hand to his lips as we join the back of the crowd. His beard scratches against my skin, and his warm breath feathers over me. I have to focus on each footstep to keep from stumbling. He keeps my hand close to his face as he whispers, "You're doing great, Nor."

He really does see through me so easily. I'd be annoyed if I wasn't so in love.

He chuckles softly, squeezing my fingers before lowering our joined hands to swing between us. "I know you, Nor. And I love you." My brows pinch as I glance at him. I'm pretty sure I didn't say that out loud. His smile grows to a grin. "You're an open book—to me at least. It's almost like I'm in that busy mind of yours. Later, I'll find some time to quiet those thoughts ... or at least give you something else to focus on."

My mind immediately goes to me on my knees before him, his large cock sliding between my lips, making him groan so beautifully. My boot catches on an uneven cobblestone, and I trip. Valsan holds me up, and my cheeks heat as I say, "Shit, you're distracting."

A darker heat pools in Valsan's eyes. "See, it's working already. Now just imagine all the ways I will—"

The people in front of us slow, and I just now realize more people have joined the crowd, closing in behind us. The main gates of House Drakam stand tall but broken from Miles' magic, though makeshift spikes and lumber shore the breach as much as possible. Guards stand at attention.

Val dips his head, his hair falling over his face as we shuffle forward, bodies pressing in from every direction. I don't like this. I feel trapped. My hands start to sweat, and when we can't move forward any more, Val gives me a little squeeze, his shoulder bumping mine before he leans down. "Deep breaths, Nor."

I do as he says as the crowd begins to quiet. Luckily, I'm fairly tall, so I can see over most of the heads in front of us. And there, behind the semi-safety of the twisted bars of the gates, Lord Drakam stands on what looks like a small table that must have been brought out from the estate.

The Channel mage and leader of this territory raises his hands, and absolute silence falls around us. I swallow my anxiousness. We're nearly three blocks back, but I know without being able to see him clearly that Severn has four stars climbing his forearm. Not only can he Channel the magic of anyone around him, it's rumored that once he has control over a power, he amplifies it as well. I wonder how far his reach goes? If he had his magic right now, could he Channel my magic from this distance?

Severn's voice rings out, and everyone cranes their necks, as if seeing him better will help them hear him. Lord Drakam presses his hand to his chest, looking every inch the concerned ruler as he says, "My people. I feel your fear. I understand your pain. Our gifts have been stolen from us."

Some grumbling starts up to our right, and Severn lets the people stew for a moment before he holds up his hand. "Now, it would be one thing if we had turned on the gods, if we had forsaken the teachings and lost our way. But no! This is not a punishment from the gods. Our gifts were taken by a mere human. A woman."

Murmurs rise through the crowd, and Severn pats the air with his palms facing us. "My people. Please. Remain calm. I'm sure many of you were at the Games and saw the horrific explosions. Lord Aloposon and a few of the guards from Kapros worked with me to try and contain and capture the Void, but we were unsuccessful."

I grit my teeth, but Val's thumb brushes back and forth over the back of my hand, and I force my jaw to relax as Severn goes on.

"It seems that the Void has somehow slipped through Alopson and has been spotted here. But please, do not over-worry yourselves. I know it is painful to be without your gifts, but I ask that you remain calm during this trying time. I ask that you keep the candles burning at the chapels, that you keep your prayers turned towards the gods. I already have my guards spreading out throughout our great city. Even without magic, they will keep you safe. And please"—he dramatically clasps his hands and brings them in front of his chest as if he's pleading with the people—"if you see the Void anywhere, do not engage. She is very dangerous. I do not know what she will do or how far she will go to hold her power over us."

He pauses, his head bowing, and the crowd goes absolutely silent, waiting. When he lifts his head, his voice booms out. "This is the first time I myself have dealt with a Void, but I have done my research, and I have found some knowledge of this Forsaken power."

My head snaps around to Val. Could he be telling the truth? Does he know something about Thaeia's power? Val keeps his eyes on Severn, and I turn back to the Lord of Drakam as he says, "I believe I know how to deal with her magic." *Well, I don't like that.* "I will do what I must to protect you, my people. All I have ever done, has been in service to you. And I ask that you now do the same. Do your duty to your family, your neighbors, your territory. If you see or hear anything suspicious, tell a guard. Be vigilant and safe as you move about your day. I recommend you try to stay indoors as much as possible, maybe close your businesses until this is sorted."

People nod, serious looks on their faces, and a few look around as if they expect to see Thaeia there among them in the crowd. And now that I think about it, that would be something she'd do. I look around, hoping beyond hope ...

Lord Drakam goes on. "Above all else, I need you all to pray, pray that the gods will help us eliminate this abomination, this evil that's trying to rip away everything the gods have blessed us with. Pray the gods will guide my hand to rid us of this Void and return peace to our land. Please return to your homes and spread the word to those who did not come here today. Pray. Be safe. Be vigilant. Be strong."

With a solemn dip of his head, Severn reaches down, and I just now notice his captain, Silas, who reaches up and takes Lord Drakam's hand. A cheer begins near the front of the crowd, and like a wave, it catches and swells as people chant Lord Drakam's name, fists raised.

Val's hand twitches in mine, and when I glance at him, his face is pulled into a serious expression. He shakes his head, whispering, "Well played, Severn."

Silas helps Severn down off the table, and the two stride back into the estate, several guards following, but most pressing through the now-open gates, directing people to return home. I can't find Owen, Miles, or Aimee in the press of the crowd, and I wonder how we're going to meet back up with them. Val turns, moving with the people back into the city. A majority of the crowd immediately starts heading towards a chapel, the line quickly growing past the gleaming columns and down the stairs as people go to pray ... to pray for their magic ... to pray for Thaeia's capture and death.

I must have been gripping Val's hand pretty tight, because he pulls me into his side as we move past the cross street and the chapel disappears from view. His lips brush against my ear as he says, "They're just scared."

So was I, for so many years, but I knew I was wrong. Still, I guess I can't cast stones, even though I really, really want to. Aimee, Miles, and Owen join us, our group melding back together, and we all quietly make our way down the street. A few citizens mill around, speaking in hushed tones, gazes darting around as if Thaeia might pop out of the shadows and kill them on the spot.

A door slams to our left, and when I turn to look, an angry set of eyes stares out at us from between heavy folds of curtains. When they catch me looking, they dart back, letting the fabric close over the window. The crowd around us slowly thins as people peel off and either head towards one of the other chapels or to their homes.

My fingers clench Val's hand. He glances at me, and even though I know he knows, I say it anyway. "We need to find her."

He nods, but doesn't say anything. I bite my lip, looking down the long street spilling before us—just one of hundreds in this city.

How the fuck are we going to find her in time? There are five of us. Severn has his entire force of guards, plus now he has the whole city looking for Thaeia. And what about Halee? How is she tied up in all this?

Aimee steps under the overhang of a bookstore, the

interior dark, the door shut tight. Miles slumps against the wall next to her, and Owen, Val, and I join them in the narrow slice of shadows.

Aimee crosses her arms. "What now, Captain?"

Valsan drops my hand, rubbing his palm over his face, scratching his beard. "After that speech, I'm inclined to think he doesn't have Thaeia."

Owen nods. "I agree. That whole thing felt like damage control."

Val's head bobs in confirmation, but a frown pulls at his lips. "Still, I think we need to get inside the estate. See what's really going on. See if we can learn what happened, and maybe something will lead us to Thaeia or Halee."

Glancing around at the near-empty street, recalling Severn's words, I sigh. "Yeah, seems as good a place to start as any. Searching the city doesn't exactly feel efficient or safe right now."

Val smiles at me before his face falls back into a more serious line. "Exactly. Time is of the essence. Thaeia and Halee need us."

Miles growls, his arms shaking from how hard he clenches his hands at his sides. "If she's been hurt in any way ..."

There's death in eyes and a promise in his words.

We let the silence hang for a long moment before we push out of the shadows and begin to move once again towards House Drakam. I rub my left wrist. The longer Thaeia's Void hangs around my shoulders, the heavier it seems to get. At this point, I don't care one lick about my magic. For her Void to have reached this far for this long ...

Thaeia, whatever has happened, please hold on. We're coming.

CHAPTER 6

KEIR

To avoid the wider, busier streets of the city, we've been sticking to the narrow side streets. As slight as Halee is, my arms are starting to ache, and my skin is sweaty and itchy from this heavy pullover. It would be easier to carry Halee over my shoulder, but for some reason that feels ... wrong, irreverent or something. But her body is starting to go stiff, and all the warmth is gone. We need to get to Layla's fast and figure out our next move. Hopefully she'll help us.

And I have to figure out how to deal with Thaeia and her ... request.

Soon after we started making our way from House Drakam, I slowed to allow Vesper to take the lead, whispering the location of The Dragon's Breath Tavern. I let Thaeia move ahead of me as well, not wanting to force her to walk behind me and have to see Halee, but also not trusting her to bring up the rear. But as Thaeia passed me, her eyes were glassy, and she swayed slightly. I wanted nothing more than to abandon Halee and scoop Thaeia into my arms and take her away to somewhere safe ... wherever that may be. I'd take her across the sea if necessary. I wouldn't stop until all threats to her were nothing but a bad memory. But that wasn't an option, so I followed my broken Fox Slayer, missing my Spirit hounds who usually always watch my back.

Vesper slows, then stops, drawing me out of my thoughts. Two wicked-looking knives flash into her hands, and I instinctively reach for my magic before I remember. My gaze lands on the back of Thaeia's head, her wavy hair tangled and knotted down her back. Her left arm is no longer stained with ... whatever that was, but little smudges remain on the tips of her fingers. Wet blood blooms across her shirt and down the side of her pants where that bastard Sidian stabbed her. At least it looks like the bleeding has slowed, but she doesn't seem to notice, or care. She just stands there, almost like she's waiting for the threat to come around the corner and end her suffering.

Reluctantly, I shift Halee to my shoulder and reach for the sword I don't have. Damn it. Walking on the balls of my feet, I come up behind Thaeia, touching her shoulder to let her know I'm here. She doesn't react. She's not okay, and it's slowly killing me that I can't do anything for her right now. I drag my hand down her arm, then the outside of her thigh. I slip one of her throwing knives out of her sheath, gripping it tightly. Still, she doesn't move.

Vesper stands at the street corner, back pressed to a wall, body tense. Thaeia and I wait, and with each second my body winds tighter, ready to snap. Finally, Vesper shakes her head and starts to back up. When she reaches Thaeia, she keeps going, but Thaeia just stands there, blank eyes staring into nothing. Vesper grabs her arm, and starts pulling her back down the street and I move with them, trying to stay as silent as possible.

Once we're a full block away, Vesper whispers, "There was a crowd moving towards House Drakam. Looked calm enough, but still. We should go around."

I nod, amazed at Vesper's skill. Something must show on my face, because a little smile quirks her lips. "Believe it or not, this is not my first time hunting or being hunted. Being a Poison mage exposed me to some ... *unsavory* characters. I've made good money doing unsavory things." She raises a brow, her smile growing with a glint of mischief. "I hid in your estate for weeks, and no one knew."

"You hinted at that earlier. How? Why?"

She tsks, shaking her head. "Now, now. I'm not about to reveal all my secrets."

My next thought almost has me stumbling. "Nisha. Was that you?" Vesper cocks her head, and I elaborate. "The Alopson council member who was murdered outside my library."

The confusion melts from her face, and she waves a hand. "Oh, her. Yeah. She'd been sniffing around, but that night she was ready to act. She'd already told some of your other councilors about her suspicions of you hiding Thaeia. She was coming for her. So I handled it." Her posture is relaxed, and she has a slight smile on her face. She may as well be talking about the weather, not murder. Her smile falls slightly. "Sorry if it caused you some trouble."

She doesn't seem sorry. I take time to think about it,

replaying everything that happened after Nisha's body was discovered. We make it another two blocks before I answer. "I find myself stuck. I can't condone murder, but your actions uncovered the treason before it could take hold in my House. Though, you could have revealed yourself to me and told me what was going on."

She shrugs. "You were busy."

Thaeia has been quiet this whole time. When I look at her, her eyes are still vacant, her feet moving automatically alongside us. Vesper follows my gaze, and all amusement leaks from her face. She looks at me, concern flashing in her eyes. She picks up the pace, and at least Thaeia is aware enough to do the same to keep up. My free hand reaches for her, to comfort her, to snap her out of this, to do ... something. But I'm still gripping her small knife, and I'm holding Halee with the other, so I let my arm fall back to my side.

The hottest part of the day comes and goes as we pick our way through the streets, avoiding pockets of people making their way towards the estate. I'm not sure what's going on, but luckily, with seemingly everyone's attention on House Drakam, we're able to move more quickly, rounding a final corner. I tap Vesper's shoulder, nodding ahead. "That door."

She heads down the tight alley, Thaeia shuffling along behind her, and I bring up the rear. A bag of trash lays torn open, the stench wafting up, causing my eyes to water. Then my eyes prick painfully for a completely different reason as I realize Halee will start to smell before too long. I know what Thaeia wants me to do, and my stomach roils with the apprehension of her begging me again to reunite Halee's Spirit with her body. My arms begin to shake at the thought.

Vesper grabs the handle of the thick wooden door and turns it slowly. She ducks her head inside before popping back out. "Hallway. Looks empty."

I shift Halee, moving her to carry her against my chest once again. I tense as I pass Thaeia, but she remains deathly still, eyes on nothing. Or maybe not nothing. Maybe she's stuck in her memories. Wherever she is, her mind is not in a good place. She needs help. I press Halee's body against Vesper. "Take her. I'll go and see if Layla is here."

I worry for a second that it will be a struggle for Vesper to hold Halee's dead weight, but she takes her easily, holding her in her arms as if Halee's just sleeping. With one last glance at Thaeia, I slip inside the tavern. The hall is indeed empty, and I move down it quickly and silently. A kitchen opens to my right, and I take a mere second to scan the room. Empty. Moving on, I open a door to my left. Supply closet. Empty. The next door on my left is an office. Empty. The main room looms ahead, but there's no hint of the usual sounds of a tavern in the late afternoon hours of the day. It's eerily quiet. I press my hand to the swinging door on my right, peering into the men's bathroom. The smell of bleach hits me, but that's all. No one here. Slowly, I open the door of the women's bathroom. Again, empty, but then a voice comes from farther down the hall.

"You better have a good reason for lurking around my tavern."

I let the door go, and it swings on its hinges. I raise both my arms, forgetting I still have Thaeia's knife. I drop it, the metal clattering to the floor with an almost deafening sound in the silence. Opening my hands to show

I'm not a threat, I say, "Layla, it's Keir Alopson. We need help."

She lowers the crossbow she had aimed at my chest and puffs out a breath. "Gods, Lord Keir, you scared the shit out of me."

I raise a brow at her crossbow. "Fooled me."

She glances at the weapon, shrugging. "Good. I've only used this thing three times in my life. Hated it each time. Wasn't eager to use it again."

"But you were willing. That's good."

"What's this about you needing help?" She walks down the hall towards me, lowering her voice. "Does this have something to do with the magic blackout?"

I nod. "It's okay if you want to stay out of it."

She looks over my shoulder. "She here?" I nod again, and Layla purses her lips. "I gave her my token. I meant it when I said my door is always open to her. And that goes for you as well, Lord Keir."

"Thank you." Bending down, I retrieve Thaeia's knife and walk back down the hall with Layla at my side. "Are there any patrons here right now?"

"No. No renters right now, and I kicked everyone out of the bar and locked up. Things were in a panic when magic went out. Didn't want my place smashed up, so I told everyone to leave."

I nod. "Any idea what's going on at House Drakam? It seemed like the entire city was heading there."

She shakes her head. "Sorry. No. I closed myself up in here." She looks around at her cozy tavern. "Gotta protect my baby."

"Sorry to bring this to your door, but we needed somewhere to go, and Thaeia thought of you, and ...."

She places a hand on my arm before dropping it. "It's fine."

I open the door, holding it wide, stepping back to let Vesper and Thaeia in. Layla gasps when she sees Halee in Vesper's arms. "Oh. Oh, gods. Oh, no." Her fingers reach for Halee's neck as if she's going to check for a pulse, but then she sees the slash cut across her neck. Her pained eyes fly to Vesper's face. Vesper just shakes her head. Layla seems to steel herself with a nod, turning back down the hall. "This way."

Instead of going towards the main room, Layla turns into the kitchen, leading us across the room to a set of stairs tucked behind a wall in the back. It's tight, and Vesper struggles to walk up the stairs sideways so she can fit with Halee in her arms. We come to a landing, and when I look down the hall, I recognize the few rooms Layla has available to rent. But we don't go down this hall either. She continues up to the third floor, the sound of our boots on the aged-wood steps the only sound. Layla unlocks a door and shoves it open. "In here."

Once we're all inside, Layla closes the door behind us, and the lock clicks. We're in a simple bedroom, a blanket pulled neatly to the fluffed pillows on the bed. A single window lets in light and a little breeze, though the air is hot and does little to cool the small but tidy space. Vesper crosses the room with Layla, their boots silent on the cream and green rug covering the polished wood floor. Layla points at the bed. "You can lay her there."

Vesper hesitates. "You sure?"

Layla just nods, walking through an open door. There's a squeak of a faucet, then the rush of running water. A second later, it turns off, and Layla returns with a glass.

Vesper carefully lays Halee's body on what I assume is Layla's bed. Layla holds out the glass of water to Thaeia, but Thaeia doesn't move. She just sways slightly, staring right through Layla. I take a step towards her, but Layla shakes her head, so I stop. She grips Thaeia's hand, putting the glass in her palm, physically wrapping her fingers around it as she says, "Here, Shanty Princess. Drink this."

Thaeia doesn't smile at the nickname Layla gave her in the desert the night she got drunk and sang sea shanties at the top of her lungs. She got the nickname, Fox Slayer, the following night. I'd smile at the memory if Thaeia didn't look so utterly broken right now. Like a doll being controlled by strings, she lifts the glass to her lips and drinks. She gulps it down until it's empty. Layla takes it back. "Good. Now, let's get you cleaned up and take a look at that wound. Okay?"

Again, Thaeia doesn't respond. I ache to go to her, to wrap her in my arms, to tell her everything will be okay. But I can't, because it won't. Layla's got her right now, and I let the tavern owner steer Thaeia towards the bathroom. She places her hand on Thaeia's back, soothing her as she closes the door, shutting them in, and me out.

Vesper's hand on my arm startles me. "Hey, you should sit down. You don't look too steady. She'll be fine." I frown at her, and she frowns back. "Yeah, okay, maybe not fine. But she'll come out the other side."

"Maybe."

"I'd agree with you, except, I know she'll make it out because she has people like you in her life. People who care. People who will stick around no matter what."

I get the impression Vesper is speaking as someone who has been abandoned in the past. I pat her hand that's still resting on my arm. "You've been there for her since the attack at the Coliseum—watching from the shadows. Why?"

She shrugs, trying but failing to hide the embarrassment that flashes through her eyes. "The explosions were meant to take her out. I figured if I stuck close, she'd lead me to those responsible."

"So, revenge?"

She picks at the hem of her sleeve. "Something like that."

I leave it at that, though I suspect Vesper's motives are less self-involved and have more to do with loyalty to a friend. I'm not sure Vesper is used to having friends. She pulls her hand out from under mine, turning around, clearing her throat.

I fold myself into a chair that faces a small fireplace. It's angled so I have a line of sight to the closed bathroom door. I set Thaeia's little blade on the small table to my right, then with nothing to occupy my hands, my fingers scrape and pick at the upholstered edge of the arm of the chair. My knee bounces as I wait. On the other side of that door, water is running again, and by the strength of the sound, it must be a shower or bath. Vesper presses her hands to her lower back, stretching before sitting on the floor, leaning against the bed without disturbing Halee's body.

I make it another ten seconds, but the silence on the other side of that door is deafening, screaming through my ears. I lunge to my feet and cross the room. I half expect the door to be locked, but when I turn the handle, it swings open. Layla's hand is splayed on Thaeia's naked back, leading her into a running shower, steam billowing around my Fox Slayer. When Layla sees me, she drops her hand, and Thaeia just stops, standing in place, swaying, gaze going through the damp tiles of the shower wall.

Keeping my eyes on my Fox Slayer, I want to bark at Layla to get out, but she's helping us and doesn't deserve my anxiety-induced impatience, so I say, "Please leave."

Layla hesitates for only a moment before silently leaving the bathroom, nodding at some bandages and gauze on the counter before softly closing the door behind her. Thaeia doesn't move. The water spills down the side of her body, but it's like she doesn't know where she is. Or just doesn't care.

Gratefully stripping out of the itchy pullover, I yank my shirt off with it, tossing both to the floor. I toe off my boots, letting them clatter where they fall. Quickly shucking off my pants, I walk into the blazing hot shower, wincing at the sting. I wrap my fingers around Thaeia's arms, pulling her fully under the water with me. My hand trails down until I come to the stab wound in her side. The water runs pink, and I notice the cut is clean, not jagged or torn. Sidian's blade went straight through, missing all the vital bits. When my fingers edge closer to the wound, her flesh flinches, her first reaction to anything in hours.

I lift my gaze to her face. She's looking through me, her hair plastered down, water running unchecked down her face. I press my palm to her cheek. "Thaeia." Nothing. "Thaeia." Nothing. I trail my hand around her face, holding the back of her neck. "Fox Slayer, tell me what you need."

Finally, she blinks at me. "I need you to fix Halee."

CHAPTER 7

NOR

WE'VE NEARLY CIRCLED the entire estate, and my thoughts keep spiraling. If Thaeia is in there, and if I can just get to her, I know we can fix this, together. But that's a lot of 'ifs.'

Aimee draws us to a stop, nodding at a large tree with a little smirk on her lips. "They should really cut that down."

Owen snorts. "Or at the very least trim those long branches." He points at a thick limb, stretching and tapering over the high border wall.

Valsan looks one way then the other. From here, we can't see the main gates, but there are little flashes of movement between distant buildings as people continue to make their way back into the city after Lord Drakam's speech.

Valsan keeps his voice low. "Now. Over then west. There's a staff entrance near the kitchens."

Owen boosts Aimee up, and she grabs a lower branch, throwing her leg over, then pulls herself up to the next limb. Staying low, she crawls carefully, the tree creaking, and I doubt it will hold Valsan's weight. I wonder if it'll even hold mine. Aimee makes it across, and she lowers herself to the top of the wall then drops to the other side. Owen helps Miles up next, who repeats Aimee's moves until he too is out of sight.

Valsan gives me a little shove forward. "You next."

I step into Owen's laced hands, the tree bark digging into my palms as I haul myself up. The branch groans, but holds, and then I'm dropping softly onto the grounds of House Drakam, startled to find myself alone. But then I feel stupid. Of course Aimee and Miles aren't just standing around waiting for the rest of us. I head west as I hear someone scrambling up the tree on the other side. Rounding a corner, I duck between some hedges, jogging in an awkward crouch. A pebble bounces off my arm, and when I turn, Aimee waves me over from the shadows of a deep-set doorway. I hurry over, noticing the thick wood door is open, and Miles is in the dark hall beyond.

A few seconds later, Owen joins us, and Aimee turns to me. "Any idea where your girl might be?"

My brows furrow. "I've never been to Rokvale before, nonetheless inside House Drakam. And I'm not a homing pigeon. I have no idea."

Valsan chuckles, joining us. Everything goes pitch-black as he closes the door, and it takes a few long seconds for my eyes to adjust as Aimee clicks her tongue. "Okay. Okay. No need to get snippy."

I sigh. "Sorry. I want to find her as badly as you all do. I'm just frustrated."

Aimee pats my shoulder like I'm a child, which does

nothing to dampen my irritation. But then I notice Miles striding down the long hallway. Owen starts after him, mumbling, "He's going to kill someone."

Aimee shakes her head. "Or he's going to get himself killed."

When we round a corner to our right, the kitchens open up on our left. There's no one here. A pot boils over, flames flaring, steam billowing. A burnt piece of meat sits black and charred on a skillet. There's an abandoned fish, only half filleted, lying on a wood board. Owen strides around a large island, snagging an entire loaf of bread. He bites into it, ripping off a giant piece, chewing loudly, crumbs flicking from his lips. Aimee tsks, and he holds out the loaf to her. She shakes her head with an eye roll, but takes it, tearing into it with her teeth.

Valsan nudges me, and when I turn to face him, he holds out his hand. I lift my palm, and he hands me a slice of peach half coated in chocolate. I glance around, wondering where he found something so decadent. He leans in, whispering, "A little sugar boost for you. Something sweet to keep you going." As I watch, he brings a second slice to his mouth, wrapping his lips around the chocolate-coated fruit. I could think of something else that would keep me going ... I nearly groan as peach juice slides into his beard. His thumb catches it, and he sucks it clean with his eyes on me.

Fuck.

Valsan's gaze flicks to the piece of fruit still in my hand. "Eat up."

I would if I could. I'd eat him all day and into the night. I pop the fruit into my mouth. It's almost too sweet with the natural ripeness of the peach and the richness of the chocolate. But Val is right. We're all going on very little sleep, and this sugar rush will help, at least a little.

Valsan's lips quirk. "Good boy."

Oh. Now he's playing dirty.

He picks up his pace, all teasing wiped from his face as he crosses the kitchen. He peeks around the corner, then waves us forward. Aimee's teeth crunch around a solid hunk of chocolate, some of it smearing her lips, but she licks them clean. Without breaking stride, Owen shoves his hand into an open sack, and without looking, tosses a handful of whatever he grabbed into his mouth. I think they might have been crackers from the sound of his chewing. Dusting his hands off on his pants, Owen keeps his voice low as we make our way down yet another hall. "The safe rooms?"

Valsan nods.

Safe rooms? I expected Valsan to have at least a little knowledge of this place since he would have come here on occasion on captain duties, but why would Owen know such things?

Val pauses at an intersection, listening. Aimee cracks her knuckles, looking antsy, ready to smash some skulls. When Val determines the way is clear we continue on until we come to a large room—what looks like a salon or sitting area or small entertainment space of some sort. But it's a wreck. What happened here?

Some of the furniture is turned over, and a corner of the large rug is flipped up. There are even a few discarded weapons lying on the floor. Bending down, I grab a sword, swinging it a few times, learning its weight. Val turns to me, and I hand his dagger back to him. "I'm more comfortable with this."

He nods, the tiniest bit of heat in his eyes. I can't help

but recall when we sparred together outside that inn on the way to the Games. The rain had hit so suddenly, and then ... our first time together was a rush of hands, and lips, and teeth ... desperate to be close to each other. Our soaked clothes were peeled off, the heat of the shower no competition for the heat of our bodies as he took control, sinking into me, driving me into the tiled wall.

I clench the hilt of the sword to clear my mind as we leave the disheveled room behind.

Valsan leans in. "The Lord's Hall is just ahead. That's where Drakam receives guests and hears grievances. Official business. We have a similar setup at House Kapros. Beyond the Lord's Hall there's a set of rooms. They have reinforced walls and doors and have their own specially assigned guards."

I nod. "So basically where the important people go when shit goes south."

Owen chuckles and Valsan smiles, saying, "Yeah, pretty much."

A series of doors spills down our left, only one open, and that one barely cracked, but as we pass, I see a long room running parallel with this hall, windows looking out onto a lush garden. The Lord's Hall perhaps?

We keep going until Valsan stops and turns. My brows scrunch as I follow his gaze to the pretty paper plastered to the wall, the gold scroll pattern climbing a deep green background. There are little dragons on the wallpaper giving a nod to the Dragon of Drakam. It's pretty, but I can't figure out what has Valsan so entranced. He runs his hands over the wallpaper, whispering, "It's been a while ... The latch is here somewhere."

Unease has my shoulder blades pinching together as I lean in, keeping my voice low. "What's to say we won't be met with a crossbow bolt to the chest if you just open this secret door and walk right on in?"

Valsan's fingers continue to search the wall, and he opens his mouth to answer, but then a shout from the other side of the wall has us all freezing in place.

"What did you just say to me?"

There's a muffled response, but it's cut off. "I don't care! FIND HER!"

I turn my wide eyes to the group, and Owen mouths, "*Lord Drakam.*"

My eyes go even rounder. It seems that Lord Drakam expended all his calm on his speech at the gates. The voice behind this wall is angry, panicked, afraid.

A different voice stutters, "My Lord, sh … she's not in the estate. We've se … searched everywhere."

Severn Drakam's voice booms through the wall again. "I know that already! Send everyone out to the city. Lock it down. Use the people. Feed their fear of her. I want them turning on their neighbors to find her and turn her in. Do what you have to do. Find her. Bring the Compulsion mage." My eyes go wide, and Val tenses. There's a pause, and I know we're all holding our breath. Then Severn's scream hits a fevered pitch. "NOW!"

There's a shuffling of feet, some moving away from us, some moving closer, and I have to assume there's more than one way out of that room, but at least some of the guards in there are about to come rushing into this hall. Miles' eyes light up with wicked excitement, but Valsan snaps a quiet command. "We've learned what we needed. There are too many without our magic. Go, now."

Miles deflates slightly, and I wonder if he's going to defy his captain. I can't say that I'd blame him. Severn Drakam is on the other side of this door, and we still don't know where Halee is. But at least we've learned Thaeia was in the estate but got out.

Miles is wound tight, ready to snap at any moment. He struggles for a moment as he tightens his left fist, relaxes it, then tightens it again. But he turns away from the door, and we run. I grab the edge of the wall to propel myself around a corner without slowing down, and it's a good thing because a lot of footsteps pour out of that hidden room behind us. We run, and I blindly follow Aimee, tempted to discard my found sword so I can move faster, but I have a feeling I might need it.

The late afternoon sun slants through the western-facing windows as we haul ass through a small dining hall. Owen barrels through a door shoulder first, and tumbles into the next room. I catch the flash of rich fabric in deep greens, and a gold statue of a dragon climbing the wall. I want to stop and take it all in, but I don't dare. I just keep running, and we leave the opulent room behind, finding ourselves in yet another hallway. I'm hopelessly turned around. I couldn't find my way back to the kitchens if my life depended on it.

I hope my life doesn't depend on it.

"Oomph." I slam into Owen's back as he skids to a stop to keep from running into Aimee. Miles is standing before her, still within the shadows of the hall. I feel Val's imposing presence behind me as we peer into an open room, and inside it ... wait. What am I looking at?

The room is packed with people, and by their clothes I'd guess they are staff. I'm not sure what this space is normally used for, but right now, it's being used as a holding room.

Dozens, maybe scores of staff kneel in neat rows across the back wall. Green-clad Drakam guards stand before them, weapons raised. An older woman in the front row of the staff members cries softly, hugging a young boy to her side. His wide eyes stare up at the tip of a sword pointed right in his face.

What the fuck?

Valsan's hand wraps around my bicep, pulling me back a step. I hadn't realized I'd moved, and that blunder gives us away.

"Captain Valsan?" An older guard with grey streaking her light brown braid, lowers her weapon, striding towards us as we all spill out of the hall into the large room. Other guards shift to face us, a few pointing their weapons at us. One of the kneeling staff—a man about my age—leaps to his feet and takes off at a sprint. To go where or to do what, I have no idea, but the guard that was heading our way pauses, raising her hand, aiming her small crossbow and pulls the trigger as she calmly asks Valsan, "What are you doing here?"

The man grunts, his body tensing as the bolt slams into his back. He stumbles and falls. The old woman in the front row pulls the little boy's face into her chest, trying to shield him from the violence happening right before him.

Shit. She shot that man in the back with barely a glance. What the fuck is happening?

The guard lowers her weapon, reloading it while aiming a hard glare at the cowering staff members. Turning back to us, she looks Val up and down. "You really shouldn't be here."

Val waves his hand at the kneeling prisoners, because that's obviously what they are. "What is going on here?"

She shakes her head, but someone else answers for her.

"The Void has slipped from her cage. We just want to know who helped her." Silas strides into the room like a strutting peacock. I want to use my Gravity magic to crush his smug face. "But maybe it wasn't the staff after all. How fortuitous that you're here. Did you help your little friend escape?" He tilts his head with a smile. "No. You wouldn't be here if that was the case." Silas spins like a dancer to face the staff. "So ... who was it?"

The little boy trembling in the old woman's arms shouts around his sniffles. "We didn't do anything! We don't know what you're talking about!"

The woman slaps a hand over his mouth, but his eyes hold impressive defiance. A guard raises his hand, and the boy flinches.

Oh, fuck no.

I don't think, I just move. I'm across the room in a sprint, slipping past hands trying to stop me. All those years training with Saph snap into place as my body shifts with muscle memory. I grab the guard's wrist, twisting back and up until I hear a satisfying pop. He screams, dropping his weapon to clutch his dislocated shoulder. I slam the hilt of my sword into his temple and kick him. He falls to his side, curling into the fetal position. Two guards grab me, hauling me back, but I spit at the fallen guard. "He's a little boy! How dare you!"

I know what it feels like to be struck by someone bigger, older, by someone who is supposed to protect you. Struggling against the grips on my arms, I kick into the air, trying to rip free. The guard on my right squeezes my wrist so hard, my sword clanks to the floor.

Silas chuckles. "Let him go."

I tug my arms free, rubbing my wrist, glaring at the guards as they step back. Silas chuckles again, a cruel smile on his face as he turns to Val. "I knew you were tied up in this, Valsan. You helped that bitch escape the Akareth desert, and now she's killed Sidian."

Who's Sidian? Wait. Isn't that the name of one of Lord Drakam's sons? Damn it, Thaeia, what's going on?

Silas looks around our group. "Where's the little love-sick lord?" My brows pinch. *Keir?* Silas swings his sword in a lazy arc. "I'm sure he'll show up soon enough. But right now, I'm gonna enjoy thi—"

The Drakam captain lunges to the side, but the chair tumbling through the air clips him in the shoulder. Miles follows his thrown projectile, his face red with rage. "Where is she! Where is Halee?"

The whine of metal meeting metal screeches through the air as their swords clash. Silas leans in with a sneer. "I don't know what you're talking about."

"Bullshit!" Miles shoves him back, following with a swing so fast, I can barely track his sword. Silas blocks it, his face shifting from amusement to anger as the two slash and stab at each other.

A man in the center of the kneeling staff members leaps to his feet, several others following his lead. He barrels into a startled guard, shouting, "Run, Lily!"

A woman with shoulder-length brown curls stumbles to her feet. Her eyes are wide and terrified as she grabs the old woman, helping her to her feet, and drags her and the little boy from the room.

I duck under a swinging punch from a guard, kicking her knee out from under her. I hear the slice of a blade whistling through the air, and I'm not sure if I have enough time to get out of the way. And then Val is there. The guard falls to the ground, his sword clattering from his dead fingers. Valsan yanks me to the side. "Are you okay?"

I nod and we shift. Back-to-back, we keep the guards from chasing down the staff members who are trying to flee. Some are fighting, picking up fallen weapons, trying to hold their own against the Drakam guards.

Gods. This is insanity.

Miles and Silas are still hacking at each other. Valsan is no longer by my side. He has his muscular arms around the throat of a giant of a man. Valsan squeezes, and the guard claws at Valsan's forearm, getting a hand around Val's fingers. I hear a pop, and Val winces, but doesn't let up. The guard's struggles get weaker until he finally goes limp, and Valsan releases him just as a small woman runs up behind him, a metal mallet in her raised hand. I begin to call out, but Valsan turns. I don't know what look he aims at her, but she stops mid-stride, her eyes going wide. Slowly, she lowers the mallet and backs away, running from the room.

With a rush of running feet and clanking weapons, more guards flood in from a side hall. I notice a few shifting their holds on their weapons as if they're uncomfortable wielding them. And I guess they might be if they've relied on their magic their whole lives. I mean, we all did. I look around at the chaos tearing through this opulent room.

This. This has always been Thaeia's life. But this is also why she's so strong. She's only ever had to rely on herself. Just her. Her own strength, her own power, her own bravery. No magic, no gift to fall back on. Just her.

Glass shatters to my left, and when I turn, Owen is standing on the sill of a broken window, a small trickle of blood dripping down his arm where he must have cut it on the glass. He helps a few of the staff climb up, but a guard breaks from the fighting, rushing towards them. Owen actually rolls his eyes, waiting for them to get closer, then leans down, grabs the guard's wrist, and twists. I hear the snap of bone from here, and they scream, dropping their dagger and hugging their arm to their chest. Owen scowls, "Shame on you."

Aimee sprints across the room, a sword clattering off her back, her Petrified skin deflecting the blade. Without slowing, she leaps through the window. Shit! What if we're on the third story or something? She's going to break her legs. Valsan pushes me, propelling me forward. He runs at my side as we race towards Owen. Glancing over, I see Miles and Silas still swinging at each other, but their movements are slower, and Silas is panting. For a second, Silas' eyes track us as we sprint across the room, and I hope Miles uses this opening. But Silas shifts his gaze back to Miles, and I see his mouth move.

Miles stops, sword frozen mid-swing. The muscles of his back tremble, and Silas smiles, lowering his sword.

Valsan barks, "Miles!" Silas raises a brow in challenge, and Miles shifts his grip on his sword, rising to the balls of his feet, but Valsan calls out again, this time his voice is calm, commanding, almost quiet. "Miles."

Amazingly, Miles backs away, and when Silas makes no move to follow, Miles turns, sheathing his sword, and runs to the broken window where Owen still waits. Owen grabs Miles' hand, pulling him up.

Silas turns, pointing his sword at me, saying, "I'm going to find your little Void, and once Lord Drakam has what he wants, I'm going to cleave her head from her body."

Rage and fear mix in equal amounts in my chest,

making me dizzy for a moment. He'd be dead right now if I had my magic ... but maybe I'd be dead if Silas had his. I hold on to the fact that Thaeia is alive and Drakam doesn't have her. There's still time. We just have to get out of here and find her.

From the corner of my eye, I see something flying through the air. Silas stumbles back, his hand pressing to his gut. When he pulls it away, his palm is coated in blood, and there's a dagger sticking out of Silas' stomach. I whip my head back around. Miles nods at me then jumps out the window.

Well, okay then.

Owen tugs me onto the windowsill, and I release a breath as I see the four-foot drop. *Okay, not a bone-breaking fall.* A grunt draws my attention. Silas stumbles back again, falling against a wall, hands grabbing at the thick fabric of the floor-to-ceiling curtains, trying to keep himself upright. I hope he's stupid enough to pull that dagger out. Maybe we'll get lucky and he'll bleed out before magic comes back and a Healer can fix him.

A guard rushes to his side, supporting his captain, helping Silas limp away.

I take one last look over my shoulder, relieved to see almost all of the staff have fled. With a deep breath, I jump out the window, and Valsan is right behind me. He grabs his crooked finger and pulls. The joint realigns with a little crunching sound and I wince. He seems okay though as he presses his palm to my back, and we move, Owen dropping down and jogging to catch up. We run through the grounds. Looking over my shoulder, I frown. We're not being chased down. Val presses his hand to my back again, whispering, "I know. We'll keep a lookout to make sure we're not followed."

I nod, unable to shake the feeling of eyes watching us. That can be the only reason Silas is letting us go, right? He's hoping we'll lead him to Thaeia. But what else can we do?

We run until the eastern gate comes into view. There are only two guards, but still, I sigh. I'm so tired.

For the third time today, a guard calls out, "Captain Valsan?"

We slow, and Owen finishes wrapping a piece of cloth around his arm, blood staining the blue fabric as he ties it off. Valsan strides to the front of our little group, taking the lead. His posture is tall, his broad shoulders flexing. Some of his hair has come loose from its tie, and a few strands blow across his face. Godsdamn, he's sexy when he bows up all intimidating. He cracks his neck. "I'm not here to fight." There's an implied, *Don't make me hurt you.*

The two guards shuffle in place, obviously uneasy about everything that's going on. I wouldn't want to stand against Valsan either. But I'm sure they have their orders. Shockingly, the guard on the right lowers her short sword and waves at the gate. "Let them through."

The other guard steps in front of the iron bars. "I don't think we should—"

The first guard aims a hard look at him. "I was put in charge here. We have our orders and they don't concern Captain Valsan or his guards. Let them through."

The man bravely blocking our way doesn't move for a long second, but then shrugs and steps aside. "Fine. But you're taking the heat for this."

Unlike the main entrance with the large double gates that could fit four carriages abreast, this is a solitary narrow gate barely wide enough for a single horse to get through. The gate swings open on silent hinges, and we squeeze past, Valsan whispering his thanks before it clangs shut behind us.

Unlike House Alopson which sits to the north of their capital with an expanse of desert buffeting it from the tight but orderly blocks of stores and homes, the Drakam estate is right in the middle of Rokvale. Here along the east wall, there's a thin stretch of spindly trees between the estate wall and the city. We weave through the thin copse, and in a matter of minutes we're once again walking through the now nearly empty streets of the city.

Up ahead, Owen leans towards Miles. "What did Silas say to you?"

Miles shakes his head, and for a moment, I think he won't answer, but he says, "It doesn't matter. He was lying. Trying to get a rise out of me." He doesn't sound as confident as he thinks he does, and worry sends a sinking pit of iron deep in my stomach.

Aimee stops in the long shadows of the early evening, crossing her arms. "So."

We huddle around her, and Valsan softly claps his hands, a gesture he used to do all the time, and I feel strangely grounded now that he's done it again. He says, "They are searching for Thaeia which means she is alive … or she was. We need to find her before Severn Drakam or his guards do. She is our objective. And hopefully Thaeia leads us to Halee." I don't miss the slight tightening of Miles' shoulders. Aimee sees it too, but stays silent. Valsan looks at each of us, and I do the same. We're a mess. Hair wild and tangled, skin dusty from the road, blood flecking some of our clothes. There are shadows under everyone's eyes, and just that realization makes exhaustion slam into me.

Fuck, I'm so tired. When did we sleep last?

Valsan claps his hands again, then rubs them together. His gaze is on Miles, but he speaks to all of us. "I know you want to keep going. So do I. But we're near our limit. We should rest, or try to rest at least for a little while."

Miles doesn't respond, and it looks like he's lost in thought, and not good thoughts either if his ever-increasing scowl is anything to go by. Aimee nods. "Our horses are probably gone, either spooked or stolen, but I'll go check just in case. Meet you at The Dragon's Breath?"

Valsan says, "Owen."

Owen claps Aimee on the back. "Let's go."

The two peel off, and I hear Aimee say, "Do you need stitches?"

Owen shakes his head. "Nah. It's not too deep. The bleeding's even stopped."

The two quickly disappear down the street and around a corner, and I pinch the bridge of my nose. The Dragon's Breath rings a bell in the back of my mind, but my tired brain struggles to recall where I heard that name before. Miles, Valsan, and I head in the opposite direction of Owen and Aimee, and when Valsan picks up his pace to catch up to Miles, I hang back. Valsan speaks with Miles in hushed tones. Every now and then, Miles nods or shakes his head, but beyond that, he doesn't respond. My attention wanders to the eerily quiet streets. This time of night, it should be bustling with people heading home from work, restaurants should be filling, taverns should be pulling mugs of ale, and children should be running and laughing down the walkways. But it's oddly still.

Light from down a side street draws my gaze to a stark white chapel. There's a line of people spilling down the steps, and a slow trickle of people leave from the other side, slowly making their way home, I presume. The rest of the city is so dark, the chapel seems to glow. As we continue on, I look around once the light of the chapel is well behind me. There's no one out in this part of the city. The doors are closed, drapes pulled tight. The flicker of light behind windows is even far and few between, as if people are afraid to call any kind of attention to the fact that they are home. As if they are afraid the Void will come stealing into their homes. Severn has made Thaeia the boogie man, and it just makes me so angry. All of this is so unfair.

I take a few slow breaths, keeping a steady distance from Val and Miles as I let the silence of the city wrap around me. If I closed my eyes, I could pretend I'm back home on Oxtara with the night insects buzzing as the sun sets into the ocean. But, if I did close my eyes right now, I might fall asleep standing up.

Valsan's voice draws my attention. "Doesn't look open. Though I'm not surprised."

When I glance towards where he's looking, I see a wooden sign hanging over the walkway. The emblem jogs my memory. The bar tent at the Games. This must be her tavern.

Checking to make sure the street is clear, we cross and stop at the thick wood door. As Valsan knocks quietly, I pray to the gods that someone is here and that they'll let us in. The stifling silence draws out, and just as Valsan goes to knock again, footsteps sound from inside. They take their time approaching the door, and then they fall silent. We wait. And wait.

"Captain Valsan?"

That seems to be the phrase of the day.

The three of us spin to the left. A pretty blond leans against the corner of the building, a dark alley stretching behind her. Her arms are crossed, but there's a smile on her face—the barkeep. She shakes her head. "I shouldn't be shocked to see you here. I should have guessed you'd be tied up in all this."

She sounds like she's talking about more than the magic blackout, but now that the idea of a bed has entered my brain, my thoughts are slow and sluggish, unwilling to grab on to anything for more than a second. The blond tavern owner tosses her hair over her shoulder, waving us over. "Come on then. Around back. You all look ready to drop. Your friends are upstairs."

At that, Miles sprints down the alley, nearly shoving the woman out of the way. A sense of relief almost buckles my knees, and Valsan sighs behind me. He reaches around me, placing a hand on the woman's shoulder. "Thank you, Layla."

His hand drops, and she leads us upstairs, her head drooping slightly, her shoulders hunching. We round the landing, and I expect her to lead us to the rooms on the second floor, but she continues climbing, so Val and I follow as she quietly says, "I don't know how much you know, but I think I should warn you—"

There's a loud thump overhead, and in a flash, Valsan has a dagger in his hand. Layla turns, arms raised in reassurance, but Valsan pushes past her, taking the remaining stairs three at a time. I frown at Layla in apology, following Val.

The single door at the top of the stairs is open. Valsan's broad back blocks my view of the room, but when he turns, there's such sadness in his eyes, I can't force my gaze to look beyond him. I don't want to know what's in there. Staring at the love of my life, I focus on my breaths. *In. Out. In. Out. Out. Out. How do I inhale? Oh, gods.* Valsan's hands cup my cheeks, and I manage to suck in a breath. He leans into me, his lips brushing mine in a tender kiss. His fingers tighten on my face, his thumbs skimming my cheek, trying to comfort me from a pain I don't yet know. He wraps a hand around the back of my neck, fisting my hair, holding me as he whispers, "I'm so sorry."

CHAPTER 8

THAEIA

KEIR GENTLY CLEANS my stab wound, and the entire time I just stare at the shower wall, concentrating. I don't worry about the fact that there's not much pain as Keir's fingers wipe the dried blood from my skin. I don't concern myself with the fact that my *father* is hunting me down—I'll worry about that later. No, right now, I need to get my stupid Forsaken power under control so Keir can fix Halee.

I try imagining the Void sucking back towards me. Nothing. My left hand flexes as I try to pull it in like a petulant horse. Nothing. I've been trying for hours but it's as if whatever was inside me burst free and refuses to come back. I can't keep my mind from circling back to that moment when the magic blade sliced into Halee's neck. I see her pain and fear over and over and over. I need to fix this.

A towel wraps around me, and I look down. I'm standing in the middle of a bathroom, the water is now shut off, and Keir has his arms around me, drying me off. Blood trickles down my side, and he grabs a bandage he got from somewhere. He secures the thick cotton to the front and back of my side with a sticky bandage. I am slightly concerned that I don't remember when or how this happened, but there's no room to obsess over it right now.

Keir says something, but I'm too focused on trying to rein my Void in that I don't hear him. He presses some clothes against my chest, and I catch them as he steps back. Pity. It's there in his eyes, and I hate it. As I shake out the shirt, he steps back towards me, but I hold out a hand. "I can do it."

"Really? You haven't done anything for yourself in hours. I'm only trying to help, Thaeia."

I throw the clothes on the floor, shoving a finger in his face. "*I'm* trying! I'm trying to get my Void under control so you *can* actually help." He winces, and I back up, lowering my voice. "I didn't mean it like that. I appreciate everything, Keir. I really do. But time is of the essence right now. I just need to figure out how to get your magic back."

He steps into his pants, avoiding eye contact, and I take a few seconds to appreciate his strong body before he covers his nakedness. The wound in my side pulls with a twinge of pain as I manage to get the tight shirt over my head, but hey, it's clean. We finish dressing in silence until we're just standing there, facing each other. Keir runs a shaky hand through his wet hair.

"Thaeia, I—"

There's a loud thud of something hitting the floor in

the next room. Keir steps in front of me, swinging the door open. Immediately, his shoulders relax as he says, "Miles? Captain Valsan?"

What?

Keir steps into the room, and I skirt around him. Miles is on his knees in front of the bed, his gaze on Halee, tears silently streaming down his cheeks. His arms hang at his sides, and he looks how I feel—broken. Valsan stands in the doorway, but his back is to us.

I blurt out, "What are you guys doing here?"

From around Valsan, Nor's voice cracks as he calls out, "Thaeia?"

"Nor?"

Nor goes to move around Valsan's broad back, but the captain grabs his shoulders. "Wait, my love."

But Nor's gaze lands on me, and he smiles, obvious relief on his face as he says, "Oh, thank fuck."

I'm so happy to see him, a smile lifts my cheeks, but then I feel guilty for that moment of happiness. Nor's gaze slides to Miles and beyond. When he sees Halee, a moment of confusion crosses his eyes, but then he really looks. He sees. His eyes go round, and he stumbles forward. Valsan catches him, pulling him against his chest, one strong arm wrapping around the front of Nor's body. Nor's pained eyes come back to me. "What happened?"

Miles crawls forward, his trembling fingers reaching for Halee's hand. She must be pretty stiff and cold by now, because he almost recoils when he touches her. His tears fall faster but still silent.

Holding up my hands, I calmly say, "It's fine. It'll be okay."

Nor says, "What?"

Miles just shakes his head, leaning his forehead against the bed, hand gripping Halee's tightly. Valsan keeps his voice low, saying, "I'm glad you're safe, Thaeia." I nod in thanks, then he asks, "What do you mean? What'll be okay?"

I gesture at Keir. "He is going to fix Halee."

Miles groans, but keeps his head down, and I wonder why he's still so sad.

Nor's brows raise as he asks Keir, "Really? You can do that?"

Keir shakes his head again, and Valsan joins him, both men trying to rip away the last shred of hope I'm clinging to. There's a gasp behind Valsan, and I just now notice Layla standing by the door as she looks to Keir. "You can't."

Keir takes a slow breath. "I kno—"

I can't stand to let him finish, so I jump in. "Where's Vesper?"

Nor says, "Vesper?"

Valsan continues to rub Nor's arm. "The Poison mage?"

Layla steps around Vaslan and Nor, straightening an already tidy desk. "She left. Said there was something she had to do, and that she'd be back after nightfall."

Nor wraps a hand around Valsan's arm that's banding his chest. "When did you run into her?"

I shrug. "She followed me after the Games. Apparently she—" I wave my hands. "That doesn't matter right now. Where were you all when you lost your magic?"

Valsan rumbles, "A few hours from the Kapros border."

I slump. "Damn. That far. I was hoping if I went out of the city then Keir's magic would come back so he can—"

Valsan moves around Nor, but shifts to take his hand, keeping them connected as he says, "I can't confirm how far your power extended, but I'm afraid it might be countrywide." *Damn it. I need to figure out how to pull it back in.* Curling my fingers into my palms in my old habit, I try to concentrate on my power or whatever it is, but Valsan continues. "But Thaeia, it doesn't matter. Even if you were able to go far enough, Lord Keir can't—"

I start to tremble ... from anger or fear? I can't tell anymore as Keir presses his hand to my shoulder. "I can't bring her back, Thaeia."

Shaking my head, I back away from his touch. "You mean you won't. Why? Why are you doing this?"

He grits his teeth, nodding. "Yes, you're right. I won't." He takes a step towards me, but stops when he sees the obvious rage in my eyes. "Fox Slayer, I would never deny you, but in this, I must. I'm so sorry. I wish ..."

Layla crosses her arms, mumbling. "Thank the gods."

I spin on her, spit flying from my lips. "What do you mean? *Thank the gods?* He could fix her. He could ... but he's standing here telling me he won't. And you're thankful!"

Keir takes my shoulder, pulling me around. "Please, just let me explain."

I try to yank out of his grip. My throat burns with unshed tears, and I'm so furious, the room is starting to go dark. "Go on then. Explain to me how you won't save my friend. How you won't save *me*?" My voice sounds strange, and everything around me is just swirling black. I hear a grunt, and Keir's hand slides from my shoulder.

From behind me, I barely hear Nor say, "Um, Thaeia?"

I think Valsan says something, but I can't hear him over the rush of my blood. Keir won't help me. And that means Halee …

Pain erupts in my side, and I start to double over, but then my head snaps back as a fist connects with my jaw. I blink, trying to figure out what's going on and who I need to start swinging at, but then my arm is wrenched up my back so hard, I'm afraid it's going to pop out of the joint. I cry out as I'm dragged across the room. Why isn't anyone helping me?

I register Nor's voice behind me. "Come on, Void. With me. We have some things to figure out."

As he drags me from the room, I see Miles, Layla, and Keir passed out on the floor. Valsan is on his hands and knees, panting, his eyes on Nor. He nods, and I feel Nor nod back as he walks us backwards down the stairs. It's awkward and painful, so I try to pull out of his hold. "Nor, let go."

He actually tightens his hold. "No. We promised each other we'd be there for each other if ever we needed an ass-kicking. Well, Void, here I am."

I struggle harder. "Seriously, Nor. Let go!"

He spins, shoving me down the last of the stairs. I tumble down them, hot blood soaking my shirt once again. I press a hand to my wound as I get a foot under me. Kneeling, I try to stand, but Nor lands a solid kick to my non-injured side. I topple over, but use the momentum to roll to my feet. I'm a bit dizzy as I lift my fists, ready to fight as I scream, "Fuck you, Nor! It's HALEE! I have to fix this!"

I swing, but it's sloppy and he slaps my punch away. "Oh yeah? You're going to fix everything by almost killing everyone else in that room up there?"

"What?"

He pauses, tilting his head at me, eyes landing on my left hand. "What do you remember?"

Not this again. I roll my eyes, hiding my hand behind my back, but not before noticing the blue-black stain swirling all the way past my elbow. "I remember Keir refusing to step up and be useful."

He tsks. "Easy there, Void. He doesn't deserve that. Don't self-sabotage. I'm sure he has his reasons."

The room wavers as tears pool in my eyes, but I refuse to let them fall. "What reason could there be to not save her? She was innocent!" I lose the battle, and my tears fall, dripping off my chin. "It was my fault. She shouldn't have been there. My father, he ... that bastard ... he ..."

A hiccup steals my words, and Nor stumbles back. "Your father? What? What the fuck happened?"

He crosses the room, reaching for me, but I back up. "It doesn't matter. Keir needs to do this." A sob bubbles up from deep in my chest. "Why won't he do this?"

Nor reaches for me again, and when I don't move, he cups my arm. "You need to let him explain."

My chest hurts so much, I actually look down, expecting to see my heart spilling out to land on the floor. "Oh, gods, Nor. He's not going to bring her back. He's not going to ... Halee ... she's ... she's really ... she can't be ..."

Nor's arms wrap around me, and we both fall to our knees. It hurt when I saw the light leave Halee's eyes, but there was a sliver of hope in the back of my mind. But now ...

When I feel Nor shudder with his own tears, I break. My throat goes raw as I scream into his chest, fisting his shirt. His sobs join mine, and his sorrow makes it too real. I can't breathe. Snot runs down over my lips, and I choke as I try to inhale. First Saph, then the attacks at the Coliseum, my father, and now this. There's too much pain, too much grief. There's not enough room for air. My fingers tingle, and little white stars dance behind my tightly closed eyelids.

And then, nothing.

CHAPTER 9

KEIR

AWARENESS COMES BACK SLOWLY. Honestly, I'm surprised I'm not dead. When Thaeia's eyes turned black and that deep voice layered over hers again, I was sure that was it. Her power hit me like being kicked in the chest by a horse.

Groaning, I push to one forearm, looking around the room. Miles is laid out on the floor near the bed. He's so still, I worry Thaeia *did* kill him. But then his chest rises on a shallow inhale. Thank the gods. Getting myself up to sitting, I see Layla, her back propped against a wall as she rubs her head. She's pale and obviously unsteady, but alive.

"You okay?" Valsan's deep voice draws my attention just as his large hand cups my shoulder. He's the steadiest of us in this room. No surprise.

I nod, asking, "Where is she?"

"Nor wrestled her downstairs. Literally." He shakes his head, wincing. "Shouldn't do that. Still a bit dizzy. Anyway, I don't know how he was able to stand against her ... whatever that was, but he got her out of here. They're downstairs ... at least I think they're still down there. It's been quiet for a while."

Propping my elbow on my knee, my gaze flicks to Halee's body, and I drop my head in my hand. Fuck.

"She might be ready to listen now." Valsan is trying to be reassuring, but I'm not as confident. And even if she does listen, will she understand? "Can you get up?" With his help, I get to my feet. We brace against each other for a moment, both of us letting the spinning in our heads come to a stop. He chuckles. "She really packs a punch, literally and magically."

I manage a small smile, but I can't seem to joke about Thaeia's power. Whatever it is, it's not under her control, and it's dangerous. Valsan must read the trepidation on my face, because he sighs. "Yeah, I know. It's not great. But I have to believe we'll figure this out."

I let his words bolster me, standing a little steadier. Yeah. We'll figure it out, because the alternative is ... her power completely unleashed. Valsan moves to Miles, kneeling over him. My heart aches for the kind Plant mage. If he wasn't there yet, he was on the way to falling in love with Halee. And I think she was right there with him. Thinking about losing Thaeia like that ... so suddenly and not being able to be there for her ...

The room spins again.

Miles stirs, gripping the blanket draped over the bed, pulling himself to his knees. A half groan, half sob tears from his chest, and I feel his sorrow in my very bones.

Valsan keeps his voice low and calm. "Come downstairs. Layla will stay with her."

He glances at the tavern owner who's looking a bit more steady. She nods, waving her hand. "Go. Help yourself to whatever at the bar. You all need to work through some stuff. But hey"—she leans her head against the wall—"bring me back a shot of something. Or maybe a bottle. Yeah. A bottle."

Miles shakes his head. "I don't want to leave her."

Valsan presses his hand to his back. "I know. But we need to talk some things through, together, as a team. As a family."

Miles' hands bunch in the blanket, but then he slowly stands and wordlessly shuffles to the door and down the stairs.

Before I follow, I ask Layla, "You sure you're okay here?"

She nods, waving us off again. "Go on. Someone can fill me in later."

"Thank you. We'll figure something out and be out of your way as soon as we can."

She shrugs. "No rush. Take your time. I'm not planning to reopen till everything has calmed the fuck down."

I take a few steps closer to her, kneeling so she doesn't have to crane her neck to see me. "We appreciate everything you've done, but we can't risk you and your tavern. A lot of people saw Thaeia at your bar tent in Akareth."

Valsan shifts behind me, the wood floor creaking as he says, "Keir is right. Severn made quite a speech to the people and basically—in a politically correct way—declared a witch hunt on Thaeia. It won't take long for the guards to come here looking ... or worse, for an angry mob to come breaking down your doors."

"They can try." A shadow of defiance flares in Layla's eyes, and I don't doubt she'd be a force to recon with if anyone threatened her or her tavern. But I don't want it to come to that. And neither does Valsan, so we leave the Clever mage in her bedroom, Halee's body laid out on her bed.

As Valsan and I walk into the main room of the tavern, I'm slapped in the face with the sight of an unconscious Thaeia in Nor's lap. Panic and anger drive me forward, but Nor holds up a finger with a small shake of his head. I stop, but it feels like my heart keeps going, slamming into my ribs to try to get to her.

My Fox Slayer groans, her eyelids fluttering open. "How long was I out?"

Nor answers, "Not long. Just a few seconds."

She stirs, trying to sit up, but Nor holds her still as she asks, "Did the magic come back while I was out?"

As they talk, I skirt around them, going behind the bar. I duck down, rummaging through cabinets.

Nor says, "Nope. At least not in here."

Thaeia sighs. "Damn it."

I find what I'm looking for and stand. With the little med kit in my hand, I glance back at the two friends. This time, when she moves to sit up, Nor lets her. Thaeia's eyes find me, and for a moment, I hope. But there's a flash of pain and betrayal in her gaze before she looks down at her lap. That one glance strikes me deep, and I'm tempted to rub my chest to try to ease the agony. She still thinks I'm denying her something so important. She honestly believes I'm *choosing* Halee's death. In Thaeia's eyes, I'm killing Halee over and over each time I refuse her. She doesn't understand. I *need* her to understand. I can't breathe when she looks at me like that.

Nor grunts as he stands, but Valsan is there to help him up. They both look exhausted. The shadows under Nor's eyes look darker in the unlit tavern. His hair is disheveled, and he seems downright beat down by life, but a grin brightens his face as he holds out a hand to Thaeia, helping her up. She avoids making eye contact with me as she sits heavily on a stool. Nor moves behind the bar, and I pass him on my way to Thaeia. Bottles clink as he rifles through them, setting one then another on the polished wood top.

Placing the kit on the bar, I aim my gaze to Thaeia's bloody shirt. Gods, I wish she'd go one godsdamned minute without getting herself hurt ... physically or emotionally. My anger turns to the gods. *She's had enough, don't you think?*

Though I'm shaking with anger at Sidian for doing this to her, at her father, at ... everything in this fucked up situation, I keep my voice low and calm. "Thaeia, that needs to be stitched up."

When she reaches for the kit, I put my hand over it, pulling it back. "You don't have to do it." *You don't have to carry everything on your own. You have people who care about you. I care about you, Fox Slayer.*

Valsan places a hand on her back, and she stiffens for a second before relaxing as he says, "Let one of us do it. All guards are trained in basic medical care."

Silently, she nods, and Valsan looks to Miles. "You up for it? I'd do it, but you're better at stitches than me."

Thaeia looks at Miles, and the depth of pain I see in her eyes ... it's beyond words. Miles grabs the kit from under my hand, and I almost snag his wrist. He's too grief-stricken to do this right now. Too tired. Too angry. My gaze snaps back to Thaeia as she grabs one of the bottles, pulling out the cork with her teeth then takes a big swallow. Miles doesn't look at her as he threads a needle with surprisingly steady hands. Still, out of all of us in this room, is he really the best one to do this right now?

Thaeia leans back, lifting her shirt to just under her breasts. The stab wound I'd bandaged is bleeding freely again. Luckily Sidian struck just below her previous injury, but now she'll have a new scar, one that has Halee's death stamped on it.

Miles places his fingers on either side of the cut, pinching the edges together. She hisses, and without looking up at her, Miles says, "This is going to hurt."

She looks at his bent head. "I know."

I grit my teeth harder with every stab of the needle into her skin, but Miles makes quick work of the front, tying off the stitching and cutting it with one of Thaeia's knives. Without a word, he grabs her shoulder, pitching her forward. I catch her grimace before her hair falls over her face. Miles starts sewing up the exit wound.

This feels like penance, like she's allowing Miles to help her but only because it's hurting her. I hate it. I hate everything that's happened, and I feel so useless. And scared—scared of what I'm about to tell them. I've never told anyone this story except my father, burying it in a box in my mind, a box that only opens in my nightmares. But they need to know. She needs to know ... to understand. *Please let her understand.*

Instead of taking the seat next to my Fox Slayer like I yearn to, I go back around the bar, standing next to Nor, bracing my hands on the wood surface. Nor slides a bottle in front of me, asking, "Drink?"

I don't even bother reading the label or smelling the contents. I just grab it, bring it to my mouth, and tip it back. Rum burns down my throat and warms my belly. I involuntarily shudder as I set the bottle back down. Thaeia grabs it, taking a few deep swallows before passing it back to Nor. She glances at me as Miles finishes, putting new bandages over the neat stitches. Thaeia lowers her shirt, then places her hands on the bar, not quite reaching for me as she curls her fingers into her palm, whispering, "Sorry."

I crack my neck again, and when that does nothing to ease my anxiety, I grab the other bottle on the bar since Nor is currently taking a swig from the rum. Whiskey sets my throat on fire. Shit. I should stop before I get too drunk to say what I need to say with any kind of coherence.

My fingers clench around the whiskey bottle, and the glass actually groans from my grip. Letting it go, Valsan takes it, throwing back a small swallow, then Miles takes it next. He stumbles to the nearest table, pulling out a chair with a loud screech, then flops into it, tilting the bottle back and taking several long pulls.

Okay. Here goes.

I force myself to look Thaeia in the eyes, and am surprised when she meets my gaze and holds it. She begins to say something, but I hold up a hand. "May I explain?"

She closes her mouth, nodding. Her face is blank, unreadable, but at least the look of betrayal is gone. That's something, and all I can do is pray that if not now, at least someday she'll understand.

"I tried to bring someone back when I was younger." I feel everyone's eyes on me, but I keep my gaze locked on Thaeia. "When I was just thirteen, I was already pretty powerful in my magic, and as you can imagine me as a teenager, I was quite cocky about my ability." My attempt to lighten the mood falls flat, so I clear my throat and keep going. "Anyway, a friend died. Well, I say friend. I think over the years I've built him up into a friend in my mind. He was an acquaintance—the son of one of my father's advisors. We were supposed to be studying with the other kids in the estate, but the two of us snuck out and went riding. It wasn't the first time we had done so, but as we raced into the desert, his horse hit a letchwe worm hole. Those creatures rarely burrowed so close to the city, so it wasn't something we typically looked out for. It was such a freak thing."

I pause as that moment plays through my mind. The horse flipping tail over ears. Its piercing scream. The way it thrashed its head in the sand.

"Anyway, he went flying. The horse broke its leg, and my friend hit the sands hard. I heard his neck break. It was ..." I press my fingers into the bar to keep from trembling at the memory as I go on. "He was dead before his body fully settled against the dune."

I reach for the rum bottle, but pull back, needing to just get through this. "I panicked. I'd like to say I did what I did because I cared about him, that I was trying to save him, but I was scared. I was terrified about what my father would do when he found out. I didn't want to be blamed. I was selfish, only thinking of myself and how that poor kid's death impacted me." I rub the back of my neck, both ashamed and disgusted with my actions back then.

I take a deep breath. "So, I jumped off my horse, calling his Spirit."

The liquor in my stomach roils as I recall what happened next. I breathe through the nausea, keeping my eyes on Thaeia as I grip the edge of the bar tighter. "When a Spirit has recently passed, they don't always know they're dead. And even if they do, they are rarely coping well, especially if it's violent. His Spirit came to me screaming. For some reason, only animal Spirits make noise. I've never heard a mage's Spirit make sounds or talk, so to hear this ... noise coming from him was shocking. It was only in my head, but it was deafening and terrifying. He kept grabbing at his neck, but his fingers kept passing through. The sounds coming from him were ... inhuman."

I shudder, recalling his wailing screams in my head.

"I shoved his Spirit into his body, thinking that would fix everything." Thaeia watches me, her eyes shimmering with the beginnings of tears, but she doesn't say anything. "His tortured screams were no longer just in my head. His choked shrieks echoed across the dunes as he writhed on the sands, eyes rolling back in his head. He jerked to his feet, his body not moving right, like it was still empty and was being moved by a puppeteer. His head fell to the side, his neck of course still broken and unable to hold it up. He screeched at me, his eyes wild, his mouth just hanging open."

Nor whispers, "Gods."

Finally, I break Thaeia's gaze, dropping my eyes to the bar. "To this day, I don't know how he did it, but he fell on his still-struggling horse, and with his bare hands, snapped the animal's neck. I was so horrified, I threw up. When I straightened, his cloudy eyes were on me. He charged me, moving unnaturally fast through the deep sand. He had a hand around my throat in the blink of an eye, and so I ripped his Spirit from his body. He collapsed at my feet, empty once more."

I take a deep breath, gaze slowly climbing back to Thaeia's face. A single tear tracks down her face already streaked with dried tears. Slowly, I reach across the bar, needing to touch her so badly, my chest aches. But I won't cross that line unless she lets me. Thankfully, she doesn't pull away, and my fingers slide over the back of her hand, resting there.

Miles stumbles behind the bar, dropping his now-empty bottle on the counter with a clatter. He drank the rest of that? There was still half left. Without looking, he reaches under the bar, grabbing another bottle. Staggering back to the table, his chair screeches across the floor as he slumps into it, taking several big swallows of liquor.

Thaeia turns her hand, brushing her fingertips over the inside of my wrist, drawing my attention from Miles back to my Fox Slayer. I drop my gaze to our joined hands as I say, "It wasn't him. His Spirit had no time to adjust, to settle. Some never do. And what I did to him ... it broke him. I know because I called his Spirit a few years later. It was fractured, his form sputtering." I look back up, meeting Thaeia's gaze. "A Spirit's flames are usually bright and steady, but his looked like fire struggling to stay lit in a rainstorm, and the center of his flames crackled black. Not even half a second passed before he tried to attack me, his Spirit hand grabbing and slipping through me. I released him immediately and haven't called him again. Even years later the guilt still haunts my dreams."

The room is deathly silent. Thaeia's hand trembles under mine as her voice cracks. "Even if we find a Healer for Halee's body?"

I squeeze her hand, willing her to understand as I shake my head. "Healer magic needs something to work off of. There's no life in Halee to Heal." I lean closer to her, desperation making my voice pitch higher. "Please believe me when I say I did my research after what happened that day in the desert. Even if a Spirit were to be put back into a whole and unharmed body, there's something that breaks the connection between body and Spirit during the transition to death. That body up there is no longer her Spirit's home. The two no longer fit together. I ... I can't do that to Halee. I won't. Not even for you. I'm so, so sorry, Thaeia. Please believe me. If there was a way to truly bring her back, I would."

Tears fall unchecked down her face, and I realize I'm crying too, but I don't wipe them away. Nor wraps an arm around me, hugging my shoulder. Valsan pulls his stool closer to Thaeia, and rubs her back, his eyes on me. He nods, understanding and sympathy clear in his gaze. Miles stays where he's seated at the table, tossing back another swig of the liquor. He sways in his chair, then folds his forearms on the table and his head falls onto them. The movement causes the bottle to tip on its side, but only a little booze drips out as it rolls and stops against Miles' crossed arms.

Thaeia doesn't say anything, but she squeezes her fingers around my hand, and I have to lock my knees to keep them from buckling in relief.

After a few moments of silence, and everyone has had a chance to absorb my story, Nor releases me, taking another drink. His worried eyes flit to Thaeia, then Miles. He dashes a tear from his eye, and his voice is sad as he asks, "So, um. What should we do with Halee?"

A little sob breaks from Thaeia, but Miles doesn't react, and I wonder if he's passed out. I rub my thumb over the back of Thaeia's hand as she whispers, "We should bring her home." With her free hand, she wipes the tears from her face. "But it's not safe for me to go there, not yet. I need to settle things here first." As she finishes her statement, anger laces through her voice, and I glance at her left hand, but it remains her usual golden tan.

Nor shifts. "I could—"

Valsan aims a hard glare at him. "Not alone."

Nor's eyes go soft as the two share a moment, but then he clears his throat. "Even so, it would take several days to get home. And in this heat …"

We all read between the lines. Halee's body won't be in great condition by the time they get to Oxtara. Normally, if a body needs to be transferred long distance, magic is used.

I glance at Thaeia, saying, "If we can figure out the magic, one of my Spirits could—"

Nor tilts his head. "Or Aimee could Petrify her."

"Aimee could petrify who?" We all turn to see Aimee and Owen striding from the hall leading from the back entrance. I sigh. They don't know yet.

Owen looks around, a grin pulling at his lips. "You all drinking without me? I'm pretty tired, but I can rally." He winks at Thaeia. "Glad to see you alive and well."

She blinks rapidly as tears fill her eyes. Owen's expression turns panicked as he holds up his hands. "What? What'd I say?"

With one last little pat to Thaeia's back, Valsan shoves off his barstool and jerks his chin to the stairs. "Come on. There are rooms on the second floor. We all need some rest. I'll fill you two in."

Valsan grabs the half-empty bottle of whiskey, I presume for Layla, and the three start to climb the stairs. Owen stops and looks over his shoulder at Miles. "He okay? Should we bring him up?"

Valsan pauses before saying, "No, he's not okay. And

yes, we should get him in a bed." Owen jogs over, concern on his usually carefree face as he maneuvers the passed-out Miles over his shoulder, and they all quietly make their way up the front stairs instead of going through the kitchen.

The resulting silence is broken by Nor, who whispers to Thaeia, "So, um, you said something about your father earlier ..."

My hand involuntarily tightens around hers, and she looks up at me, understanding passing between us. I may not know it all, but my father filled me in on enough, enough to have me racing across the country to get to her ... but not in time. I round the bar, pulling Thaeia into my side, and she sinks into me. Honestly, I don't know how she's still in one piece. Rubbing her arm, my lips press to the side of her head, whispering into her hair, "I'm here, Fox Slayer."

She turns into my chest, and I look over at Nor. "Is there any way that story can wait until we've all had a little sleep?"

Nor nods, running a hand through his messy hair. "Yeah, yeah. I'm exhausted and honestly probably wouldn't be able to process one more piece of information anyway." As he comes around the bar, he punches Thaeia in the shoulder, playfully but fairly hard as he says, "Hey, Void, get your shit together."

I'm about to snap his wrist, but Thaeia chuckles. "Thanks for kicking my ass."

He waves over his shoulder as he climbs the stairs. "Anytime."

CHAPTER 10

NOR

I'M PULLED from sleep with a deep ache in my heart. My head hurts from crying, and my eyes feel swollen. What woke me?

Valsan's lips brush my neck as he whispers, "You were having a bad dream."

His beard scrapes against my skin, and I press back into his strong body. I don't recall my dreams, but the sorrow squeezing my chest tells me he's right. Val's lips trail down to my shoulder, and when I shift, his hard cock nestles perfectly between my cheeks. He chuckles darkly, but keeps his touch and kisses light.

The bed shifts as he props himself on an elbow to stare down at me. My heart actually skips a beat as he brushes my hair off my forehead. His eyes search mine as he asks, "Go back to sleep if you can, Nor. You could use the rest."

I know my eyes are darkening, but he just continues to comb his fingers through my hair. With him propped over me like this ... with his hands on me ... sleep is the last thing on my mind right now. Reaching back, I press my palm to his cock, moving my hand to his base then back to his head. He groans, and the sound shoots straight to my balls. Only hesitating for a moment, Val grabs my wrist, pulling it away from his cock. With one hand, he holds both mine hostage over my head where I still lie with my back to him. Leaning down, his hair tickles my neck and shoulder, stirring my growing desire. His voice is calm and deep. "I love you, Nor."

"Fuck." Tears burn my eyes, but I'm tired of crying. "Please, Val."

There's some shifting behind me, then my eyes close on a punched exhale as Val kisses my shoulder and languidly slides a finger inside me, some slick substance easing his way. His voice is raspy with emotion as he says, "I'm here, Nor. I've got you."

"Gods, yes, Val. I love you so much. I ... If you ... If I ever lost yo—"

His teeth clamp down at the base of my neck, then he eases the pain with gentle kisses. "Try to turn it off, Nor. Focus that beautiful mind on me." He shifts again, sliding out of me. I look over my shoulder to see him dip his fingers into a small bottle of oil.

"Where did you—"

I gasp as he presses back inside me. Lazily pumping, he says, "Kitchen." A second finger slides into me, and my eyes close. My cock bobs against my stomach as I rock into his thrusting fingers. "You left the room? I must have really been out."

He nibbles my ear. "Don't worry. I didn't leave you for

long." He scissors his fingers, stretching me, and my eyes roll back. Precum drips down my length as my breaths turn to pants. He whispers, "Never for long."

There's a promise in his words. My body and my heart melt for him. The pain, and sorrow, and anger over Halee slips to the back of mind as I find a few moments of reprieve in Valsan's arms.

I nearly moan in protest when he pulls his fingers out of me, but then he grips my inner thigh, rolling me onto my back and settling himself between my legs. The sight of his muscular chest and abs flexing over me has my mouth watering, and my pulse beating tingling pleasure up my cock.

Wordlessly, he hooks the back of my knee over his elbow, opening me, and I clench in anticipation. He grips his cock, stroking his hard length a few times, coating himself in oil until he's glistening. His eyes are on my ass as I flex to try to roll my hips, needing him. Lining himself up, he holds the head of his dick against me as he leans down. Valsan presses his lips to mine, and I open on a groan. Our tongues tangle and taste as he slowly slides inside me.

It's exquisite. The stretch. The feel of being filled by him so completely.

My cock jerks, more precum dripping onto my stomach, smearing into my skin where our bodies are pressed together. He kisses me like he's consuming me, and I gladly let myself go. Our pace is slow, every roll of his hips scraping my inner walls, inching closer and closer to *that* spot. Using the leverage of his hold on my leg, I push into his grip, lifting my hips to grind against him with his languid thrusts.

Breaking the kiss, I suck in air, tilting my head back.

He immediately takes advantage, running his beard down my throat, kissing and licking my neck. His pace starts to pick up, and sexy grunts escape his lips as he punches his cock deep, the sound so erotic, it pushes me closer to the edge.

The pleasure is building, and the friction of my dick pressed between us is good, but I want more. I go to wrap my hand around my aching length, but I'm left completely empty. Valsan's wet dick bobs before him as his dark green eyes find mine. He crawls … actually crawls around me like a panther stalking its prey. A shot of desire curls up my spine, the pleasure so intense I nearly come just from the look on his face. His muscles ripple with each pass of his arms and legs as he stalks around me towards the headboard. He bites my shoulder with a growl, and it's too much. I grip my cock, stroking hard. But I only get one good pump in before his hand wraps around mine.

With a shake of his head, he leans in. "Not yet, love."

Like a king sitting back on his throne, Valsan settles against the headboard, his legs spread, his cock standing at attention. He fists himself, tilting his chin at his dick. "Come and sit on this." Eagerly, I move to straddle his waist, but he grips my hips, turning me so my back is to his front. He pushes me forward, giving himself a good view of my ass. His large hand grabs and squeezes one cheek before he spreads me. He groans, rubbing the tip of his cock against my hole. "This way I can go deeper." He pushes his head past the tight ring of my opening, then wraps his arms around my chest, grabbing my pecs and pulling me back. I grunt as I'm slammed down, his cock filling me as he hugs me to his chest, growling in my ear, "This way, I can do this …"

He threads his legs between mine, then bends and plants his feet into the bed, spreading us both wide. I'm shaking from the sensation of holding him so deep inside me. We're not even moving, and my ass is squeezing him with each of my panting breaths. If I don't come soon, I might very well pass out.

I grip his hand against my chest, begging, "Please, Val."

Without warning, he bucks into me. Over and over his hips snap up, using the leverage of his feet pressed into the bed. With my legs spread over his thighs, I'm held in suspension as he drives into me, his thrusts picking up speed. We're both grunting and moaning. Sweat pours down my back where our bodies are pressed together. One of his hands slides up my chest, circling my neck.

I'm at his mercy. There's nothing else. There's no one else. Nothing except this man matters. I'm obsessed. I'm in love. I'm ... I'm ... ohhhhh fuuuuuck.

He squeezes my throat, and the world goes hazy and a little swirly. His frantic thrusts turn to desperate rolls of his hips grinding into my ass. He uses his grip on my neck to tilt my head so he can growl directly in my ear. "Now, Nor. Paint your chest with your release. Let me see it. Let me feel you shudder around me."

"Yes, sir." The words fall from my lips, and his grip tightens even more. Stars dance behind my closed eyes, and it's like my blood catches fire. Sparks of pleasure bloom low in my belly, then expand and explode. My balls draw up, and my cock kicks with the force of my orgasm. Cum coats my sweaty chest as I come without even touching my dick. Valsan pumps once, twice, then holds himself deep. His hand releases my throat, but his other arm pulls me even tighter against his chest as he releases inside me. I feel his cum leaking out and dripping between my cheeks. His cock pulses and kicks, and I groan at the feel of him owning me so thoroughly, so completely.

We both come down slowly, our muscles relaxing with each breath. He keeps me wrapped in his arms, but stretches his legs out, flexing his feet, his toes curling in a strange way. He hisses, his leg shaking as he says, "Cramp."

I laugh, shifting off him. I cross my legs, sitting between his, and rub his twitching calf muscle. He bows his back. "Fuck, fuck, fuck, that hurts. Why does that hurt so bad?" But there's a smile on his face, and with my next pass over his leg, the muscle releases and he sighs. I keep rubbing, because it feels good to touch him.

We sit in silence for a while, and I marvel at how comfortable it is being with him. I glance out the small window, but the sun has set and clouds have moved in. "How long did we sleep?"

"Mmmm." The soft moan comes in response to my massaging fingers moving down his leg to his foot. "A few hours. Four at least. I'll let the others keep resting, they could use it, but I need to go check on Layla and see if I can quietly assess the state of the city."

I poke the bottom of his foot with a dramatic roll of my eyes. "And I didn't need more sleep?"

He jerks his foot from my hands, sitting up and gripping my chin. "No. You needed my cock."

"Mm-hmm." I brush his lips with mine then pull away, chuckling at his cocky grin. He knows he owns me, and I'm okay with it. I kiss him again, a slow meeting of lips meant to convey my love for him. When we finally pull apart again, I shuffle to the edge of the bed. Standing, I stretch. The little bit of sleep did some good—but Val's cock did wonders.

I stride to the door with a smile, gripping the handle as I say, "Let me grab a shower, and I'll join you. Maybe Thaeia will wake soon. I'm more than a little curious to know what she was talking about with her father." When she spoke of her father, the tone of her voice suggested it wasn't good. But still, if her discovery has something to do with everything that's going on, we should know.

Before I'm able to open the door, Valsan is right behind me, pressing a kiss to the back of my neck. "You're just so irresistible." He slaps my ass, and the sting has me jerking forward, but my cock wakes up, starting to harden as the burn melts into a fluid pleasure. He reaches around me, opening the door. "Come on. I'll wash your back."

Yes, sir.

I follow him like the eager puppy I am. We walk down the hall towards the communal bathroom wearing nothing but matching sappy grins. Our bare feet pad quietly against the smooth wood floor. As I follow him into the bathroom, a moment of guilt kicks against my heart. In spite of everything that's happened ... even with Halee ... with her death weighing heavily on my heart, I'm happy. I'm grateful for Valsan and his love. I'm ... I'm just so ...

After turning on the water, Valsan turns to me, a teasing smile on his face, but it quickly falls when he sees the look in my eyes. He rushes to me, cupping my face, wiping away the tears I tried and failed to keep from escaping. "Oh, my love, what's wrong?"

I just shake my head, angry at myself for ruining the moment, but I force the words out, I force myself to be honest. "I'm happy. What's wrong with me?"

He pulls me to him, his fingers combing through my hair. "It's okay. It's okay to feel it all. You can be sad and happy at the same time. You can be angry and peaceful. You can feel guilty and grateful. It's okay. Shh, my love. It's okay."

When my tears slow, I lift my head, running my fingers through his beard and up into his long hair. "I love you. So much. Thank you for seeing me."

"Always, Nor. Forever."

Forever.

CHAPTER 11

THAEIA

I HAVEN'T SLEPT. I don't know if I'll ever be able to sleep again. At least not without seeing Halee's face in her last moments. As that image plays over and over in my mind, I must make some noise of protest because Keir stirs next to me in the small bed. His bright blue eyes blink open, and when he sees me with my back leaning against the head-board, he frowns, sitting up.

"Did you sleep?"

I shake my head, and as he scoots closer to me, the book he'd been reading clatters to the floor. He'd been trying to read me to sleep, and usually, that works, but he passed out before I did, the open book falling over his chest. It was cute, and as I stared at him, my heart settled for one blissful, peaceful moment.

"Fox Slayer, you need sleep."

I shake my head again. "I can't." Tapping my temple,

I fight against the tears that want to fall. "She's in here. I see her, Keir. She was so afraid. Her last moments were filled with fear and confusion and pain." Anger boils inside me, and I grip the sheets, pretending not to notice the midnight blue creeping up my fingers. "Her last moments should have been years and years from now, in her bed surrounded by family to send her off to the Everafter." I grit my teeth, my jaw aching, my head pounding as I practically growl, "I'm going to kill him, Keir."

"Okay."

The rage that was building comes to a standstill at that simply said word, and then it all drains away. I'm left dizzy as I stare at him, blinking in confusion as I ask, "Okay?"

His fingers thread through my left hand, and the inky darkness recedes. His other hand cups my cheek as he nods. "Okay." I'm blinking too fast, and I must look flabbergasted because he smiles. "You really do need some sleep."

I frown. "Keir, why are you here?"

His brows furrow, and I expect him to pull away, but always surprising me, he moves closer, his hand caressing down my cheek, along my neck until it settles on my shoulder. "I couldn't let you face him alone. I'm sorry I wasn't there for you, Thaeia. I got held up at the bord—"

"No, Keir. That's not what I meant." I wave a hand at my chest. "Why are you here, with me? Why are you helping me? Why are you so invested? We haven't known each other that long. I'm a nobody from a tiny island. Well, I guess I'm a Draka—." Bile rises in my throat, cutting off that name. I shake my head as if to expel the very thought. "No. No. I'm not a Drakam. I'm just Thaeia from Oxtara. I'm Forsaken. And apparently I killed someone with this power, whatever it is, this darkness. I'm dangerous. You're the heir to Alopson. You—"

Keir shakes me. "Hey!" The venom in his voice has me focusing on his face. He's angry. "Stop. Take a breath and try that again."

I just stare at him, unsure of what he wants, and he just stares back. After a while, he raises a brow as if in expectation ... of what? I take a deep breath and look at him. Really look at him. His hair is mussed from sleep, but his eyes are clear and intense as he keeps his gaze on me. Those eyes. So blue. Like home. Like clear seawater with the sun shining through to the soft, sandy bottom. The first moment I laid eyes on him, I was intimidated ... who wouldn't be? I mean, he's Lord Keir Alopson. He was entirely captivating, but I quickly learned he was so much more than his stunning looks. He's kind, and smart, and funny, and oh so dirty in bed. And ...

I let myself get lost for a moment in his eyes. He cares ... for me. And I care for him. A lot. Do I love him? Isn't it too soon for that? All I know is that when my world fell apart, my friends were there for me. Keir was there for me. He still is. But this darkness inside me, this power, what if I hurt him? What if I kil—no. I can't. I won't.

I'm so afraid ... of myself.

"Fox Slayer."

The command in Keir's voice rips me from my spiraling thoughts, and I look back up at him. Both his brows are raised now, waiting, letting me work this out. My gaze travels to where his ten stars climb down his inner arm to his wrist. Without thinking, my fingers reach for him, tracing the tattoo. KVERETH. Spirit. I look back up at his face.

"Thank you. Thank you for being here. For ... everything. You ground me, and every moment I'm without you feels empty and ... wrong."

He nods. "There you are."

I take a slow breath. "And I'm sorry about what you went through as a kid ... about your friend. And I'm sorry for ... no, I'm not sorry for asking. I didn't know. I didn't understand. But I do now." I grab his wrist, holding on to the place that marks his magic. "I understand, Keir. I hate it, but I understand." A breath punches out of him, and his hand tightens on my shoulder. Tears actually rim his eyes, making them shine even more like the ocean. My hands frame his face, his beard scratching my skin. "Oh, Keir. I'm so sorry."

He dashes his tears away with a little smile. "Fox Slayer, I'm supposed to be comforting you."

It's fitting that one of my favorite places to be—sitting on my wave board with the sparkling waves lapping over my legs—is mirrored in this man's blue eyes. He feels like home, and I'm falling fast. Maybe I've already fallen.

Leaning forward, my lips tingle with anticipation of his mouth on mine, but then the door swings open, hitting the wall with a thud. We pull apart, on alert, adrenaline coursing through me so quickly the room goes into hyper-focus.

Vesper stands in the doorway, and she has the decency to slap a sheepish look on her face before holding her hand out in front of her, pretending to shield her eyes, but I see her looking. And I can't blame her. Keir's muscular torso is on full display.

Peeking through her fingers, Vesper says, "Sorry, kids. But we need to move. The Drakam guards are headed this way. They're knocking on doors, asking questions, poking around. We probably shouldn't be here when they get to this street unless we're itching for a fight—which I'm all for. Still, we should go."

Her eyes land on me, and the delicious anger begins to build again. *Let them come. We'll kill them all.* Vesper's gaze flicks to my left hand, and her eyes go wide with a flicker of fear before she replaces it with a forced smirk. "That's a dangerous look you have in your eyes, Void. I like it, but a word of advice. Before you go charging in with no regard to your own life, know that your friends are going to follow. You have people to take care of. Think before you act because you are *responsible* for more than just yourself."

Her words hit me like a boulder, and I struggle to take my next breath as Keir actually growls next to me. Vesper just plants her hands on her hips, keeping her gaze on me. "Now, to me, it seems this"—she waves a hand at me before putting it back on her hip—"power of yours stems from strong emotions. Right now, I imagine rage and pain are ruling the roost." She pauses, but when I don't answer, she takes that as an affirmative and nods. "So, find your calm, or at least a balance. Own your shit. Fix it. And let's get out of here. We have maybe ten minutes before the guards get here. Let's go."

And with that, she turns, walking down the hall. A second later another door slams open and Owen yelps. "Hey! I'm all for a lovely lady coming into my room, but warn a fella."

Vesper chuckles, but then her soft voice carries down the hall as she asks, "He okay?"

It's silent for a moment before Owen says, "No. I don't think so."

Miles must be sleeping in the room with Owen. Good. He probably shouldn't be alone right now. None of us should. I scoot out of bed, wincing at the pain pulling at my stitches. Miles did a good job. The scar will probably be barely noticeable ... at least on the outside.

"Here." I turn at Keir's voice, and I scramble to catch the thrown shirt against my chest.

I smirk, pulling Layla's tight tunic over my head. I frown at the bloodstains. Shit. I'll have to buy her a new one. Sliding Keir's shirt on, I smirk. "Always dressing me in your clothes, lordling." My response is half-hearted, but I'm doing the best I can right now.

He stalks to me, eyes darkening. "Well, since there's no time to sink my cock into your pussy and my teeth into your skin, then this is the next best way to claim you, Fox Slayer."

My heart races, pulling me further out of the cloud of darkness I've been existing in as my core clenches with the need to be filled by him. I lick my lips, loving the way his eyes track the movement. Tilting my head, I manage a genuine smile. "You say the sweetest things."

He chuckles, running his hands through his hair. "Fuck. Those lips."

I smirk. "No time. Apparently, I'm being hunted."

I meant it as a joke, sort of, but Keir's teasing evaporates, and he quickly pulls on his own shirt and shoves his feet into his boots. "You're right. Let's go."

We rush down the stairs to the sound of voices coming from the main room. Everyone is here ... well ... Halee's absence hits me hard, which makes me remember Saph is gone too. I press a hand to the wall, waiting for the spinning to stop. Keir rubs my back, shielding me from the others with his body. His lips press to my hair as he whispers, "Just breathe. Take your time. I'm here." I fist his shirt, clinging to him as he kisses my head again then just rests his lips against my temple.

Slowly, I bring my breaths under control, and Keir follows me into the room. The conversations die off, and Keir heads to the bar. All eyes land on me as Keir comes back around and hands me a glass. I take a sip, smiling at the mint sprigs floating in the water. It's cool and refreshing and just what I needed. Drinking down half the glass, I snag a mint leaf and chew it as I look around the room. I try to steady my nerves.

"You all need to know what happened while I was in House Drakam. I went to—"

Layla rushes in, waving us towards the back hallway. "Not here. No time. Follow me. The guards are close."

Aimee runs down the back hallway, and the rest of us follow Layla. I clench my fists, hating that I'm running, that I'm hiding yet again. I want to be the one hunting. I want to run them down. *We want to taunt. We want to hurt. We want to* kill.

Keir looks over his shoulder, concern in his eyes as he looks at my left arm. I don't bother looking. I know what I'll see. Nor grunts behind me. I almost yelp as he slaps the back of my head. "Knock it off. That hurts."

Owen chuckles, but when I glance back, he's rubbing his chest, and there's pain in his expression. Just seeing his usually cheerful face like that has my bloodlust evaporating, and everyone sighs.

Damn. I need to get this under control. I need to get *myself* under control.

No, what we need to do is unleash ourselves and show them all what Forsaken means.

I shake off the voice in my head as Layla goes into a supply room. We all come to a comedic halt, Nor bumping into my back. Val and Owen thud to a stop out in the hall since we can't all fit in here. Before anyone can ask why we're trying to cram into this small room, Layla pushes her shoulder into a cabinet and it slides along the wall revealing a door in the floor. Moving quickly, she grabs the handle and yanks it open. Her actions are smooth and practiced, making me think this isn't the first time she's used this room to hide things or people. Who is this tavern owner?

Holding the door open with one hand, she ushers us forward. "Hurry. Down here. You'll have to be quiet. This room is right under the tavern bar and is not soundproof."

Keir starts down the stairs, and my boot hits the first tread, but I pause, looking back in a panic. "Halee."

Nor gives me a little shove. "Miles already went back for her."

I stumble down a few steps before jogging down the rest. The hidden room is dark, and the dirt floor muffles our footsteps as the others join us. The ceiling is low to the point Valsan, Keir, and Nor have to duck their heads. It's a surprisingly large space though. There are a few crates in a corner, but other than that, it's wide open. Looking up, the underside of the wood planks of the tavern floor makes up the ceiling. Little streamers of dim light filter through the cracks.

Aimee jogs down the stairs, several packs slung over both shoulders. A few seconds later, Miles hurries down the stairs with Halee in his arms, and the door thuds shut, cutting off the little patch of light from the storage room. A loud scraping noise accompanies the cabinet sliding back into place. Valsan crouches, resting his forearms on his thighs, and Nor lowers himself to one knee next to him. Aimee, having dropped the packs to the dirt floor, posts up close to the stairs, leaning against the wall, arms crossed. Owen rests a shoulder against a support beam, and Vesper sits, tucking one leg under her, bending the other to plant her foot on the ground and rests her elbow on her knee. Miles sits against the back wall, holding Halee. He bows his head over her, his shoulders shaking with his silent tears, and my heart breaks again. How many times can a heart break? How many pieces can it shatter into before they no longer fit back together?

Keir wraps his arms around me from behind, ducking to rest his cheek against mine. He squeezes me, his thumb rubbing my stomach over my shirt. He doesn't say anything, just holds me.

We all look up as the front door of the tavern slams open and dozens of boots thunder across the floor. That was close. Layla's calm voice carries down to us. "We're closed."

A familiar voice has my shoulders bunching in Keir's hold. He grips me a little tighter as Captain Silas says, "Now Layla, you know you're never closed to the guard."

Vesper stands, her fists balled at her sides, a death glare aimed at the ceiling. Valsan shares a look with his guards, but I can't read their expressions other than they seem surprised to hear Silas' voice. I'm not. He's like a cursed coin ... always showing up.

"What do you want, Silas?" Layla's composed tone makes me picture her casually wiping a glass as she speaks.

Silas' voice goes deeper. "Captain."

I can practically hear Layla's eye roll as she says, "*Captain* Silas."

Silas barks, "Spread out. Search the place."

Dust billows down on our heads as the guards do his

bidding, but Silas must stay in the barroom, because he says, "Seems odd you'd be closed. Doesn't seem good for business."

Layla sounds unconcerned with his questioning as she says, "I don't have any renters right now, and the bar does the most business at night. I'm not a breakfast joint, though if you're fishing, I have some biscuits and ham in the kitchen ..." There's a pause before she goes on. "Besides, what with the magic blackout ... tensions are high. I thought it best to shut my doors. An angry mob is definitely not good for business."

Silas' voice drips with overconfidence. "The city is calm. On alert, yes, but you have nothing to fear."

"Then what's all this?"

There's a long pause, footsteps moving overhead. Then Silas says, "She spent time in your tent, didn't she Layla?"

A glass clinks as she says, "Who? When? I have a lot of patrons, Silas. Quit being obtuse."

He chuckles. "That's what I like about you, Layla. Always to the point." A cork pops. "The Void. I'm talking about the Void. You know her."

"She enjoyed a few rounds. A lot of people did. It was the Games, Captain. I don't go for shits and giggles. I go to make money, and that means selling drinks, lots of them to anyone who wants them."

"Have you seen her since?"

A muted crash comes from what sounds like the second floor, and Layla sounds angry now. "You break it, you buy it."

Silas' voice drips with mirth. "Have you seen her, *Layla*?"

Aimee shoves off the wall, and Owen silently cracks

his knuckles. Valsan frowns, his gaze locked on the ceiling where Silas' voice is centered. Nor's gaze is on the dirt floor, but his back muscles are pulled tight with tension, his left hand flexing. Vesper's scowl has darkened with murderous intent, and she wiggles her fingers as if she'd like to Poison Silas right here. I'm with her.

The voice in my head chuckles, pushing against my skin from the inside. *Yes. Drain him, slowly. Watch him go weak with terror. Make him fall to his knees at our feet.*

Yes. That sounds perfect.

I didn't realize I was smiling until Keir's hand grips my face, turning me to look up and back at him. I snap out of my dark thoughts as he breathes a whisper, "Don't leave me, Fox Slayer. Stay here. You're mine, and I won't let you go. Now show me those pretty gold eyes."

His chest rises behind me, and I inhale with him. Slowly, the tingling in my hands recedes, and Keir nods. When I look around the room, I expect to see a mix of concern and fear, but as I meet each of their eyes, they nod encouragement at me. Vesper was right. My friends are with me, they are in this fight. Looking around, I take a moment to appreciate how much my life has changed since I took the leap and left Oxtara. Never in a million years would I have guessed things would have turned out this way, but despite everything, I'm grateful. My friends are here, supporting me.

It feels as if my heart actually sighs. Something clicks into place. This. This is my family. People I can count on without having to ask. People who have my back. I can't let them down. I won't. They're mine.

A sensation starts tingling along my skin. It's almost like the feeling I get when that perfect wave comes along and my feet hit the board just right. That feeling I get when I'm dancing with the ocean as water crashes around me, and the sun sparkles above me.

My hair actually lifts off my shoulders then settles as the sensation dissipates into nothing. Everyone's eyes go wide, and there's a few muffled shouts and cheers from above and even from outside. Bright red catches the corner of my eye, and as I look down I see Keir's Spirit flames licking along his arms ... against my body!

He releases me, stepping back, shock on his face, Gren and Hich at his side. They are so close I could run my hand through their heads. Before I can process what happened, Valsan rushes over, throwing his arms over Keir, bending his body over him. Valsan whispers, "Put it out." His gaze flicks to the ceiling where the cracks of the floor planks could reveal Keir's telltale red glow.

Shit.

Keir drops his head, concentrating, but nothing happens. Boot scuffles overhead precede Silas' voice. "Well, that's interesting." He's moving closer to above where we are as he says, "Ahh, there you are."

CHAPTER 12

KEIR

My magic is resisting me. It won't go out. Shit. Shit. Shit. Hich and Gren circle my legs, and I mentally tell them to stay quiet. Silas' boots thud right overhead as he says, "There you are. That's better. Ahh, magic, how I missed you. Now the bitch won't be able to hide from me."

Gods, I thought he saw my flames, but he was talking about his magic. Still, the thought of being the one who exposes us all only makes me panic, and unfortunately my Spirit fire responds, flaring brighter.

Shit!

Thaeia's Void slips over me like a blanket, and the flames go out in a blink, my hounds puffing into red and black smoke. I lift my head, and my Fox Slayer is there, chewing on her bottom lip. She dips a little nod to me, and I press my palm to my chest as I mouth, *Thank you.*

Nor comes up behind Thaeia, his head slightly ducked

to avoid hitting the ceiling, and taps her on the shoulder. She turns, and Nor's dimple creases his cheek as he smiles down at her. Holding up his left hand, little grains of dirt float up from the floor and dance around us before settling once more. Wait. Nor still has his magic? I look around the room, each person nodding at us.

How is she doing this? I look down just to make sure ... yup, no Spirit fire. This room isn't that big, everyone is well within Thaeia's previous twenty-pace range, yet here we are. Her power is evolving. She drops her head, her hair hanging over her face to hide her gold eyes from me. Her fingers curl into her palms, and I know she's unsettled. I reach for her, but a voice overhead stalls my movement.

"Captain, the second floor is clear, but the beds look like they've been slept in."

There's a shuffling of feet, and all our gazes track the sound as it gets closer to where the bar is. There's more clinking of glass as if Layla is cleaning or setting up for the day, business as usual.

Silas must make some expression at her because she sighs. "I haven't stripped and remade the beds from my last renters. What with everything going on, making beds didn't seem like a high priority."

Silas hums in answer, then it sounds like several guards enter the room, and a male voice says "Captain, third floor is clear."

Layla's voice drips with a teasing lilt. "Ah Leon, I should have known you wouldn't pass up a chance to rummage through my things. Do I need to check your pockets for my underwear?"

There's a beat of silence, and Owen turns red trying to hold back his laughter.

It's Silas who says, "Guards, go out and search the alleys, nearby streets, and buildings. Everything."

Layla's voice sings out, "Bye Leon. See you later?"

Cheeky Layla.

There's stumbling overhead, then running boots thunder across the floor sending a shower of dust down on our heads as the guards rush out the door. Owen throws his arm over his face, muffling a cough. We all freeze, looking up, waiting for Silas to rip the floor apart to get to us. But nothing happens.

Layla says, "If that's all, Captain, I need to finish preparing for the day. As you said, I should be op—"

She's cut off by something, and we stand frozen in the tense silence. A second later we hear, "Ahhh, good ale as always, Layla."

Owen rolls his eyes, and I shake my head. Of course the Drakam captain is drinking on the job. Another voice breaks into the room upstairs. "Captain, there are horses around back in the stable."

Shit. My eyes travel over our group and land on the pile of packs leaning against the wall. I'm glad Aimee is such a quick thinker. We're all tense, and Vesper holds up her left hand, pointing at her wrist then up at the ceiling with a question in her eyes. That would solve our current problem, but Valsan shakes his head, holding up a finger, silently telling her and everyone else to wait.

Silas moves slowly while saying, "Thank you. Go out and join the search." The guard rushes out, their footfalls fading, but Silas' boots thud in a languid rhythm towards the back hall. "Layla dear, what are you hiding?"

Sweat rolls down my back, sticking my shirt to my skin. Aimee is at the foot of the stairs, a blade in her right hand, her left hand raised and ready, her skin grey like rock. Owen slowly tracks directly under Silas, his gaze glued to the ceiling. Vesper stands opposite Aimee across the stairs, a gleeful grin on her face as she bounces on the balls of her feet. She's scary. I'm glad she's on our side.

Nor shifts closer to Thaeia, flexing his left hand before balling it in a fist and holding it in front of her. She grins around the worry in her eyes and bumps his knuckles with hers. Valsan takes two steps into the center of the room, and that's all it takes to draw everyone's attention. He holds up both hands, palms patting downwards, mouthing, *Calm.* Everyone settles slightly, but Owen continues to track Silas' lazy stroll through the tavern.

Thaeia turns to me, and I look down at my Fox Slayer. I'm shaking with the need to grab her and run. To run and run and run until no one and nothing can hurt her again. I have found this perfect woman, but the gods keep pushing, keep poking, keep tearing at her. I'd call every Spirit in the Everafter and rip the heavens apart if I thought it would give Thaeia some peace.

She taps my boot with hers, bringing my attention out of my thoughts and back to her face. Touching her left wrist, she then points at the ceiling, her finger following Silas' movements. She looks back at me, her brows pinched in question. I look between her wrist and the ceiling again before realization hits. My knees pop as I kneel and drag my finger through the dirt spelling out Hunter, then drawing a little star with the number four next to it.

When I look up, Thaeia's eyes are wide, and I nod. Yeah. It's not great. Silas has Hunter magic, and he's very, very good at finding what he wants. She points at her wrist again, then up at Silas. She closes her fist in a pulling motion, her brows raised. I shake my head, and she frowns. She could try to take Silas' magic, but who knows what would actually happen. And if his magic suddenly goes out again, I'm afraid that would just raise his suspicions.

Silas makes his way towards the kitchen, his boots thudding slowly, in no rush. He's in Hunter mode. My back starts to ache from the tension, and my eyes track his progress, but he only goes halfway across the room before he turns back. Silas stops, and I'm staring so hard at the ceiling, it's a wonder I'm not burning a hole through the planks. His boots start to thud again, moving only two paces towards the back door before backtracking again.

Shit.

I'm not sure if she means to do it, but Thaeia shifts closer, seeking comfort, and her arm brushes against mine. She's trembling ... from fear? Adrenaline? Rage? Probably all three. I want to look at her, but I can't seem to peel my gaze away from where the sounds of Silas's steps are steadily making their way to the storage room.

I don't know if the others are holding their breath, but I realize I am. I exhale slowly, moving in front of Thaeia. I know she'll hate it, but I just can't help myself. Surprisingly, her warm hand presses to my back, and she stays behind me.

We're all so quiet, I can hear the door to the storage room open with a soft brush of wood against wood. Silas enters the room, and Owen stops at the base of the stairs as Silas makes a tight circle.

Layla tsks. "Unless you need a restock of cleaning supplies at the estate, don't know if this room will be that useful to you."

Silas pauses, saying nothing for a long while before he hums in interest. Vesper has a 'fuck it' look on her face, and she takes one silent step up, but Owen grabs her arm, shaking his head. She scowls at him, and he turns a little green, but he doesn't let her go. Vesper doesn't come back down, but she doesn't try to go up any farther either.

Everyone is practically vibrating with anticipation, well, almost everyone. My gaze slides over my shoulder. Miles still sits against the back wall, his head bowed, his body curled over Halee's body. He isn't moving. He's just there with her, and I get the feeling he's ready to join her if it comes to that.

No. We won't lose anyone else!

Thaeia notices where I'm looking, and her gaze drops to the floor, but not before I see the flood of guilt in her eyes. I lean down, pressing my lips to her ear, and I can't help how pleased it makes me when she shivers slightly from my touch. I whisper, "If Silas finds that door, give me my magic back. He won't make it past the first step." Her eyes snap to my face. She looks back and forth between my eyes, searching for ... something. Hesitance? She won't find it. Slowly, she nods, biting her lip. I tug it out from between her teeth, as I say against her mouth, "You can do this, Fox Slayer." My lips find hers, and she leans into the kiss. It's not wild or desperate. Our tongues don't lick or seek entrance. We simply breathe each other in, our lips pressed softly together.

I pull back just enough to look her in the eyes, and she licks her lips with a more determined nod. That's my girl.

The hidden door rattles as the large cabinet above shakes. Silas grunts, and it sounds pained. Is he hurt? Valsan steps forward on silent feet. He moves Owen out of the way so he can stand at the foot of the stairs. One slow, silent step at a time, he starts to climb. Vesper throws her hands up in frustration, waving at Valsan's back, her eyes wide with indignation, as if to say, *Why does he get to go?*

"Captain." Thaeia jumps as a new voice calls out from upstairs near the front door of the tavern. Silas moves around the storage room in another slow circle, then the voice calls out louder, "Captain Silas?"

Silas curses, and his angry stomps take him from the storage room, but he slows on a stumbling step with a pained grunt. We stare at the spot where he stopped, then follow his now limping strides down the hall, and back into the main bar. He shouts, "What!"

"Someone three doors down says they might have seen something."

Silas growls. "Did you question them? *What* did they see?"

There's a pause, then the guard says, "They, um, they wanted to speak to you. They were wondering if there was any kind of reward?"

I clench my hands. Greedy motherfuckers. I doubt they actually saw anything, but what if they did?

Silas growls. "Fine. I'll deal with them." There's another pause, then he says, "Layla, that Void is dangerous. She can't be trusted. There are things about her you don't know."

Layla asks, "Like what, Silas?"

"Just, for your own safety, you need to tell me if you see her. That Void is dangerous, and she's trying to spread lies about Lord Drakam. She wants to tear the entire country apart."

"She's just one woman."

Silas tsks. "After what just happened with everyone's magic, can you really say that? You know I'm right, Layla."

There's a wooden knock, like Silas is rapping his knuckles on the bar as he says, "I can make it worth your while."

"Money?"

"If that's what you want."

Every one of us take a step towards the stairs. My hackles are raised, and I'm about to tell Thaeia to release her Void, but Valsan looks over his shoulder down the stairs, shaking his head. We all go still again, but you can cut the tension with a knife.

Layla's voice comes from behind the bar. "I'll let you know if I hear anything. Drunk people talk."

"Indeed they do. Thank you, Layla. Be careful. Like I said, she's dangerous." And with that, he leaves and the door clicks shut, but I have no illusions that he won't return. He's on our scent, and it's only a matter of time before he Hunts us down.

We all remain tense and silent, not trusting that the Drakam guards won't come barreling back into the tavern. Layla doesn't move overhead. A minute passes. Then another. My muscles are wound so tight, I feel like I might snap. Half an hour passes in agonizing silence, then Layla makes her way to the storage room, and the cabinet scrapes across the floor. Valsan is there to help her lift the hatch, and dim moonlight spills down the stairs. Valsan backs against the wall, letting Layla make her way down to us, and he closes the door, following.

Layla runs her hand through her long blond hair, her blue eyes tired as she says, "Well, that was unpleasant."

Owen claps her on the back with an uneasy chuckle. "Thought you were going to sell us out there for a moment"

She grins up at him. "Nah. I do just fine. I don't need Silas' blood money." She looks at Thaeia. "Besides, I get the feeling Drakam is hiding something big if he wants to get his hands on you so badly."

Layla raises her left arm, the word CRAQAR wrapping around her wrist. Clever. She shrugs. "Anyway, the good captain seemed to be in pain." She raises a brow, but I have no idea what could be wrong with Silas.

Owen tsks. "Yeah, that's because he caught Miles' dagger ... in his gut. Honestly, I'm surprised he's up and about. Without magic, he couldn't have been Healed yet."

Vesper snarls, "He's got that mean blood in him. Won't stay down till you make him."

I get the impression Vesper's mind is currently cycling through all her options of 'putting Silas down.' She's got that gleeful look in her eye that's more than a little unnerving.

Layla shrugs, unable to hide the mirthful smile on her face as she says, "That explains it. He kept pressing his hand to his stomach." She rubs the back of her neck, tilting her head towards the hatch at the top of the stairs. "Well, now that magic is back you'll be glad to know the cabinet is spelled to be unmovable by anyone but me, and the hatch is similarly spelled. Of course, if the magic had still been out, I would have been more worried about Silas finding you all." Layla turns back to Thaeia. "So thanks for sorting that out."

Thaeia shifts, and even in the dim light of the room, I notice her blush. She opens her mouth to say something, but Owen cuts in. "So, um, I'm just gonna ask. Why is Lord Drakam hunting you? What happened?"

CHAPTER 13

THAEIA

I PHYSICALLY SHRINK AWAY from the question. Will they look at me differently? Treat me differently?

The voice in my head whispers with a laugh, *We are different. We are special. More.*

I clench my teeth. *Shut up. Go away.*

I can't. I'm you.

But this ... whatever it is in my head, doesn't feel like me.

Owen holds up a hand, his face turning serious. "I'm sorry, but by the look on your face and by everything that's going on, we kinda need to know."

Keir's hand presses to my lower back, and I relax just a little. Tilting my head up at him, I bite the inside of my cheek, wondering ...

I picture the 'Void blanket' I threw over him, then I imagine pulling it off, letting it slide up and over his head, letting it pool on the floor. As I stare at him, there's a rush over my skin, like the blood in my veins is speeding up, coursing through my body. It's dizzying, and my breaths come faster. Keir's Spirit flames burst to life, crawling up one side of his body, across his head, and then down the other, just as I imagined the 'blanket' moving and falling.

Everyone is silent, but I don't look around. I keep my eyes on Keir. He doesn't look at his flames, he doesn't even glance at his hounds now circling our legs. Keir keeps his gaze on me, a soft smile lifting his lips. The ruby-red color of the Spirit fire reflects in his eyes. His fingers brush across my cheek, and for a split second, I wonder if the fire will hurt. But there's nothing, not even a warm tingle other than the usual rush I get when this amazing man touches me. His eyes are filled with ... love? He says, "I knew you could do it, Thaeia. You are a wonder."

We stare at each other for a second, then Nor's quiet voice breaks the moment. "See? I knew you'd get a hold of it sooner or later. Just took you sixteen years ... Void."

My lips twitch with a smile as I turn to face him. "I'm not really sure how I'm doing it. It still feels a little out of my control, but it seems like if I'm calm enough, I can ... coax it to do what I want?"

Nor smirks. "Calm, huh? Well, then we're all in trouble." He laughs, grabbing my arm, pulling me to him, and I hold him tight. His fingers splay across my upper back as he whispers into my hair. "You'll figure it out. You're amazing. I'm so sorry. For everything. All those years. I—"

I pinch his side, pulling away so I can look at him. "We're past it, Nor. I love you. Always have. Even when I hated you."

His bright green eyes shimmer with tears, but he blinks them away with a nod.

On a slow inhale, I turn, stepping back to face the group. "Okay, let me explain." I shake my head, an inappropriate smile threatening to lift my lips as I say, "No, there's too much. Let me sum up."

Keir chuckles at the reference, and I don't know why I'm surprised he got it. He does love to read.

I grit my teeth then say the words that burn my throat. "Severn Drakam is my father." Wide eyes blink at me from around the room, stunned looks on everyone's face. But I don't give them time to react beyond that. The story spills out so I don't have to think about it for long. "Apparently all the Drakam males produce"—I point at myself—"this. If a female is born to their line, they are Void. There's a long, drawn-out history of the fucked up shit that went down years ago, but basically for the past however long, the Drakams have been killing off their female babies, claiming that Drakam males can't sire girls. Father dearest thought me dead until the Games. Surprise fucker. So then I guess he got the wild idea that he could use me, well, my power anyway. He ... Halee ... He used her to goad my power out of me." I force myself to turn to Miles' tear-streaked face. There's rage in his eyes, but at least I think not all of it is aimed towards me. "I tried, Miles. Really. I tried so fucking hard. I couldn't stop him. I ..."

He holds up a hand, shaking his head before breaking my gaze. Miles bows over Halee once more, and I take a deep breath, turning back to the group. I sniff back my tears, replacing them with anger at my father as I say, "Severn won't want his dirty secrets to get out, so he needs to shut me up." My fingers curl over my palm, reaching for the sleeves I no longer wear. "So, that's it. Oh, and there's a woman being held by Drakam. Her name is Fara." Nor's eyes get even wider. "I'm not sure if she's even still alive, probably not, but I need to try to help her, to get her out of there. I think she's the reason I'm alive." I look around nervously, but force my posture to remain straight. "I'm not asking you to—"

Owen tsks. "Don't even bother finishing that sentence. That's some fucked up shit you just told us. What kind of friends would we be if we walked away now?"

I look around the group. Owen's signature grin is in place, but behind it is determination and support. Aimee's arms are crossed as usual, a hard look on her face, but she nods at me. Vesper winks from where she's leaning against the far wall. I don't know what has her so invested in all this, but it seems she's sticking to me until she's satisfied. Valsan's arm is around Nor's shoulders, rubbing his arm with his thumb, and my love for them both lightens the load from my shoulders. They smile at me, and Nor holds out his fist. I grin, mimicking him, sending him an air bump. When I drop my hand, my gaze lands on Miles. Layla is crouched next to him, whispering something to which he nods once. His head lifts slightly and I stiffen, guilt turning my stomach inside out. His pain-filled eyes hold mine. The deep shadows on his tired face make him look haunted, and his jaw flexes as he grinds his teeth together. There's a promise of violence in his eyes, and when he nods at me, I know he's in this fight for Halee and will stop at nothing until she is avenged.

Keir stands still next to me, his steady presence like a balm. Gren barks at me, and I chuckle. He steps closer, his head reaching above my waist. His flames lick harmlessly against my body as my hand trails through the little flames that flicker along his head. I can't feel anything, but as I pass over his ears, he tilts his head as if leaning into my touch.

Owen clears his throat, and we all turn back to him as he says, "We knew something was going on. Before we ended up here, we did a quick tour of House Drakam." He winks at me. "Must have just missed you. Anyway, your father ... nope, gross, don't like that. Severn Drakam came out to the gates and spoke to the people. It was with the pretense of keeping everyone calm, but in reality, it was him directing the building anger of the crowd away from himself, and at, well, you."

I shake my head, my fists clenching tighter. "Of fucking course."

Valsan says, "The people know you're in the city and that you are responsible for taking their magic."

I throw up my hands. "It wouldn't have happened if Severn hadn't—"

He holds up a palm. "I know. I know. But now that we know the whole story, I think his speech was him trying to get out in front of you. To discredit you if you were to start telling people what he's been doing all these years. And now, after what happened with everyone's magic, even if they were to believe you, I'm afraid most people, at this time, would side with Severn."

I begin to pace. "People can't be okay with their lord *killing babies*."

"No. But they won't see it like that. Not with the fear and anger at losing their magic so fresh. They'll see him saving them from the so-called terrors of the Voids."

Vesper whistles. "Well, shit. What do we do now?"

Valsan goes to clap his hands, but pauses right before his palms meet, his gaze flicking to the ceiling before landing back on us. "Now, we plan. We think of ways to expose Drakam and clear Thaeia's name."

Miles' rough voice cracks from behind us. "Exposing him won't be enough."

I agree. My father has to die.

Vesper coughs, grabbing everyone's attention, but her eyes are on me. "So, your"—she flicks her gaze to my left hand—"power. You got a leash on it now?"

Her harsh tone has the others frowning at her, but I see the fear behind her eyes. She saw. Both her and Keir know what this power inside me is capable of. Before I catch myself, my fingers curl, reaching over my palm once more. I try to inflict confidence in my voice, but it comes out too soft, too timid as I say, "I'm not sure."

Vesper sucks in a sharp breath, clenching her jaw before saying, "Get sure."

Nor takes a step towards her. "Hey. Poison mage or not, watch your tone."

She sneers at him. "Or what, *Gravity* mage? Think you can crush me before my Poison touches your pretty skin?"

"Yes."

I step in front of Nor with my arms held up. "Hey. Stop. Vesper is not wrong." Nor looks like he's going to push back, but I drop my arms and hang my head. I don't want to say it. I don't want them to know. But ...

Vesper shifts. "There's a good godsdamned reason the Drakams are so afraid of Thaeia." She turns to me with a frown. "They need to know. If you don't tell them, I will."

I look at Keir, and he nods. Needing the support, I step towards him, and he doesn't hesitate. Threading our fingers, he pulls me to his side, rubbing his thumb over the back of my knuckles. I look back at Vesper.

"Actually, yeah. You tell them. I still don't remember everything, and you're right. Everyone needs to know, to understand. You saw it. You felt it." My hand tightens around Keir's as I look up at him. "You both did. And a few of you experienced a piece of it upstairs."

Layla tsks. "That was just a piece?"

She sounds terrified, and I guess she should be. Keir's free hand wraps around the back of my head, pulling my face to his chest. It's strange having his fire swirl and lick around me without actually feeling it. It's strange to have active magic so close, pressed right up against my skin. It's beautiful. I breathe him in—leather and dried grass. He kisses the top of my head, whispering, "I'm here."

And that's all I need.

After a moment, he releases me, and I step back, ready to face my friends once more. Vesper nods at me, then tells them everything. My eyes get wider as she describes what I did, how my skin swam with midnight-blue shadows, how my eyes bled black, how even my voice changed, and I'm pretty sure I know what that voice sounds like ...

Mmm. Yes, you do.

When Vesper recounts how my touch seemed to spread the darkness onto Sidian, a shiver ripples down my spine. The voice in my head chuckles. *You won't admit it to them, but you enjoyed it—the power. You let me take the reins because you knew what had to be done. And you liked sitting in the back of my consciousness, in the dark, watching me punish him. You've convinced yourself you've somehow kept your hands clean because you let me take control. But never forget, I am you. You are me. And* we *are powerful.* Mentally, I shake my head, but the voice just tsks. *That's fine. You can deny it. I'm well practiced in patience. You'll come around.*

I realize Vesper has stopped talking, and though I really don't want to see the expressions of horror on my friend's faces, I force myself to look at them. They are all a little wide-eyed, but Aimee is as stoic as always, arms crossed. Valsan seems more curious than afraid. That tracks. Nor rubs the back of his neck, and doubt rears its ugly head. This is what he was afraid of. Maybe not this specifically, but the unknown of my Void. And apparently, he was right. I am dangerous.

Yes, we are.

I need to control it. I can't hurt them. I won't. I'll die before I let that happen.

Pfft. I won't allow you to die, not now that I'm free.

Nor breaks the silence. "So, that's what happened upstairs? You don't remember?"

I shake my head. "At House Drakam, all I remember is walking down the hall, then seeing Sidian. Then I was on the ground in a different room. Same with upstairs. I was so"—I duck my head and angle away from Keir—"angry. And then you were wrapped around me, dragging me downstairs."

Keir tugs my arm, and when I don't turn, he grips my chin with his free hand, forcing me to look at him. He doesn't say anything, just holds my gaze until my shoulders drop, and he nods, releasing me.

Nor rubs the back of his neck again. "Well, that's ..." He drops his hand, shrugging, but there's a tiny smile on his face that tries to hide his fear. It's something. At least he's not attacking me or running away. I'll take it.

Owen barks a laugh before slapping a hand over his mouth, eyes flying to the ceiling. There's no one up in the tavern though. He strides over to me, clapping my shoulder. "That's badass, that's what it is." My breath puffs out, releasing even more of my tension. Good old Owen. His smile drops into a more thoughtful expression as he looks me in the eyes. "Seriously, Thaeia. Your power sounds terrifyingly amazing. And Sidian had it coming." A noise bubbles from my lips, something between a laugh and a sob as he says, "We've got your back. We'll help you in any way we can."

He pulls me into a hug, dragging Keir with us, and I tell myself I won't cry, but I do. Nor wraps his arms around us from behind me. Valsan comes over, a smile on his handsome face as he says, "This is so fascinating. I'd love to work with you, see what kind of control we can help you gain." He wraps his arm around Nor from the side, hugging Owen with the other.

Vesper jumps onto the pile with a laugh. "Group hug? I love it!"

I hear Aimee snort a quiet laugh before she joins us. I'm so relieved, and dare I say happy. Layla chuckles, "You all are too cute."

But her voice brings the realization that Miles isn't in the hug with us. And neither is Halee.

Just like that, the gloom of grief casts its shadow over me. Keir must feel the change in my body, because he breaks from the hug, and everyone backs away. My eyes slide across the room. Aimee presses her hand to my back, pushing me forward, and I resist. I can't. I ... Oh gods ... I can't ... Oh Halee. Halee. Halee. I'm so sorry. So sorry. I ... I ...

CHAPTER 14

THAEIA

Gently, Aimee keeps urging me forward, walking with me until we're standing right in front of Miles and Halee. Miles must know we're here, but he doesn't move. He doesn't look up. He just holds her. Aimee kneels, her hand resting on his shoulder. He flinches as she says something to him, but he keeps his head bowed over my friend's body.

Eventually, Miles nods. Aimee scoots back, and Miles shifts, lowering Halee to the floor. He reverently brushes her curls away from her face, arranging her hands over her chest, then presses a quick kiss to her forehead. He goes to sit back on his heels, but he sways and falls to his ass, his grief-stricken gaze screaming with sorrow as he looks at her.

Aimee looks at Layla who's sitting cross-legged against the wall a little ways away from Halee. Layla nods, and

Aimee presses her hand to Halee's arm. Nausea roils in my stomach as I realize Halee's skin is now a little puffier, and her blood has started to settle creating deep purple bruising. From where Aimee touches her, Halee begins to Petrify, the hardened surface spreading quickly until she looks like a stone sculpture. It's cowardly of me, but she's easier to look at like this. Like this is just a likeness of her, not actually her.

Running her fingertips over Halee's stone body, Aimee's voice is quiet but calm. "You are safe, Halee. We will take care of you here. There's nothing left for you to worry about. Your friends are here. We love you. You are safe."

I'm breaking, shattering. There's not going to be anything left.

There's a soft shuffling behind me, and Valsan asks, "You sure, Layla?"

She smiles, looking at the captain standing behind me. "I'll watch over her until you can take her home."

I shake my head, hiccupping around the tears that are building in my throat. "We can't ask you to do that."

She smiles. "You didn't, Shanty Princess. I offered. You really need to get better at accepting help, yeah?"

I take a deep breath. "Thank you."

Vesper shuffles forward, and for the first time since I've known her, she looks uncertain. Her boot toes the ground as she looks down at Halee and says, "I didn't know you, but I watched you. You were ... kind. To every one. You always seemed to have this ... happiness inside of you, and it made me want to know you. I wish I'd had the chance."

She steps back, and I hear her cross the room, and when I look over my shoulder, she's sitting on the bottom step, knees pulled to her chest as she hugs her shins. There's some inner turmoil slipping through her eyes.

Forcing my gaze back to Halee, words build inside me, sitting heavy on my tongue. Lowering myself, my knees hit the dirt floor, and I place one hand on Halee's stone arm. "I'm so, so sorry, Halee. I ... I will make sure the one responsible pays. You will be avenged. But more importantly, I promise to get you home safely. I will take you to your parents. I'll make sure they know how brilliant you've been these past weeks. I'll tell them about your star, and how we all celebrated on the side of the road, how happy you made everyone. Because you did, Halee. Wherever you went, whoever you were with, you made everything better." My voice cracks, but I have to keep going. I have to tell her. "You were my friend. Through it all, you stood by me, you defended me, you ..." I swallow, my throat burning, my eyes spilling tears. "You were the best of us. I hate that you're gone. I hate what was done to you. And I HATE myself for not being able to save you."

My fingers slide from her, falling to my lap. "I'm so sorry. I love you, Halee, and I hope one day, your spirit will forgive me. I miss you so much."

I can't take the pain that's ripping my stomach apart. I hunch over, hugging my waist, and of course Keir is there. He kneels next to me, hugging me as he whispers, "When she's ready ..." I fall into him, those three words both giving me hope and breaking my heart.

Nor kneels on the other side of me, resting his hand on Halee's stone hair, the curls still so lifelike. His voice is quiet and filled with emotion as he says, "Thaeia is right. You were the best of us. So kind. So bright and happy, but also fierce." He chuckles sadly. "You always followed your heart." He looks at me. "I wish I could have been as brave as you, Halee." Dropping his gaze back to her, he runs his hand down her hair. "But I will strive to always be better. I will always ask myself if what I'm doing, if what I'm saying, if who I am would make you smile. Because if you were smiling, everything was okay. I miss you, Halee."

Tears splash onto his lap, and he lets his hand fall away. Valsan comes around, sitting next to Nor. "Halee, I only knew you for a short while, too short a time. But Nor is right, you made everyone around you happy. I'm honored I was there for your first star. I'm honored to have known you. You will be remembered. Always. Everyone in this room will carry you in our hearts forever."

I bite my lip to keep the loud sob in my chest from escaping. Keir presses his lips to my temple, wiping a few of my tears away with his thumb.

Owen comes to Keir's other side. There's a crackling sound, then Ice builds in his hand, and I startle. It's still shocking to have people working magic when I'm so close. After a few moments, a crystal bird sits in Owen's palm. No, not a bird, a prazar. The thin wings are tucked to its back, its head cocked to the side, its tail feathers spread like a cape behind it. Owen sets the Ice prazar on Halee's chest right above her crossed hands. "It won't last. The beauty of this little prazar will melt away all too soon, like you." There's a bite of anger in Owen's tone as he goes on. "You were taken too soon, little Halee. We are rarely ready to let our loved ones go." My mind flits to Saph, and my grief doubles. "But losing you, Halee, has hit us all very hard. The pain may fade like my Ice, but your memory will live on." He presses a hand to his heart. "I promise, Halee. You will be avenged, and I will carry you here"—he thumps his chest—"forever. I promise."

There's a moment of silence before Keir shifts. I didn't

realize how much I was leaning on him until I nearly fall over when he shuffles forward sightly. Settling back on my shins, I watch as he holds out his left hand and places it on Halee's hands below the Ice sculpture which is already starting to melt. Gren walks right through Keir since there's not any room for him to walk around. The large hound bows his head, sniffing at Halee before laying at her side, his body half in and half out of Keir. I topple back when Hich's head pokes through mine. He sits, head tilted down at Halee, then he lets out a little whine that stabs me in the heart.

Some silent communication happens between Keir and his hounds. Keir nods, and Hich disappears. With his eyes on Halee, Keir pulls his hand away, but a piece of his Spirit fire stays behind, burning and flickering over Halee's heart. "This will burn with my magic, leaving a piece of all us with you until we can take you home. It will stay true as long as I have my power. We are with you, little warrior. You are goodness and joy and light. You are loved."

I'm staring at the little flame dancing on Halee's chest when Keir turns to me. "Hich asked to stay on the other side. He's going to watch out for her. He will be there for her, Thaeia. She's not alone."

I keep my eyes on the flame. It blurs and focuses then blurs again as tears form and fall unchecked down my face.

There's a long stretch of silence as we all sit in our shared grief. Nor and Valsan are in a tight embrace, supporting each other through this moment. Then Miles shifts from where he's been sitting silently at Halee's head. Like his arm is too heavy to lift, his hand drops to the dirt floor. Then his fingers curl, digging little grooves. We all scoot back when tiny green shoots push through the ground. Grass appears, forming a blanket under Halee, and flowers bloom in bright colors. Thin vines climb up her sides, clutching to her like I know Miles wants to. Delicate white petals unfurl from the vines, their light scent filling the room. Halee is hugged by color and life and beauty.

A single star flower blooms near her cheek. Its bright purple petals are so saturated, they look like velvet. The purple bleeds to a soft yellow towards the center. These flowers only bloom on Oxtara. Miles has given her a piece of her home until we can take her there.

This pain is too much. I don't want to face this anymore. I want to be anywhere but here. But I also never want to leave.

Miles' voice is husky from grief as he touches her cheek. "Flowers bloom without fear of death ... but why did your radiance have to be taken so soon?" He clears his throat, sniffing. "I only told you the one time. I wish I'd said it more. I love you, Halee. I always will. It sounds silly, and I know you'd laugh at me for saying this, but I honestly didn't know what true happiness was until you. My life was great, but then I met you, and it was spectacular." His voice cracks, and his red eyes fill with tears. "Oh, gods, Halee. How do I go on?" Falling forward, he presses his forehead to hers. "I miss you. This hurts, so much. I wasn't there for you. I let them take you, and I wasn't there." His arm curls under him, and he grips his shirt. "Every time I take a breath, it rips me apart and I wish it would stop. But I'll hold on to this pain. I'll carry it and deliver it to Severn." His free hand digs deeper into the dirt floor, then he just sort of goes limp, his body slouching. "And then your friends and I will take you home. I'll meet your parents just like we talked about. I'll see the North Shore bay you wanted to take me to. I'll try the fried fish at The Kitchen, and I'll save you a sweet roll. I'll climb the tallest hill and watch the sunset with you in my heart." He turns his tear-streaked face towards me, and I whimper as he says, "And I'll make the garden in front of Thaeia's house, just as you planned it."

I can't keep it in. My sobs wrack my body. It's hard to breathe as Miles leans back over Halee. "Her garden will be the most beautiful thing on the island. Just as you were the most beautiful thing in my life."

We're all crying. Our sniffles are the only thing breaking the pain-filled silence. I'm not sure how long we sit there, but eventually, my tears slow, and I take deep breaths to try and calm myself. I look around at my family and a shiver curls down my spine.

I may be Forsaken, but one thing's for sure, if the gods do indeed exist, they did one thing right by me by putting these amazing people in my life.

CHAPTER 15

NOR

WE'RE all milling around the basement. It's been hours since we rushed down here, and we're all in different phases of disbelief over Thaeia's story: anger at Drakam for what he's done, grief over Halee, and a tiredness that seems to come from the bones.

I shift, absently hovering one of Thaeia's throwing knives above my palm. At first, using my magic, even in a little way eased my anxious mind. But as I flip the blade over and over in midair, I realize my tension is spinning back up. Snagging the hilt out of the air, gripping it tightly, I just blurt out, "So, plan of attack? How do we get to Severn, and how do we kill him?"

Vesper adds, "Then what? Who will lead Drakam? Will it even be Drakam anymore if there's not a Drakam to rule?"

All eyes shift to Thaeia, and she holds up her hands,

her eyes wide. "No. No. I don't want it. I won't take it. Just ... No."

Vesper chuckles. "Okay, calm down. No one is asking you to 'take the throne,' but do you have a plan?"

Thaeia shakes her head. "I'm no strategist. When I 'stormed the castle' as they say, I was working off of pure fury and luck. And well, that didn't work."

Exhaustion pulls at my eyelids. The few hours of sleep felt great at the time, but it wasn't enough. I glance at Miles, unsure if he's slept at all beyond passing out last night.

Valsan rubs his palms together. "I need to find a way to contact Lady Kapros."

Layla shakes her head from where she's sitting on the stairs. "That's going to be difficult." She's been carefully coming and going the past few hours. The tavern is still closed, and all seems quiet, but we don't dare leave this hidden place in case Silas comes back, which we all know he will. "People are staying inside for the most part, but there are already alleged sightings of the Void." She rolls her eyes. "Physical blockades are being erected throughout the city, and the barricades around House Drakam are ... borderline excessive. The guards are crawling all over Rokvale, and well, Captain, you are a known associate of Thaeia's. All of you are. I can try to get a message out, but just know it'll probably be intercepted by Drakam's guards. They're monitoring everything."

Vesper cracks her knuckles. "Well, we can't stay holed up in here forever."

Keir taps his boot on the floor where he sits against a wall, Gren laying at his feet. "There's also my father. I haven't contacted him, and he'll use that to his advantage."

Shit. I keep forgetting Keir is like the prince of Alopson. He's so laid back, so ... normal. Will his father invade Drakam if he thinks Keir is being held against his will?

Valsan walks over to Layla, crouching so she doesn't have to tilt back to look at him, and they speak in hushed tones. My boots have worn a little path in the dirt from my pacing, but if I stop, I might collapse. Every time I think about Lord Drakam, my magic thrums with the need to crush him. The question is, do I squish him slowly? Let him feel his bones crack and his blood race? Let him experience his lungs crushing? Or do I just ... pop? End it? That would probably be the best. While torture would be fitting, dragging it out serves no real purpose. I flex my hand. Instant explosion it is.

Valsan chuckles over his shoulder from where he's still crouched next to Layla. "You have a murderous look on your face, Nor."

I smile, shrugging. "Just thinking through my options on how to kill Severn."

Vesper laughs. "Hey, me too!"

We chuckle, just casually laughing about murder as I go back to pacing.

Owen drops his head back, looking at the ceiling. "Well, with magic back, we can try to sneak into House Drakam. Valsan has Confusion. Vesper has Poison—not that I'm asking you to kill any guards, maybe just make them sick. You know, keep them distracted. Nor has Gravity that can hold them back and shield us. I can shield as well. Miles can sic his Plants on any attackers. Keir can bulk our numbers if needed with his Spirits, and Aimee can Petrify herself and can take point. And of course we have Thaeia in an emergency."

Vesper taps her chin. "We'd need to be ready for traps.

I only explored a small section of the estate while looking for Thaeia, but I came across three triggers. Don't know what they do, but I can't imagine they're any fun."

Layla leans to the side to look around Valsan. "Let's call that plan B."

Owen raises a brow. "So what's plan A?"

Valsan stays crouched, but pivots to face us. "We give Layla a few days. Three days. She's Clever." He winks at her, and a tingle of jealousy rises unwanted. I shake it off, trying to bury my insecurities. Layla smiles at us, lifting her left hand, the tattoo wrapping around her wrist spelling out the ancient word for Clever. Valsan continues, "And she knows this city, its people. She's asked for three days."

I stop my pacing. "To do what?"

Layla drops her hand. "To assess. To see if there are sympathies to be found in favor of Thaeia. If I don't have anything concrete after three days, we'll"—she grins at Thaeia—"storm the castle."

Vesper groans. "Well, I for one am hoping for plan B." She has a slightly crazy look in her eyes, and not for the first time, I'm grateful she's on our side.

Valsan stands, ducking as he helps Layla up. She brushes off her pants before climbing the stairs as she says, "I need a few hours sleep. It's almost dawn. It's still pretty quiet out there, so I feel fairly okay with you all going up to grab blankets and pillows and such. You're welcome to grab a shower too. Just don't dawdle, and no lights. And maybe not all at once, yeah?"

Valsan props one foot on the bottom stair. "Thank you, Layla. For everything."

She waves over her shoulder before pushing the door open. "Keep this cracked and the cabinet pushed to the side. If the door closes, the spell snaps in place and only I can open it." She uses the handle of a broom to prop the hatch up, then disappears from view.

Valsan looks around the room. "I'll go grab some bedding. Owen, Nor, want first shift at the shower?"

Owen sniffs himself and grimaces. "Yeah." His stride seems tired as he climbs the steps, pausing at the top, tilting his head, listening. Then he climbs out and I follow the sound of his footsteps across the ceiling until they start to fade up the stairs to the second floor.

Valsan crosses to me, his hand wrapping around the side of my neck. He goes to pull me closer, but I place my hands on his chest. "I'm not at my freshest right now. Let me go clean u—"

His lips press to mine, and he hugs me close. His mouth caresses mine, his lips sucking my bottom lip. It's an intimate kiss without the frenzied tangle of tongues or the nipping of teeth. It's gentle, slow. Valsan breaks the kiss, nuzzling his cheek against mine, our beards scratching together. He whispers, "If I want to hold you, Nor, I'm going to do so. If I want to kiss you, I will—as long as you want it."

A sliver of fear and uncertainty stabs at me, but I promised to be better than my fears, so I make myself hold his gaze as I say, "Forever. I want you forever."

He leans in for another kiss, but stops with his lips hovering over mine. "Good. Because that's what I want too."

A blush of pure pleasure heats my cheeks. I don't know if I'll ever get used to Val saying such things to me, but I hope not. The rush I get just from his words of acceptance and love ... it's addictive, and I never want to be without it.

He squeezes my ass. "Go shower. But be careful. Stay alert. Get back as quickly as you can. We can't chance being found. Not yet." I nod, and he nods back. "When you return, you'll sleep. You, Vesper, and Thaeia will sleep first."

"But—"

He shakes his head. "If you recall, we are guards of Kapros. And Lord Keir has trained with his guard since he was a child. We may be just as tired as you, but we've also trained to function off little-to-no sleep. We'll be okay for a while longer."

Aimee speaks up, her voice hard, but there's a hint of desperation in her eyes, and I think being cooped up down here is getting to her. "Let us do our jobs."

Like the rest of us, she needs something to do, to distract, to feel useful. I understand that, so I nod. "Thanks."

I climb the stairs as silently as I can, using my magic to lighten my steps and muffle any sound I might make. Straining to listen, I creep through Layla's tavern, but the only thing I hear is a shower running upstairs. It's dark, so I run my hand down the wall as I approach the bathroom on the second floor. I reach for the door, but it swings open, and steam billows out followed by Owen. He rubs a towel over his wet hair, another wrapped around his hips. I don't think I ever realized how muscular he is. He's lean, but the muscle definition is impressive. He smirks, slapping my shoulder. "I appreciate the compliment." My brows scrunch, and he laughs, gesturing at his naked torso. "Your appraisal was very flattering." I blush, backing up a step, but he just grins at me. "I know you're happily taken. No worries." He presses a hand to his chest dramatically, a wistfulness in his voice. "One day, I'll find the someone or someones"—he winks—"who looks at me like you and the captain look at each other."

I'm not sure what to say to that, but he walks past me with a wave. "Shower is all yours. The water is spelled to stay hot, so don't worry about the others. They'll get a hot shower too."

Before he's even done talking, I'm pulling my shirt over my head, tossing it on the floor. I quickly shed my boots and pants, then I'm standing under the heavenly spray of hot water. I know Val said not to take too long, but this feels *soooo* good. I keep my senses tuned though, listening for trouble. Leaning my head back, I let the water hit my face, the burn almost too much, but I need it right now. I need something to wash away ... everything.

I clean myself quickly, then take another minute to just enjoy the water, but a groan of a floorboard has my hand reaching for the faucet. I turn off the water and listen, my magic ready. Footsteps approach, and Vesper appears in the doorway, eyes averted, hands on hips. "My turn, big fella."

Big fella? I snort, reaching over the fogged glass, snagging a towel. I wrap it around my waist and step out of the shower. "All yours, but hey, maybe don't just appear unannounced."

"I know what I'm about." She's reaching for the hem of her shirt before I can take another step, and I look away, snatching up my clothes and boots before hurrying towards the door as she says, "Hot water, come to mama."

I chuckle as the sound of the water turns on behind me, and as I step into the hall, Vesper moans loudly. I know the feeling.

A glance at the balled-up clothes in my hand causes me to grimace. I'm clean and warm and I really, really don't want to put these dirty clothes back on. The clothes in my pack aren't that much better, but it is what it is.

I startle as Valsan silently pushes out of one of the rooms. How does a man that size move so quietly? His arms are full of blankets and pillows. He pauses when his eyes find me. His pupils dilate as his gaze travels down my wet body, and it's as if he can see right through the towel wrapped low on my hips. Fuck, the way he looks at me. A half smile pulls at his lips as I reach out to take some of the pillows, but he shakes his head, jerking his chin towards another bedroom. "Go grab a few more blankets and pillows. I want everyone to be as comfortable as we can make them. I know waiting is hard, but it's a good opportunity to rest. We'll need it."

The thought of going up against House Drakam steals some of the relaxation the shower gave me. I quickly gather bedding, piling it high to the point I can barely see in front of me. As we make our way downstairs and across the tavern, I notice the faint lightening of the sky outside. Another day. Maybe this one will be quiet for a change. Probably not.

I swallow the sigh of frustration and exhaustion as we duck into the hidden room below the tavern. I dress in the cleanest clothes I have in my pack as Val passes around the bedding. Keir takes two blankets and pillows, setting up a little area for him and Thaeia. Vesper comes down with a towel wrapped around her hair, a tired smile on her face, wearing the clothes she had on before. Taking a pillow and blanket from Val, she tosses both on the floor. Flopping down, she literally rolls herself up in the blanket and closes her eyes as soon as her head hits the pillow. My jaw drops as seconds later, little snores come from her lips. That fast? Now that's talent. I wish I could do that.

Aimee tucks a blanket around Miles' shoulders before guiding him to lay down. She gently lowers his head to a pillow, making sure he's as close to Halee as he can be. The flowers shift and actually move out of his way as he presses right against her, draping a piece of his blanket over her like I saw him do so many times during our travels. For a moment, I wonder if Keir's little flame will go out, or maybe burn the blanket, but it just keeps on flickering through the fabric. Tears prick my eyes, and I turn away. There are moments when it doesn't feel real—that Halee can't be gone—denial shielding me. But then there are times like this, when the realization hits me like a rogue wave pulling me under.

She's gone.

Fuck! I promised to look after her. I swore ...

I don't see Valsan coming through the tears in my eyes, so my breath punches out in surprise when he hugs me. "What happened to Halee is no more your fault than it was Miles' or Thaeia's. *All* the blame lies with Severn."

I nod into the crook of his neck. Logically, I agree with Val, but the guilt ... it just won't let go. I don't think I'm ready to let it go. I need to feel guilty, to punish myself in this small way. How else could I live with myself?

One by one, everyone takes their turn in the bathroom. Valsan even drags Miles upstairs. Both men return with wet hair, and Valsan looks a little more awake, but Miles ... the shadows under his eyes are darker than ever, his hair hangs dripping in front of his face, his shoulders slumped. He shuffles back to Halee's side, dropping to the floor and covering them both with his blanket, cutting himself off from the rest of us.

Thaeia, having waited for the others to go first despite Val's orders, makes her way upstairs. She's only gone for a minute before Keir looks up at the ceiling, his fists bunching. He strides across the space, climbing the stairs. Good. She needs someone. Keir will take care of her while making sure she doesn't do something stupid—like try to sneak out on her own to try and spare us or some shit. She'd do it. The self-sacrificing idiot.

Val's deep voice is low but commanding, snapping me away from the point on the stairs I was staring at. "Nor, try to get some sleep."

Yes, sir.

Laying down, I toss and turn for a while, missing Val's arms wrapped around me. I hug my blanket, wishing it was Val's back I was pressing my cheek to. I slip into sleep, but immediately try to wake myself up. I'm home. My father is waiting for me, and at his side stands Severn. There are bodies strewn across the living area of my home. Halee lies lifeless at Severn's feet, and I look from body to body, I can't hold back my screams as I see Aimee with her neck snapped, her sightless eyes staring at me. Owen is impaled on a spike of his own Ice. Vesper is dead in a pool of her own vomit and blood. Miles' eyes have nearly popped from his face from the pressure of the vine that's wrapped around his throat. And Valsan ... I can't. Movement draws my gaze. Thaeia steps around my father, standing at Severn's side. Her eyes are black, her left arm swirling with inky shadows. Red, flaming Spirits pop up all around the room, their eyes hollow, their lips pulled back in silent screams. My father laughs, and I pinch myself, trying to wake up as he points at Val's body. "See what you did?"

I shake my head, noticing the broken bones and the burst blood vessels. Valsan has been crushed to death. By my magic. I fall to my knees, hoping the pain of hitting the polished floor will wake me. No luck. I plead with Thaeia, "Take it. Take my magic. I don't want it. Take it away."

She smiles, reaching for me, her stained finger touches my forehead, then trails down my nose. Thaeia turns into Valsan, and he smiles down at me, cupping my cheek, and I relax. The dream fades. I fall into the darkness, hoping I stay in the nothingness and far away from my nightmares. Vaguely, I feel an arm around my waist. Breath puffs against the back of my neck, I smell woodsmoke and leather. Val is here.

I sleep and dream no more.

CHAPTER 16

KEIR

I press my naked body to Thaeia's back. I just need to touch her. I'm wound so tightly, and it's all for this woman. She keeps getting knocked down. How much more can she take?

She doesn't seem surprised by my presence. She sighs, not in relaxation but in resignation. Damn it, I was right. I swallow my anger, focusing instead on her wet skin. My lips press to her shoulder, then I move her dripping hair out of the way, pressing a kiss to her neck, whispering, "You will hurt them more deeply if you leave. They deserve retribution too." She stiffens, and I chuckle. "Ah, Fox Slayer. When will you learn? You are mine. I am yours. I will always protect what's mine, just as you will sacrifice for what's yours."

She turns, blinking up at me, water pouring down her back as she says, "I ... I just don't want anyone else getting hurt. And not just because of my father. I don't trust *myself* not to hurt or ... kill someone accidentally. Keir, I can't chance it. I won't be able to live with myself if I hurt one of you."

I nod, knowing that feeling all too well. After the incident in the desert with my friend, I certainly didn't trust myself or my magic. I was terrified of it. Control, that's what she needs—I just need to figure out how to give it to her.

I rub soap between my hands before massaging her scalp. Staring at my hands as I run them through her hair. My Spirit fire is gone, Thaeia having taken it so the ruby-red flames wouldn't accidentally be seen through a window. My fingers dig in a little harder, and she closes her eyes and moans. Such a pretty sound. I want more. But in a minute. First ...

"We have three days. It's not much, but it's something. You will train with us as much as you can." She opens her eyes and her mouth at the same time, but I shake my head. "No. Don't argue, Fox Slayer. You need practice to build your confidence. We'll need your power in the coming days. Your *family* needs you, so you will learn what control you can."

Her voice cracks. "Family." I nod, tilting her head back to rinse away the soap. When I grab the conditioning oil and start working it through the ends of her hair, she sighs again. "But only three days. What can I possibly—"

"You won't know until you try."

My heart skips as a little smile pulls at her lips. "You sound like Saph."

"I never met your mother, but I take that as a compliment."

"You should."

We fall silent, my body straining to listen or sense if we are in danger, if someone has found us, if we need to …

"Hey." Thaeia's eyes are closed and a small frown tugs at her wet lips. "Are *you* okay?"

My fingers tighten in her hair, gripping, tugging slightly as I press my forehead to hers. "I … I wasn't there. I'm so sorry. I got held up at the border. Wasted too much time. I should have … If only I'd gotten to you sooner. Maybe … When I heard the fighting and saw you surrounded by all those guards …" I trace trembling fingers over her latest wound. "When Sidian stabbed you … I thought … I …"

She steps closer, the front of her body sliding against mine. "Keir." My gaze trails up her body until I'm looking into her golden eyes as she says, "You came. That's all I wanted. You. Thank you."

"As long as you want me, I'll be there, Fox Slayer. This … between us … happened so blindingly fast, but never once have I questioned the rightness of *us*." I scratch her scalp as I adjust my grip on her hair. Her mouth falls open, her eyes searching mine as beautiful little pants puff from her lips. My eyes search her face. "I just …"

The steam clouds around us, making this moment feel secluded, ours. Thaeia's hands land on my chest, her fingers splayed. "Keir, what do you need?"

I need to touch her, stroke her, feel her. But I shake my head. "I'm here to take care of you."

"Oh, lordling, I think—"

"No. Thaeia." As much as I love her little nickname for me, I need her to understand. "Please. Let me do this. Let me make sure you're okay, that you're safe, and clean, and warm, and fed, and rested, and … just let me, okay?"

Her eyes go round with surprise, but she nods. She

turns, and I release her hair as she fits the back of her body against the front of mine. My cock responds, nudging her. It can't be helped, because having this amazing woman in my arms ... gods. But I do my best to ignore the pulsing desire trying to distract me from my mission. I start to comb my fingers through her hair, being careful of the last of the stubborn knots, but she takes my hand and presses it to her stomach. Her hips shift. It's just the slightest of movements, but it works to nestle her ass against my erection. I nearly groan as my fingers caress her skin.

"Keir. Touch me."

Her whispered words almost drive me to my knees. Yes. How I need this. I need her. But I force myself to go still. "Thaeia, I want nothing more than to calm my mind with the feel of every inch of your body, but—"

She moves my hand down until I'm touching her tight curls. "Keir, please. Take *care* of me."

Fuck.

My fingers slide the rest of the way until I find her clit. I softly circle it before spreading my fingers to rub down either side of her entrance. Her head falls back, giving me the most beautiful view I've ever seen in my life. Water cascades down her body, the heat from the shower and the flush of her arousal pinking her skin. I gaze between her breasts, watching as I slip my middle finger inside her. We both groan at the feeling.

Her ass grinds against me, and my cock twitches with the need to be inside her. Keeping my eyes on my slowly pumping finger, I lick the side of her neck, and her head drops to the side, granting me better access to her delicious skin. She tastes like ... everything I've ever wanted.

Like life. She's alive. She's here, in my arms. I didn't lose her. And I won't.

The image of Sidian's sword rammed through her body flashes through my mind for the thousandth time. My fear escapes me on a growl, and my teeth clamp down on where her shoulder meets her neck. Something between a gasp and a moan comes from Thaeia's lips, and her hips buck. She reaches back and grabs my hair, holding my lips against her neck, my teeth in her skin as her hips thrust into my hand.

I lick the place where I bit her, inserting a second finger. Her entire body jerks as her mouth falls open in silent pleasure. Gods, that look on her face. Perfection. And I put it there. I need more.

The heel of my hand grinds against her clit. The wet sounds of her pussy sucking my fingers has me on the verge of coming. Not yet. I shift just enough to get my free hand around my length, squeezing the base, willing myself to last a little longer. But, fuck, my Thaeia tests my limits when she leans forward, slapping her palms against the shower wall. I go with her, keeping my finger's strokes even. I wrap my body around her, and I wish I could keep her here, protected and flushed from the things I do to her.

Her head turns, and her piercing eyes find mine. They're hooded with pleasure, water clinging to her lashes. Her fingers flex against the wall as I curl my pumping fingers, hitting that spot deep inside her. She gasps, her eyes widening.

"Please." One word, that's all she says but underneath, there's so much more. I've learned my Thaeia over the past weeks, and I've discovered physical touch is how she shows her affection. And she was starved of that as a child by friends who abandoned her and adults who shunned her. But at least she had Saph, and later, Halee.

Both, now gone.

My teeth grind in equal parts anger and sadness for her, but I shake both emotions off. Thaeia and I are similar in how we express ourselves. When everything becomes too much, we search for a comforting touch. When she's sad, she reaches for me, her hand brushing against mine. When she's happy, she bumps fists with Nor. She celebrates with hugs for her friends, and sinful kisses for me. She relaxes by resting her head on my chest. She sleeps with her toes pressed against my feet. She loves with her body.

But, she also disassociates with her body. She uses pleasure to take her away from her pain. And I don't blame her, but I know it's only temporary, that her grief, her frustrations, her fears ... they're still there after the orgasms have faded.

Still, I said I was here to take care of her, and I will.

"What do you need, Thaeia?"

"To forget. For just a few moments, to be free of all of this."

I stroke myself, letting the head of my cock brush against her wet heat as my fingers continue to move in and out of her. My lips brush the skin of her neck with every word. "You need me to fill you up until there's room for nothing else? You need me to hit you deep? Stroke you hard? Do you need my cock, Thaeia?"

Her head bobs in a frantic nod, her knuckles turning white where she's pressing her hands tightly to the wall. Biting down, I growl against her neck before pulling back just enough to whisper, "Use your words, Thaeia."

She gasps, one hand slipping down the wall before she

braces herself again. "Yes. Keir, fill me until there's only you."

In one swift movement, I pull my fingers out and slide my cock inside her. She flexes around me, gripping me with her inner walls, and I breathe through the intense bliss tingling from my balls. Gods, how is it that every time I'm inside her feels better than the last?

My hips grind against her ass without my permission, my body searching for release. She groans, pushing herself back so I go even deeper. "Fuck." I growl, grabbing her hip with one hand, my other landing over hers, interlacing our fingers against the wall.

My hand on her hip pulls her back with my thrusts, and her ass jiggles every time our bodies slap together. Thaeia throws her head back, her breaths coming faster as she quietly chants my name. "Keir, Keir, Keir, oh gods, oh fuck, Keir, Keir, Keir ..."

I release her hip so both my hands press into the wall as I push her body against the tile and unleash on her. *More, more, more. Mine, mine, mine.* My hips pound relentlessly, my cock swelling even more as euphoria begins to bloom in my belly. I need her to come. Right the fuck now!

Bracing on my right hand, my left arm snakes between the wall and her body. My fingers find her clit, and I press down, hard. I rub in tight little circles until I hear *that* sound—the little squeak that trills from her throat as her body tightens. She grips my cock as her orgasm trembles through her.

I'm lost to her. My building pleasure erupts, curling my toes, tingling over my scalp, pulsing through every inch of my body. I come, riding my orgasm with hers, filling her until my seed begins to leak down her thighs. And I keep coming.

She sags, her back rising and falling with her deep breaths. I hold her up as I grind into her with the last of my release, my body slowly coming down from the high of being with my Fox Slayer. I kiss her neck, and she sighs, nuzzling the side of her face against mine.

Though the tension has left my body, there's an increasing pressure in my heart, and the words just tumble out. "I can't lose you. From the moment I saw you, my entire life shifted. Never in a million years would I have thought I'd find someone like you. Someone who would capture my heart so quickly and so effortlessly. I was yours the first time you smiled at me. And the first time our lips pressed together, you became mine. Thaeia, tell me you understand. You. Are. Mine."

Her hand cups my face, keeping us pressed together as she whispers, "Yours."

I'm still inside her, and my possessiveness preens at that softly spoken word. My cock twitches as I turn my lips into her cheek. "Promise you won't leave me, that you won't leave us. Promise we'll do this together." My hands tighten against her. "Promise me, Fox Slayer."

She shifts, pressing her lips to mine. My tongue strokes, and she opens. My hips begin pumping lazily as we kiss deeply. Pulling back slightly, I look in her eyes. "Promise me."

"I promise."

A little chunk of anxiety breaks and falls away from my heart, because I know she means it. I hear it in her voice and see it in her eyes.

The water is too hot, and my Fox Slayer is too flushed, so I turn it off. The resulting silence is startling, only broken by her panted breaths as I continue to slide my hardening cock in and out of her. The water rolls down the walls, dripping down the drain as the steam begins to fade. I take her slowly until we're both falling apart once again. This orgasm is softer, spreading through me like the warm burn of a shot of whiskey. The pleasure settles in my fingers and toes, and I finally pull out of her.

As I run a towel over her then myself, I notice her eyes blinking slower, her movements sluggish. Good. I smile as I help her thread her arms through a clean shirt. One of mine of course. She mumbles something about it smelling good, like me. Gods, this woman. Dressing quickly, I tuck her against my side, peering out the door, looking up and down the hall before pulling her along and back down to the hidden basement.

Our group is half-asleep, half on watch. From where he's seated next to a sleeping Nor, Valsan nods at me. His hand rests on Nor's waist, who I imagine is sleeping better knowing his man is there. A simple touch can have the strongest of impacts—I glance at Thaeia—I should know.

I guide Thaeia to the little pile of blankets and pillows against a side wall. Vesper snores softly, only her hair peeking out of her blankets. Miles is curled against Halee, and my heart weeps … for him, for Thaeia, for Nor, for Halee's family …

Thaeia's hand grabs mine, pulling my attention back to her. Without a word, she pulls me down with her. Rolling onto my back, I pull her against my chest, tracing light circles over her upper arm. I press a kiss to the top of her head, and when she lets out a slow exhale, relaxing completely into me, I whisper, "Sleep. I've got you."

And I do. I always will as long as there's breath in my body.

CHAPTER 17

NOR

ONE DAY. Only one day has passed in this hidden underground room, and I think we're all going a bit crazy. I force my leg to stop bouncing with anxiety so I don't wake Val, but a few seconds later it starts up again and I have to focus to keep still. He finally went to sleep a few hours ago, and I'm only able to calm down by looking at his peaceful face. At some point I stopped wondering how I got so lucky to have someone like Valsan love me, now I'm just grateful.

I'm not sure what time of night it is, but the daylight streaming through the cracks in the ceiling faded a while ago, and Layla hasn't lit any torches. Aimee stands on the first step leaning against the wall, arms crossed as usual. Vesper sits at the bottom of the stairs, knees bent up to her chest, her eyes darting every now and then to Owen who snores softly in the back of the room. I'm not sure if Miles is asleep or awake, but he hasn't moved in hours, curled in his blankets, back to the room, his body pressed against Halee. Keir and Thaeia sit with their backs against the opposite wall, their heads bent towards each other, passing whispers back and forth. They're cute, and I hope they get a chance to just ... be together. I hope we all get the chance.

But then their whispers turn heated. Keir rolls his eyes at Thaeia, and I fully expect her to smack him, but she just drops her gaze.

Uh oh.

Keir looks at me, jerking his chin, telling me to come over. Great, I get to mediate the lover's quarrel? Carefully, I extract myself from Val's side, double-checking that his breathing stays even in sleep. I duck my head and cross the room, squatting in front of Keir.

"What's going on, you two?"

Keir's posture is relaxed, his forearm braced on his bent leg, but there's fire in his eyes as he says, "You know Thaeia the best out of all of us here. And well, I'm not going to pull punches, you spent years experiencing her Void and fearing her power."

Thaeia's head snaps up, and now she does smack his shoulder. "Keir."

I wave a hand. "No, he's right. So, what's the question?"

He looks me in the eyes, silently telling me to be completely honest. "Is Thaeia's magic evil? Has the power of her Void filled her with darkness? Is she corrupted?"

My eyes pop wide, and my head snaps to her. She won't meet my gaze, but I catch her fingers curling into her palms. She actually believes this? I drop to my ass, crossing my legs. Leaning forward, I take her hands, knowing all too well what it feels like to spin out in your own thoughts. "Hey, what's going on in that head of yours, Void? You can't honestly think you're evil."

Thaeia keeps her eyes on our joined hands as she shrugs. "The darkness of my power literally stains my skin, Nor. I ... I killed someone and I don't remember it. That sounds like corruption to me. The voice ... in my head ... is it actually my magic talking to me, or has my mind fractured from the trauma? And if that's the case, I shouldn't be anywhere near any of you—a crazy person with killer Forsaken magic. You all should have me chained to the wall."

Keir tsks at her as I grab her chin. My grip is hard, and I mean it to be. I force her gaze to meet mine. "What the fuck are you talking about? Where is Thaeia? Where is the girl who didn't let the islanders talk shit about her, me included? Where is the woman who trained every day to get stronger, faster, smarter? Where is the woman who held her head high every damn day even when she was shunned by her friends and neighbors? Where is the Thaeia who kicked my ass over and over?"

I pinch her chin harder until she scowls at me. "Where is the woman who went into that arena, hungover as fuck, and faced the infamous Lord Keir?" A small smile tugs at her lips. "Where is my best friend? Because she would never say such things about herself."

She sighs. "Nor, I'm trying, but I *killed* someone and don't. Remember. It."

Now I understand Keir's earlier eye roll. Releasing her chin, I take her left hand and hold it up. "Show me."

She tries to yank back, but I hold tight as she shakes her head. "No, Nor."

"Show me"—I meet her gaze—"I dare you, *Void*."

Thaeia's eyes narrow, but then her gaze softens and

her shoulders slump. Her fingers flex in my hand and pretty blue-black ink stains her skin, working its way up her knuckles. It climbs her arm, revealing her reverse tattoo, the word, KURKODAM scrolling around her wrist. The color stops halfway up her forearm, and I squeeze her hand. "More." She shakes her head, and I give her arm a little shake. "More, Thaeia. All the way."

Her angry eyes snap to mine, and while her tone stays quiet, that creepy double voice layers over hers as she hisses, "More, Nor? You want us to drain you?"

"Thaeia, do *you* honestly think you'll drain me? That you'll kill me?"

"I ..."

I smile at her. "Go for it. Show me. We've both waited all these years to know what your magic really is. Let me see."

She blinks at me, and I know she's recalling all those times we spent on her beach as kids, laughing and joking about getting our magic when we turned twelve ... all those times we played on the jungle paths, shooting imaginary magic at each other ... all those nights curled up together on her worn couch watching Saph make little metal animal figurines for us, eager for our own magic.

The midnight blue swirls up her arm, over her shoulder, and across her chest. Her eyes bleed black, and my magic snuffs out. Tingles spread through my fingers, and when I look down, the inky shadows are creeping onto my skin. Internally, I freak out. I want to shake free of her touch, but I force myself to remain calm. Thaeia needs me right now, and I know she can do this. Well, I hope she can. If anyone can, she can.

It's getting harder to breathe, but I smile at Thaeia, though her black eyes terrify me. "Hey." Lifting her hand,

I turn her wrist, looking at the moving, swirling color. "You know what this reminds me of? The ocean at night. Sure, it's dark, and it can be scary, but look how beautiful it is. Not the pitch-darkness of nothingness. No, this holds the deep blue of a starry night."

Thaeia looks at her inked skin like it's the first time she's really seen it.

I relax my hand around hers. "What were we taught as kids when we were given our first practice wave boards?"

When she speaks, it's just her voice this time, and even more of my tension melts away when she says, "Don't fight the waves."

"Exactly. The ocean is too powerful. We respect it. We find its rhythm. We move with it. We try to become one with the power." Her gaze lifts to mine, her eyes still black, but there's hope in them now as I say, "Ride it, Thaeia."

The ink bursts over every inch of her skin, her hair lifting and floating around her face. Vesper gasps in alarm, but I ignore her as I brace, waiting for that scraping, sucking sensation to drain me. It never comes. Instead, my magic churns back to life in my gut, and I smile. She looks at Vesper, who shrinks away from her gaze, but Thaeia raises a brow at her in question. Vesper raises her left hand and shakes her head. Then a second later, a light green Poison mist drips from her fingers, and Vesper grins, giving us a thumbs up.

But then Thaeia's voice changes again with a growl. "More." She shakes her head as if she's fighting with herself. I don't let her go. I won't. Keir places his hand on her arm, and she tenses, gritting her teeth before her hair settles and the blue-black ink drains from her skin, down her arm, into the tips of her fingers until there's not a trace left.

I release a slow, strained breath with a shaky smile. "There you go."

Her hand trembles slightly in mine, but she smiles at me. "I didn't lose control that time. I was here the whole time. I ... I rode the wave, Nor."

She falls forward, wrapping her arms around me, and I hug her to my chest as she climbs into my lap whispering, "Thank you, Nor."

We hold each other for a long moment before I whisper back, "No problem, *Void*."

She chuckles, slapping my chest before scooting back. Turning to Keir, her cheeks warm with a blush as she says, "And thank you."

He strokes her face tenderly. "Of course, Fox Slayer."

Their hearts are in their eyes, so I shift back, getting to my feet, my job done. Keir asks her to describe what her power feels like, and as they fall into a whispered conversation, I walk away, knowing Keir has it from here. My best friend is in good hands.

CHAPTER 18

NOR

CAREFULLY, I slide down the wall next to Val. I don't want to wake him, but I can't hold back the desire to touch him. I rest my hand on his calf where he's curled up beside me, my thumb brushing little strokes to ground me. As much as I didn't want Thaeia's show of power to unnerve me, I'm unsettled. I have to trust her. She needs me to trust her. But what if …

A strange crinkling noise distracts me, and I look down at Val. *Where is that sound coming from? His pocket? Whatever this is, I can't imagine it being good. No. Just no. Nope. No.* It's getting louder, and I press my hand against his pants trying to figure out what it is so I can stop it and keep it from waking him.

Too late.

Val stirs, his hand landing over mine where it rests

against his pocket. His eyes are still closed, but a little smile tugs at his sleepy face. "What are you slipping into my pocket, Nor? Secret love notes?"

I wish. No. I have a feeling whatever this is will wipe that smile from his face, and I hate it. I think about lying, but brush that thought off. When I don't answer, his eyes blink open, and sure enough, that lovely teasing smile melts away as a concerned expression hardens his face.

Damn it. Why can't we just be left alone for one gods-damned second. Let the man sleep!

Val pushes to a sitting position, but keeps his leg pressed to mine, maintaining contact. He keeps his voice pitched low so as not to disturb the others, but Aimee looks our way as he says, "What is it, Nor?"

I glance at his leg. "I didn't put anything in your pocket. A noise just ... started. Came out of nowhere."

Slowly, Val reaches into his pocket. His body tenses against me, but his face remains impassive. How does he do that? I can feel the anxiety and anticipation showing on my expression. His fingers curl into a fist inside his pocket, and he takes a deep breath, whispering, "Someone really wanted to get a message to me."

I try to think of good reasons someone would expend that much power to send a message directly to Val. I fail. Messages sent by Transportation mages are usually sent to a specific place, a place the mage has been and knows well. It takes a lot of magical power to Transport even a single piece of paper across long distances. For someone to focus on Valsan and be able to send a note to him without knowing precisely where he is ...

Val shifts against me as he pulls the paper from his pocket. His large hand delicately opens the single fold, and his eyes begin to scan the words. I don't read it, but I can see the message is short, only a few sentences. Val's body goes still, and his breath catches as his fingers dent the paper. *Of course it's something bad. Why wouldn't it be?*

Aimee has crossed the space, and now crouches in front of us. "What is it, Captain?"

Val's grip goes slack, and my heart plummets to my toes when a single tear tracks down his face. He passes the slip of paper to Aimee and immediately reaches for me. I take his hand and just hold it, unsure of what to do. He's trembling, and I really, really wish I had ripped that note out of his pocket and shredded it before anyone could read it.

Aimee crumples the note in her fist as she whisper shouts, "What the fuck!" Vesper, Keir, and Thaeia look our way, and I just shrug with a shake of my head at Thaeia. Owen stirs, but stays asleep. Miles doesn't move. Aimee stands, pacing three steps one way, then back. She runs her hand through her short dark hair. "I don't care what that fucking note says. And the Kapros guard won't follow that order either, Captain. There's no fucking way."

Keeping my grip on his hand, I reach with my free one, and Aimee stops her pacing long enough to toss the paper at me before resuming. I manage to flatten it out by pressing it against my thigh, because there's no way I'm letting go of Val. My eyes skim the words, then I read them again, and again. This can't be right.

My gaze snaps to him then to Aimee and back to Val. "Maybe this is a trick. Severn trying to draw you out. Maybe ..."

Val shakes his head, his hair falling around his dejected face. "That is Lady Kapros' seal. It's not impossible, but would be very hard to fake. I have to assume the letter is real."

Aimee stops, facing us. "Well, fuck that, *Captain*. If you're out, then so am I."

I read the words again as Owen wakes and everyone but Miles comes over, looking down at us, surrounding us in a little semicircle. Owen yawns, scratching his chest. "What's going on? I was in the middle of such a nice dream. A dark-haired beauty was just about to—"

Aimee growls, "Lady Kapros discharged the captain. Said she didn't give him permission to go back into Drakam, and that if he had been in 'possession' of the Void, he should have brought *it* to House Kapros instead of letting *it* wreak havoc on the country. She said she'd find someone else who could 'follow orders and act in the best interests of Kapros.' The bitch."

Thaeia gasps, and Vesper shakes her head. Owen takes a step towards me, arm held out, so I pass him the paper. He reads it once, crumples it up and tosses it on the ground. Now both him and Aimee are pacing like caged animals. Owen waves a hand at the discarded paper. "I mean she has tried to undermine your orders and advice before, but this ...?"

Vesper interlaces her hands behind her back, stretching with a little smile on her face. "Well, this kinda frees you up, doesn't it?"

I can't help but agree with her, but I don't say anything because I know Valsan is devastated. He loves being a captain, and from what I've seen, he's a damn good one. The guards—and not just his—love him, respect him.

Owen spins, halting his pacing to stare at Val. "Well, I'm with Aimee. If you're out, I'm out."

Val starts to shake his head. "You all weren't mentioned in the letter. You can go back, keep your jobs, your pay. You shouldn't throw away—"

Owen snorts. "Don't bother finishing that statement, sir."

Valsan shifts his gaze to Aimee who just shakes her head, her lips pressed into a determined line.

Keir steps forward. "I'm sorry, my friend. I can send a letter to Lady Kapros to explain the situation. My father will vouch for you. We can fix this."

I flex my core and brace as Val leans into me, using me as leverage to get to his feet. His hand never leaves mine, and he tugs me up with him. Facing Keir, Valsan clasps his shoulder. "Thank you, but ... I think for now at least, we let this be. There are more important things for us to focus on than my status. It's just a job after all."

He sounds sure, his voice even, his posture tall other than the fact that he has to duck to keep his head from brushing the ceiling, as do Keir and I. But I see it, the deep hurt inside him.

Keir looks like he's about to respond, but the telltale sound of the cabinet being moved overhead draws all our gazes. As one, we move closer to the stairs, staggering our positions, bodies tense, ready for anything. Layla rushes down the stairs, the hatch closing behind her, but the look on her face does nothing to ease the tension in the room. She pauses two steps into the basement, her gaze flicking between us. "What's happened?"

Valsan waves her off. "Nothing of importance right now. What is it, Layla?"

She sighs, tugging at the end of her braid that's slung over her shoulder. "I thought it was strange that Captain

Silas hadn't returned, or at least sent his guards to tear this place apart, but I just found out why.

She pauses dramatically, which only serves to annoy everyone in the room. Vesper snaps her fingers at Layla's face. "So?"

The barkeep glances between Keir and Val. "Drakam is under attack from both the north and the south." Her gaze lands on Keir. "Your father claims you're being held against your will." She turns her attention to Thaeia. "And Lord Alopson officially charged Lord Drakam with being responsible for the attacks on the Colosseum. The Alopson guards broke through the border an hour ago and are headed here, to the capital."

I shift to face Val, squeezing his hand. "Well, this is a good thing, right? At the very least it'll distract Silas and his guards and maybe keep Lord Drakam out of our hair for a bit."

Valsan nods, but his eyes are sad. "Yes, it'll distract, but violence and war are never a good thing."

I take the admonishment, but don't let it sting, even knowing fundamentally that he's right. This move by Lord Alopson is a good thing.

Aimee taps her boot on the dirt floor, her eyes flitting to the balled-up piece of paper before asking, "And Kapros?"

Layla looks at Aimee then Valsan. "Lady Kapros claimed Lord Drakam had something to do with the magic blackout, and that if he had a secret weapon capable of taking away the blessings of the gods, he needed to be stopped."

Vesper chuckles. "Won't argue with her there."

Layla goes on. "They are still fighting at the southern border, but with attacks happening from the north and the south, Drakam is spread thin. It's believed Kapros will break through soon."

I jump, tingles of surprise shooting down my spine as Miles says from behind us, "So, do we attack Severn now or wait till the Alopson front gets to the capital and use them to get into the estate?"

Vesper grins, rubbing her hands together. "I vote now. Who knows what will happen between the northern border and here. The Alopson guards could get held up, or pushed back. Drakam is distracted now. Let's do this!"

Miles turns to Valsan. "Captain?"

Val's face falls, his eyes dropping to the note. Owen steps next to Miles, leaning in to whisper in his ear. Miles' eyes go round as his gaze flicks between the paper and Valsan. When Owen steps back, Miles shrugs, cracking his neck. "So? Captain?"

A smile not only lifts my cheeks, but my spirits. Valsan is going to be just fine. He has the support and devotion of the people in this room, and I'm sure that extends to the other guards of Kapros.

Val swallows, nodding at Miles before facing Layla. "What do you think?"

She chews her lip. "Give me one more day?"

Vesper groans, rolling her eyes, but Val nods. "One. Then we move." His eyes find Thaeia and hold. After a moment, they nod at each other and Val turns to Keir. "You can go. If you need to. Or at the very least send word to your father. There's no need for your people to put their lives on the line."

Keir actually chuckles. "Nah. My father has had designs on Drakam for years, maybe his whole life. I'm just an excuse. He knows why I came here." His hand rubs down Thaeia's back as he continues. "We have a system.

We've had it since I was a child. If I'm ever in trouble ... well, too much trouble to get out of ..."

Vesper snickers. "You mean if your life is on the line."

Keir nods. "Yes. If my life is in danger, one of my Spirits will alert my father. It was a promise I made in exchange for more freedom outside House Alopson." He turns to Thaeia, keeping his hand on her back, and his eyes stay on her face as he says, "Besides, I'm not leaving. Like you said, Captain, there are more important things at stake right now."

I nearly swoon at the look in Keir's eyes. Damn. He loves her. One look at my best friend tells me she loves him too.

A little squeeze on my hand draws my attention to Valsan. He looks at me, and for a moment, I get lost in the forest-green depths of his gaze as he says, "Is there any way I can talk you and Layla into taking Halee home ... now?"

I'm shaking my head before he's done talking, my palm pressing to his beard, my thumb running over his lower lip. "Not a chance."

I keep my eyes on him as Layla says, "Nope. Not leaving."

Valsan takes a deep breath, fighting a smile that's quivering his lips. "Okay. One day." He presses a quick kiss to my lips then steps away, clapping his hands in his familiar gesture. "We're all agreed?"

Everyone nods, and Vesper cracks her neck and her knuckles, looking much too gleeful. "Yesss. I'm going to dance around his convulsing body as my poison slowly eats away his insides."

Owen laughs, "Gross."

Miles shuffles back to Halee, sliding down the wall to

sit at her head. His hand falls to her petrified hair, his gaze on her frozen face as he says, "Get in line. Severn is mine."

His voice is so cold, I nearly shiver. Looking at Thaeia, I can't help but think if anyone is owed Severn's painful death, it's her. But one thing is for sure, Lord Severn Drakam is not long for this world.

CHAPTER 19

THAEIA

VALSAN TWIRLS his finger in the air, silently telling me to go again. We've been training with my power for hours, and it's still hit or miss. Valsan points his right hand at himself, Nor, Vesper, and Keir, then points his left hand at Owen and Aimee. Owen and Aimee get magic, no one else does. Got it.

I huff a breath at the tip of my nose, knocking away the bead of sweat that was tickling me. Shaking out my arms, I crack my neck, wiggle my hips, and then lift and shake first one leg then the other. Where Nor says he feels his magic in his gut, and Valsan's sits in his head, mine seems to come from ... everywhere. My entire body aches with the effort to direct my power.

Quiet footfalls sound from overhead again, and it's a struggle to keep from looking up. For the past hour or so there has been activity up there, and I'm not the only one itching to know what's going on. I know we're all on edge, but I need to take advantage of every minute I have to practice, because once I go out there ...

I focus on Owen, as I drape the 'blanket' of my Void around everyone in the room. That's the easy part. Well, sort of. It's easier than what I have to do now. I squint, imagining pulling the Void off of just Aimee and Owen. My left hand lifts, and I clutch at thin air, pulling back on the darkness in my mind, trying to get it to come away from the two guards. Owen smiles, lifting his own hand, little Ice crystals coating his fingertips. Aimee nods, her arm turning to a bark-like substance. But then Nor tsks, and he shoves me back with his Gravity just as Keir's flames burst to life.

Damn it.

Everyone's magic puffs out as my Void settles around the room. This seems to be its natural state, keeping me in the bubble of 'protection' that I've been in my entire life.

Good. You've realized I am protection, not a curse.

Internally, I roll my eyes at the voice in my head. *It can be both.*

A soft chuckle in my head is my response, and for the hundredth time, I wonder if I've gone mad.

You're only mad if I am.

Before I can argue with myself further, Valsan twirls his finger in the air as he's done over and over for the past several hours. Everyone moves, taking up different positions around the room. Valsan plants his hands on his hips and raises a brow at me, ready to go again. I wipe the sweat off the back of my neck as he points his right hand at Keir, but then pauses at the loud noise overhead.

The hatch opens, and I sigh, thankful for the break as Layla comes down. Yet more footsteps echo across the ceiling, and all I can imagine is Layla's place being filled with guards ready to tear her tavern apart until they find us. But the tavern owner is calm as she joins us in the dark basement. She opens her mouth to speak, but a loud crash sounds upstairs, and I jump, adrenaline tingling down my arms and legs. The room goes into hyper-focus and all I see are my friends, my family ... Halee. Never again.

I blink, and when I look around, the room has changed. Nor is down on one knee, head bowed, back heaving with his panting breaths. Valsan is at his side, his broad hand rubbing his own chest as his other rubs Nor's back. Layla is laid out on the stairs, Vesper is braced against a support post, Aimee has a hand pressed to a wall, and Owen's sitting on the ground, his feet splayed out before him, his face pale. Miles is the only one who hasn't moved, but that's probably because he was already lying down.

Shit.

I try to shake off the adrenaline, but my eyes keep flicking to the ceiling. It's quiet once more, but I'm too on edge. Layla grunts as she stands back up, holding out her hand like I'm a spooked horse. "It's okay, Shanty Princess." She points up. "They're all friends. Trust me. Okay?"

Trust her? Pfft. Trust the power, the darkness, the magic.

I tell myself to shut up as I hold up my left hand. The blue-black, smoky ink is nearly to my elbow. Shit. There's not enough time. I can't control it—not like I need to, I'm going to hurt someone I don't want to hurt. I can't do this. When I look back at Nor, it's as if our roles growing up have swapped. I know there's fear in my eyes, because as afraid as I am of losing my friends to Severn or his guards, I'm even more terrified of being the one who will hurt them. But instead of the fear and hate I so often saw on

Nor's face when we were kids, I see confidence, patience, love. From where he's still kneeling, he smiles weakly at me, whispering, "You've got this. Remember what we practiced. Breathe. Don't fight it, ride it."

Anger builds and turns inward. I speak either to myself or my power, or to whomever is in my head ... I need to get the message. *These are my friends. They are off limits. My power will only be used to protect them, never to harm. Never!*

There's what I can only describe as a mental eye roll and a sigh. *So dramatic.*

I feel the power pulling back, sucking inwards like sand churned up in the water as the tide rushes in. My skin feels raw from the push-pull of my magic. Nor gets back to his feet. Crossing the distance between us, and he claps my shoulder, leaning in, keeping his voice low. "Good work, Void. You brought it under control faster that time."

I'm cut off from responding when Layla waves at us. "Come on. You all can come upstairs now."

Aimee crosses the room, kneeling at Miles' side, her hand resting on his shoulder. She says something to him, and without responding, Miles shifts, pushing himself upright. Aimee helps him stand, and I nearly gasp. Dark shadows ring his eyes, and his hair is tangled. His skin is pale, and his lips are cracked. His gaze trails over Halee before he shuffles across the room.

Valsan says, "Aimee," and she silently moves to the stairs, taking the lead as Layla disappears back through the hatch. Vesper is hot on her heels, her eyes lit up with the anticipation of finally doing something. Keir gently pushes me forward, and I start climbing, hearing the rest of our group following.

My eyes don't need to adjust to being out of the dim basement because it's dark up here too. As we pass the kitchen, the smell of earthy soup and fresh bread has my mouth watering, and I gaze longingly at a large pot bubbling away on the stove. We're almost halfway down the hall when someone taps my shoulder. I turn to see Keir, his arm outstretched with a small roll in his hand. I look around, trying to figure out where he snagged it from, but he just shrugs with a grin, placing the hot roll in my hand. Gods, this man. I tear the bread open, steam billowing from the pillowy insides, and the yeasty scent wafts up my nose. I take a big bite, and Keir leans in. "It's not chocolate or popped corn, but I figured it would do."

I act before my brain can catch up. With a fistful of bread, I grip his shirt, pulling him to me. My lips brush his, leaving behind a few crumbs. He smiles, licking his mouth, and my eyes track every movement of his tongue. He chuckles. "You can have *this* snack later. First, let's see what's going on, hmm?"

I nod, still slightly in a lust haze, but I'm snapped out of it when the sound of unfamiliar voices drifts down the hallway. Layla stands in the center of her tavern, moonlight spilling over her face, turning her blond hair silver. I freeze at the edge of the hall, unable to step into the main room where dozens of people stand, all eyes shifting and landing on me.

Shit. What is this? Has Layla sold us out?

Aimee and Vesper are already positioned in front of me, and Keir quickly joins them. I feel the rest of my friends at my back. I'm surrounded by my family, and I will protect them no matter what. I'm not losing anyone else.

My power scrapes against my skin, and this time I

welcome the discomfort. I'll deal with any amount of pain to keep my friends safe. Several people in the crowd frown, but no one reacts beyond that. Before my panic can fully rise, Layla comes over, her smile still in place as she holds up her hands. "Not to worry, Shanty Princess. As I said, these are all allies. They have been warned to expect ... inconsistencies with their magic while here." She pauses in front of Aimee, tilting her head up at the taller woman. "You've trusted me this far." Aimee holds her ground for a long moment before shifting. Still, she keeps her eyes on Layla as she approaches me. Putting her hand on my arm, Layla leads me into the room. My heels dig in, and my back stiffens. I hate that everyone is looking at me. I hate everything about this. When we reach the center of the room, Layla stops, but keeps her hand on my arm as if she knows I'm a flight risk right now. I pivot, realizing my friends have all hung back, blending into the crowd that's now circled around Layla and me. I feel so exposed, surrounded by these strangers.

You're not alone. You've never been alone.

I grit my teeth. *You don't count.*

The voice in my head huffs as Layla rubs my arm. She says, "Thank you all for coming. I know we had planned on gathering tomorrow, but with circumstances as they are ..." I look at her, wondering what is going on, but she keeps her eyes on the small group as she continues. "You all are here because you have questions. Some of you were at the Games, and what you saw, what you experienced doesn't match up with what our lord has told us." She looks around, a kind smile on her face. "I appreciate the bravery it took for you all to come here tonight, and I hope to reward you with the truth."

She turns to me, and I can't help but cringe. If only I

had Invisibility. Better yet, if only I'd never left Oxtara. I glance at Keir and regret even thinking that. Nor takes a step towards me, but I shake my head, and he stops. As much as I appreciate the support, I need to face this, face who I am, what I am.

Who we *are.*

Layla leans into me, the rest of the room eerily silent as she says, "I won't force you to tell your story, but I think it's time for them to know, for the country to know what was done to you, to your sisters. It's time for Severn to be exposed. It's time for you to take back your power, and let us all do the same."

I can't help but feel a little blindsided. My fingers curl into my palms, and I want nothing more than to run all the way back to Oxtara, collapse on my beach, and stare at the stars until the sun comes up. But I can't go home until *he* has paid for what he did to me, my sisters, my mother, Saph, Fara ... Halee. At this point, I almost don't care about my tragic backstory. Severn murdered Halee. He has to pay.

This isn't about me anymore, but if my story will rally the people against Lord Drakam, that's just more of what he deserves. I step away from Layla, and she drops her hand. I can do this.

We can.

I almost smile at the voice in my head as I make a slow turn, looking around the room. "My name is Thaeia, and Severn Drakam is my father."

CHAPTER 20

THAEIA

The room is nearly empty except for my friends and the last few of the civilians waiting to slip back out into the night. I feel like I talked for hours, but it must have been less than twenty minutes. The rest of the time was spent growing more and more frustrated at the questions being hurled my way that I had absolutely no answers to. Finally, Layla managed to get everyone to quiet down, and a plan began to form. It's a good plan ... risky, but if it works ...

I roll my shoulders, and Keir rubs my back, pressing a kiss to my temple as a woman comes over—what feels like the hundredth person tonight. She smiles, holding out her arm, and I barely manage to keep from sighing in exhaustion as I shake her hand. I think she introduced herself as Ann during the meeting, but I'm not sure. A quick glance reminds me she has Lyrical magic, and I have no idea how that will be helpful in a fight, but I don't say anything. I just let her spew her platitudes at how sorry she is for me, how angry she is on my behalf ... The same sentiment has been on repeat all night, and I'm tired. I'm sure they mean well, but they're not really doing this for me. And that's okay. They need somewhere to focus their fear and anger, and for once, it's not aimed at me, so ...

She walks off with a strained smile and a wave, and I steal my spine as the last person makes their way over to me. I take in his wild brown hair, sticking out in all directions, and the bags under his eyes. He can't be that much older than me, but he looks ... worn down. I lean into Keir, whispering, "What was his name?"

"Cardan."

I have no idea how he remembers these things, but I guess that's a skill you have to hone when you grow up in politics. Cardan's face lifts in a warm smile, a small gap showing between his front teeth. He holds out his hand, and I take it. I manage not to grimace at his sweaty palm, and I distract myself by glancing at his tattoo. It wraps around his wrist twice, and I can't make out the entire word, but I catch KVREO before he drops my hand. I'm forced to look away from his wrist as he says, "Thank ya for coming forward and telling ya story. It was very brave of ya."

I just nod, uncomfortable and exhausted from this whole thing. Cardan's eyes flick between Keir and me, and he shifts his weight from foot to foot. I get it, meeting Keir for the first time is certainly daunting. I know I was starstruck. My lips quirk in a little smile as Cardan wipes his hands on his pants and holds out his palm to shake

Keir's. I bite the inside of my cheek. Why didn't I get a palm-wipe? I got the sweaty handshake.

From the corner of my eye, I watch as Keir smiles and responds to Cardan's stumbling words. I'm not really listening, just observing Keir and how effortlessly he engages with people. After a few more exchanged words, Cardan backs up, almost bowing to Keir as he wrings his hands. "So, uh, I guess I'll be seein' ya tomorrow night."

Keir nods with a friendly expression. I can do that. Pressing my hand to Keir's back, I let his solid presence ground me as I smile at Cardan and say, "See you later. And thank you."

His eyes go round, and his gaze drops to my left wrist. Thankfully, the swirling ink stayed clear during the entire meeting, so Cardan is met with nothing but clear, unmarked skin. His eyes jump back to my face, and he smiles sheepishly, scratching the back of his head as he continues to back away. "Ah. Yeah. Sure. Of course." And with that, he spins, waving at Layla who's behind the bar, and he shuffles quickly down the back hall and out into the night.

And finally, it's just our small group once again. My thumb absently rubs Keir's lower back, and I step a little closer to press against his side. This position forces my hand to climb between his shoulder blades, and I shift so my nails scrape lightly across his soft shirt. His upper back bows into my touch, and I smile. He's like a cat—loves scratches. His favorite is when I run my fingers through his hair, scraping his scalp as he reads to me.

I continue lightly trailing my fingers over his back as Miles pushes off the wall where he was leaning. "Come get me when it's time." And with that, he crosses the room and shortly after, the sound of his boots echo down the stairs to the basement.

The clink of a bottle brushing against a glass is the only sound in the room as the rest of us just stand here for a moment, trying to take everything in. Layla throws back her head, swallowing whatever drink she'd poured herself. She holds up the bottle, waving it towards us, but we all shake our heads. She shrugs, pouring herself another. Layla holds the full glass by the rim, swirling it slowly. "That went better than I'd hoped."

Valsan nods, but Vesper cracks her knuckles as she says, "Still don't like that we're waiting."

She'd been against waiting until nightfall tomorrow. Vesper was ready to charge House Drakam right now, magic blazing, but she was outvoted ... again. Honestly, I'm surprised she didn't just go out on her own. Even though she's stuck with us to this point, she still feels like a lone wolf, used to being on her own. She's helped us so much, but for some reason she doesn't feel like a part of our group, and that bothers me.

Owen chuckles, but it sounds tired. We're all tired. He rubs the back of his neck. "You'll have your chance soon enough, Viper."

"It's Vesper."

He raises a teasing brow. "What'd I say?"

She points at him, her cheeks turning red, but Valsan holds up a hand. "From what we were told tonight, Silas did not go to either border, but instead is running things from House Drakam. Alopson's forces are about a day from pushing through to the capital here, and Kapros is still fighting at their border." I don't miss the slash of pain that spears through his eyes at the mention of Kapros, but he quickly wipes it away. "Those that came here tonight risked much, and have pledged to gather as many as they can to our cause. But they only have this one day, so we can't expect many more than who came tonight. For now, we should rest and get ready for tomorrow."

Just him saying the words causes a sweat to break out under my arms. I can't rest. I can't stop. I can't close my eyes. I shake my head. "I need more practice."

Keir crosses his arms. "You need sleep."

"I CAN'T!" I didn't mean to shout, but every time I close my eyes for too long, all I see is Halee's fear-stained face and all that blood. The room is silent for a long moment, and I shake my head. "Sorry." I let out the long sigh that I've been holding as I shift my weight from foot to foot. My fingers curl into my palms as I say, "I've called Severn Drakam my father, but he's not. I hold no misguided thoughts that he can be 'saved.' I don't want anything to do with him, with his name, with that family." I look around the room. "I already have a family. I guess ... I guess I just don't want any of you to think I'll hesitate or ... I don't know. I just want him dead. I want his sons dead. I want his entire bloody legacy wiped from this country."

Aimee tilts her head. "And your mother, Lady Drakam, if she still lives?"

I lick my lips, a pang punching against my chest. "Saph was my mother. And while I don't know if my birth mother deserves to die, I won't lie. I can't help but feel she should have ... known somehow and done something. I know I'm being unreasonable, and I don't know what she's been through all these years, being told time and again that you're pregnant with a girl, knowing the baby won't survive. But still, shouldn't she have asked questions?

Shouldn't she have pushed back? Refused the drugs? Run away? Something?"

No one has any answers for me, and I don't expect them to, so I let my rant trail off, dropping my head. "Anyway. Let's go kill my family I guess."

I laugh, the sound coming out a little maniacal, but the others chuckle along good-naturedly. Valsan takes Nor's hand, leading him towards the stairs to the second floor. "We're sleeping in a proper bed tonight. Aimee, take first shift. Owen take over in the morning. I'll relieve you at lunch." I notice he leaves Miles out of the rotation, but no one says anything as they all disperse.

Layla grabs the bottle by the neck, swinging it in the air. "I'm off to bed too."

As her footsteps fade, I turn to Keir, focusing until his red flames flicker along his skin, and Gren rubs against his leg. Sorrow claws at my heart, and I rub at the spot. Hich is still on the other side ... still looking out for Halee.

Keir strides over, and Gren bumps his head against my hand. I don't feel anything, but I appreciate the gesture all the same. My fingers comb through the fur sticking up on the dog's head, and his tongue lolls out with happy pants. Keir takes my hand, drawing my gaze to his beautiful blue eyes.

"Probably shouldn't chance calling attention to ourselves. I doubt anyone is out on the street, but—"

"Shit. Sorry." For some reason, the Void is easier to manipulate with Keir. It wraps around him like I want it to, and Gren and his flames extinguish. Keir means safety to me, and maybe my magic feels safe with him too. I bite my lip. I should probably stop thinking of the Void as its own entity. It is me. I am it. At least I think it is.

I wait for some sarcastic response inside my head, but there's nothing. And a second later, Keir's finger traces over my cheek, and I'm thoroughly distracted as he whispers, "It's a good plan, Thaeia. As good as we're going to get right now. We can do this. You can do this." I nod, the unease I felt during the meeting settling over me again. I hate that we're involving civilians. I hate that I'm involving anyone at all. This should be between me and Father dearest. But people were hurt at the explosions at the Coliseum, people died. Severn has been ruling Drakam built on generations of lies and murder. For those who are seeking the truth, who am I to deny them retribution?

And like Layla said, I have to get better about accepting help.

Keir pulls me from my thoughts as his face turns serious, his eyes hardening. "Thaeia, if you start to lose control, if you can't keep Lord Drakam's magic in your Void, you make sure I don't have my magic."

My lips part, but he grips my shoulders and shakes me. "I'm serious. Lord Drakam *can not* get ahold of my magic. He can't have access to the Spirits."

I swallow. Just thinking of Severn using his Channel magic to steal Keir's magic, wielding all that power ... all the magic of the Spirits ... There's no winning against that. No. I have to keep Severn under my control, inside my Void. "I won't fail, Keir."

While we practiced in the basement, we learned that even if someone has their magic close to me, even if they're touching me, magic still doesn't work *on* me. Nor could hold my hand and depress the dirt into the ground, but he couldn't make me float or manipulate the Gravity around me. Owen could have his right hand on my shoulder and call Ice to his left, but the Ice wouldn't touch me.

So at least we know Severn can't steal and control the Void. So that's something.

Keir's gaze jumps back and forth between eyes, but the hard look there doesn't dissipate at my reassurance. Instead he says, "Promise me he won't get my magic. Or I'm not coming."

I nearly stumble back. Not coming? My chest tightens, and I can't seem to take a full breath. Keir keeps his hold on me, but softens his touch, rubbing his thumb over my shoulder. "It's that serious, Thaeia. You know." He ducks his head so his eyes are level with mine. "You know that I'm with you." Slowly, the panic seeps away, and I nod. He nods back. "But I won't put everyone else in danger. If Severn gets my magic ... Thaeia, he could wipe out everyone."

Not could ... would.

I clench my hands. *Not helpful.*

Keir tilts his head, worry creasing his brow. "Still hearing the voice?"

I nod, but shrug, trying to seem unconcerned. "It's nothing. I've always had a vivid imagination."

He purses his lips, but doesn't say what I'm sure he's thinking. He's worried. And maybe he should be, but a snarky voice in my head is the least of our worries right now.

After a second, he steps closer. He smells like dirt and sweat from being down in the basement for so many hours, but under that is his familiar leather and dried-grass scent. It's faint but there, and it calms me like nothing else can. Clarity. That's what Keir gives me. His lips press to the top of my head, and tears burn my eyes and sting my throat. I won't lose him. I won't lose anyone else, but especially him. His hand caresses down the side of my face, tilting it up so he can kiss me. It's gentle. Soft. And too brief. When he pulls away, I go to follow for more, but he chuckles. "I've had to pee for what feels like half a day. I'll meet you in one of the bedrooms on the second floor? We should at least try to get some sleep." He holds up a hand before I can protest—though I wasn't going to. "Please, just try. For me."

I bite my lip, nodding, not trusting myself to say anything.

Spinning, he rushes across the tavern, hunching over slightly as he whines. "Gods, gotta go. Gotta go. Gotta go."

I giggle, wondering if he'll even make it to the bathroom on this floor. My smile falls as I'm met with the silence of the empty room. Are we really doing this? We're going to stride out into the middle of the street and everyone is going to let their magic loose. We're going to draw Silas and his guards, and hopefully Severn out of his estate. I won't face him within the walls of his sanctuary where who knows what traps he may have set for us. No. I'll face my *father* in the streets where his people can see.

It's so quiet, I'm able to hear the soft rustling coming from outside. Rising to the balls of my feet, I tiptoe to the window and look up. There's the first phase of our plan. Moonlight illuminates the fluttering pieces of paper dipping and dancing through the air. The winds of the oncoming storm grab and throw the papers to the streets, flyers sticking to rooftops, drifting and landing against windows. One of the people who came to the meeting was an Air mage, and I can see the ordered line of papers seemingly parading through the sky as she directs them to disperse all across the city.

Those flyers contain my story—a condensed version. Whether people believe it ... I guess we'll see. But at least it will be out there. I smile up at the dancing papers. It's a small thing, but knowing how much this is going to piss off Severn makes me really happy.

And tomorrow, I'll kill him.

Will it be that simple? No. But as long as he's dead at the end, that's all that matters. He won't be captured. He won't get to live with the guilt of what he's done. He won't get the chance to repent. He's had his entire life to make things right.

I stare at the ceiling. How has my life come to this? Unwanted anger spikes through me as I think of Saph. She could have told me. She *should* have told me. I get that she wanted me to grow up away from the danger and violence of House Drakam. But still.

My thumbnail scrapes at the base of my pinky finger where her ring used to sit. She was a good mother. She loved me, and I miss her. So much has happened since I left my island home, but in reality, not much time at all has passed since Saph's death. How much more am I supposed to take? What more will I have to endure? I clench my fists at my sides, recalling Severn's smug smile. I want that smile to turn to screams of pain, gasps of agony, whimpers of suffering. But more than anything, I just want him gone, dead, no more.

I blink, dragging myself out of my murderous thoughts and sigh. I take one last look at the fluttering flyers spreading through the sky before I turn, ready to go up and try to sleep. A little smile lifts my mood. I can think of something that might help me relax. The stirrings of desire tumble through my gut, but then my stomach rumbles, reminding me that the little roll I had earlier was not enough.

I slip into the dark kitchen. The pot that was bubbling earlier is cold and silent, but the heavenly smell still hangs in the air. I open the cold box, grabbing a thick slice of some kind of meat. There's a loaf of bread on the counter, so I slap together a sandwich, spreading some spiced oil over it before shoving it in my mouth. I'm chewing loudly, and crumbs tumble onto my shirt and down to the counter, but I don't care. No one is here to admonish my table manners. I lick my fingers as I head back to the cold box, pulling out a bunch of mint and pinching off a few leaves. Shaking some salt into my palm, I sprinkle some water on the salt, then rub the mint into the wet mixture and scrub that over my teeth. Dipping my head under the faucet, I take a big mouthful of water and swish it around, then lean over the large kitchen sink, pursing my lips to spit.

Taking a breath of minty air, I head upstairs to find Keir. As I pass a door on my right, I slow down when I hear the telltale sound of flesh slapping flesh, accompanied by dual masculine groans. My mind immediately imagines Nor and Valsan together, and a single pulse of pleasure hits me low and deep. The thought of the two muscular men wrapped in each other's arms in ecstasy plays through my head just as another moan, a feminine one this time, comes from the door across the hall. I wonder who's in there, and are they alone or are others in our group hooking up? I shrug, moving on. Whatever. Good for them.

I pass two more doors, these silent, until I come to one that's cracked open. I peek inside, ready to slap my hand over my eyes if I end up seeing something I shouldn't, but it's just Keir, pulling back the blankets and sheets on the bed. I slip into the room, closing the door behind me, and I lean against it, a smile on my face. He looks at me, his own smile lighting up his eyes, and he crosses the room. His hands brace on either side of my head, and my lips part as I tilt back, offering.

His eyes dance as he lowers his head. "You need sleep, Thaeia, but when you look at me like that ..."

Guilt slicks through me like oily mud. "I'm sorry, Keir. You're tired, too. I can behave myself." I smile, trying to sound nonchalant. "Let's sleep. You're right. We need the rest."

I go to move past him, but he shoves his thigh between my legs, grinding me into the door. I groan at the friction, and Keir smiles. "Like I'm going to let my Fox Slayer go to bed all needy and wanting my cock."

I lick my lips again, trying to find the strength to tell him no, to tell him we should just sleep. But I'm a weak woman when it comes to my lordling. My hips roll against the press of his leg, and he chuckles darkly. Gripping my ass, he hauls me up, and I wrap my legs around his waist. He shoves me against the door, pressing his hard length against my clit through our clothes, and I whimper. "Less clothes. Naked." I pant, "Now."

He chuckles again, lifting me away from the support of the door, carrying me across the small room. Dropping me on my back on the bed, his fingers curl under the waistband of my pants, and slowly, with reverence in his eyes, peels them down my legs. I gasp, arching into his touch as he crawls up my body, taking my shirt with him, until I'm bare before him. He steps back, just looking.

I wiggle under his gaze. "You're still dressed."

He hums. "And you're still coherent enough to notice. That won't do."

"Wha—Ahhhhh!" His head dives between my thighs, and he licks me, flattening his tongue against my pussy before spearing it inside me. I buck into the pleasure, then he flicks my clit before sucking it into his mouth—hard. I see stars, actual stars. From where Keir's skillful mouth works me over, shooting daggers of pleasure streak through my entire body. It's so good. Almost too much, on the verge of pain.

I stuff my fist into my mouth to try and stifle the cry that comes from my mouth as he thrusts a finger inside me while his tongue continues to lap and flick at my clit. He groans, the vibrations sending the next wave of pleasure even deeper. I can't breathe, it's so intense. I don't want to breathe. All that matters is the orgasm I'm chasing. It's so close.

His finger leaves me, and I watch as he sucks it, swirling his tongue all while the thumb of his other hand continues to strum my clit. My legs are shaking, and the pleasure is hovering at the edge of climax ... right there. Then he's back on me, his tongue thrusting into me, his thumb pressing and circling, and then his wet finger finds my asshole. I push my hips into his mouth, groaning, and when he chuckles darkly against my pussy, I jerk in his hold, my body overloaded with pleasure.

With a slow lick on my clit, he presses his finger into my ass, and I hiss at the sting. He lifts his head, his other hand tracing the lightest of touches along my inner thigh as he says, "Relax for me, Fox Slayer."

He licks me again, and I gasp. "I ... I can't. It's too much."

Keeping up his soft sucking and licking, he hums

against my pussy. "You can." With heroic concentration, I force my muscles to relax, and his finger slides in past the first knuckle. My mouth drops open at the fullness as he pumps slowly, humming again. "Yes. So good."

I look down at him just as he lets a thick stream of spit slip from his lips. It drips onto his pumping finger, and he adds a second. I bite my lip, pushing into his gentle thrusts as I pant, "Gods, that's ... do it again."

He hollows his cheeks and spits again, this time scissoring his fingers in my ass, stretching me. The sound that comes out of my mouth is part moan, part gasp, part shriek. The pace of his pumping fingers picks up, and with a growl, he dives back between my legs.

Keir uses his free hand to hold my thigh down, opening me for him to feast on. He licks and sucks and pumps his fingers. My body is vibrating, pulsing, throbbing, aching for release. And then he rubs his beard against my pussy, and I shatter. Pleasure pulls me apart until I'm floating. I don't want to come back down. I want to stay here in this place where I feel so good. But I do. The pulsing bliss fades, and my back relaxes from where it was bowed off the bed.

Licking his lips, Keir stands. He quickly strips out of his clothes, wiping off the fingers that were teasing and stretching my ass just moments before. Slowly crawling over me, he nips at my lips, and I can smell myself on his face, and if that's not just the sexiest thing in the world ... I lift my head, taking his mouth with mine so I can taste myself on him. He groans, and I answer with a whimper. My arms wrap around him, as he fits his hips between my legs, his hard cock pressed between us. I trail my lips over his jaw and up to his ear. I nip at him, and his cock kicks against my stomach. I lick the shell of his ear, wrapping my legs around his back, hooking my ankles together.

"Inside me, Keir. I want to watch you fall apart while your cock throbs inside me, emptying yourself until I'm leaking with you."

"Fuck." He grinds against me, and with the next roll of his hips, I angle myself, lining up so his thrust pushes him inside me.

CHAPTER 21

KEIR

SHE'S SO TIGHT, so perfect, so ... *mine*. She challenges me, she makes me laugh, she just makes everything ... brighter, sweeter ... just *more*.

I pull back just enough to watch my cock slowly sliding in and out of her. My length is drenched in her wetness. I can't get enough of her. Planting my forearms on either side of her flushed face, I roll my hips into her, rubbing my pubic bone against her clit just the way she likes. Her lips drop open, and sweet little breaths pant from her mouth, her breasts swaying with every slow thrust.

I trail my fingers down the side of her face, and she leans into my touch as I whisper, "So beautiful. You feel so good, Thaeia." My lips press to hers, gentle at first, then seeking, licking, nipping, tasting. I interlace our fingers, stretching her arms over her head, and her breasts lift with the arch of her back. Holding both her wrists in one hand, I trail my other down her arm as I continue lazily pumping my hips. Gooseflesh chases my touch as I cross her collarbone and down. I cup one breast as I lower my head and suck her nipple into my mouth.

"Keir. Oh, yes. Yes."

I nip the swell of her breast, watching as her skin turns red with my little love marks. Slowly, I work my way up the column of her neck as she writhes beneath me. I bite her earlobe, pulling a gasp from her lips before I whisper, "I know you're close. You're squeezing me so perfectly. You're perfect for me, my Fox Slayer."

Her eyes find mine, her hips lifting as much as they can to meet my slow thrusts. Her fingers flex around my hand where I still have them placed above her head. She licks her lips, and with my next thrust, I roll my hips against hers, and she groans deep and sensual. My balls draw up at the sounds of her pleasure, bringing me close to the edge as well. I want to fall with her. Always.

But the look in her eyes changes, and she bites her lip. She keeps grinding against every pump of my hips, but all of a sudden, she seems unsure, hesitant. I release her hands so I can hold her face. My thumbs brush her cheeks, and I press a soft kiss to her lips. "What is it, Thaeia?"

She takes a slow breath, and it stutters on the way in. Her fingers tickle along my sides as she reaches up and slowly wraps her arms around my middle. Little pinpricks of pain light up along my back when her nails dig in slightly, and that faint bite along with the spreading pleasure makes me dizzy. I keep my thrusts slow, hitting her deep each time, waiting.

Her legs fall open even wider, and the wet sound of my cock sliding into her over and over drives my pulsing pleasure even higher. She hugs me close, our faces just a breath apart as she whispers against my mouth, "This is such a cliche time to say this, but, I think ..." She gasps as I roll against her clit, and my cock twitches in anticipation. Is she going to say what I think she is? I wanted to say it first. She pants around her building pleasure. "I think I love you, Keir."

Fuck. My hips pick up the pace of their own accord. My body responds to her words, needing to be one with her, to show her I love her too. As I drive into her, words continue to spill from her. "It's probably too early, too fast. And things have been crazy, and who knows what's going to happen. And then after—"

I crush my lips to hers, thrusting my tongue into her mouth then pull back. Our noses brush with my thrusts as I grin. "Say it again."

"I ... I love you, Keir."

"Fuck, Thaeia." My mouth takes hers again, consuming her lips, her tongue, her moans, her pleasure. She tries to throw back her head as her pussy starts to pulse around my hard length, but I hold her fast, kissing her like our lives depend on it. I bite her lower lip, sucking it, then dive back into the wild kiss. She cries out into my mouth as she comes. Her release squirts between us as her body goes tight.

We hold each other close as she trembles under me, and I only make it two more hard thrusts before I'm chasing her. Sheer bliss shoots up my spine. It's so intense I jerk against her, my arms almost giving out. Spurt after spurt of cum fills her until it's leaking onto the bed.

We stay locked together as I brush a few sweaty

strands of hair from her face. Rolling us, I relax into the pillow, holding her against my chest. Wrapping my arms around her, I kiss the top of her head, whispering into her damp hair, "I love you too, Thaeia. And the timing was perfect. Though if you want to tell me again after the orgasmic bliss has faded, I won't complain."

She giggles, pinching my side, and I grip the back of her neck. She lifts her head, and I don't think I've ever seen a more beautiful sight. She's flushed and sated. Her hair is mussed, and her eyes are shining with love—for me of all people. She scoots up my body, causing me to slip out of her, and more of my cum drips out of her. Pressing a kiss to my lips, she smiles against my mouth. "I'm still pretty high from that orgasm, so I guess I'll save it."

Hooking my leg through hers, I flip us again. She squeaks a laugh as I press her into the bed. "Say it anyway."

She melts under me, her eyes going soft and serious. "I love you, Keir."

My cock jumps at her words, and she looks down between us. I shake my head, shoving my half-hard cock down. "Nope. We need sleep." She laughs, and the glorious sound does nothing to dampen my growing arousal. I roll again, this time pulling her with me to the edge of the bed. I stand and help her up. "Why don't you run to the bathroom while I change the sheets."

She glances at the rumpled bed. "We did make a mess."

I kiss the side of her neck. "That's how you know it was good."

She lets her head fall, inviting me to lick and suck along the column of her throat, but I manage to keep it to one quick kiss before I bend down and retrieve my shirt. Shoving it into her arms, I nudge her towards the door. "Go on."

She slides my shirt over her head and leaves. I make quick work of the bed, finding fresh linens in a cabinet in the corner. When Thaeia slips back into the room, her hair is a little less tangled, and her thighs are slightly damp from where she must have washed them off. *Pity, I would have liked to lick our combined releases from her skin.* I scowl at my cock. *No. Stop it. We need sleep.*

I slip into my pants, keeping them unfastened. Throwing on a shirt, I press a kiss to the top of her head. "Go ahead and tuck in. I'll be right back."

She mumbles something as she pads towards the bed. Climbing in, she tucks the blanket up to her chin and snuggles into her pillow. Her eyes are closed, and her breathing is already evening out as I slip into the hall. I'll use the bathroom real quick, and get back to my Fox Slayer. Thoughts of getting a few hours sleep with her wrapped in my arms has me relieving myself then eagerly wiping myself down with a wet cloth.

Stepping back into the hall, my Spirit flames flicker to life, sputter, then come back full force with a shot of power down my spine. With a deep breath, I snuff out my magic, frowning at Gren as he disappears with a growl. My palm itches. A wince pulls my face tight, and I press my hand against the wall. Pain scrapes against the inside of my skull, and when I try to shake it off, the hall goes swirly, and I just barely keep from sliding down the wall to my knees.

Something's not right.

KEIR

I SCREAM inside my head as I walk down the hall against my will. I want to reach out and slam my hand against our bedroom door, but my body just keeps going. I grit my teeth as I make my way down the stairs. I try to call out, but the words stay lodged in my throat. The tavern is quiet as I walk down the back hall and out into the rear alley. Every step takes me farther from Thaeia, and every stride stabs me in the heart. But I just keep going. A little black cat pads from an even narrower side alley. Its ear twitches, and it flicks its tail before sauntering off. I stop, facing the dark alley, and a second later, someone shuffles from the shadows.

His hair is even messier than it was at the meeting, and nervous sweat has soaked through the front of his shirt. Cardan shifts his weight from foot to foot, wringing his hands before shoving them in his pockets. I reach for my magic, but Cardan shakes his head, and I release the weak hold I had on my power, Submitting to him.

Shit.

Cardan turns to me. His face is pale, and he only holds my gaze for a second before looking at the ground. He nods down the dark alley, away from the tavern. "Sorry 'bout this. I have kids, though. I have to do as I'm told."

I try to ask him who sent him, I have a good guess, but my mouth stays shut. My body shuffles along obediently, thoroughly stuck within Cardan's Submission magic. Cardan follows, and as we move farther and farther away from the tavern, the 'should haves' start parading through my mind. I should have been more on guard. I shouldn't have let him touch me, shake my hand. I feel the pull of his magic in my palm. I shouldn't have asked Thaeia to take my magic. I should have tried harder to break something, make some sort of noise on my way through the tavern. I should never have left Thaeia's side.

I try everything I can think of to break free, but it's like I'm in a dream—no, a nightmare. My body isn't my own. And what's scarier, the longer I'm under Cardan's control, the less I seem to care. How long until it's not just my body, but my mind that simply wants to do whatever Cardan says?

Little pieces of paper flap and flutter through the air, one floating down right in front of me. I step on it as I make my way down the empty street. I tread on Thaeia's story, on her heartbreak.

The faintest hint of blue tinges the horizon, and the edge of the dusty outer ring of the sister star peeks over the profile of the buildings surrounding us. This is a nice time of morning. The new day is beginning, but it's still quiet. The heat hasn't broken through yet, and the shadows are blurred. Everything seems softer right now.

I bite my cheek. *Focus, Keir. You have to break free. You have to …*

We're circling the large Drakam Estate. I don't like it. The wood and stone and metal make it look heavy, bulky. Nothing like the smooth, sleek lines of my home. The desert is a harsh place to live, but it's beautiful. Just like … like …?

I blink, shuffling along. There's a barricade ahead, and for a moment I consider turning around, but for some reason I keep going. I turn sideways to squeeze through sharp stakes jammed into the ground, crisscrossing to block the way. The side of my shirt snags on a sharp edge, and the fabric tears. Damn. I like this shirt. Wetness drips down my waist, and when I look down ... I'm bleeding? Oh well. I'm through, but now there's a new obstacle before me. I haul myself up and over what seems like a hastily constructed barrier wall. It wobbles under my weight, and there's an itch in the back of my mind like I should know why these barricades have been put in place. But I shrug it off because it's nice to be out in the early hours with nowhere in particular to go, just yourself and your thoughts.

"That will be all, Cardan." The voice comes from the shadows. Cardan? I look behind me, and sure enough, there's a man wringing his hands, his brown hair sticking out in all directions. He looks nice, though a bit nervous. Should I be worried about the voice from the shadows?

Cardan shifts his weight, looking around. "And my kids? My mum? My sister?"

The voice in the shadows sighs. "You know the deal."

Cardan slumps and drags his feet as he walks past me. A hand emerges from the shadows, and when it lands on Cardan's shoulder, he flinches. The voice says, "That's a good lad. One of my guards will take you to your room."

Cardan slips away without another word. Hmm. Seemed like a nice fellow. I hope he finds his family.

"This way, Lord Keir." I follow the voice into the shadows, through a gate and into a garden, my shirt beginning to stick to my skin with my sudden sweat. A grey cloak flutters behind the man in front of me, and something about that garment makes me pause. Wait. This ... this isn't ...

I stumble, panic clawing at my chest. Severn turns to me, a cruel smile on his face. His dark hair is slicked back under the hood, and his brown eyes appear black in the shadows.

And I just stand still, Submissive, unable to move, to call my Spirits, to wrap my hands around Severn Drakam's neck and crush the life out of him.

He smirks. "I see the hate in your eyes, young lord. That's okay. I am Channeling Cardan's magic, and as long as the simpleton is within my estate, I have control over your absolute Submission."

My lips part, but no sound comes out. I try again, and Severn smiles. "Didn't you wonder why I didn't kill *her* when I had the chance?" He chuckles, waving a hand. "You know me, Keir. I'm not one to waste an opportunity. Now, come along." He turns, striding along a dirt path, little balls of vibrant moss creeping over the border. Without my permission, my body follows as we weave through the trees and shrubs and flowers, the blooms still closed tight in the dim light of the early morning. Severn keeps talking, seemingly loving the sound of his own voice, proud of his scheming. "I'll admit, I panicked a bit when she just showed up at the Games. I had to scramble to get my mercenaries into place. That whole business with the explosions was such a messy ordeal. But then, I saw. I watched."

He pauses, turning to face me, and my body draws to a halt. I'm forced to stand there before him. Severn's gaze travels down to my toes then back up. "You, Keir. I saw the way you looked at my daughter."

I strain to reach for him, to claw his eyes out of his skull, to rip his tongue from his mouth so he can never call her that again. Thaeia is not his daughter. She is nothing of this man. I manage to raise my hand a fraction of an inch, but Severn frowns, and with a flick of his left fingers, all my anger melts away. It's such a nice morning in this peaceful garden.

Severn smiles, patting my cheek, and though the gesture is kind, like something my mother used to do, coming from this man, it feels ... wrong. He drops his hand and continues down the path, a solid wood door ahead of us. He says over his shoulder, "Why settle for just her power when if I was patient enough, I could have yours as well?" *No.* "And maybe even that Gravity mage's too. He's got potential, and I just know I could do great things with that power. I was sure you would show up with my daughter when I took that little Animal mage." He shrugs, and I see red. How can he stand there and talk about Halee like she was nothing? He uses his thumbnail to pick nonexistent dirt from his other nails. "But, like I said, I'm a patient man." He smiles, and that's when I see it, the resemblance. The way his cheeks lift is similar to Thaeia, and it makes me want to vomit. He waves a hand at me. "And here you are."

I shiver in fear and disgust. This can't be happening. Nausea burns my gut, and I sway with dizziness before I have to press a hand to the wall to steady myself.

Severn slips a key into the door, and it swings open, saying, "Come on then."

I can't go in there. I can't ... I fight the desire to follow, to Submit. Movement beyond Severn draws my attention, and Silas' voice grates down my spine. "Was he where I said? All go according to plan?"

Severn waves at me. "Indeed. Please see our new guest to his *quarters.*"

Silas chuckles, followed by the screech of an iron door swinging open. "With pleasure." He sweeps his hand into the stone cell, bowing with a mocking grin. "Your room, your lordship."

I hesitate only for a moment, then realize that room doesn't look *so* bad. There's a bed and a little sink and toilet in the corner. I shuffle in, stopping in the center of the small space and turn. Severn gestures. "Take a seat." I back up until my legs hit the bed, and I sit with a squeak of the springs. His eyes land on my ripped shirt and the blood staining it. He tsks. "Seems you were clumsy getting through my barricades. I'll send a healer down here to get the poison out of your system. Can't have you dying on me and taking away your precious magic."

Well, that explains the sweats and dizzy spells. Under the bravado, Severn is scared, and that makes me want to smile. But Silas presses a small stone in the wall, and a thick white mist comes pouring out of the ceiling. I hold my breath, but Severn's voice stops me as he says, "A nice deep breath now, Keir. Can't have you using your magic once I release the Submission magic."

Does that mean he can only Channel one power at a time? My question fractures and floats away as I inhale deeply, sucking down the sweet scent of the drug. The cell starts to turn blurry, but a little corner of my mind feels like mine once again. My flames sputter to life, and Gren whines. I bite my tongue until I taste blood, fighting against Severn's Channel magic just long enough to mentally link with Gren. *Nor. Get Nor.* I've sent Gren after Nor before. He'll know what to do.

Silas slowly begins to close the solid iron door of my cell. Behind him, Severn walks off, his voice trailing down the dark hall. "Around the clock watch on him. I'm going to play with my new magic before a certain daughter of mine comes to rescue the man she loves."

Thaeia. No. Please.

Just before the door clangs shut, the red flames of *my* magic flare to life out in the hall. He has it. Lord Severn Drakam has my magic. Thaeia's *father* laughs. The wickedly gleeful sound echoes off the stones and against my skull. I feel myself falling, slumping over on the bed as the drug takes hold.

We've lost.

CHAPTER 22

NOR

I STRETCH, keeping my eyes closed against the light of the morning sun streaming through the window. I'm not ready to wake up. I'm still tired, and Valsan is pressed against my back, one muscular hairy leg shoved through mine. I could stay here for at least a few more hours. Or the rest of my life.

Screwing my eyes shut even tighter, I nestle down into my pillow. The light behind my eyelids gets brighter. I groan, turning my face into the pillow, pulling the blanket over my head.

A loud bark jolts Val and me out of bed. Val has pushed me behind him before I've even blinked, even though I technically have the stronger defensive magic—I love every protective bone in his body. We're both naked, and his dried cum still coats my chest, and my cock is still slick with oil. I do my best to shake off the memories of sliding into his ass last night and using my magic on him until he came all over us both. I need to focus on the here and now.

What the hell woke us up?

"Gren?" I push around Val and approach the flaming Spirit hound. A sinking sensation plummets from my throat to my stomach.

"Nor!" Valsan calls after me as I rip the door open and run down the hall. He follows as I throw open the next door I come to.

Owen groans, blinking at my naked body before shoving to sit on the edge of his bed. "What's going on?"

I run from his room, charging into the next one. Empty. Val grabs at my upper arm, but I keep barreling down the hall, calling out, "Thaeia!"

Slamming through the next door, Thaeia rubs her eyes, blinking at me before she slaps her hand over her face. "Gods, Nor. Put some clothes on. That's not how—"

"Thaeia, where's Keir?"

Her eyes flick to the empty bed beside her. When she looks back at me, there's panic crawling into her gaze as she glances at Gren. She clutches the loose shirt she's wearing to her chest as she gets up. "I ... I don't know. I fell asleep. He went to the bathroom. Said he'd be right back." She grabs a pair of pants. "I don't even know if he came back at all. Fuck! How long was I asleep?"

"I don't know, but let's not panic just yet." Though that's exactly what I'm doing right now.

She sweeps a hand at Gren before jamming her legs into her pants. "No? Why is Gren here and not Keir?"

Fabric presses to my chest, and when I look down, Val holds a shirt to my body. He's fully dressed and has my pants in his other hand. I take the shirt, missing the armhole twice as Val says, "Aimee is already searching the nearby alleys and streets. He definitely is not here in the tavern."

Thaeia hops around the room as she puts on her boots. "Fuck! Fuck Severn! Fuck! This is what I get for sleeping, for thinking I could take one godsdamned minute of rest! FUCK!"

Vesper pushes into the room cracking her knuckles. "Let's go."

Valsan blocks the door, arms crossed. "Wait. Just hold on. This is an obvious trap. Severn knows you'll come for Keir, but with access to Keir's magic …" Thaeia groans, pressing her palm to her forehead as Val says, "We have to be careful here."

Thaeia drops her hand, her eyes finding me. "I promised him. This was the one thing Keir said couldn't happen. Severn couldn't get a hold of his magic. He made me promise. Fuck!" She shakes her head, heading towards the door, the look in her eyes telling Val to get out of her way. "I have to go. I have to stop Severn. This has to end."

Val puts a hand on her shoulder. "Not at your expense."

She rears back. "So at Keir's?"

Val shakes his head. "Think about it, Thaeia. He won't kill him, not with access to that kind of power. And he knows you'll come."

From out in the hall, Owen says, "Seems like Lord Drakam wants his cake and to eat it too. Keir's power plus a way to control the Void. I think the captain is right here, Thaeia."

I turn to stand next to her, lacing our fingers, Gren still at my side. I squeeze her hand as I look at Val. "So, what do we do? We're obviously not going to leave Keir in Severn's hands."

Thaeia's hand trembles in mine, and the press of her Void slides over me. She rolls her shoulders. "Sorry, it's slipping from me."

I squeeze her hand again. "It's okay. Just try to pull it back. You can do it."

Valsan shifts, moving out into the hall. "Let's go downstairs. It's too crowded in here. Owen, go get Miles. Aimee will be back soon, and who knows, maybe she'll have found Keir."

I take a step towards the door, but I'm halted by Thaeia's hand in mine. Turning, I'm met with sheer terror on her face. She's so pale, it looks like she's about to pass out. Her entire body trembles as her wide eyes dart from my face to Gren then back again. Her breaths are shallow. I step closer to her, rubbing her arm with my free hand. "Thaeia?"

"Severn. He has Keir's power. The ... the Spirits." *Ohhh fuuuuuck.* "Halee ... what if ... oh gods, what if ... Halee. I can't let him ... I WON'T let him." She knocks into me, slamming her shoulder hard into mine, and before I can recover, she's out in the hall. She breaks into a run, sprinting down the stairs, screaming, "No! NOT HALEE!"

I stumble down after her, Gren letting loose a bark. I try to catch up as she barrels through the tavern, yelling, "I won't let him hurt Halee anymore. She should be safe from him. She should be safe from everything, from ..." I hear the unsaid word—her. "I won't let him touch Halee's Spirit!"

Thaeia sprints towards the door, and instinctively I reach for my magic to stop her, forgetting she'd run right through any barrier I throw up since magic still can't touch her. Damn it. I glance around our group, but it's as if everyone is moving in slow motion. She's fast, but so am I. Putting on a burst of speed, the distance between us closes. Owen freezes the wood floor in front of her, maybe hoping to slow her, but as soon as her boots touch down, the Ice disappears like it was never there.

I'm close, but she must feel me gaining, because without looking back, she starts to pump her arms harder, trying to pull away. Her shoulders bunch, and she screams, "No!"

Blue-black inky shadows burst up her left arm, over her shoulder, and across her neck. A pulse of power hits me in the chest, and Gren flickers out then pops back beside me. Thaeia's power burst stops me as if I ran into a wall. I grunt, careening back into Val who catches me. He's always there to catch me. Thaeia's hand slams into the door, shoving it open. *Shit. People are going to see her. The guards will find her.*

But then Aimee is there, seemingly out of nowhere, blocking the doorway. No magic, just muscle. Thaeia careens into her, and Aimee wraps her arms around her chest, picking her up. "You're going to get yourself killed."

Thaeia throws her head forward, slamming into Aimee's nose. Blood spurts, and Aimee swears, her grip loosening just enough for Thaeia to jerk free. I sprint forward, this time able to grab Thaeia before she can take off. She spins, swinging a fist at my face, but I duck as I kick her leg out from under her. We both topple, rolling around the floor, pulling hair, landing weak punches because we're too close to get any kind of wind up. *Ah, just like old times.* I grunt as she gets a knee into my gut, but I manage to wrap a hand around her throat. I squeeze, shouting, "Thaeia, stop!"

She snaps her teeth at me, but the black in her eyes bleeds away, and I can't help but notice that even though her power had pushed all the way to her eyes, it didn't scour my insides or strip me of my strength this time.

Some of the fight leaves her, and her body starts trembling again, the shaking getting more intense with every moment that passes. I sit us up, holding her shoulders as she shakes her head. "I can't do this, Nor. It's too much. I can't take anymore. I've reached my end. I ..."

Her voice trails off as she drops her head. I lean in when she remains silent and nearly unmoving. "Thaeia?" No response. Gripping her shoulders, I give her a little shake. "Hey." She remains sitting, but she's limp. I tilt her chin up. Fear burns hot and sharp through my entire body as I'm met with completely black, unblinking eyes. I shake her harder. "Hey! Thaeia!"

Valsan kneels next to me, snapping his fingers in front of her face. Nothing. Then Owen clears his throat. "Um. Not sure if we should worry, or be *more* worried, or ... well, Vesper's gone."

I look around, and sure enough, no Vesper. Well, that's just great.

CHAPTER 23

THAEIA

IT'S DARK, but it's neither cold nor hot. Holding up my hand, I'm relieved I'm able to see my fingers wagging. I turn a slow circle. Wasn't I just in The Dragon's Breath Tavern with Nor? Should I call out?

No need to shout. I'm right here.

A form slowly comes into focus a few paces in front of me. I don't know how I can tell, but I know they are facing me, and if I could see their face, they'd be smirking.

"Who are you, and where am I?"

I've told you before, I am you, you are me. And as to where you are ... well—they gesture around the vast darkness around us—*we're in your head.*

My brows pinch. In my head? So, it's finally happened. I've cracked. I've gone mad. But what if I'm stuck in here permanently? With myself?

"What happened?"

I get the sense that they are rolling their eyes. *Always closing yourself off from the dirty parts of life.*

"That's not fair. My life has been mostly dirty parts, especially lately."

Okay, fair point. Still, you can run and hide here every time things become ... too much.

"I don't mean to. I just appeared here. I don't like this any more than you do." The form just gives me a mirthful chuckle. I spin, eyes finding nothing but darkness. "Fine. So how do I control, well ... you? How do I keep myself from ending up here? How do I manipulate the Forsaken magic?"

I don't know.

"What do you mean, you don't know!"

I don't know because you haven't figured it out yet.

"I still don't understand who or what you are. Are you my magic? Or ... what?"

The blurry form shrugs. *I guess, in a way. After Halee, your mind kinda ... split.* Fractured into pieces is more like it. *You gave me an identity. You used me to give yourself permission to do what you didn't have the heart to do.*

Shaking my head, I back away. "No. That's not right. I'm more than ready to do what's necessary."

I get that smirking feeling again. *Really?*

Waving my hand at them, my voice gets louder. "You can't be made up. You have a voice. I've heard you. Other people have heard you speak through me."

They cock their hip. *It's truly amazing what the brain can do under duress. You needed power. Here I am. You needed to strike without a conscience. I did that for you.* I shiver, recalling Sidian's dried body. *See! That, right there! You recoil at what I did, but ... and hold on because I'm going to blow your mind ... that was all you.*

I ... I don't ...

You don't remember? They tsk, the sound one I've made on several occasions. *Saph would be disappointed. She didn't raise you to run from your problems. In fact, it was quite the opposite, yes?*

Anger tingles through me that they would bring Saph into this, but then I realize I brought Saph into this. Because if what they said is true, this whole thing is just ... me. My thumb rubs at my pinky where Saph's ring used to sit. Images of Sidian and me fighting scroll through my mind. I jolt as I recall his sword plunging into my body ... and how I didn't care. I remember smiling as I touched my stained finger to his throat and watched the swirling blue-black ink cling to him, draining his life.

The form takes a step towards me. *See?*

I clench my hands, shaking my head. I liked it better not knowing, not remembering. I liked blaming my actions on someone else, even if they were in my head.

You're better than that. We're better than that.

Their body starts to sharpen at the edges.

I picture Saph's determined look, doing her best to prepare me for what was to come while letting me have a semi-normal life. I picture her smile as she fixed us sandwiches to take to the beach. Then I picture Nor, his grin aimed at me, his fist raised ready and waiting to bump mine. I know he's with me right now, holding me on the floor of the tavern. Nor is with me, and that gives me ... peace.

The form takes another step towards me, and I can make out their hair, dark and wavy.

I picture Valsan, his warm laugh, and his eyes filled with love for Nor. I picture Owen, flirting and joking and smiling. I picture Aimee, arms crossed but with a tilt to her chin that says she's got my back.

The form is closer now, and they're wearing the same clothes as me.

I balk when I think of Halee, but I force her image to play across my mind. I see her bright smile, her blushing cheeks, and her shy glances at Miles. I picture Miles, trying to hide his obvious affection for my friend, but unable to do so, his crush on her just as evident as hers on him.

I am standing before myself. The other me smiles. With a nod, she holds up her hand, palm towards me. I hesitate, and the other me tsks again.

Keir's face lights up my mind. His smiling blue eyes, his dark beard that tickles and teases, his laugh, the way he feeds me, his loyalty to his friends, his dedication to his people, his immense power, his kind heart, the way he loves me …

My palm presses to the other me's hand. The midnight-blue ink bleeds over our joined hands, down our arms, over our shoulders, stopping at our necks. The other me grins. *Feels good to put yourself back together, doesn't it?*

I smile back at myself. "Yeah, it does." I tilt my head, and she mirrors me as I ask, "So does this mean I can control it now?"

The other me chuckles with a shrug, our hands still joined. *I guess you'll find out.*

I shake my head, my chuckles joining hers. "Okay then. How do I—"

The other me fades as if she's being sucked into my body through our clasped hands. The darkness around me swirls, and I'm forced to close my eyes against the wave of dizziness that threatens to drop me to my knees.

Everything goes silent for a long moment. Opening my eyes, I find myself on the floor, Nor's grip on my shoulders so tight it hurts. "Ow, ow."

Instead of letting me go, Nor's hands clench even tighter. "Fuck, Thaeia! You were, I don't know, catatonic. We couldn't ... you were ... Fuck."

Bumping his forehead with mine, I whisper. "I'm sorry. Everything, it's just ... I think I finally broke." Gren tries to press his head to my side, but it just ends up going through me. Still, I smile at the Spirit hound until I remember ... Keir.

From where he's kneeling next to Nor, Valsan places his hand over Nor's where he's still gripping me. Nor relaxes slightly as Valsan says, "You don't have to keep going, Thaeia. This fight is as much ours as it is yours. We can—"

I shake my head. "No, I ... wherever I went just now, I think, maybe I might have sorted some things out."

Nor chuckles. "That's the least confident statement I've ever heard."

I can't help but smile at him. "Well, I just had a strange conversation with myself in a Void within my mind."

Tilting his head, Nor asks, "So?"

I shrug. "No idea."

We both laugh as he playfully shoves me. I squeak in surprise as I'm lifted off the floor. Nor takes Owen's offered hand as Valsan sets me on my feet. I can't help it. My gaze turns towards the door as if I can see House Drakam beyond, and Keir inside its wood and stone walls.

I have to do *something*.

CHAPTER 24

KEIR

CONSCIOUSNESS COMES SLOWLY AND PAINFULLY. My head pounds, and the sweet scent of the drug coats my tongue. I know even with my eyes closed that I'm not alone in my cell—if I'm still in the cell, which I assume I am. Keeping my eyelids shut, I take a few slow breaths. My side no longer hurts, and the nausea from earlier is gone.

Severn's voice, though quiet, bounces off the stone walls and makes the ache in my head worse. "I know you're awake, son of Alopson."

I swallow, trying to wet my dry throat, but my voice still cracks. "I'm aware that you're aware." I keep my body relaxed, even as I feel the tingle of my magic in my spine.

There's the sound of shifting clothing, and the slight squeak of maybe a chair. A rhythmic noise makes the space behind my eyes throb in pain, and if I were to guess, Severn is impatiently tapping his foot on the floor. But honestly, I think if I were to open my eyes right now, I'd vomit, so I keep them closed.

After a few long minutes pass and I still haven't said anything, Severn sighs, the chair groaning again. His voice is a little closer as he says, "Tell me how to control them."

My lips twitch with the urge to smile.

The leaders of the territories have always tried to be cryptic about the extent and power of their magic. Until this past Games, no one knew my father had such an expansive reach with his Emotion magic, and that he could hold it for such an extended amount of time. And until now, I assumed that when Severn Drakam used his Channel magic, that he could pull several powers at once as long as they were within range. But now, I don't think that's the case. He may be able to cycle through magic quickly, dropping one to Channel another in rapid succession, but I don't think he can use more than one at once. Though I'm not one-hundred-percent sure about that.

I fold my hands over my chest, settling into the lumpy mattress, knowing if I look relaxed, it'll piss Severn off.

I've also learned that while Severn is Channeling magic, he's more or less sharing it. Though that makes it sound like the exchange is mutual. It's not. But I still have access to my magic even while Severn is Channeling it. It doesn't have the same punch of power I'm used to—it feels like when I'm close to a magic burnout, weak and kind of sputtery. But I have it, and I know what to do with my magic. *I* know how to use the power.

I remain silent as I collect my thoughts, letting Severn stew in this cell with me. Finally, with another squeak of the chair, he says, "You will tell me how to control the Spirits, Keir."

My brows climb my forehead, but I keep my eyes

closed, letting a small smile lift my lips. "Why don't you start small, you know, like a newly hatched letchwe worm, or a baby hagraven."

He's silent for a while, and I almost open my eyes just to see if his face has turned red with anger yet. He catches me off guard when the bed dips near my shoulder. My eyes pop open to see Severn leaning over me with a sneer on his face. "You'll tell me how to control the Spirits, how to wield their magics ..." I force my face to remain relaxed as I wait for it ... "or I'll rip that little Animal mage friend of yours out of the Everafter and experiment with her Spirit until I figure it out."

Fast as a snake, my hands wrap around his throat. He reels back, but ends up taking me with him. I'm not letting go. I use his momentum to shove him back, squeezing harder until my knuckles turn white and the skin around his neck turns red. His mouth falls open, but instead of fear, there's amusement in his eyes. My magic comes back full force, but Severn Channels a new power, and it must be Strength or something in that realm. One of his hands grips my wrist, and my bones crunch. I scream, trying to keep my choke hold, but my wrist snaps, and as my hand falls away, he slams the heel of his palm into my chest. I fly backwards, my head smacking against the wall before I crumple to the stone floor. The small cell spins around me, and I feel the wet heat of blood dripping down the back of my head. I try to breathe through the nausea.

A hand wraps around my throat, and I'm lifted completely off the floor, my toes scraping the stones as Severn holds me up one-handed. Releasing me, he grins as I stay suspended in the air as he drops the Strength magic and Channels something else, something that keeps me floating, my arms pressed to my sides, my head unable to move.

He steps closer, poking me in the chest, and I wince, pretty sure my breastbone is cracked. Cocking his head to the side, he says, "Tell me how to control them, and I'll leave your little Animal mage's Spirit alone."

Blood drips down my back, and the room is still spinning, and being suspended isn't helping. I look at Severn, at his straight black hair with little wisps of grey at the temples, at his dark brown eyes, and his lean, tall figure. His white teeth are stark against his rich brown skin, and I can't believe I thought I saw Thaeia in that smile. There's nothing of this man in my Fox Slayer. She's so much ... *more* than him.

I smile, picturing my fierce Thaeia, how she taunted me in the arena during the Games. How she allowed herself to trust me to get her out of the desert. How she marveled at my library. How she worried over her friends at every turn. How she looks when she comes for me.

Raising a cocky brow at Severn sure to piss him off, I say, "You control them like this." My Spirit flames flare bright, and I finally get the panicked look from Severn that I've been waiting for.

CHAPTER 25

THAEIA

I CAN'T THINK about anything beyond ... Severn has Keir. That's it. That's all my brain can process right now. Everything in me wants to run out the door, sprint down the street, and don't stop until Keir is back in my arms.

Keeping within the shadows, I look out the window. Heavy clouds have moved in fast, reflecting my mood perfectly, dark and unpredictable. The wind whips scattered flyers across the street, one snagging on a lantern post, its edge flapping wildly. I have to angle myself, but I can just barely see the estate gates and the towering House Drakam. It's just a few blocks away.

Keir's in there.

I jump, my heart racing as a thud comes from the back door. Adrenaline snaps through me with a dizzying rush but instead of fear, I only feel anger. I'm tired of being afraid. I'm tired of ... everything. The now familiar feeling of sand scraping against my skin lets me know my power is flaring. Sure enough, when I glance down, the tips of my fingers have swirling inky shadows climbing towards my second knuckles.

You know we can stop whatever that is, right? Just let me go.

I clench my hands, knowing I shouldn't but kinda wanting to.

"Are you all just going to stand there and watch me struggle or is someone going to help.?" With a grunt, Vesper stumbles into the tavern, falling to her knees. And she's not alone. The cloaked person she's supporting with an arm over her shoulder slumps to the floor, falling on their side.

Keir? I dash forward, slipping past Nor. Valsan and I reach Vesper at the same time. I hold her shoulder as Valsan gently looks over the person lying at Vesper's knees. My hopes dash and break as I realize the person is too small to be Keir.

Owen kneels next to me, pressing his hand to the Poison mage's back. "You okay, Viper?"

She grunts. "It's Vesper."

He smiles. "I know. What happened?"

Vesper stretches, cracking her back as she says, "Went for a little stroll around House Drakam. Poked around. Found her." She jerks her chin at the person still curled up on the floor. "She's weak and a bit battered"—Vesper looks at me—"but she's alive. Said her name was Fara."

My eyes go wide as I spin around to look at the woman now cradled in Valsan's arms. There are bruises on her face, her right eye is swollen, and her ear is crusted with dried blood. She blinks, her head lolling before she's able to focus on me. I place a gentle hand on her upper arm, trying and failing to keep my fingers from trembling as I ask, "Fara?"

She gives me a weak smile, reaching for me, but she winces and drops her hand. "I knew Rhenara would keep you safe."

Rhenara. Saph's real name. Fara's face turns blurry as tears fill my eyes. I brush them away, stroking her arm. "You'll be alright. We'll find a Healer."

Layla says, "I have a Healer friend that owes me a favor. I'll get word to her."

Valsan asks, "Can she be trusted?"

Layla nods. "To do her job and keep her mouth shut? Yeah." She looks at me. "But maybe you stay out of sight while she's here."

I nod as Miles presses his hand to Fara's shin, looking at Valsan. "I can take her upstairs. Get her cleaned up and into a bed."

Carefully, Valsan shifts Fara into Miles' waiting arms. But he only takes one step before Fara snaps out her hand with a little grunt of pain. She fists my shirt with surprising strength. "Come with me. There's so much I need to tell you. And I'd like to know about you, dear girl. And about Rhenara."

I swallow, nodding as I pat her hand. "We will talk, I promise, but let's get you Healed first, and then get some food in you so you can rest. We'll have time. Later."

She drops her hand, nodding, her voice fading with her strength. "You're a good girl. I'm glad I got you out. I'm glad you were safe." And with that, her head falls to the crook of Miles' arm, and her eyes close as her breath evens out in sleep. Miles pats her gently as he shifts her a little higher in his arms, then quietly goes upstairs.

My gaze swivels back to the door. Vesper's hand curls

around my forearm. "I tried to find him. But I found her instead. Thought I should go ahead and get her out while I could." She lets go of me, waving in the general direction of the estate. "We could ... you know ..." She smiles, leaving the offer open to take me into the estate to go find Keir. She says, "I took care of the guards at the gate." She holds up a hand before Owen can say anything. "I didn't kill them. They're just hallucinating their balls off. Probably be tripping for a few hours unless the Void here saps my magic Poison out of their system."

"The guards at the gate are—" Owen barks out a laugh. "Hallucinating their ..." He doubles over with his laughter.

Vesper shrugs, but I catch the faint blush to her cheeks. "They'll have a headache and their sense of taste will probably be all fucked up for a few days, but they're alive." She grins, rubbing her hands. "Unless you wanna go ahead and eliminate the threat while we have the upper hand?" She nods maniacally, her eyes wide with glee.

I shake my head with a little laugh, and she throws up her hands. "Aww. Come on. I'm sure they have orders to capture or kill all of us."

Shaking my head again, I say, "Let's keep the murders to a minimum. But we do need to find Keir. We need to get him away from Severn."

She starts striding towards the door. "Well, come on then. I at least know where he's not." She keeps her eyes forward, but raises her left hand. "You just make sure I keep my magic."

I follow Vesper, and I glance at my left hand, wondering if I'll be able to control myself when I see

Severn again. And then I wonder if I want to control myself. *Does that make me as bad as my father?*

One: don't call him that. Two: maybe, but sometimes you need to be a monster to beat a monster.

While talking to myself, I failed to notice Nor. He grabs me, and I tug against his hold, but he doesn't let go. Gren looks up at me with puppy eyes as Nor says, "Thaeia, you can't just go out there and stroll down the street and knock on the door."

Three soft knocks rap on the tavern doors, and we all freeze. *Well, that was ...* No one moves. I don't think any of us are even breathing. Layla hurries across the room, holding up a finger, silently telling us to be quiet. Valsan gestures, and we all scatter to the edges of the room, pressing against the walls, trying to sink deeper into shadows. Nor is next to me, our arms pressed together. His fingers lace through mine, and he gives me a little squeeze.

As soon as Layla reaches the door, her posture snaps straight. She shakes her braid over her shoulder and down her back. Opening the door just wide enough for her body to still block the inside, Layla says with a cheery voice, "I'm sorry, but we're not open right now."

A deep female voice comes from outside. "Would you have rooms to rent this evening?"

Valsan pushes away from the wall, Owen and Aimee following. Valsan crosses the room, but Nor and I stay where we are. He reaches over Layla's head, wrapping his large hand around the edge of the door. "Daria?"

"Valsan?"

He pushes the door open a little more, dipping his head at Layla who steps back. A tall blond woman pushes into the tavern. Her long hair is braided tightly to her scalp, and it falls over her shoulder. Her pale skin and plain clothes are slightly dusty, indicating days on the road. Scanning the room, her posture says she's ready for anything. Four other people come in after her, spreading out but staying near the door which Valsan closes and comes back into the center of the room.

Valsan clasps her arm. "Good to see you, Daria. You made good time."

The captain of the Alopson guard is here. My first thought should be that she'll help rescue Keir. But it's not. My first thought is she's here to take Keir home. Then where does that leave me? Gods, I'm selfish. And I have more important things to concentrate on right now.

Daria glances at the four behind her, and I assume they are Alopson guards as well, but you couldn't tell by their dress. They're all in plain clothes, travel worn and dusty. One of the men has prominent pit stains, and the woman has a small hole in the knee of her pants. Daria says, "We're the advance team. Scouting to see what we're up against. There are so many blockades in this city, especially the closer you get to House Drakam, you'd think Severn is expecting the entire country to storm his gates."

The man closest to the door turns to me. "You her?" I'm so tired. I don't want to do this anymore. I want to go home. Nor steps in front of me, and the guard raises his hands. "All friends here."

Daria spares me a quick glance, and I can't read her expression before she looks around the room. Her eyes fall back to me, and I brace, waiting for her to ask where Keir is.

The silence stretches.

Layla's behind her bar, pouring drinks. No one takes one though, we just stand around the large room until

Daria turns to Valsan. "Captain, have you heard anything about the fighting at your border? Have your guards broken through?"

Valsan frowns, pulling the tie from his hair before running a hand through it. "They're no longer—"

Aimee crosses her arms. "We haven't heard anything new. We don't know if they're through or not."

I blurt out, "Did you lose your magic?"

The five Alopson guards face me, and I swallow, resisting the urge to back away from their stares. But my back's against the wall. There's nowhere to go. One guard cocks his head at me. "You really are that Void woman?"

I raise my left hand, my skin unmarked, my power behaving for the time being. "Guilty."

His eyes go wide, then he lifts his left hand and starts to ... Expand. He just gets bigger. And bigger. His muscles swell, and he grows at least three feet. Then as fast as it happened, he shrinks back to his original size with a smile. "Sorry. Had to check."

I shrug in understanding. "That's pretty cool, how you can"—I open my arms, spreading them wide—"puff up like that."

He laughs, the sound warm and kind. "Yeah. It can come in handy."

One of the other Alopson guards slaps him on the back, speaking to me. "You should see him when he uses his full power. He can grow taller than the Drakam Estate."

My eyes pop as I imagine this man lumbering through a city at that size. He could crush several homes with one step. The Expanding guard shrugs off his companion's hand. "I'm Marcus by the way." He points to the guard next to him. "This is Taos. And that's Anton and Eva over there."

I nod at each, then Marcus says, "To answer your earlier question, yeah, we all lost magic there for a while, but"—he waves a hand at me—"seems sorted now, yeah?"

I waggle my hand with a shrug. "Eh. We'll see.

Daria frowns. "That's not reassuring. Maybe you should ... remove yourself from the situation."

I read Daria's tattoo. ORRIKEUM. Allusion. A fancy word for suggestion. My hands land on my hips, and I raise my chin. "Maybe you should—"

Owen raises a hand with a chuckle. "Let's calm down."

One of the Alopson guards laughs. "Owen, my man, you just told two women to calm down. You got a death wish?"

Owen shrugs with a smirk. Daria glares at me, then her green eyes flick to Gren who's still at Nor's side. She looks back at me. "Where is Lord Keir?"

CHAPTER 26

THAEIA

The room goes quiet, and Daria just waits. Layla tips back her head, swallowing a shot of something. Valsan takes a step towards Daria. "Why don't we all sit? There are some things you should know."

Daria holds my gaze with a glare as she moves further into the room, her hand landing on the back of a chair. It scrapes quietly against the floor as she pulls it out, and she takes a seat but keeps it far enough from the table to allow her to leap up if necessary.

I fight with myself to keep from curling my fingers into my palm as I take a step towards the table where Valsan, Daria, Owen, and two of Daria's guards now sit. Aimee remains standing as well as the other two Alopson guards. Nor stays near me, and Layla remains behind the bar cleaning glassware that I doubt needs actual cleaning. Why is it that bartenders seem to clean to de-stress? Actually, having something to do with my hands sounds nice right about now.

I stop a few paces from the table. "About Keir."

"What about me?"

I spin around so fast at the sound of Keir's voice, my hair smacks me in the face. He's here! Standing at the end of the hall, one arm is tucked against his chest, his other hand braced against the wall, his breathing a bit labored ... but he's here!

Layla sighs, "Why do I even bother locking that back door?"

But I'm across the room in a flash, barely noticing Daria and the other Alopson guards standing and moving towards him. They can wait in line. My hands land on his chest—his solid chest, but he hisses in pain and I leap back. "You're here. Are you okay? What happened? I was sure Drakam had you."

Keeping one hand pressed to the wall, he takes the single step that separates us and brings the other to my face. "I'm here. I'm fine. Well, I will be. I'm sorry. Drakam did have me." My eyes go wide, and my fingers curl into his shirt, but his gaze flits over my head. "Layla, I'll not lay this at your feet, but know that one from the meeting, Cardan, betrayed us. He used his Submission magic on me, delivered me to Severn."

Layla swears, and Owen smacks the table. "Son of a bitch!"

From a few steps behind me, Daria asks, "Are you okay, Lord Keir?"

Keir dips his head. "I'm fine. It's good to see you, Daria." His gaze moves beyond her. "You too, Taos, Marcus, Anton, Eva."

A chorus of "my lord" comes from behind me.

I can't stop looking at Keir. His Spirit flames flicker over his skin. His brilliant blue eyes look down at me, and though there's a smile on his face, I see the pain he's trying to hide. I run my hands over his cheeks, his beard scratching me. "You're not okay. Do you need a Healer? One is on the way for Fara."

"You found her?"

"Vesper did while she was looking for you."

His gaze goes back over my head. "Good at getting into places, huh?" Vesper chuckles, and I imagine her shrugging. Then Keir's eyes are back on me. "I'm sorry. I should have known better than to let my guard down. I let Cardan shake my hand. I let everyone at that meeting shake my hand. I felt it. His magic." He holds up his hand, staring at it. "Here, in my palm. I didn't *want* to leave, but ... I did because he wanted me to."

Carefully, I run my fingers over his skin. I can't stop touching him. Until this moment, I didn't realize how little I expected to actually get him back. After everything that's happened, I didn't think I'd ever see Keir alive again. I'm trembling with the realization, and one of my hands continues to comb through his beard while the other lowers to rest lightly on his stomach. "It's okay, Keir. Please don't blame yourself. I was ... I was so scared. Did Severn ... did he ... your magic ... Halee ..."

He frowns, tucking some hair behind my ear. "He tried to Channel my Spirit magic. He threatened to use Halee, but—"

We both look down as Gren growls. He's pacing, trying to get between us but is just walking back and forth through our legs. I take a step back, giving the hound some room, but instead of staying closer to Keir, he moves with me. My eyes go round as the hound stands between me and Keir, his lips pulled back, another deep growl coming from his chest as he glares at Keir.

What the fuck?

Keir's brows furrow. "What's wrong, Gren?"

The hound growls again, actually snapping at Keir with a bark. Daria's voice is closer than it was a moment before as she says, "That's not good."

I look down at the hound, running a hand through his head. "What's wrong, big fella?"

He gives a little whine, circling my legs, then sits at my side, watching Keir. While he's still acting strange, he's at least settled a little, so I take Keir's hand, leading him towards the table where the others were sitting. As we approach, Daria pulls out a chair for Keir, waiting for him. The other Alopson guards take their seats as well as Owen. Nor and Valsan trail behind Keir and me, and Miles comes back downstairs heading straight for the bar, the presence of the Alopson guards as well as Keir not phasing him in the least. He props himself on a stool, not quite sitting, not standing either.

Keir stumbles, drawing my attention back to him, and I wrap my arm around his waist. "Keir?"

His hand slides over mine. "I'm okay. Well ... There are a few broken bones, and there was this gas. I think some of the drug is still lingering."

I try to take more of his weight. "Gods, Keir. You should sit."

He shakes his head. "I'd rather stand." He glances at the waiting chair. "I think sitting would hurt worse."

A look of obvious concern crosses Daria's face, but she sits at the table with the others. She looks Keir over from head to toe. "How'd you get away?"

Keir rubs his temple. "I'm ... it's a little blurry ... from the drugs, I guess. Severn wanted me to tell him how to control the Spirits. He could call them, but he couldn't direct their magic." His eyes clear of the pain slightly. "I had him. I was still stronger than him even while he was Channeling me." He shakes his head. "I ... I don't remember, but the Spirits must have helped me."

Miles, with a hand around a mug of something asks, "Is he dead?"

Keir turns to him, but he must move too fast because he winces. He shakes his head. "Wait. Why am I waiting?" He chuckles, and his Spirit fire flares. Two Spirits pop into the room, but I'm the only one who jumps. Damn, I'm on edge. One of the Spirits comes up to Keir, bowing his head slightly before holding his flaming hands over Keir's body, moving slowly from head to toe. The other Spirit bows as well then disappears. Keir looks at the ceiling. "She'll heal Fara. I assume she's in one of the bedrooms upstairs?"

I nod, and with another pass of his hands over Keir, the Spirit backs up, bowing again. Keir places his hand over his heart, bowing back, and the Spirit fades into nothing. Keir rolls his shoulders with a little sigh. "That's better. I should have done that right away. I guess the drugs made me slower than I thought."

He turns back to Miles. "As to your question. I'm not sure if Severn is dead. But I want to say no. I don't recall killing him anyway."

Valsan rubs his hands together. "I don't like it."

I wave him off, turning to stand in front of Keir. My hands go back to his face. I stare at him, taking in the little crinkles at the corners of his sea-blue eyes, the dark scruff of his beard. How his hair is a little longer than when we first met. I think I like it this length. His full lips draw my attention, and I swallow. I don't care that I can feel everyone's eyes on me. I rise to my toes, and Keir leans down to meet me. Our lips brush, and I nearly whimper. I didn't think I'd ever get to kiss him again. To hold him. To hear his rumbling voice read me to sleep ...

I kiss him again and again before I pull back slightly. From my peripheral, I see Gren walking through our legs again, but I ignore him as I stare into Keir's eyes. "I don't think I'd survive losing you too."

His fingers trace my cheek. "If I could promise you that I'll never leave you like that, I would. But I do promise that while there's still breath in my body, I'll always find my way back to you, Thaeia." He winces slightly, and I wonder if the Healer Spirit missed something, but then the look is gone.

I bite my lip before saying. "That's enough. And I promise the same. I love you, Keir."

The words are barely out of my mouth before his eyes go wide. Gren barks, menacing growls coming from his snapping jaws. Keir's hand grabs my throat, and he pushes me back towards the front door. I'm stumbling, clawing at his grip, gasping for air, then a flash of something shiny catches my eye.

A blade. One of Saph's blades is raised in Keir's hand, and it's plummeting towards my heart.

CHAPTER 27

KEIR

Someone stop me!

Valsan jumps to his feet, yelling, "Compulsion magic!"

But I'm on my Fox Slayer as soon as she tells me she loves me. Of course Severn would use those words from the woman I love as a trigger. My hand is wrapped around the knife that I only now recall Severn sliding into a small sheath at my lower back. I'm plunging the blade towards Thaeia's heart, and her wide eyes just look at me, pleading with me to stop.

I can't. Someone, please.

Owen's Ice snaps around my arm, stalling my movement, and I breathe a sigh of relief, but it's short-lived. My magic flares as the Compulsion digs deeper. *She must die.* Dozens of Spirits pop into the room, one melting the Ice. A blast of Anton's Lightning magic hits me. Thank the gods he doesn't hit me full force or I might be dead, but still, the sharp burn of electric shock sizzles against my skin. He's unable to get in another hit because one of my Spirits is on him in the next moment. Aimee comes for me, hand reaching, ready to Petrify me, but again, a Spirit intercepts her too.

I must have some control over myself, because there are many more-powerful Spirits I could call but don't. Still, everyone in the room is fighting one or two of my Spirits, leaving me free to swing the knife at Thaeia. She manages to kick her hips back enough so that I miss her, but I still have a choke hold on her throat. I squeeze, screaming in my head to stop, to let her go, to turn the blade on myself instead. Anything but this.

I push her so hard, we tumble through the door, rolling across the walkway into the street. Nor yells from inside. "Void him, Thae—!"

Something cuts him off, but he got the important bit out. *Yes, please.* I try to plead with Thaeia with my eyes as I shift the knife, holding it overhand as I kneel over her, holding her down so I can drive it into her chest. *Please!*

Thaeia chokes out a scream. Her entire body turns a midnight blue, her hair floating around her agonized face. Her Void punches into me, and the Compulsion snaps. I drop the blade as Thaeia's power explodes, spreading from where she lies on the ground. I can actually see it, the pulse of her Void spreading outwards like a shock-wave. She's still screaming, that eerie voice layered over hers. I release her as her back arches off the cobblestones, and the force of her power actually lifts her completely from the ground. I reach for her, but another pulse slams into me, this time from the outside in. It pushes against me, and with a dizzying pop, my Spirit fire flares back to life.

I look down at her. She's panting, reaching a shaking hand towards me. I take it, holding her sweaty palm in mine. Kissing the back of her hand, I struggle to find the right words. How do you tell someone you love you're sorry for trying to kill them?

Amazingly, a weak smile lifts her lips. "Are you okay, Keir? Is it gone? The Compulsion?"

I nod, pressing another kiss to her palm. Gren whines, circles us, and I stroke a hand through his body. "Thank you, friend. You tried to warn us."

"Keir?" I look down at my Fox Slayer, concern ripping through me at how pale she is. "I think ... is this magic exhaustion?"

Her eyes flutter closed, and I scoop her up, standing. Before I can head back into the tavern, I notice people in the streets. Damn it. I've compromised us all. We've drawn a crowd.

Pointed fingers aim at Thaeia. One woman stands in her doorway, one of the flyers from last night held tight in her hand. She looks at the paper then at Thaeia, then back to the paper. A group of three, then four, then five start down the street, slowly, cautiously headed our way.

From behind me, I hear, "That's her! The Void."

Then another voice rings out, "Guards!" Shit. Green-clad guards standing behind the obsessive blockade in front of the estate gates turn at the shout.

More join the call, but the woman steps from her doorway, holding out the flyer. "Is this true?"

A young man bursts from a clothing shop, the store still dark inside. He waves another flyer over his head. "Lord Drakam is a murderer!" The street is beginning to fill, and unfortunately, there are more angry eyes aimed our way than sympathetic ones.

Thaeia stirs in my arms, and when I look down, she presses her hand to my chest. "Let me down."

I frown at her. "I don't think—"

"Keir, let me down."

I set her on her feet, my hands hovering to catch her should she fall. She's a little unsteady, but she turns a slow circle, facing the growing crowd. A man yells, spit flying from his lips. "We can't let her get away! Hold her until the guards get here!"

Several citizens raise their left hands against Thaeia. I growl, my Spirit flames flaring several feet into the air. A few people back up, eyes wide, but not enough. I'm in control now. Scores of Spirits surround Thaeia and me. I smirk, watching through the ethereal bodies of the Spirits as the entire crowd retreats several steps, some outright running away. And then our friends are there. Valsan strides through the wall of Spirits, coming to our side. Aimee is right behind him. Owen stays outside the circle, but his left arm is raised, ready. Miles is there too, along with Daria and the other Alopson guards.

The air around us shimmers and sparks and sizzles with Anton's Lightning magic, and Energy courses through my body as I see the flare of Taos' magic illuminate his hand with golden sunlight. I take Thaeia's hand, and through the translucent shield of Spirits, I see several Drakam picking up their pace to reach us. One sneers at us, well, she's trying to through the fear in her wide eyes. She raises her left hand again, but she stumbles back, rubbing her eyes, then holding out her hands like she can't see. I grin, knowing Eva has her with her Sight magic.

I call out, "Daria, if you would."

She calmly walks past our group, not raising her left

arm. She doesn't even flex her fingers, but I know she's calling up her Allusion magic. With a steady voice, she says, "People of Drakam, go home."

A few of the guards and most of the remaining citizens begin to shuffle away. With the barest of movement, Daria flicks her hand behind her back, and my guards know what to do. Anton slowly walks up to me, and without a word, wraps his hand around my arm and starts pulling me down the street back towards the tavern, his dome of lightning crackling and moving with us. I let him guide me away from the danger, as is his job, but I bring Thaeia with me, keeping my grip on her hand. I don't know if I'll ever be able to let her go again.

As a group, we begin to creep away, but Valsan stays with Daria. She says something to one of the Drakam guards, but her voice is so low and calm, I can't make it out. He starts walking back towards House Drakam, but when the others hold their ground, Valsan takes another step forward. A second later the remaining green-clad guards look around, brows furrowed in Confusion as they wander off into the city, scattering like lost kittens.

We're almost back to The Dragon's Breath when Valsan and Daria join us once again. I release the Spirits, and my guards drop their magic, eyes still scanning the street. A gust of wind cools my skin and sends a few of our flyers from last night fluttering across the street. One catches on Marcus' leg, and he leans down, retrieving it. His eyes travel over the words, over Thaeia's story before he says, "Saw these last night." He looks at Thaeia. "This all true?"

Instinctively, I bow up at the implication that we lied, but I breathe, trying to calm down. It's a fair question because it's kind of an unbelievable story.

Thaeia cracks her neck. "Unfortunately."

Marcus shakes his head. "Damn."

Owen pauses. "Yeah, man. It's fucked up." He waves a hand at the tavern. "And I think it's safe to say this place is compromised."

Then movement draws our attention and we turn, looking down the long street towards House Drakam. A thick mist begins to curl out and surround the estate, and in a matter of seconds, House Drakam, the guards, the gates, and the barricades are cut off from view by the thick, swirling fog.

Owen sighs. "What fresh fuckery is this?"

Thaeia's hand tightens around mine, and when I look down at her, I resist the urge to hold her even tighter. Not because she's filled with uncontrollable rage, or the opposite and on the verge of passing out. No. She's calm. Too calm.

My Fox Slayer stares down the street as if her vision can pierce the fog and see through the estate right to where her father hides within. Our friends surround us, eyes locked on the shrouded estate, when the ground shakes and a deep rumbling comes from House Drakam.

CHAPTER 28

NOR

I HOLD out my arms to keep my balance, and I flex my left hand, using my Gravity magic to stabilize everyone else. Around the perimeter wall of House Drakam, giant black thorn-like shapes spear out of the ground. They are so thick, I wouldn't be able to wrap my arms around them. Even from this distance, I can see a bright green ooze dripping from the wickedly sharp-looking tips of the thorns.

Vesper chuckles. "Looks like daddy is a little scared."

I tilt my head down at Thaeia. She looks ... tired. "Hey."

She turns to me, and I don't think I've seen her look so dejected since her twelfth birthday. I hate it. I hate all this. Raising my fist, I hold her gaze. She stares at my clenched hand, taking a long moment to gather herself. I wait. I'll wait as long as she needs. Keir stands at her side, a strong presence lending her strength just by being here for her. Our other friends surround us, everyone silent.

Thaeia takes a slow inhale, and on her exhale, some of the fight comes back into her eyes. She stands a little taller, and with a tiny nod of her head she bumps my fist with hers.

I nod back, dropping my hand.

Here we go.

Flexing the fingers of my left hand, I grab hold of my magic, yanking it from my gut. The rush of power tingles over my skin and makes my blood rush. With a burst of my Gravity magic, the cobblestones before us crack, sink, then fly to the sides of the street as if dug up and pushed aside by some giant invisible hand. The wave of power barrels down the street, tearing up the stones, some hovering and tumbling in the air. Our flyers from the night before flutter and whip around as they ride the pulse of power. It reminds me of riding my board back home, and I recall Thaeia and I sitting on our boards, soaking up the sun, waiting for that perfect wave. My magic slams into the giant thorns, crushing the ones in my wake. It disperses the fog, punching a hole through the swirling mist which allows us a clear view as my magic tears through the blockades sending wood and metal flying in all directions. The gates go next. The metal crumbles, curls, and bursts open, but I don't stop.

The stone driveway breaks apart and churns under the power of my Gravity magic. The wide steps leading to House Drakam crack and sink. Then with a thunderous crack, the giant twenty-foot-high doors rip right off their hinges.

My panting breaths are loud in the resulting silence. There's sweat dripping down my face, and my shirt is soaked through. The fog begins to close back in around the estate, and the thorns grow back thicker and farther down the street, closer to us. But I accomplished what I wanted. I turn to Thaeia and smile brilliantly as I say, "Knock knock."

Vesper laughs, slapping me on the back before darting ahead of us, shaking her hips as she dances down the ruined street. "That was amazing!"

Owen starts after her, calling, "Vesper, wait."

Val chuckles as he comes up next me, his hand pressing to the back of my sweaty shirt. "That's one way to do it."

Daria says from behind me, "So I guess this means you all are going in now?"

I struggle to shift my gaze away from Val. Mmm. He's so beautiful. I shake my head, trying to focus, but my body is a little sluggish after using so much magic so quickly. He brushes a piece of sweaty hair off my brow as he shakes his head, answering Daria. "Not quite."

Vesper spins a circle in a giant hole in the street, her arms held wide. "Look at what he did! Tore this shit up!"

Owen crosses his arms. "Focus, Viper. We have a plan, remember?"

She stops her twirling, her shoulders drooping dramatically. "But ..." Owen shakes his head, and she actually stomps her foot. "Seriously? Come on. Nor just blew the place wide open. We can walk right in."

Daria clears her throat. "So, there is a plan?"

Owen says something to Vesper to which she rolls her eyes but follows him back to our group. Before Val can divulge our plan to Daria, Thaeia holds up her hand. When all eyes turn to her, she shifts, but speaks quickly and clearly. "If this works, I'll keep my Void reined in as much as I can, but when my emotions run high, I might still have trouble controlling it."

Vesper snickers. "What she means is when she lays eyes on daddy, all bets are off, and you'd best be grabbing weapons, because who knows what's gonna happen with your magic."

Thaeia shrugs, because Vesper's not wrong.

Our attention is pulled to House Drakam once again when a loud bell tolls deep from somewhere within the fog. It reverberates through the city, and the tone hasn't even dissipated when several people step out into the street. They come from all directions, flexing and raising their left hands at us as the gigantic thorns spread up the street, punching through the ground, blindly aiming for our group. My muscles bunch. The citizens are going to get caught in the deadly thicket curling and growing and reaching for us. But then the angry growth of thorns slows, then stops. Miles grunts, staggering back a step with his left hand raised. "I've got it."

One problem temporarily taken care of, but then the people in the street start running towards us, their magic flaring.

Shit!

Valsan steps forward. "Let me." A few of the citizens closest to us pause, brows scrunching in Confusion, but others push on towards us. Daria joins Valsan, using her Allusion magic as she says, "Turn back. Go home. You don't want to do this."

A man to our right whimpers. "Don't want to. Must."

I swear. "Shit. More Compulsion magic." My Gravity magic swirls, and I shove the closest threats back.

I can't help it, I shiver, recalling the hold the Compulsion magic had over Keir and what it almost made him do.

Thaeia calls out, "Get ready for a blackout. I'm going to try to break it."

I'm so proud of her. Her voice is confident, even if she isn't. Blue-black ink climbs to her forearm, and the steady press of people halts. Some slump in relief then run off, but more than a few stay, angry eyes turned on our group. One woman points and screams, "It's her! It's the Void! We have to stop her! Guards! Guards!" She raises her left hand, but nothing happens.

Emboldened by her outburst, citizens begin to approach again, pressing in from every direction. Owen shifts his weight from foot to foot. "Come on, people, don't make us hurt you. You read the flyers. You know what Lord Drakam did."

A person in the back of the crowd yells, "We know that woman stole our magic, our gifts! For all we know, those flyers are nothing but lies, slander. Lord Drakam warned us. He said she was trying to tear our country apart!"

Another voice rings out. "Protect House Drakam!"

Yet another shouts, "House Drakam!" Until everyone is chanting the words, marching towards us with increasingly angry looks. I have a feeling the only thing keeping them from charging us is the fact that no one has magic. Thaeia still has us all in her hold.

I press closer to Thaeia, trying to keep my eyes focused on the threat, but we're surrounded. Val and Daria back up, and our ranks close in tighter, and I just now notice a few of the people from the meeting yesterday have joined us—I just hope we can trust them. After what happened with Cardan and Keir ...

Keir bends down to Thaeia. The wind picks up, almost stealing his words, but I hear him say. "Thaeia, can you give me my magic? Just me?"

That would be a huge help. Keir could probably disperse this rabble singlehandedly. Thaeia bites her lip, eyes focused on the advancing crowd. She gives him a little nod, but then cries out as a rock slams into her temple.

Keir grabs her, spinning her under his arm, shielding her with his body and three Spirits appear, shielding them both. I spin in the direction the throw came from. A small boy stands in a doorway, his eyes wide, another rock in his hand. That was a perfectly timed and thrown hit. I'd be impressed if all this wasn't so fucked up. He drops the other stone and runs away. Probably a good thing, since Thaeia has lost her focus. I hope she's okay, but I'm distracted as my magic bubbles in my gut, which means ...

I go to turn around, but sticky web-like threads wrap around my legs, and I nearly topple over. Clouds swirl overhead, and a small funnel begins to dip out of the sky towards us. Marcus is three times his usual size. Owen is freezing people to the ground as fast as he can, but the humidity keeps them from remaining stuck for long. Aimee, her body a light grey color with her Petrification magic, darts into the crowd. Those she touches lock up, temporarily turning to stone.

Valsan kneels, quickly slicing the webbing off my legs before rising and spinning, putting his back to mine, left hand raised, a dagger in the other. Vibrant green vines punch out of the ground, as Miles wraps two and three people up at a time. Lightning cracks and booms into the broken street before us as Anton fights to keep the crowd back.

Two people charge from behind, but they slow, then stop, scratching their heads in Confusion before walking off. A shadow falls over us, and when I look up, a woman with wings for arms swoops towards us, but then she flaps erratically, blinking as Eva's Sight magic blinds her, and she falls to the ground beyond us.

Valsan shouts at Taos, pointing at me. "Can you give him a hit? He can shield us, but he's running low."

Taos nods, placing his hand on my shoulder. I tense, not sure what to expect as his hand starts to glow. It gets brighter, like sunlight spilling from his palm. But there's no heat, just a rush of Energy.

He pulls away, and I smile. "Thanks."

With a quick nod, he turns, reaching up to place his hand on Marcus' hip, repeating the process. I feel renewed, and when I reach for my magic, it comes easily. A bubble of Gravity snaps around us, and the citizens' magic bounces off, unable to reach us. Though, they still try. A large puddle of ... something black and oily-looking slinks towards us and starts climbing my invisible Gravity wall. I shiver, feeling like the sludge is coating my stomach. It burns. But I grit my teeth and hold my magic.

A small group charges towards us, but they quickly stop, Confusion blanketing their faces before they wander off. The giant poisonous thorns start to spread in our direction again, and Miles snarls, getting them under his control once more. Aimee darts into the thorny tangle, petrifying the largest ones to nullify their poisonous tips and keep them from pressing any closer.

It's pure chaos, magic flaring everywhere. It's all happening so fast. My eyes start to water, and the buildings around us start to vibrate. All the windows around us shatter, glass exploding into the street as a Sonic wave rolls towards us. I feel my Gravity bubble crack, and I drop to a knee, my fist slamming into the ground. But still, I hold my magic.

Taos' Energy magic slides into me again, and while it helps, it's not nearly enough. The stones under our feet start to shift and ... melt. I start sinking as a Fire mage shoots spears of flames at us. Owen freezes them as quickly as he can, but a few slip through, hitting my magic with searing heat.

I grunt, now on both knees, my trembling palms submerging in the quicksand beneath me, but I hold my magic. I won't fail my friends. I won't fail Thaeia. I won't. Sweat drips off my nose, and Keir shouts, "Hold on, Nor!"

A second later, Keir's red flaming Spirits pop up all around us, creating a wall just beyond my Gravity shield. They lift their left hands, and their magic joins the fray. The paper flyers come spearing through the air from all over the city, swirling into the faces of any citizen that gets too close. A few people struggle to pull their shoes from a sticky substance that appears in puddles on the street. The glass from the earlier explosion lifts into the air, forming into one giant shard, like a jagged blade the size of a prazar.

My vision blurs, and I blink away the sweat that's threatening to drip into my eyes. Apparently, Keir's pissed. He's not done. In front of the fighting Spirits, he calls up Spirit animals of all kinds and species. They burst forth all around us in a tight circle, snarling, barking, baying, and growling to keep the citizens away from us.

Yet another Spirit pops into our group, and Vesper startles, "Holy shit!" The Spirit moves next to Keir who holds out a hand, and the Spirit hovers their palm over his. When Keir speaks, his voice booms out so loud, everyone jumps, hunching in on themselves, covering their ears. I glare at him. A warning would have been nice.

Keir bellows, "Severn Drakam, come out and face us! Face your daughter! Face the truth of what you've done!"

As his voice dies off, utter silence presses in on us. At least the ground has stopped sucking at my hands and knees. The rabble that was eagerly attacking us just a moment before has turned to face House Drakam as if they expect their lord to come striding down the street.

Will he?

The deafening stillness goes on and on for what feels like hours, but I know it's only been a few minutes when a form appears in the fog.

Holy fuck. Is Severn really coming out to face us?

The person strides towards us, their pace slow but confident. The citizens back away, hugging the sides of the street. A few just run off, not willing to stick around and possibly get caught in the crossfire.

Daria tsks, and Owen rolls his eyes as Captain Silas swaggers down the street—a cursed coin ... always showing up. Silas rolls the fingers of his left hand, flexing them one after the other like he's stroking the keys of a piano. Valsan told me his Hunter magic makes him shrewd and observant, and when he locks onto his prey, his strikes rarely miss. He holds out his arms, a wide smile on his face, scores of Drakam guards following slowly behind him as he yells. "You will face *me*, Void, and you will die. My lord need not concern himself with you anymore."

CHAPTER 29

KEIR

THAEIA LOOKS UP AT ME, her hand pressed to her head. The cut isn't bad, but head wounds always bleed so damn much. She asks, "What do I do? Do I take the magic?"

Daria, who's right behind me lays her hand on Thaeia's shoulder. "Wait."

I bow, bringing my lips to her ear. "I wish one of my Spirits could heal you."

She shakes her head. "I'm fine. Just a little bump. Focus on protecting the others."

"I'll protect you first, Fox Slayer. Always. But yes, I've got the others as well."

I kiss her cheek and step back as Valsan weaves through our group, stopping at the edge of Nor's Gravity shield. He touches the barrier, and when Nor doesn't drop it, Valsan angles his head down at Nor where he's still on all fours. "Let me through, Nor."

Without lifting his gaze, Nor shakes his head.

Valsan keeps his hand on the shield as his voice drops. "My love, let me through."

A tear splashes to the melted cobblestones under Nor as he chokes out. "You better fucking come back."

"To you, always."

Another tear hits the ground as Valsan's hand pushes through the barrier. The Kapros captain strides forward, the wind whipping his hair around, his broad body tall and full of confidence. There's an odd shimmer around his body, and I'm pretty sure Nor has wrapped Valsan in his own personal Gravity shield. I don't know how much longer Nor can pull his magic, but Taos is helping.

With a casual grace, Valsan reaches back, tying his hair back as he says, "You will face me, captain to captain."

Silas smirks then lets loose a cruel laugh. "Word is you are no longer captain."

My guards shift and gasp. Daria leans in. "What is he talking about?"

My hand finds Thaeia's back, and I stroke my fingers over her shirt, needing the contact as I say, "Lady Kapros dismissed him."

Daria tsks. "Well, that was stupid."

Despite the circumstances, I smile, completely agreeing with her. She strides past me, her long blond braid swaying down her back as she follows Valsan, calling out, "You will face us both, as *captains*." She pulls a crumpled flyer out of her pocket. "I'm assuming you knew about this ... about what your lord was doing?"

Silas' eyes narrow on Daria then flick to us before he smiles, but it looks forced as if his lips are in pain making the gesture. "Daria, I'm glad you and your little ... advance party made it through my lines. Now I'll have the pleasure of cutting you down myself."

Daria scoffs, her posture completely relaxed as she waves at the scores of guards standing several paces behind him. "With threats at both your borders, I'm surprised you're here, nonetheless that you have so many guards to spare to watch your back."

Vesper covers her mouth as she says rather loudly. "Ooooh." Owen smacks her shoulder, but he's smiling at her.

Silas, to his credit, doesn't react, he simply says, "Those little skirmishes will be put down before long." His eyes shift to Valsan. "Both of them." He spreads his arms. "So what are you waiting for?"

Daria balls up the flyer, tossing it on the ground since Silas is obviously going to ignore her earlier question. Placing her hands on her hips, she nods at the estate behind him. "Well, to start, I *suggest* you go take a seat on one of those poisonous thorns surrounding your coward of a lord."

Silas takes a step back and turns around, but his shoulders bunch, and he growls, "You and that fucking Allusion magic." He spins back around, a dagger appearing in his hand. It flies end over end, and with his Hunter magic, I know it'll be near impossible for Daria to dodge. Before I can call a Spirit to help, Nor grunts, and the blade stops midair, shivering for a moment before falling to the ground.

Silas glares at our group standing several paces behind Valsan and Daria. "You need your little *friends* to help you, Daria?"

Valsan crosses his arms, and Silas frowns. He looks left then right, then spins around looking up then back at the mist-shrouded estate. I almost laugh at his obvious Confusion. While his back is turned, Valsan charges.

One of the Drakam guards shouts, "Captain!"

Silas whips around, sword in hand this time. He swings. His aim is true, and Nor screams, "No!"

But Silas ... stumbles. His angry eyes find Thaeia, and when I look at her, there's a wicked smile on her face aimed at the Drakam captain. My flames still lick over my skin, and Ice crackles along Owen's hand, but it seems my Fox Slayer has taken Silas' magic. He lifts his left hand, and my pulse kicks at the blue-black stain on his fingers. Silas' face pales, and he staggers again before clenching his fist, charging the two captains before him.

Valsan deflects a thrust from Silas' sword, and Daria dances in with a sharp jab to Silas' ribs. She hasn't drawn either of her weapons yet, using hand-to-hand to humiliate Silas in front of his guards. She actually slaps his hand as he tries to slam the butt of his sword into her face, and she ducks under his elbow, landing another hard punch to his side. Valsan lunges, landing a slice of his dagger across Silas' shoulder while Daria says, "Guards of Drakam, you're needed at the estate."

Silas roars, "Don't any of you move!" but all but a handful of the guards turn and jog into the fog. The stain on Silas' fingers climbs to his wrist, and he groans with a shout of rage, charging into the fight once more.

A growl draws my attention back to Thaeia. Her eyes are black, watching Silas, and that eerie double voice says, "End him."

Her hair starts to float around her head, and I reach for her, but Nor collapses, distracting Thaeia. The black drains from her eyes as she rushes to his side. Anton shouts with a crack of Lightning, "Captain!"

My head whips around at the fighting trio. Valsan has a dagger in his lower stomach, and Daria has a matching blade in her thigh. The midnight-blue stain is gone from Silas' skin, and his movements are sharper, faster. With a small flex of my hand, a Healer Spirit appears between Daria and Valsan. Daria has already yanked the blade from her body, and the Spirit makes quick work of her wound. And a good thing too, because Silas is there again, but Daria is quick enough to meet his sword with hers. Valsan grunts as he pulls the dagger from his stomach, and blood pours down his shirt. The Healer Spirit turns to him, and I turn my focus back to Thaeia.

Taos is pushing his magic into Nor, and while a little color flushes his cheeks, he doesn't stir. Thaeia grips Nor's shirt, taking a slow, deep breath, her clenched hand shaking. She raises her gaze to Silas, but Vesper clasps her shoulder. "Wait."

Thaeia frowns but nods. A gleeful smile spreads Vesper's lips and she jogs out of our group. But instead of heading into the fight like I expected her to, she darts to the right, slipping down a side street. I never know what that woman is going to do.

Valsan and Daria continue to dance, dodge, deflect, parry, thrust, and swing at Silas. But he's holding his own. I should just end this. My flames grow brighter, and I'm about to send as many Spirits as it takes to bring Silas down, but the few remaining Drakam guards gasp, clawing at their throats as they fall to the ground. They writhe, a few foaming from the mouth, more than one vomiting bile. The commotion is enough to distract Silas, and Valsan slashes his dagger across his middle. Silas hisses, jumping back before the blade can go deeper.

The Drakam captain glares at Daria and Valsan. "Once

I'm done putting you two in your place, I'll kill that Void and any of her other friends that get in my way."

Vesper appears behind where the struggling guards squirm and scream on the ground. She chuckles, the sound dark and deranged, catching Silas' attention. Her arms are spread wide, and a dark green mist clings and circles her fingers. She steps around the Poisoned guards, her shining eyes on Silas as she says, "You set those explosives at the Games."

Silas swings his sword, splitting his attention between the two captains and the Poison mage. "You're crazy."

Vesper rubs her hands together, her smile growing. "Probably, but that doesn't mean I'm wrong."

Silas shakes his head. "I didn't."

She tsks like a mother disappointed in her child. "Then you gave the order at your lord's command."

Silas glares at her all while deflecting strikes from Daria and Valsan, his Hunter magic giving him hyper-focus. Thaeia remains kneeling at Nor's side, and I stand over them with Taos, Marcus, Anton, and Eva around me, at the ready. Those from the meeting that had joined us have backed away or left. Aimee and Miles look prepared to run to their captain's side at any moment. Owen only has eyes for Vesper.

The Poison mage stops several paces from the captains as if they aren't in a fight for their lives. She tilts her head at Silas. "You killed my friend. Admit it."

Silas chuckles as he leaps away from Valsan's sword and ducks under the swing of Daria's blade. "I don't have time for you right now. Be a good girl and go—"

Silas' eyes go wide, and he stumbles, vomiting blood. Daria and Valsan freeze, watching as Silas staggers back another few steps before falling on his ass. Sores erupt with pus and blood all over his body, and he screams as Vesper stands over him. She looks down at Silas. "You will have the time to confess, *Silas*."

The way she says his name has a shiver running down my spine. Owen actually chuckles, "She's scary."

I think he likes that about her.

Vesper kneels over Silas as his left hand starts to rot, the fingers turning a dark grey, curling inward. She looks him over from head to toe as he writhes on the ground in agony. "There were two women out late the night after Thaeia's triumphant debut at the Games. Everyone was partying hard, and I was no exception. My friend and I were catching some fresh air, trying to clear some of the rum from our systems."

Her gaze stays on Silas, but Vesper's tone has gone distant as she loses herself in her memory that none of us knew about. "We wandered into the arena. We knew we weren't supposed to be there, but that's the fun of it." Her gaze hardens and she pokes his forehead, eliciting a scream from Silas as his eyes start to bleed. "It was dumb luck. I stumbled into one of the passageways to be sick. I puked my guts up." She laughs. "Much like you are right now." Her smile falls. "I left my friend in the center of the arena. She wanted to see if she could open the hatch to see the Game cup."

Vesper nudges Silas with the toe of her boot. "I shouldn't have left her. When I came back out, she was gone. I searched and searched. All night and into the day. Even as the team competition started, I was searching the passageways of the Coliseum. That's when I found it. A bundle of explosives. I ran, and you know who I found?" She waves her hand. "I'll tell you. A pair of Drakam guards. You and one of your lackeys. As I ran up, you walked off with that stupid swagger of yours. I told your guard what I found, and he assured me he would take care of it."

Owen starts to walk towards her as she says, "Your guard patted my back and thanked me. Then the explosions went off, and guess whose body I found in the rubble? Sheri—that was my friend's name. She was broken and burned, but I found it, the stab wound. No one believed me." She glares at Silas. "I know it was you. Say it."

Silas grunts, and Vesper growls. "Say it. Admit you killed her. Or you gave the order. Admit it!"

"I ... we couldn't let the Void—" Silas' words are cut off by his wracking coughs, blood spurting from his lips.

Owen shifts, and Vesper glares up at him. "Are you going to try to stop me?"

He smiles at her. "Me? Try to stop a Viper from striking? That would be stupid."

She beams at him, leaping to her feet. Silas screams then dissolves into a disgusting pile of goo as Vesper throws her arms around Owen's neck, kissing him. He wraps his arms around her back, lifting her off the ground as he deepens the kiss.

Anton retches next to me, and Daria's nose scrunches at the sight of Silas' liquid remains as she says, "Gross."

Owen and Vesper continue to devour each other's faces as Valsan turns and races back to us. He kneels at Nor's side, brushing his hair back, so much love in his eyes, it's almost painful to look at. As if he senses the touch of his love, Nor's eyes blink open, and his palm covers Valsan's hand.

Valsan smiles at him. "There you are. You did so well, my love."

Nor grunts, sitting with help from Valsan and Thaeia. She holds his hand as he holds Valsan's. Nor asks, "Silas?"

I lean down, wrapping my hand around Thaeia's upper arm, pulling her to her feet and tucking her against my chest. I kiss the top of her head as Valsan nods at the pile of sludge that was Silas. Nor grimaces, turning pale, but then he sees Owen and Vesper. The two finally come up for air, and Vesper spins, practically skipping back to our group, a chuckling Owen trailing behind her. Nor's brows pinch. "When did those two become a thing?"

Valsan shrugs. "Who knows."

Thaeia's hands fist my shirt, and her lips press to my chest. I grip the back of her head, holding her to me. But she pulls back, head swiveling towards the shrouded estate. Stepping out of my arms, she weaves through our group, purposefully striding towards House Drakam. The midnight-blue shadows climb to her elbow, but then she shakes her arm, and the darkness retreats until it's just her natural skin color once more.

I take off at a run, catching her quickly, grabbing her arm, spinning her around a little too hard. "What are you doing?"

The others have stayed back, and she waves her free hand down the street. "*My father* obviously isn't coming out. So I'm going in."

Back in our little group, Vesper dances, wiggling her hips. "Fuck yeah!"

Owen chuckles, but I shake my head. "That's not the plan. We can draw him out."

She sighs, the exhaustion from earlier creeping back into her eyes. This is a tired that not even Taos could fix. It's soul deep. I stroke her cheek over the dried blood. "I understand you want to end this Thaeia, but who knows what traps he has laid in there?"

A bit of frustration laces her tone. "So what? We keep wrecking things out here? We destroy people's businesses? Their homes? We engage in a war with the people of Drakam? They didn't do anything to deserve this."

I want to remind her she didn't do anything either, and she has suffered the most.

She waves her hands. "We could stand out here and demand he face us until we're blue in the face, but he's obviously a coward. Smart, but a coward. I need to end this."

The hairs on the back of my neck stand up. My magic flares down my spine with such force, the world around me begins to tunnel. I stumble back, on the verge of collapsing. Thaeia reaches for me, concern in her beautiful gold eyes. A deep voice rumbles through the air right next to us. "Then end this we shall."

Severn appears out of nowhere, a long dagger raised in his fist.

Everything seems to slow down as fear and panic threaten to stop my heart. Severn smiles at me over Thaeia's shoulder as he plunges the blade downwards. No, no, no, no. Thaeia spins around, her eyes wide with surprise, but she's not moving fast enough. That dagger is aimed at her chest.

I hear our group rushing forward, their magic flaring, but my own power rips down my spine, stealing my breath. My legs buckle and I fall to the ground as Gren roars, pulling my magic to solidify himself. He clamps his jaws around Severn's arm, shaking his giant head. Severn screams, but instead of dropping his blade, he grabs it with his free hand. He also knows better than to look my basilishound in the eyes, so he avoids Gren's Petrification stare.

The amount of power Gren is siphoning from me is draining me fast, but I give him more. I give him all I have, giving Thaeia the time to strike. I feel myself slipping into unconsciousness as I manage to get out a whisper, "Now, Thaeia."

But she doesn't draw her blades. Her power climbs her arm, her Forsaken mark standing out around her wrist. She turns her black eyes to our friends who are rushing to our aid. But then Thaeia actually takes a step away from her father. Severn's still trying to dislodge Gren, but every time he slashes at my hound with his dagger, Gren just slips back into his Spirit form, allowing the blade to slip through him before solidifying again to tear more flesh from the man's arm.

Thaeia backs up another step, and I want to scream. What is she doing? Severn's rage-filled eyes follow her as he tries to shake Gren off him. My Spirit flames flicker over his skin, and I nearly collapse as Severn tries to Channel my magic. His pained voice echoes down the street. "I warned you what would happen if you defied me, Keir! I'll do it! I'll pull your little friend from the Everafter. I'll tear her Spirit apart!"

"No." Thaeia's too-calm voice sends a shiver down my back. The Spirit fire on Severn extinguishes. Even though Thaeia is nowhere near enough to have touched him, her blue-black inky shadows start to climb his left arm.

He bellows, managing to fling Gren off him. My loyal hound sputters as my magic starts to falter. Severn roars, spit flinging from his lips. "No! How dare you take my magic! You can't touch me. I am Severn Drakam! You are an abomination! You are a thief! You are wrong and I will save my people with your death." His face pulls back into a dark grimace. "I'll do it myself. I'll make sure to put you down for good this time, *daughter!*"

Disapproving gasps come from the few civilians hugging the walkways. Whispers begin to build of Severn and his daughter, the Void, the flyers, the secrets, the murders ... But the voices fade. It's too much. My magic is almost spent, but I manage to pull enough for Gren to resolidify, and he launches himself at Severn once more. I force myself to hold on for a few seconds. If I pass out, Gren goes with me. I need to hold on. I need Thaeia to make her move. I look at her, hoping to convey the urgency of the situation, but her back is to me.

Thaeia nods, the movement almost a bow as she takes yet another step away from Severn. That otherworldly double voice spills from her lips, but somehow I know my Fox Slayer is in control as she says, "Miles."

CHAPTER 30

MILES

A few days ago ...

THE BLANKET DRAPED *over me is hot and scratchy, but I don't move. I know I should find a way to pull myself out of this black hole of nothingness and depression, but ...*

From within the darkness of the blanket, I let my fingers trace down Halee's petrified arm. Her absence has left me empty. Her life, her joy, her spirit took up so much space in my heart, and now ... I continue to stroke her, wishing she would turn her head and smile at me, wishing she'd giggle as I trailed featherlight touches up her waist. I long to see her eyes light up in delight as her magic connected with the Animals around her. I want to feel the little skip in my heart I'd get when she'd run to Thaeia's side with a grin on her face, knowing she was going to talk to her friend about me and the feelings that were growing between us.

How do I go on knowing I'll never see her eyes darken with the pleasure I give her. Even in my own head, I know how cliché it sounds, but food has lost taste. I can't even find joy in my magic anymore because it just reminds me how Halee would beam at me anytime I made even the smallest of plants grow for her. The only thing I want is to sleep. There I can be with Halee again. I can tell her over and over how much I love her. I can see her smile, I can feel her touch. If I'm not dreaming of her, it's wasted time.

But I've slept so much, my body won't sink into the dark, it won't fall into the dreams I'm constantly chasing. If I can muster the will to get up, maybe I'll drink myself into unconsciousness again. But that would require leaving Halee.

My fingers brush up and down her arm. I need to get myself out of this darkness. I need to find the anger, the rage, or even the sadness ... something.

Movement and shuffling sounds come from behind me, and I fight a sigh—someone else has come to offer me their sympathy, or to tell me to drink some water, or to try to eat something. Or maybe it's the captain again, come to drag me to the shower. A hand lands on my covered shoulder, and Thaeia's whispered voice says, "Miles."

I hear the pain and guilt in her voice, and I understand that she blames herself and expects me to blame her as well. I think she expects me to hate her. I don't. All the blame, all my hate is reserved for Severn Drakam. Have I told her that? I'm not sure.

Thaeia shifts, sitting, keeping her hand on me. "You don't have to get up, just stay there, stay with her." She pauses, and I remain still other than the small strokes of my finger along Halee's arm. Then Thaeia leans closer, the pressure of her hand increasing. "If you want it, Severn's death is yours."

I go utterly still at her words. She's offering me revenge. She's offering me a death that by all accounts is hers to claim. But I want it. Gods, I want it. My heartbeat thuds a little faster, and for the first time in days, I ... feel.

I nod, and in case she can't see the gesture from under the blanket, I swallow around my dry throat and say, "Yes."

Her fingers tighten on my shoulder. "I'll distract him. His focus will be on me. I'll give you an opening, no matter what I have to do. I promise, Miles."

The blanket shifts and Thaeia reaches inside, her arm snaking over my waist. With a soft thud, one of her throwing knives with the interlocking circles inscribed in the blade falls to the dirt floor between my body and Halee's. I know this is one of Saph's blades—the woman who raised Thaeia, who kept her safe from Severn all these years. Thaeia whispers, "All I ask is that if possible, you use this."

Then, without another word, she gets up and walks off. I breathe through the excitement that courses through me. It's almost dizzying after spending so much time in my depression. The rage at Severn starts to trickle through, and I run my hand up Halee's arm, over her slender neck, cupping her face. I scoot closer, pressing a kiss to her petrified skin whispering, "He will die. He won't hurt anyone ever again. And then I'll take you home, Halee."

THIS IS THE MOMENT. Thaeia has stepped back, giving me my opening. Gren clamps his jaws around Severn's calf this time, blood and flesh coating the hound's sharp teeth. Thaeia's eyes find me among our friends, all of us rushing to her aid. She nods and says one word. "Miles."

With a burst of speed, I break from our group, and I

can sense them holding back, giving this to me while still having my back. Severn sees me coming. Good. I want him to see his death in my eyes. The fingers of his left hand flex, and I brace to be hit with whatever magic he decides to Channel, probably Keir's since he's so hard-up for the lord's Spirit power. But nothing happens, and I notice the shadowy stain covering his arm up to his elbow. I grin and keep going knowing Thaeia has him in her Void.

I could have already wrapped vines around his neck and squeezed until his head popped off. I could have already sent a thorn like the ones surrounding his estate right through his heart. I could have already wrapped his arms and legs in vines and pulled him apart. But I don't reach for my magic. Halee loved my magic, she said it was beautiful. I won't use it now for something so ugly. No, I barrel right into Severn's chest just as Gren puffs into smoke, and I know Keir has passed out. I'll have to thank him later.

Severn grunts as he falls to his back, and I go with him, straddling his thighs, my hands wrapped around his throat. He thrusts his arms between mine, breaking my hold, but I saw it coming. I let him think he's gaining the upper hand. I let him have his moment of hope because I needed my hands free anyway. I grip Thaeia's throwing knife in one hand and press my other against his chest.

Severn's eyes go wide as he sees the glint of the blade, and his feet kick under me. I feel a chill behind me accompanied by the crackle of Ice and Severn's lower body goes still as Owen freezes his legs to the ground. I feel my friends behind me, all of them giving me this moment. From my peripheral, I see Thaeia kneeling off to my left, hovering over the unconscious Keir, but I know her eyes are on me and her father. No, not her father. He hasn't earned that title.

Severn shifts, moving to grab my wrist, but I'm faster. Without a word, without hesitation, I slam the blade into the side of his neck. He bows under me, some of Owen's Ice cracking with the force of his struggles, but I lean into him, ripping the knife across his throat, slicing through cartilage and skin. My grip slips as blood coats my fingers, then my hand, then all the way to my wrist. A few spurts splatter my shirt, and some hot blood flecks my cheek. I keep going until his neck is gaping open from ear to ear, the wound so deep, his head is halfway cut off.

I don't know at what point he went still, but as I sit back, breathing heavily, Severn's glassy eyes stare at the sky as the first raindrops hit my head and splash into the blood pooling around Severn and me. Tilting my head back, I close my eyes and let the rain hit my skin.

It's done.

CHAPTER 31

THAEIA

It's done. The Dragon of Drakam has fallen.

I'm not sure what to do with myself. Our little group has been sitting on and around the stoop of The Dragon's Breath Tavern for the past few hours. The rainstorm passed quickly, and now little puddles dot the ruined street. There has been the occasional civilian popping their heads into the street, but none have dared come close. I expected guards to come flooding out of House Drakam to avenge their fallen lord, but they never came, and the reason comes jogging down the street.

Daria and her guards stand, striding down the road to meet the red-clad Alopson guard. They exchange a few words before Marcus, Anton, and Eva follow the guard back towards House Drakam. Daria and Taos come back to us. Taos kneels and gives Nor another hit of his Energy magic before he turns his glowing hand on Keir. Both men are awake and doing better, though they are still a little unsteady. Daria plants her hands on her hips with a smile. "Alopson has taken House Drakam."

The rest of us whip our heads to look at the estate. It's so quiet. We didn't hear a thing. Granted, we had our own thing going on out here, but still. Daria bows to Keir. "If you'll allow me, my lord, I'll go see to the organization of our new House."

Keir waves a hand from where he's seated next to me. "I'll join you shortly, but go, make sure everyone is taken care of. This needs to be as peaceful of a takeover as possible."

Daria bows again and heads back down the street with Taos following, but then Keir calls out, halting Daria several strides away. "Make sure to send a message to the southern border to stop the fighting. Drakam is ours. Kapros can keep fighting if they wish, but we will defend our new border."

Daria smiles with a nod. "Yes, my lord."

Keir sounds so much like his father ... so much like the Lord of Alopson ... which he will be one day. I don't realize my fingers are curling into my palms until Keir grabs my hand. He smiles at me, and my breath catches as his blue eyes sparkle. "You ready to go home? I'm dying to try the fried fish you and Nor go on and on about."

I take a slow breath, holding up my left hand. The pretty blue-black ink swirls and dances up my fingers, over my wrist, and up to my elbow. I twist my arm, reading the letters, KURKODAM. Forsaken. I chuckle as the sensation of *my magic* touches me. Before, it felt like sand scraping my skin raw. Now, it's softer, like sand swirling in seawater, brushing my skin as I pull back on my power and the inky shadows retreat, leaving my skin blank once more.

I smile up at Keir. "Yes, but aren't you needed here? Or back in Alopson?"

Keir shakes his head. "Daria has things well in hand. I'm sure Father will come down here soon, if he's not already on his way. I'll let Daria know where I'll be. Father can send a message if I'm needed." His finger crooks under my chin. "But right now, we need to get Halee home."

I blink at him, surprised at the absence of tears. But I'm not sad, I'm proud. I'm proud of what we all did. I'm proud to be the one who stopped the bloody Drakam line from taking the lives of any more baby girls.

And I'm excited. I'm excited to show Keir my home. He gets to his feet, looking much steadier than just moments before. Taking my hand, he helps me up, and everyone else follows suit. Looking around, I ask, "What will you all do now?"

I glance at Miles, already knowing he's coming with us to bring Halee to our small island home.

Valsan presses a kiss to Nor's temple. "I'm coming to Oxtara with you and Nor."

Nor looks up at him with a flash of uncertainty in his eyes. "Shouldn't you go to Loudare and speak with Lady Kapros? Get your position back?"

Valsan shrugs with a grin. "I'm kinda enjoying the freedom at the moment. I'll either get my job back or I won't. What's important now is getting Halee home."

Owen slings an arm around Vesper. "I'm with the captain." He grins down at the blushing Poison mage. "How 'bout it, Viper?"

She swats his stomach, but chuckles with a shake of her head. "Sure, why not."

Aimee crosses her arms, the slightest of smiles on her face. "I'm in. I'm owed some time off anyway."

Owen laughs. "That's the spirit."

Layla comes out of her tavern wiping a rag inside a glass. Always wiping something down. She tilts her head over her shoulder. "Why don't you all come in for a drink and a meal, catch some sleep before you head out? You've had a crazy couple of days, a few more hours won't kill you."

Valsan nods, clapping his hands. "Sounds great. Thank you, Layla."

Everyone files into the tavern, and Keir turns to me when I hesitate. He searches my eyes then nods before following everyone inside. I place my hand on Layla's arm. "Thank you, for everything."

She smiles, pausing her cleaning. "Anytime, Shanty Princess. Just promise you'll come visit from time to time. My customers would love the entertainment."

A laugh bursts from me as she ushers me into her tavern as I say, "It's a deal."

CHAPTER 32

THAEIA
Eight days later

My body sways with the motion of the waves as I sit on my board. The sun slowly sinks into the water, turning the sky gold and the ocean red. The people of Oxtara bob on their boards all around me in the calm bay of the North Shore. Keir's hand rests on my thigh from where he sits on his board next to me. I smile at him as his thumb strokes over my bare skin. He took to the wave board like he'd been doing it for years. Of course he did. He'll probably be riding the larger waves with Nor and me before the week's done.

I hold back a chuckle as I look over at Nor and Valsan. The captain has a death grip with one hand on the edge of his board, the other fist pressed tight to the surface. His stiff body seems to resist the motion of the waves with every ripple. Nor tries to get him to relax, to move with the ocean, but that only makes Valsan wobble and nearly fall from his board. Owen and Vesper share a board with him seated behind her, and as I watch, he presses a quick kiss to her shoulder. I hope they stay together. They seem like a good pair.

I crane my neck, looking for Aimee, finding her closer to shore. She was the most hesitant about getting on the wave board, but she did it, sticking to the shallows where her feet would touch if she were to topple over.

Turning back to the setting sun, I focus on Miles out at the front of the group. His dark hair clings to his head as he bobs in the waves, Halee's parents out there with him. Though they had every right to, Halee's parents didn't blame me when I told them everything that had happened. All my friends were there to support me as I did the hardest thing I've ever done—tell my friend's parents that she's dead because of me. But they'd both pulled me into a hug, weeping for their daughter even as they told me how sorry they were that I went through all that.

And because they are just as kind as their daughter was, Halee's parents accepted Miles, telling him he was a part of their family, no questions, no mistrust, no doubt. And the Plant mage has taken to island life in just the few days we've been here.

The last sliver of the sun sinks into the ocean, pulling me from my thoughts. As one, we all lower our left hands into the water, releasing Halee's ashes just as we did with Saph all those weeks ago. As the ashes swirl and sink, I rub the ring that's back in its place on my pinky. I'm not sure why I left it behind in the first place, but I think I was trying to leave Saph behind—to see if I could stand on my own. But Saph was always with me, and she always will be. Sliding the ring off, I twist it, letting the faint evening light catch on the shiny metal. I wonder if Saph would be proud of me.

Keir's hand squeezes my thigh. I slide the ring back on, and lace my fingers through his with a smile. Yeah, I think Saph would be very proud of me. We sit there for a long moment as the islanders paddle back to shore. Aimee joins them, quickly followed by Owen and Vesper. Valsan doesn't rush Nor, but my friend knows his captain is eager to get out of the water, so Nor helps guide Valsan back to shore. It's now just Keir, me, Miles, and Halee's parents.

With a final slow inhale, I squeeze Keir's hand. "I'm ready."

He nods, releasing me, but not before pressing a quick kiss to the back of my hand and whispering, "You're so beautiful, Fox Slayer."

Before he can shift to start paddling in, I snag his arm, aiming my gaze out at the water. "This, right here, was one of my favorite places as I was growing up. Out here, I could relax, I could forget about my troubles. Out here, I was always free. There's a time of day when the sky is clear and the sun is bright and the blue tint of the sister star's rings hang low on the horizon. The light hits the shallows right here, making the water look like blue crystal reflecting off the white sands below." I look at him, a soft smile on my face. "It's my favorite color."

Reaching over, I cup his face. My thumb rubs over the smooth skin above his beard. "The color of your eyes, Keir."

His expression fills with love that's laced with heat that pulses through my core. He turns into my touch, pressing a kiss to my palm. After another moment, we both paddle to shore, and hand-in-hand, we walk the path I traveled countless times towards my house. Well, it's now Fara's house. She didn't want to stay in Drakam, so I offered her Saph's house. Fara sacrificed so much for the woman she loved. She sacrificed her love for me, to get me out of House Drakam before they could kill me. She left the love of her life behind. She left Saph and went back to make sure the lie stayed in place. She told Drakam I was dead, and she kept her position in the House, ready and willing to rescue any other female babies born to the Drakam line, though none were.

It wasn't until the journey home that Fara told me my birth mother secretly started drinking an infertility tea after my birth and supposed death. She couldn't handle losing any more baby girls, so she made her own stand, in her own way. There's still bitterness in my heart towards the woman, but I try not to judge. I don't know what she went through, and well, I'm alive.

The house comes into view, but a frown pulls at my lips as my thoughts wander to my remaining two brothers. Daria sent out several hunting parties, with a promise to find them and bring them to justice. Shortly after we all left Drakam, or now Alopson, Daria sent word that they found evidence that Severn's two sons boarded their family's ship headed to Kivel of all places.

I smile, banishing my anger. If the storms hadn't held me back, I could be in Kivel right now, searching in vain for my family origins. Looking over at Keir and the soft flicker of his Spirit flames, Gren padding silently at his side, my smile grows. Maybe the gods don't hate me after all.

CHAPTER 33

KEIR

FARA WENT into town a while ago, shooting me a wink and a smile. I really like that woman, and I hope she finds peace here on Oxtara. It's been a week since Halee's ceremony, and we have all spent that time being dragged around the island by Nor and Thaeia. We've eaten the best seafood I've ever had, we've played in the ocean, we've strolled through town, and we've sat on the beach watching sunsets. We've even spent some time training together in Thaeia's yard, Owen of course turning everything into a game.

And true to his word, Miles grew a beautiful garden in front of Thaeia's house, the blooms bright, the greenery lush, the bushes full. And along the path leading from the beach to the back porch, brilliant star flowers bob happily in the sea breeze, Halee's favorite flower. A similar garden graces the grounds of Halee's home as well.

I glance over my shoulder at Thaeia's house from where I'm standing on her front path. She's in there, waiting for me, giving me space to …

Soft footfalls draw my attention back around as Valsan comes down the path through the lush jungle that makes Thaeia's place feel tucked away and private. I hardly recognize the man as he smiles at me with a wave. Loose shorts sit low on his tapered waist, his feet bare. A dark green sleeveless shirt perfectly reflects the color of his eyes, and his long hair hangs in waves around his face, brushing his shoulders. He looks like an islander, his naturally brown skin a little darker after spending these past days on the beaches with Nor. He looks so relaxed and … happy.

Holding out a hand, I clasp his muscular forearm, then he surprises me by pulling me into a hug, clapping me on the back. I return the gesture with a smile, and when we step back, he looks over my shoulder. "How's she doing?"

"Better. Being home has been good for her."

"Good. That's good. So, what'd you want to talk to me about?"

Gods, why am I so nervous? I take a deep breath and just get it out. "I received a message from my father yesterday."

Valsan's face drops into a serious expression. "Everything okay?"

I smile, waving a hand. "Oh, yeah, just restructuring the country." I laugh, but it's tight, and Valsan doesn't join me. My smile falls, and I fight the urge to shift from foot to foot, but I stand firm. "No, everything is going fine. There's pushback, of course, but Daria is more than capable, and my father has things well in hand. He's had his eyes on

Drakam for a long time. He's had plenty of time to think about this."

My palms are sweating, so I shove them in my pockets. "Once I return home, my father plans to temporarily move to Rokvale and reside in the former House Drakam."

Valsan nods. "Makes sense. He would want to be in the heart of his new territory to deal with any ... challenges that come up in the first few years of this transition." He smiles at me. "I'm assuming he's leaving you in charge of House Alopson in Farcrest?"

"Yes, that's the plan."

A broad smile lights up Valsan's eyes. "Congratulations, Keir. You'll do a great job."

I feel my cheeks heating with a blush. "Thank you, Valsan." I stand taller, meeting his eyes. "So, Daria is obviously staying with my father, moving part of our guard to Rokvale with her."

Valsan's smile doesn't falter. "And?"

My lips twitch. Damn it, he's teasing me. "Will you consider moving to Farcrest and being my captain? I know it's sooner than either of us anticipated, and of course you'll need to talk to Nor since this affects you both. And there will be a relocation compensation—if you want to sell your house in Rokvale or keep it, I'll make sure—"

He clasps my shoulder. "Keir." I snap my rambling mouth shut. "Thank you. I'd say yes right now, but you are correct. Let me talk to Nor. I don't want to speak for him, but I suspect he'll like the idea of being close to Thaeia."

I grin. "She said the same thing." Valsan steps back, and I rub my neck with a chuckle. "Actually, what she said was that if Nor said no, she'd kick his ass into changing his mind."

Valsan laughs. "So, I think it's safe to say you have yourself a new captain."

I don't let my hope soar too high yet. "And Kapros?"

His face falls slightly. "Honestly, I could probably get my job back, but the man who took over for me ... he's a good man."

I nod. "Ander. He was a good choice. He's no you, but I think he'll grow into a great captain."

His smile slides back to his lips. "Yeah. He'll do well ... and, well, Sodoles is changing. *We* changed it. So I think it's time for a change ... for all of us."

"I agree, my friend. Talk it over with Nor. If the answer is indeed yes, and if there are people you want to bring with you, I'll match pay with a ten percent raise and a relocation allowance."

Valsan raises a brow, and I shrug. "Cost of living is a bit higher in Alopson."

Holding out my hand again, he clasps my arm. "I'll let you know as soon as Nor and I have made a decision." He winks. "And I look forward to being your captain, Keir."

I laugh, giving his forearm a squeeze before releasing him. He spins on his heel with casual grace, waving over his shoulder. "Go fill in Thaeia on everything she couldn't hear through the door."

I laugh louder as he walks away and the jungle swallows him from view. Jogging into the house, I spy Thaeia in the kitchen. A pot clatters as she reaches up to put it away in the cabinet. I round the narrow kitchen island, arms circling her waist as I press a kiss to her shoulder. "How much did you hear?"

She chuckles. "Enough to congratulate you."

I laugh against her sun-kissed skin, breathing in her

vanilla and sea salt scent. "You're so beautiful. You're different here. Island life suits you."

She turns in my arms, wrapping hers around my neck with a smile. "It does. And I do love it here, but Keir, I'm ready to start something new." Her lips press to mine, and desire races through me.

I pull her closer, deepening the kiss, and when she rolls her hips against me, there's no holding back the growl that punches from my lips. "Here?"

Thaeia rips her shirt over her head, throwing it away before scrambling at the waistband of her pants. I chuckle as I race her to get undressed, but she beats me. I'm still trying to kick out of my shorts when her lips wrap around my cock. My knees nearly buckle. "Fuck, Fox Slayer."

She mumbles something, spit already dripping from the corners of her mouth. I reach back, bracing my hands on the counter, but keep my eyes on her. She bobs and sucks and licks. I'm already so close. It's been days since I've had her, and I have plans.

Gripping her hair close to her scalp so as not to hurt her ... too much, I pull her to her feet, kissing her, demanding she open for me. She does, and my tongue plunders her mouth as she moans. I swallow the sound, eager for more. Spinning her around, I shove her chest down to the counter. Leaning over her, I wrap her hands around the opposite edge of the narrow counter, biting her neck before scraping my beard over the mark. "Stay here, Fox Slayer."

I wait for her nod before I rise. I riffled through the kitchen our first day here, so I know right where I'm going. I pull the bottle of oil from the cabinet and she moans, her hips grinding against the cabinets. But she stays where I put her, and I smile as I drizzle oil onto the small of her back. She presses her cheek to the counter with a groan, and I slick the oil down, down, down, between her cheeks, slowly circling her asshole.

"Are you ready for me, Fox Slayer?"

"Yes, gods, yes." Her voice is deeper, throaty, needy.

I pull my hand away, and stroke my cock. She tries to look back, but she can't with her grip still on the edge of the counter. I grin, stroking myself again. "So good, Thaeia. So beautiful laid out for me."

"Keir, please."

My foot makes contact with her ankle, and I kick her legs wider so she has to rise to her toes. I press one hand to her oiled back and line myself up at her dripping pussy with the other. One hard thrust, and I'm inside her. My hips slam against her ass, and she grunts with the force. I hold myself still for a long moment, just enjoying being so deep in my Fox Slayer, enjoying the way her body is trembling with need ... need for me.

As I pull back, I slip one finger into her ass, and she groans as I slide all the way to the knuckle.

"Yes, Thaeia. What do you say if you need me to stop? Because I'm about to unleash on you."

"Gren." She tilts her head as much as she can, a smirk on her lips. "But I won't need it."

Fuck, this woman.

My hips slam into her, and I pick up a punishing pace, watching my wet cock driving in and out of her tight pussy, anticipating her ass. I insert another finger, and she takes me easily. Her toes scramble on the floor, trying to find purchase to move against me, but she can't. Over and over, I thrust into her. She feels so good, my balls draw up, and I bite my cheek, keeping my orgasm at bay.

"You're all mine, Thaeia. I want you to come on my cock before I take your ass."

"Yes, yes, yes. Fuck, Keir, yes. Oh, oh, Keir, Keir, Keir."

Hearing her chant my name with desire lacing her voice is like the strongest drug. I'll never get enough. I slide a third finger into her as I reach around, finding her clit and pressing down. She screams, her body going tight under me as she pulses, coming on my cock just as I demanded. The oil has slipped down to mix with her release and it drips on the floor. I might lick it up later.

She's still fluttering with the last pulses of her orgasm when I pull out of her. She whimpers, and my cock weeps precum that joins her cum on the floor. I draw my fingers out of her ass, lining up my throbbing cock to take their place. She's still coming down from her climax, and I take advantage of the moment. The head of my cock slides past her tight barrier, and she hisses, her legs quivering. I close my eyes, breathing through the nearly crushing grip she has on me. My hand smooths over her back.

"Are you okay, Fox Slayer?" Her head bobs in a weak nod. "I need your words, Thaeia."

"Yes, Keir. I need more. Please."

I smile, making sure not to use the fingers that were in her ass to flick her clit as I push deeper into her. "Fuck, Thaeia. You feel so good. You're taking me so well. Fuck."

"More."

My fingers plunge into her pussy as I bottom out in her ass, my hips hitting her cheeks. We both breathe out a long, "Yesssss."

I pump my fingers as I start thrusting, but I need to watch.

"Touch yourself. Get yourself off for me, Fox Slayer. I need both my hands."

"Fuck." She releases one hand, maneuvering it between herself and the counter. "I'm so full. Fuck, this is ... oh, gods."

As soon as I feel her fingers pressing at her entrance, I grip her hips with both hands. I'm mesmerized at the sight of my cock sliding in and out of her tight ass, and I pump into her, rolling against her jiggling cheeks every few thrusts. She's panting, her fingers working furiously. I reach the edge and can't stop myself from falling over.

"Thaeia!"

I slam into her as she screams, her legs giving out with her orgasm, and I'm right there with her. My cum fills her until it's leaking between her pink cheeks, pleasure flooding my body until I'm floating. It pulses through me so powerfully, I collapse on top of her, the oil slicking between us.

We stay like that for a long moment, our breathing slowing down. She tries to get her feet back under her, but she slips in the mess of oil and cum. I shift, helping support her weight as we stand. I turn her in my arms, pressing a long kiss to her lips, then the side of her mouth, her temple, the top of her head.

"I love you so much, Thaeia."

She giggles. "Of course you do. You just fucked my ass."

I laugh, shaking my head against her hair. "Even so."

She wraps her arms around me, holding tight. "Even so." She sighs into my chest. "I love you too."

I grip the back of her neck, overwhelmed with happiness and love. "How was it? Are you okay?"

Finding a rag, I run it under the faucet, then begin mopping up the mess we made. Thaeia shimmies side to side. "It stung a little at first, but that feeling of fullness was so ... It's hard to explain."

I toss the rag in the sink then turn to her with a wink. "You'll just have to show me sometime."

Her eyes go wide, and her cheeks turn scarlet. "Is that something you'd like?"

I chuckle at the look of interest on her face. "Nor and Val really seem to like it, and you just had a pretty good time ..."

She laughs. "Well, okay then."

Kissing her, I smile against her mouth. "Let's go take a shower. I'll wash your hair." I know how much she loves that.

Thaeia melts against me at the mere thought of having my hands stroke through her hair and massaging her scalp. Taking my hand, she leads me towards the bathroom, and says, "I really am excited to start my life in Alopson, Keir." She looks over her shoulder, a brilliant smile filled with love lighting up her face. "With you."

CHAPTER 34

NOR

THE ROOM IS DARK. This room in my house is always dark. The storm shutters I put in place before I left for the Games all those weeks ago are still secured in place. The curtains are drawn, and all the doors are closed except the one I came in through. My fists clench. I hate this room. I can still hear my own screams as my father punished me with his magic. No. He abused me.

With purpose, I quickly work my way around the room, removing the shutters and putting them in storage. Dust floats in the air, sparkling in the sunlight. It would be pretty if this room wasn't stained with the pain of my past. Nope, the light didn't help. I draw the curtains back over the windows, preferring the shadows. They fit my mood better right now. I shouldn't be dwelling on this. I should be upstairs finishing packing, but instead I'm standing in this fucking room.

Quiet footsteps sound behind me. I don't have to turn around to know Val is there. I can picture him—loose shorts, shirtless, barefoot ... gorgeous. I keep my back to him, asking, "What did Keir want?" I'm pretty sure I know, but I want to hear him say it. I want him to ask so I can say yes. I love Oxtara, but I also hate it here. I want something new, and I don't want the entire country separating Thaeia and me.

Val comes closer, but doesn't touch me. "Why are you standing alone in this dark room, Nor?"

I shake my head, and my shoulders slump. "Just visiting the ghosts of my past for some stupid reason." He takes another step towards me. I can feel his body heat on my back, that's how close he is, but still he doesn't touch me. He remains silent. I shouldn't dump this on him. I'm past it. Right? I glance at the corner of the room where I used to huddle in a small ball, my hands pressed over my ears to try and block out his magic. With a sigh, I rub the back of my neck. "I hate this place, but this room especially. My father ... let's just say he had very strong opinions about my magic and how weak I was. Then when Thaeia's magic didn't manifest ..." I drop my hand. "He hated her. He was scared of her." I chuckle. "Probably still is, the bastard. He put that fear and hate in me, Val. I was just a kid. He was my father. I ..."

Val takes my right hand, tugging gently. I turn, and he raises my crooked fingers—the ones my father broke and refused to allow me to get healed—to his mouth. Pressing a soft kiss to the bent knuckles, he whispers against my skin. "No child deserves to be betrayed by a parent. You certainly didn't, Nor. I'm sorry."

I lower my head to rest it against his chest. Inhaling his wood-smoke and coffee scent, though the smell of coffee is stronger from the cup he had this morning before he went to Thaeia's to speak with Keir. I nuzzle into his warmth, one arm wrapping around his waist, repeating my earlier question. "What did Keir want?"

I feel him smile as he presses his lips to my hair, his fingers now threaded through mine. "What would you think about moving to Alopson?"

I hug him tighter, finally lifting my head to look into his forest-green eyes. "Congratulations."

His free hand cups my face. "I haven't said yes yet. And I won't until we both agree."

My fingers clench around his, and he lifts my right hand back to his lips. I'm ready to say yes, to beg him to take me away from here, but he turns my hand, moving his sinful mouth to the inside of my wrist. I know my pulse is kicking against his lips, but I can't help it. Val always makes my heart race.

He steps away, and I swear he's using his magic on me, because I'm confused as to why he's suddenly leaving the room without a word. Before the panic can really settle in my chest, Val comes back holding a small box which he sets on one of the tables. As he props open the lid, I glare at the table. When I was thirteen, maybe fourteen, my father got angry over ... something. He slapped me so hard, I fell and cracked my head on the corner of that table.

I realize Val has stopped moving, and when I look at him, his head is turned over his shoulder, his eyes searching mine. He holds my gaze, saying, "Everything in here holds some pain of yours, doesn't it?"

I just shrug, letting the man I love see my vulnerability. He nods, turning back to his little box. There's a little clicking noise, then soft music starts to fill the room.

Turning to me, Val closes the space between us, his bare chest pressing against my shirt. One arm wraps around my waist, the other takes my hand, and he starts to ... dance. He moves us slowly around the room. These aren't practiced steps, just us moving together to the lazy flow of the music. I hold him tighter, and he presses a kiss to my lips. We end up back in the center of the room, just swaying in each other's arms.

After a long while, I whisper, "Thank you."

"You don't have to thank me for trying to make you feel better ... but you're welcome."

I kiss him, lightly sucking his bottom lip. "Seriously, Valsan, thank you. Not just for this. For everything. It's all been you. Everything good in my life right now was because of you."

His lips find mine, his tongue licking the seam of my mouth. "Don't sell yourself short, Nor. It doesn't matter what the catalyst was, *you* made your life better."

I groan, knowing he can feel my hardening cock. "Why are you so perfect?"

He chuckles, pressing his hips a little harder against mine. "I can't surf for shit."

I laugh. "That's true. You really are pathetic on a wave board."

He smiles, his white teeth dazzling against his skin which is darker after the past few days spent shirtless in the island sun. Suddenly, I want to banish the ghostly screams from this room and replace them with something good ... with Val ... with us. I don't care that I don't plan to set foot in this room or this house ever again. I don't want to leave it with the ghosts of my pain.

Using my magic with any kind of dexterity takes a crazy amount of concentration, but I manage to use my power to undo the fastening of Val's shorts, and my magic shoves them to his ankles. His cock springs free, and when he steps out of his shorts, I'm knocked nearly breathless at the sight of his naked body. He backs up a step, waving a hand at me with a smirk. "Your turn."

I practically rip my shirt over my head, then wiggle my hips in a little dance to free myself of my shorts. Now we're both naked, standing in the center of this room. I make the mistake of looking away from Val. My eyes dart around the room, seeing every strike from my father, every minute trapped under this magic.

"Nor, eyes on me." Val's deep voice snaps my gaze back to him. Yes. This is much better. I smile, holding up a finger, indicating for him to wait. He tilts his head, cocking a hip. Only he can pull off that look while completely naked. I send my magic to my bedroom upstairs, and a few seconds later, a small bottle of oil floats into the room. Val's brows raise, and one corner of his lips lift. "What a marvelous use of your magic, Nor."

"Just you wait." The bottle tips, the oil streams out, floating towards Val. The golden liquid hovers over his twitching dick, and I say, "This is special oil. It ... warms with skin contact."

I use my magic to slick the oil over his cock, and he groans but keeps his eyes on me. My Gravity magic strokes him, and he gasps. "Fuck, that's ..."

I grin, advancing on him. "I know."

Grabbing the back of his neck, I kiss Val, tangling my tongue with his. My cock throbs, and pleasure pulses low in my core. When we part, our breaths pant against each other's faces. I squeeze his neck, looking right in his eyes. "Yes. Let's move to Alopson."

His eyes darken. "Okay."

I shove his chest, and he backs up, then lowers himself to the floor—the same floor that met me time and again at my father's abuse. With Val laid out naked on the wood planks, I'm ready to give this room a better memory. I kneel between his legs, and he spreads them wider for me. He remains propped on his elbows so he can watch as my hands trail up his inner thighs as my magic continues to stroke him. I direct more of the oil to drip down his balls and circle his hole. Val's hips lift with my strokes, and I draw a grunt from his lips as I slide more of my magic into his entrance. My power stokes and pumps, thrusts and squeezes. He reaches for me, but I shake my head. He pauses, his gaze eager on my straining cock, but with the next thrust of my magic inside him, I expand it, making it ... bigger. He moans and falls back, pressing his head to the floor so he can grind into my magic.

"You're so beautiful, writhing under my magic, Val."

A spurt of precum drips onto his flexed abs, and I lean down, licking it up. "Fuck, Nor. Your magic feels so good, but I want you."

My fingers trail around his hips and up his sides. Anticipation curls in my belly, and my cock swells even more as I finally let some of the oil coat my length. It quickly warms, and I can't keep my groan from escaping. Val tries to press towards me as I line myself up. Bliss blooms over my entire body as I slide into him. The warm oil combined with his tight hole is nearly my undoing. I breathe through the ecstasy, my balls quivering against his ass. Val's fingers scrape at the floor. "Fucking move, Nor."

I pull back until the crown of my head catches at his rim, then I slam back inside him. Over and over, I drive into his ass. Our grunts and moans fill the room. Looking down his muscular body under mine, I suddenly hate the shadows. I throw my magic at the windows, pulling the curtains right off their rods. Sunlight fills the room, casting the love of my life in bright relief. It's not enough. The windows fly open, and the breeze spills inside.

Val hooks an ankle over my calf, meeting me thrust for thrust, then he barks out, "Use your magic on yourself, Nor. I want to see. I want you to fill yourself."

Fuck. My magic grips his cock tighter as I let a little slide inside my ass. I lose my rhythm as I concentrate on trying to thrust into him with my cock, stroke his dick with my magic, and pump my magic inside my own ass. It's ... overwhelming. I close my eyes, letting myself fall into the sensations of pleasure, bliss, euphoria ...

"Yes, Nor. That. That look on your face. So beautiful." He grabs my left arm. "And look." A fourth star is there on my forearm, and my heart skips as Val whispers, "Well done, Nor."

Looking down at him, I forget about my new star and just fall forward into the desire and love that's pouring out of his eyes. "Val."

"Nor."

The way he growls my name sends sparks through my blood. I fall, erupting inside him, my hips grinding into him. My fingers tingle, and my head swims with the orgasm crashing through me. Val arches, coming hard. With the sun streaming on his sweaty, oily body and the breeze playing with his long hair, I don't think I've seen anything so ... perfect. His cum spurts onto his chest, and I slick my fingers through it, then lick them clean. I release my magic, wrapping my hand around his cock to stroke him through his orgasm. As soon as my fingers squeeze his length, he grabs my forearm, bucking harder against the floor, another orgasm chasing his first. I watch every moment of his bliss. I soak it in, imprint it on my brain.

Slowly, his body melts back to the floor, and I reluctantly let him go, sliding out of his ass. When my cum starts to leak out, Val drops his knees to the side. He rubs his chest as he tries to catch his breath, but a wicked thought has taken root and won't let go. Bending over, I lap at my cum, my tongue flicking his hole. His entire body jerks. "Gods, Nor." I lick my release from his ass, then climb his body, my chest rubbing against his. The oil slicks between us, warming and tingling slightly, and I take an absurd amount of joy from every point of contact between us.

I must be moving too slow, because he grabs the back of my neck and hauls me up his body until we're face-to-face. He pulls me down, his eyes on my mouth. "Give it to me."

My cock starts to harden as I press my lips to his. He thrusts his tongue into my mouth, stealing my cum. He consumes me. Hooking his leg through mine, he rolls, never breaking the kiss. His spent cock starts to grow hard as well, and he chuckles into my mouth as I grind my cock against his. I slip more oil between us before calling my magic to grip us both. I only get two strokes in, but it's enough to get us both completely hard once more. Then Val sits back, grabbing my hands to pull me to my feet. Spinning me, he shoves me towards one of the open windows. I stagger forward, and his large hand presses between my shoulder blades, bending me over the sill. His finger slides into my ass, and my hands flex around the window.

He shifts, and when I look over my shoulder, I see him grab the bottle of oil out of the air. Upending it, he pours the rest over his dick and between my cheeks. Tossing the bottle aside, it clatters to the floor as he thrusts inside me, driving all the way to his balls. We both moan, then he draws back, and as he slams back inside, he says, "We're bringing that oil back with us." He pumps a few times. "A lot of it."

I chuckle between my panting breaths. "We'll buy all Hilary has."

His pace picks up. He slips a hand between us then wraps his arms around me, using his oiled hand to stroke my dick as he asks, "How much do you think we'd have to pay her to get the recipe?"

I laugh-grunt, but can't reply. I've lost the ability to talk. The sound of Val driving into me, his flesh slapping against mine, the wet sound of his hand pumping my cock ... that's all I can focus on. I even forgot about the music, still floating around the room.

Val's free hand grips the windowsill next to where my fingers have a death grip on the wood. He continues to stroke me as his cock grinds into my ass, hitting me so deep, he *scrapes* that spot. I shout, my cum spurting against the wall and down Val's hand. His release fills me as he chants next to my ear. "Nor, gods, Nor. So good. Nor. Nor. Nor."

My name on repeat, spilling from his lips, is the sweetest sound I'll ever hear. His lips brush my neck, and I let my head fall to the side with a smile. This room now has a new memory, a good one. It now has the sounds of my love for Val to cover up the screams of my childhood. I know there's still work I have to do to keep healing, to keep forgiving myself ... but right now, I'm content, happy, in love.

We untangle ourselves, and I stand, turning to lean

against the open window. I press my hand to Val's chest, letting my emotions pour out of my eyes, not that I can ever hide what I'm feeling from him. "I love you.

He takes a step back. "Stay there."

I nod, gripping the windowsill to keep from grabbing him. Instead, I do as I'm told. He hurries to his crumpled shorts and riffles through his pocket. With a grin, he comes back and grabs my hand, pressing my palm to his beating heart. "I planned to do this in two days with everyone to share the moment before we leave Oxtara. I thought it would be a good way to start our trip, our new life, but ... My gaze shifts from his dark emerald eyes to the small object he's holding between us. A ... ring. "Will you bond with me, Nor?"

'Yes' is in my throat, but what comes out is, "How long have you been carrying that around?"

He laughs, turning the silver band so it catches the light. "Don't deflect. And just to be clear, regardless of the answer, even if it's 'I'm not ready' or a straight up 'no,' I still want you to come to Alopson with me. I still want a life with you. Of course I want to be bonded to you, but my love is not conditional on—"

"Val." I curl my fingers into his chest. "Yes. Of course, yes. In fact, let's have the bonding ceremony as soon as possible." Now that he's asked, every second that I'm not bonded to him is a second too long. I already have the perfect ring in mind for him.

He closes the ring in his fist with a nod since we won't exchange our rings until the ceremony. "Whatever you want, my love. All I want is you. Forever."

"Forever."

CHAPTER 35

THAEIA

I WRING MY HANDS, shifting in place, sand crunching between my toes. It's just Keir and me here on my little beach. The sun is moments from rising, but the air is already humid. It'll be a good day to spend at the beach.

Our last day.

Tomorrow Keir and I leave for Alopson. We'll be traveling with the others, planning to spend several days in Rokvale so Keir can check in with Daria on how the transition is going now that Drakam has been absorbed by Alopson. Lady Kapros objected, of course, but in the end, the new captain of the Kapros guard, along with her advisors, got her to cease the fighting at the southern border, and a tentative peace was struck.

Valsan and Nor did take Keir's offer. I knew they would, and it made making the huge move to Alopson that much easier knowing my best friend would be coming with me. And with the two having announced their upcoming bonding ceremony in Alopson, I can't wait to get back to the beautiful desert oasis up north. Keir offered to throw the couple a party at his estate, and while Valsan protested, Nor quickly accepted the offer. Of course, Valsan relented.

I don't think I've ever seen Nor like he's been these past few days. I smile, recalling how he giddily packed his things in anticipation of their ceremony, going house hunting in Farcrest with Valsan, and making a home together. I'm so happy for him, and honestly, I'm happy for me—that Nor and I will still live close to each other.

And he has been showing off his fourth star to everyone on the island, his old cocky attitude coming back out, but now there's an underlying humbleness. His cheeks turn pink whenever someone congratulates him, and he often shuffles in place, rubbing the back of his neck when people start to make a big fuss over his new star. He's changed so much.

Vesper left the day after Halee's ceremony, much to Owen's displeasure. Though I suspect Valsan is going to ask Aimee and Owen to come with him to Alopson, and I'm sure the Ice mage will jump at the chance to stalk his Viper. Regardless, they will come up for the bonding ceremony.

Valsan already offered Miles a position with the Alopson guard, but Miles said he needed time to think it over. For now, he is staying in Oxtara for a while, taking an extended leave of absence, claiming he wants to make sure Halee's parents as well as Fara are well taken care of. But I suspect Miles is simply not ready to leave this part of Halee behind just yet.

I shift again, focusing on the moment at hand, digging

my toes into the sand as I ask Keir, "You'll be strong enough to do this tomorrow for Miles?"

"Yes, Thaeia. If you'll recall, my father is sending a carriage, so I can sleep as long as I need to recover."

Gren circles my legs, his tongue lolling with a doggy grin as he looks up at me. I curl my fingers into my palm. "And you're sure sh—"

"Thaeia." Keir takes my hands, and I look into his sea-blue eyes.

With a sigh, I nod, and he releases me, stepping back under the expansive branches of the kilap tree. The circular leaves wave like little fans in the sea breeze, and Keir takes a seat, crossing his legs. Sand sticks to his swim shorts, and the early morning light casts shadows across his bare chest, displaying each muscle to perfection. He folds his hands in his lap and closes his eyes.

Spirit fire flickers bright and clear before me, and a sob bursts from my chest.

"Halee."

She smiles at me. Hich is at her side, and she pats his head before the hound trots over to Keir and flops to the ground at his side. Gren joins them, barking in greeting. I wipe at my tears, but they keep coming. I planned what I was going to say to her, but now all the words are stuck in my throat.

I sniffle. "Halee. I'm so so—"

She holds up a translucent hand, shaking her head, her curls bouncing with flame. She's so beautiful.

I choke out. "I miss you so much."

Her smile turns sad, then she looks at Keir. Something passes between them before he says, "I'll hold my magic as long as I can."

She nods, turning back to me. With a burst of power,

Keir's Spirit fire flares, and Halee solidifies, her voice soft as she says, "I don't blame you, Thaeia. I never did."

She holds out her arms, and I run into them, hugging my friend, crying into her hair. She holds me just as tight, whispering, "I was sad at first. After the confusion, I was sad about everything I'd miss out on … mainly with Miles if I'm honest." She chuckles, and I feel the vibration against my chest. "But, Thaeia." She pulls back, keeping her hands on my arms, and I hold her as she continues, "I'm okay. Really. I am okay. You don't have to worry about me."

It's getting hard to breathe through my sobs, and she pulls me back into a fierce hug. My tears slow, then stop as I soak in the reassurance of her warm arms wrapped around my waist. Slowly, she starts to fade, my hands passing through her. I step back, giving her a genuine smile. "Don't waste too much time talking tomorrow. You kiss Miles with every second you have."

She laughs, her form wavering. "I will. I love you, Thaeia."

"I love you too, Halee. I'll see you around."

She nods. "Yes, you will."

Halee blinks out along with Gren and Hich. I look at Keir, at his sweat-slicked chest and his pale face. But he's smiling at me, and I hope my gratitude shines in my eyes as I say, "Thank you, Keir."

"Anything for you, Thaeia." He slumps over, his eyes fluttering closed, and I dash forward, catching him. I lay his head in my lap, combing my fingers through his damp hair, watching his chest rise and fall. He warned me that he would pass out after only a few seconds of pushing his power into Halee. But he held her solid form for so much longer than either of us thought he could.

I pause, looking down at him. I know every inch of my lordling by now, and there's something different. A smile lifts my cheeks. Eleven stars now climb his arm. Nor's going to give him hell. I chuckle, tracing the new star with my finger, then I lift my hand. As the tip of the sun peaks over the horizon, the pretty deep-blue color swirls up my arm revealing my tattoo.

I let my magic climb my arm and bleed across my chest, riding the wave of power. *My magic.* Lowering my inked hand back to Keir's hair, I lightly scratch my nails over his scalp like I know he loves. I watch the ink swirl and dance across my skin. I'm still learning this power, but every day it feels more like ... mine. With a smile, I let it go, pulling it back into me, and the ink slips down my arm, over my wrist, and to my fingertips until it's gone.

Tilting my head up at the quickly lightening sky, I sigh.

I was born in fear. I was saved with bravery and love. I was raised with compassion, and found my place, my friends, my family ... I look down at Keir's sleeping face. I found my love.

I also found my power and faced my darkness. But I am more than the power and darkness.

I am Thaeia. And that is enough.

THE END

ALSO BY T. B. WIESE

I genuinely hope you enjoyed this series. If you're interested, here are my other books - all adult fantasy with varying levels of spice.

Scan the code below for links to my Amazon author page where you'll find all my other books.

You'll also find a link to my website for signed paperbacks & hardcovers as well as swag.

ACKNOWLEDGMENTS

A huge thank you to my readers. Without you, this crazy dream of being an author would not be possible.

To all my beta & ARC readers, thank you! Debbie, Mackenzie, Erica, and Heather ... You had a big hand in making this series what it is today. Thank you so very much for taking the time to help me polish this story.

Thank you to Marcelle for such wonderful edits. Your encouragement and insightful notes took this story to a whole other level.

And lastly, I want to thank all my friends and family for cheering me on and being as excited about my characters as I am—I love my tribe.

ABOUT THE AUTHOR

T. B. Wiese is a military spouse, dog mom, photographer, Disney nerd, and lover of spicy fantasy. She loves animals (She grew up with dogs and working with horses, including working at the Tri-Circle D Ranch at Disney World), so don't be surprised when you find yourself reading lovable animal characters in her novels.

If you'd like to keep up to date with future releases as well as new swag and sales, sign up for her newsletter via link in code below.

SCAN THE CODE WITH YOUR CAMERA APP FOR HER SOCIAL LINKS